STAR TREK
THE NEXT GENERATION
MIRROR BROKEN

Become our fan on Facebook **facebook.com/idwpublishing**
Follow us on Twitter **@idwpublishing**
Subscribe to us on YouTube **youtube.com/idwpublishing**
See what's new on Tumblr **tumblr.idwpublishing.com**
Check us out on Instagram **instagram.com/idwpublishing**

Greg Goldstein, President & Publisher
Robbie Robbins, EVP & Sr. Art Director
Chris Ryall, Chief Creative Officer & Editor-in-Chief
Matthew Ruzicka, CPA, Chief Financial Officer
David Hedgecock, Associate Publisher
Laurie Windrow, Senior Vice President of Sales & Marketing
Lorelei Bunjes, VP of Digital Services
Eric Moss, Sr. Director, Licensing & Business Development

Ted Adams, Founder & CEO of IDW Media Holdings

ISBN: 978-1-68405-145-8   21 20 19 18   1 2 3 4

Originally published as STAR TREK: THE NEXT GENERATION—MIRROR BROKEN issues #0–5.

Special thanks to Risa Kessler and John Van Citters of CBS Consumer Products for their invaluable assistance.

For international rights, contact licensing@idwpublishing.com

Star Trek created by Gene Roddenberry

STAR TREK
THE NEXT GENERATION
MIRROR BROKEN

WRITTEN BY
DAVID TIPTON & SCOTT TIPTON

ART BY
J.K. WOODWARD

COLORS BY
J.K. WOODWARD (ISSUE #1)
CHARLIE KIRCHOFF (ISSUES #2-5)

LETTERS BY
ANDWORLD DESIGN

EDITORIAL ASSISTANCE BY
CHASE MAROTZ

SERIES EDITS BY
SARAH GAYDOS

COVER ART BY **J.K. WOODWARD**

COLLECTION EDITS BY **JUSTIN EISINGER** AND **ALONZO SIMON**

COLLECTION DESIGN BY **CLAUDIA CHONG**

PUBLISHER **GREG GOLDSTEIN**

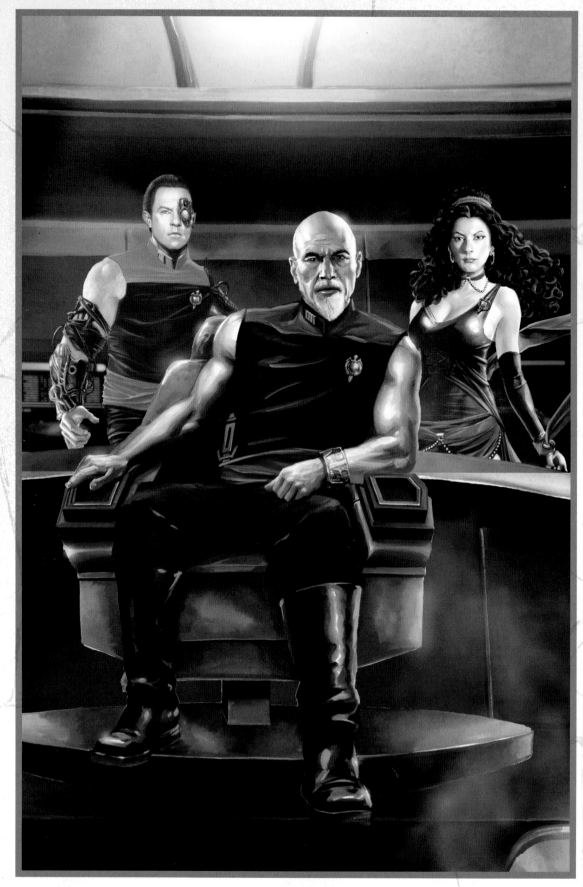

ART BY
J.K. WOODWARD

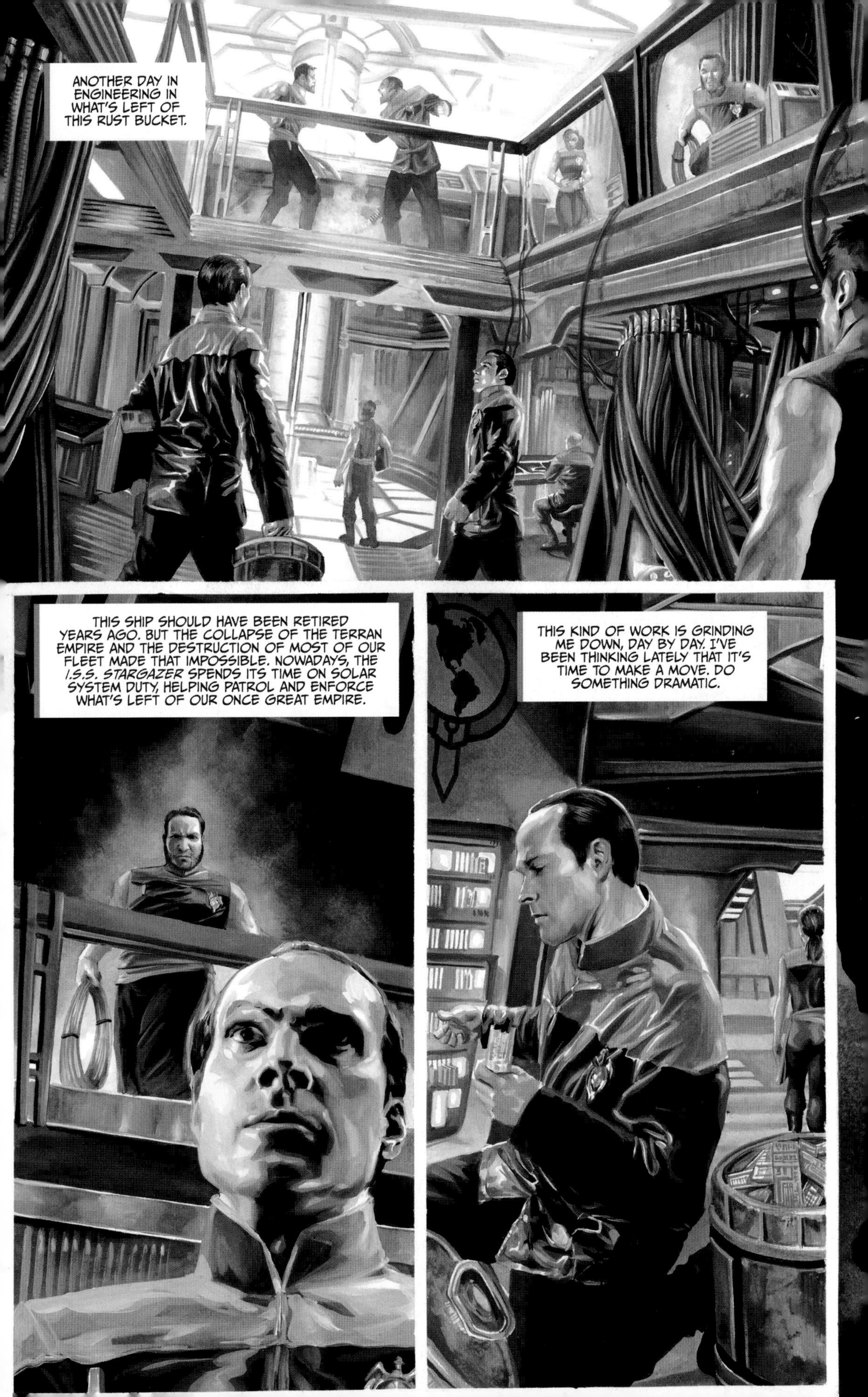
ANOTHER DAY IN ENGINEERING IN WHAT'S LEFT OF THIS RUST BUCKET.
THIS SHIP SHOULD HAVE BEEN RETIRED YEARS AGO. BUT THE COLLAPSE OF THE TERRAN EMPIRE AND THE DESTRUCTION OF MOST OF OUR FLEET MADE THAT IMPOSSIBLE. NOWADAYS, THE *I.S.S. STARGAZER* SPENDS ITS TIME ON SOLAR SYSTEM DUTY, HELPING PATROL AND ENFORCE WHAT'S LEFT OF OUR ONCE GREAT EMPIRE.
THIS KIND OF WORK IS GRINDING ME DOWN, DAY BY DAY. I'VE BEEN THINKING LATELY THAT IT'S TIME TO MAKE A MOVE. DO SOMETHING DRAMATIC.

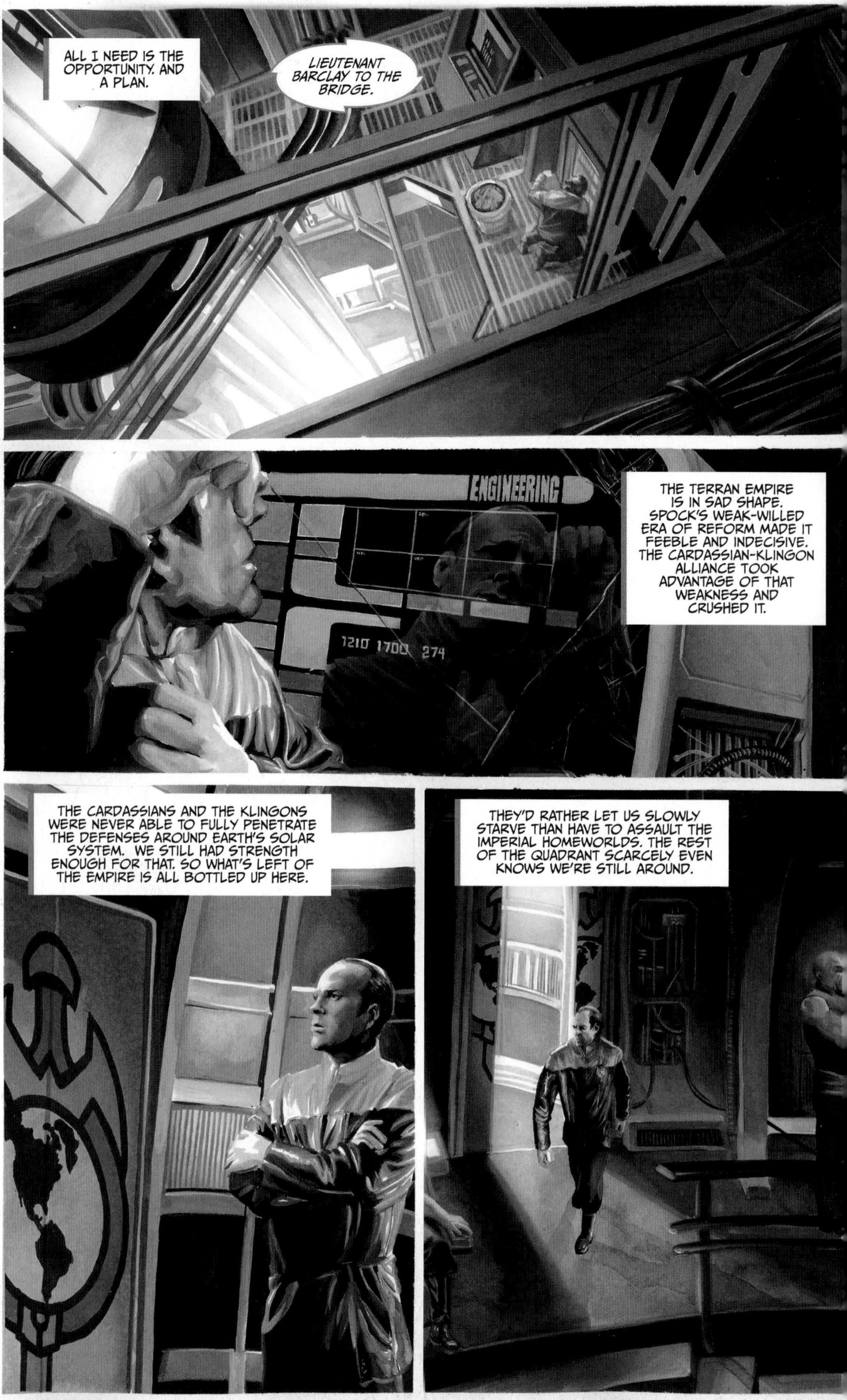
ALL I NEED IS THE OPPORTUNITY. AND A PLAN.
LIEUTENANT BARCLAY TO THE BRIDGE.
ENGINEERING
1210 1700 274
THE TERRAN EMPIRE IS IN SAD SHAPE. SPOCK'S WEAK-WILLED ERA OF REFORM MADE IT FEEBLE AND INDECISIVE. THE CARDASSIAN-KLINGON ALLIANCE TOOK ADVANTAGE OF THAT WEAKNESS AND CRUSHED IT.
THE CARDASSIANS AND THE KLINGONS WERE NEVER ABLE TO FULLY PENETRATE THE DEFENSES AROUND EARTH'S SOLAR SYSTEM. WE STILL HAD STRENGTH ENOUGH FOR THAT. SO WHAT'S LEFT OF THE EMPIRE IS ALL BOTTLED UP HERE.
THEY'D RATHER LET US SLOWLY STARVE THAN HAVE TO ASSAULT THE IMPERIAL HOMEWORLDS. THE REST OF THE QUADRANT SCARCELY EVEN KNOWS WE'RE STILL AROUND.

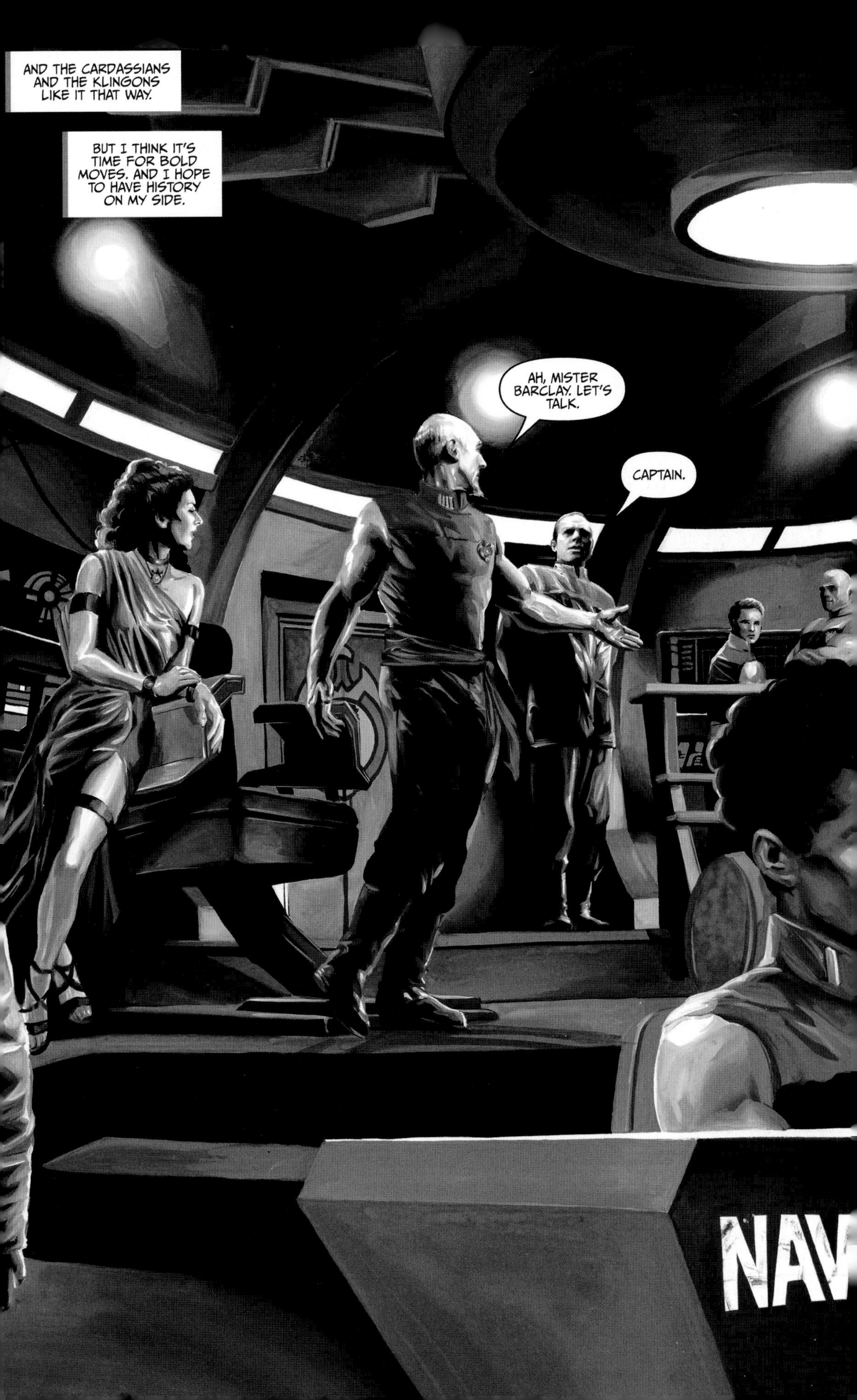
AND THE CARDASSIANS AND THE KLINGONS LIKE IT THAT WAY.
BUT I THINK IT'S TIME FOR BOLD MOVES. AND I HOPE TO HAVE HISTORY ON MY SIDE.
AH, MISTER BARCLAY. LET'S TALK.
CAPTAIN.
NAV

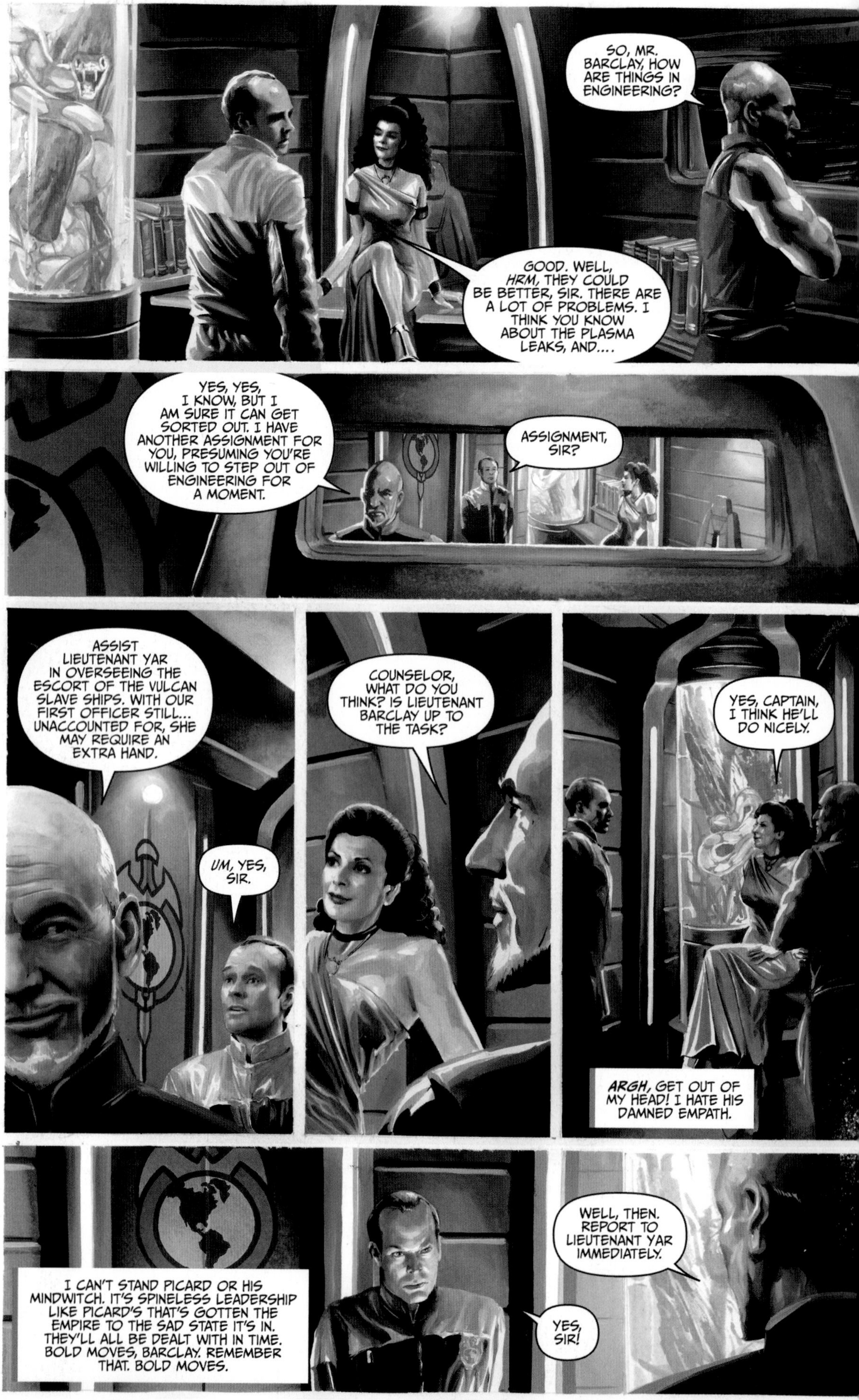
SO, MR. BARCLAY, HOW ARE THINGS IN ENGINEERING?
GOOD. WELL, HRM, THEY COULD BE BETTER, SIR. THERE ARE A LOT OF PROBLEMS. I THINK YOU KNOW ABOUT THE PLASMA LEAKS, AND....
YES, YES, I KNOW, BUT I AM SURE IT CAN GET SORTED OUT. I HAVE ANOTHER ASSIGNMENT FOR YOU, PRESUMING YOU'RE WILLING TO STEP OUT OF ENGINEERING FOR A MOMENT.
ASSIGNMENT, SIR?
ASSIST LIEUTENANT YAR IN OVERSEEING THE ESCORT OF THE VULCAN SLAVE SHIPS. WITH OUR FIRST OFFICER STILL... UNACCOUNTED FOR, SHE MAY REQUIRE AN EXTRA HAND.
UM, YES, SIR.
COUNSELOR, WHAT DO YOU THINK? IS LIEUTENANT BARCLAY UP TO THE TASK?
YES, CAPTAIN, I THINK HE'LL DO NICELY.
ARGH, GET OUT OF MY HEAD! I HATE HIS DAMNED EMPATH.
I CAN'T STAND PICARD OR HIS MINDWITCH. IT'S SPINELESS LEADERSHIP LIKE PICARD'S THAT'S GOTTEN THE EMPIRE TO THE SAD STATE IT'S IN. THEY'LL ALL BE DEALT WITH IN TIME. BOLD MOVES, BARCLAY. REMEMBER THAT. BOLD MOVES.
WELL, THEN. REPORT TO LIEUTENANT YAR IMMEDIATELY.
YES, SIR!

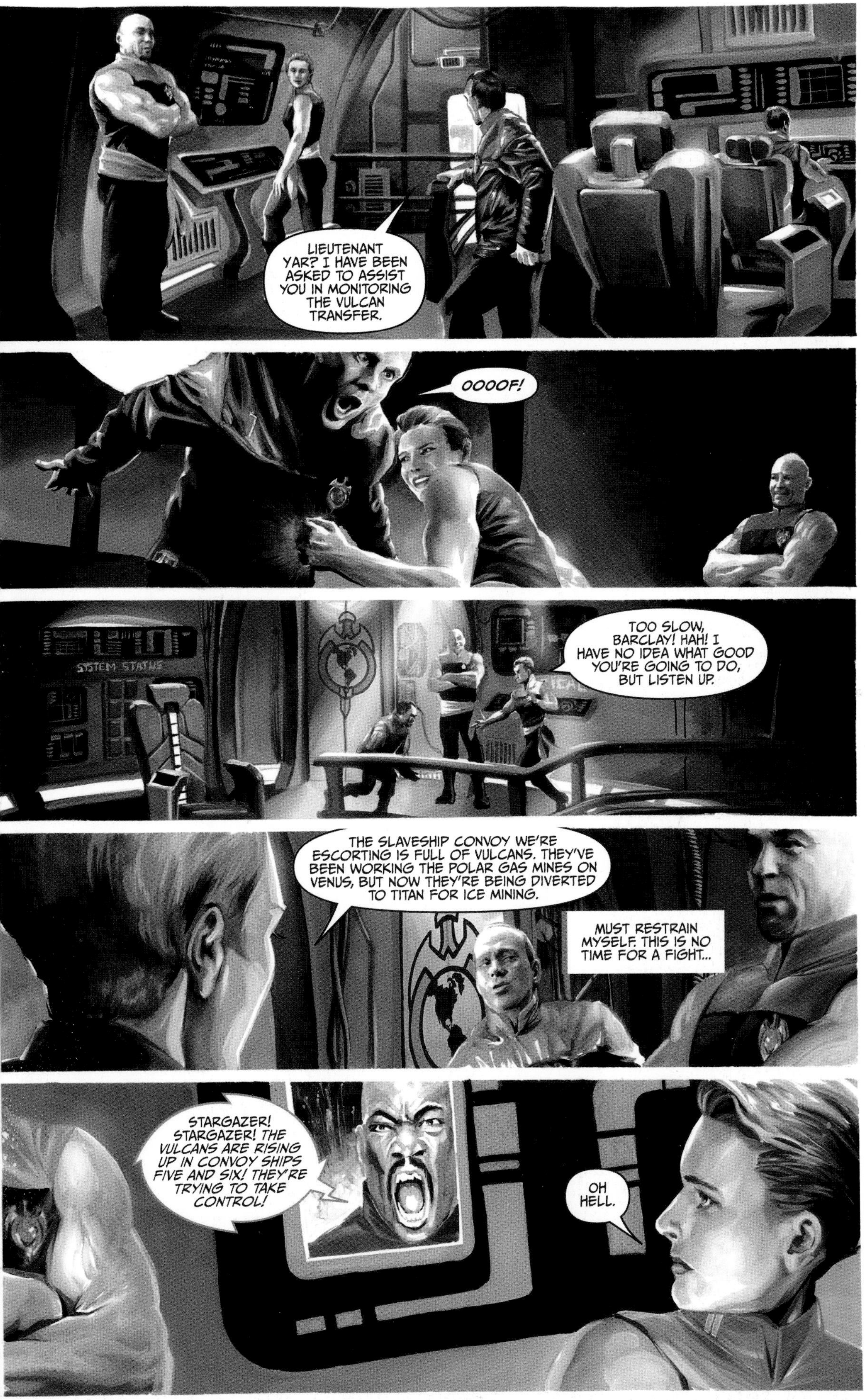
LIEUTENANT YAR? I HAVE BEEN ASKED TO ASSIST YOU IN MONITORING THE VULCAN TRANSFER.
OOOOF!
TOO SLOW, BARCLAY! HAH! I HAVE NO IDEA WHAT GOOD YOU'RE GOING TO DO, BUT LISTEN UP.
SYSTEM STATUS
THE SLAVESHIP CONVOY WE'RE ESCORTING IS FULL OF VULCANS. THEY'VE BEEN WORKING THE POLAR GAS MINES ON VENUS, BUT NOW THEY'RE BEING DIVERTED TO TITAN FOR ICE MINING.
MUST RESTRAIN MYSELF. THIS IS NO TIME FOR A FIGHT...
STARGAZER! STARGAZER! THE VULCANS ARE RISING UP IN CONVOY SHIPS FIVE AND SIX! THEY'RE TRYING TO TAKE CONTROL!
OH HELL.

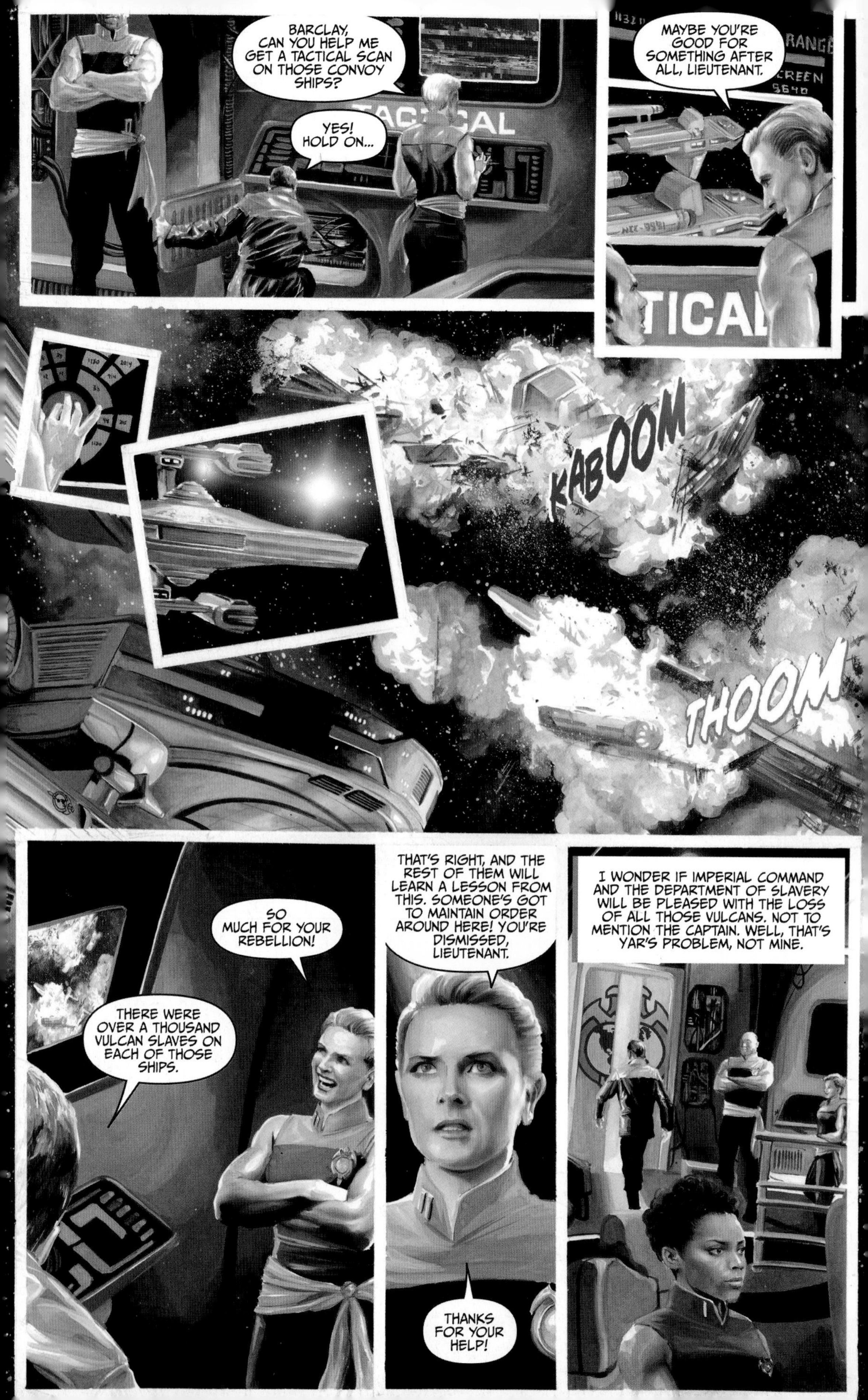
BARCLAY, CAN YOU HELP ME GET A TACTICAL SCAN ON THOSE CONVOY SHIPS?
YES! HOLD ON...
MAYBE YOU'RE GOOD FOR SOMETHING AFTER ALL, LIEUTENANT.
KABOOM
THOOM
THERE WERE OVER A THOUSAND VULCAN SLAVES ON EACH OF THOSE SHIPS.
SO MUCH FOR YOUR REBELLION!
THAT'S RIGHT, AND THE REST OF THEM WILL LEARN A LESSON FROM THIS. SOMEONE'S GOT TO MAINTAIN ORDER AROUND HERE! YOU'RE DISMISSED, LIEUTENANT.
THANKS FOR YOUR HELP!
I WONDER IF IMPERIAL COMMAND AND THE DEPARTMENT OF SLAVERY WILL BE PLEASED WITH THE LOSS OF ALL THOSE VULCANS. NOT TO MENTION THE CAPTAIN. WELL, THAT'S YAR'S PROBLEM, NOT MINE.

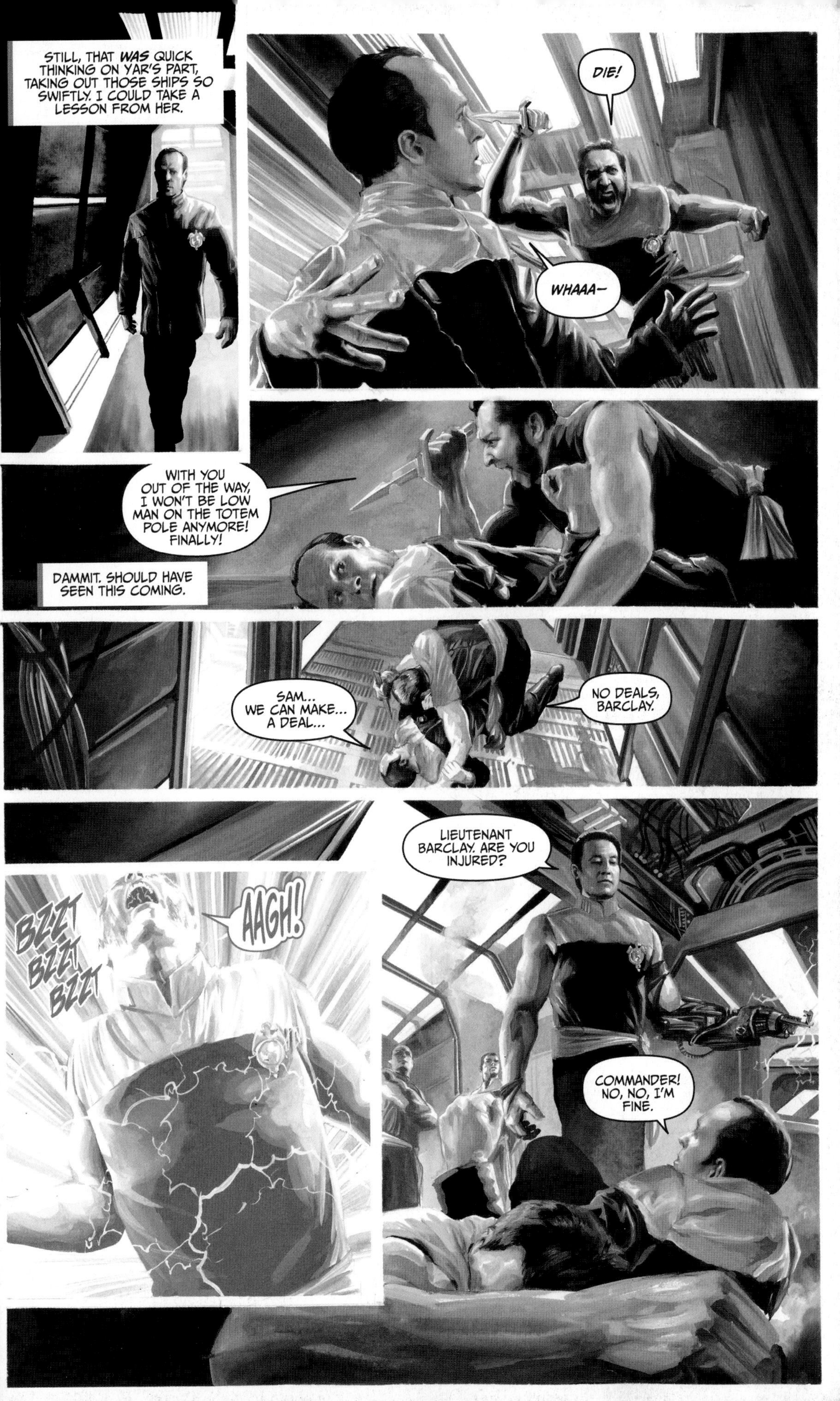
STILL, THAT WAS QUICK THINKING ON YAR'S PART, TAKING OUT THOSE SHIPS SO SWIFTLY. I COULD TAKE A LESSON FROM HER.
DIE!
WHAAA--
WITH YOU OUT OF THE WAY, I WON'T BE LOW MAN ON THE TOTEM POLE ANYMORE! FINALLY!
DAMMIT. SHOULD HAVE SEEN THIS COMING.
SAM... WE CAN MAKE... A DEAL...
NO DEALS, BARCLAY.
BZZT BZZT BZZT
AAGH!
LIEUTENANT BARCLAY. ARE YOU INJURED?
COMMANDER! NO, NO, I'M FINE.

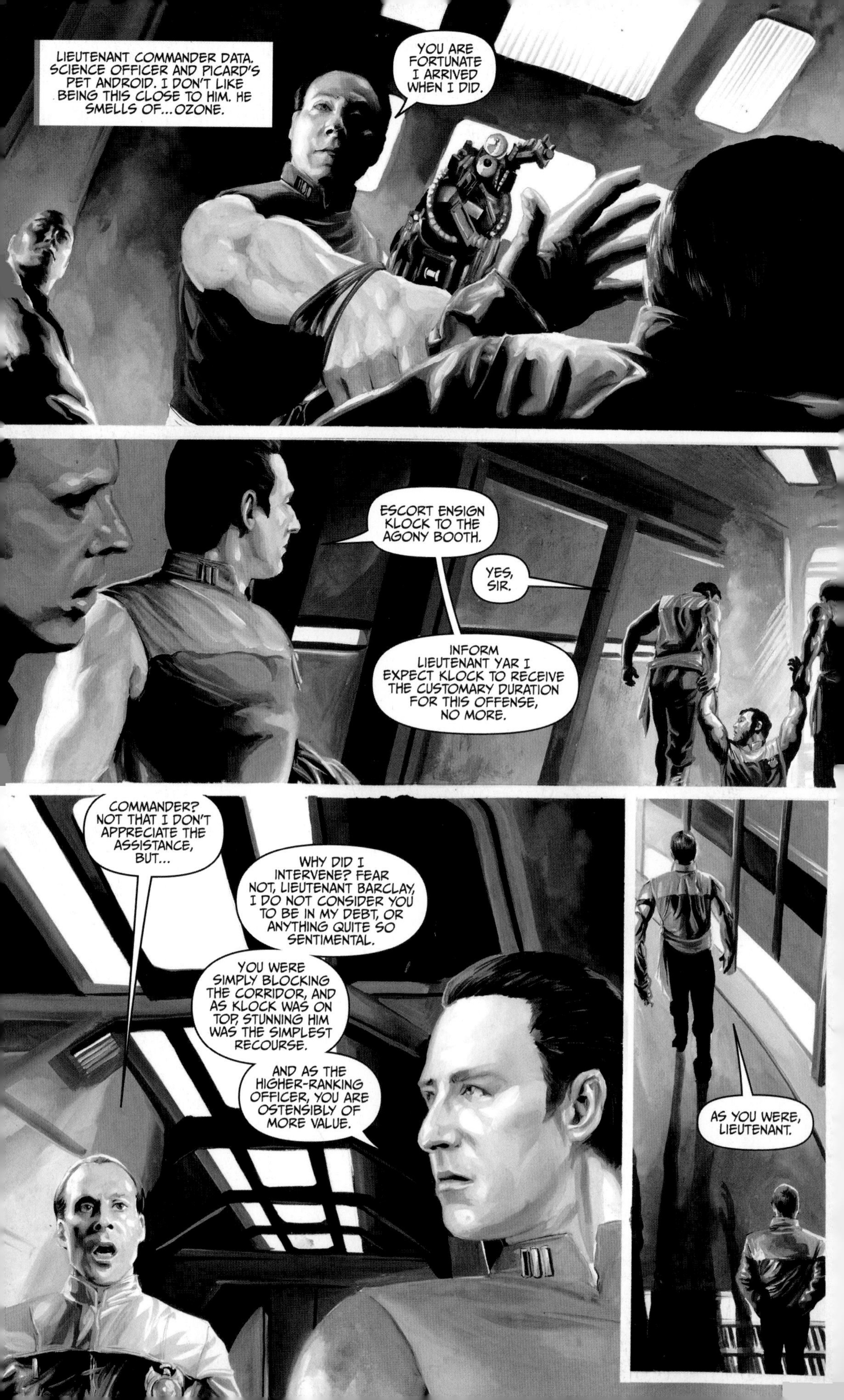

LIEUTENANT COMMANDER DATA. SCIENCE OFFICER AND PICARD'S PET ANDROID. I DON'T LIKE BEING THIS CLOSE TO HIM. HE SMELLS OF...OZONE.
YOU ARE FORTUNATE I ARRIVED WHEN I DID.
ESCORT ENSIGN KLOCK TO THE AGONY BOOTH.
YES, SIR.
INFORM LIEUTENANT YAR I EXPECT KLOCK TO RECEIVE THE CUSTOMARY DURATION FOR THIS OFFENSE, NO MORE.
COMMANDER? NOT THAT I DON'T APPRECIATE THE ASSISTANCE, BUT...
WHY DID I INTERVENE? FEAR NOT, LIEUTENANT BARCLAY, I DO NOT CONSIDER YOU TO BE IN MY DEBT, OR ANYTHING QUITE SO SENTIMENTAL.
YOU WERE SIMPLY BLOCKING THE CORRIDOR, AND AS KLOCK WAS ON TOP, STUNNING HIM WAS THE SIMPLEST RECOURSE.
AND AS THE HIGHER-RANKING OFFICER, YOU ARE OSTENSIBLY OF MORE VALUE.
AS YOU WERE, LIEUTENANT.

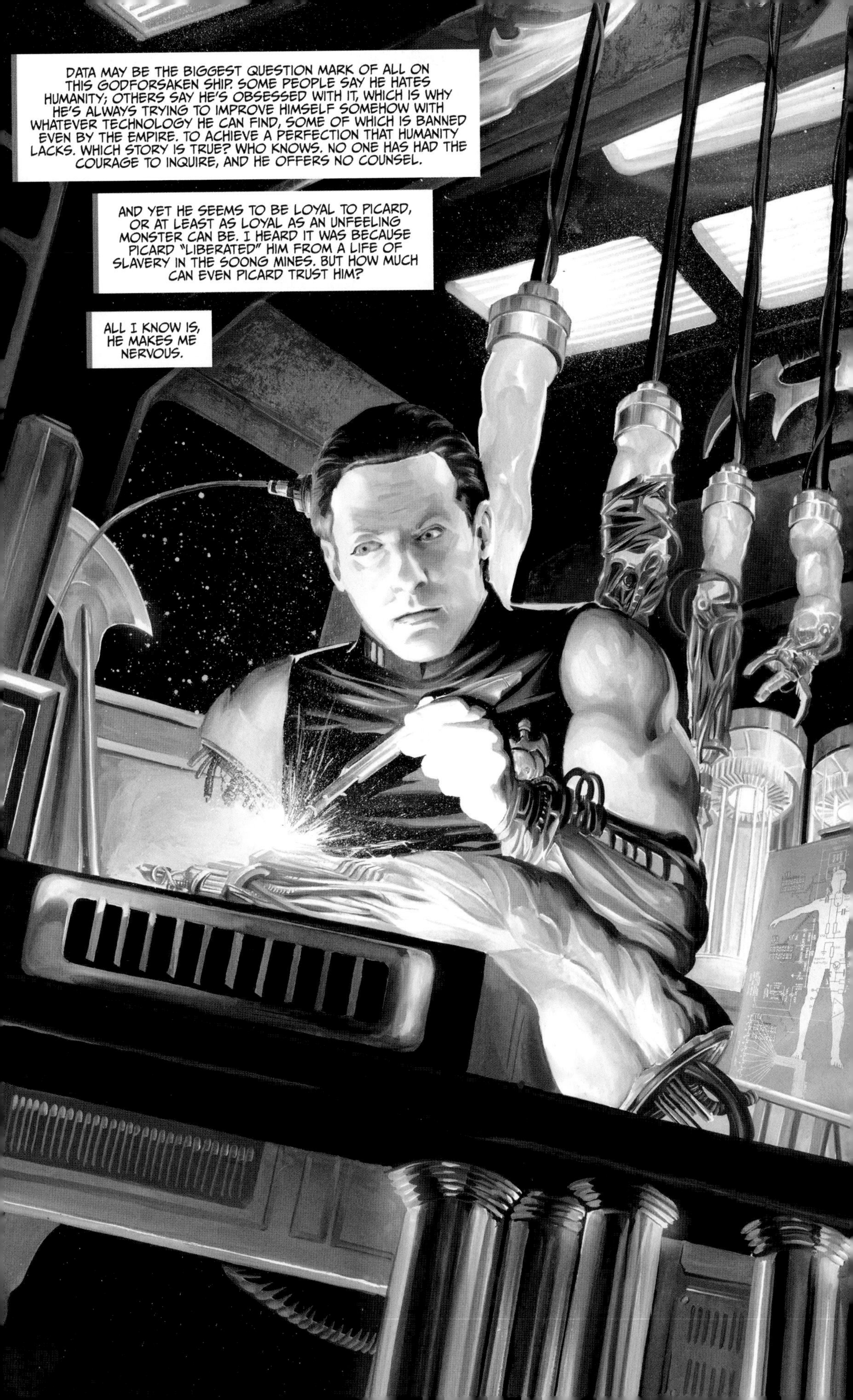
DATA MAY BE THE BIGGEST QUESTION MARK OF ALL ON THIS GODFORSAKEN SHIP. SOME PEOPLE SAY HE HATES HUMANITY; OTHERS SAY HE'S OBSESSED WITH IT, WHICH IS WHY HE'S ALWAYS TRYING TO IMPROVE HIMSELF SOMEHOW WITH WHATEVER TECHNOLOGY HE CAN FIND, SOME OF WHICH IS BANNED EVEN BY THE EMPIRE. TO ACHIEVE A PERFECTION THAT HUMANITY LACKS. WHICH STORY IS TRUE? WHO KNOWS. NO ONE HAS HAD THE COURAGE TO INQUIRE, AND HE OFFERS NO COUNSEL.
AND YET HE SEEMS TO BE LOYAL TO PICARD, OR AT LEAST AS LOYAL AS AN UNFEELING MONSTER CAN BE. I HEARD IT WAS BECAUSE PICARD "LIBERATED" HIM FROM A LIFE OF SLAVERY IN THE SOONG MINES. BUT HOW MUCH CAN EVEN PICARD TRUST HIM?
ALL I KNOW IS, HE MAKES ME NERVOUS.

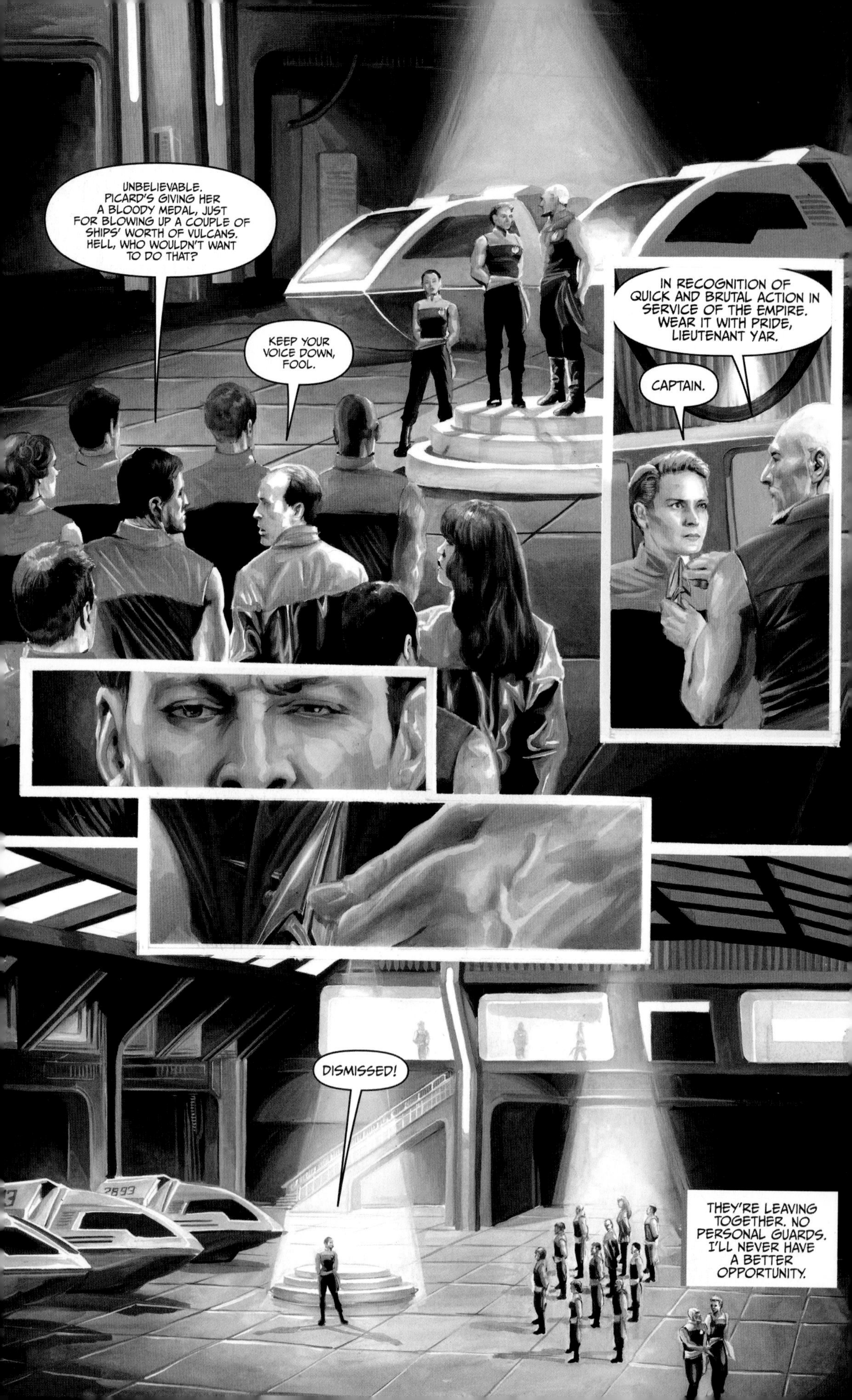
UNBELIEVABLE. PICARD'S GIVING HER A BLOODY MEDAL, JUST FOR BLOWING UP A COUPLE OF SHIPS' WORTH OF VULCANS. HELL, WHO WOULDN'T WANT TO DO THAT?
KEEP YOUR VOICE DOWN, FOOL.
IN RECOGNITION OF QUICK AND BRUTAL ACTION IN SERVICE OF THE EMPIRE. WEAR IT WITH PRIDE, LIEUTENANT YAR.
CAPTAIN.
DISMISSED!
THEY'RE LEAVING TOGETHER. NO PERSONAL GUARDS. I'LL NEVER HAVE A BETTER OPPORTUNITY.

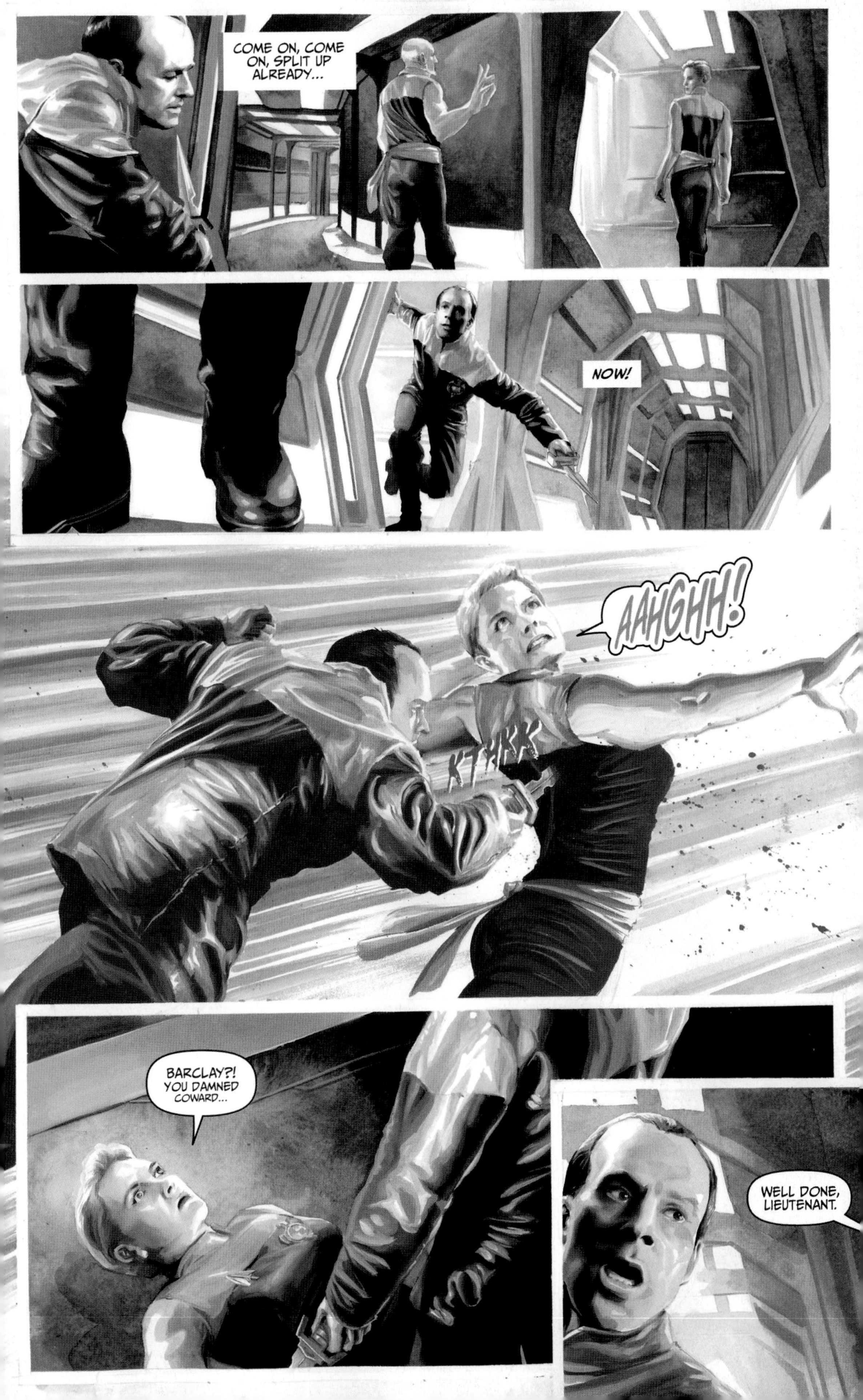
COME ON, COME ON, SPLIT UP ALREADY...
NOW!
AAHGHH!
KTHKK
BARCLAY?! YOU DAMNED COWARD...
WELL DONE, LIEUTENANT.

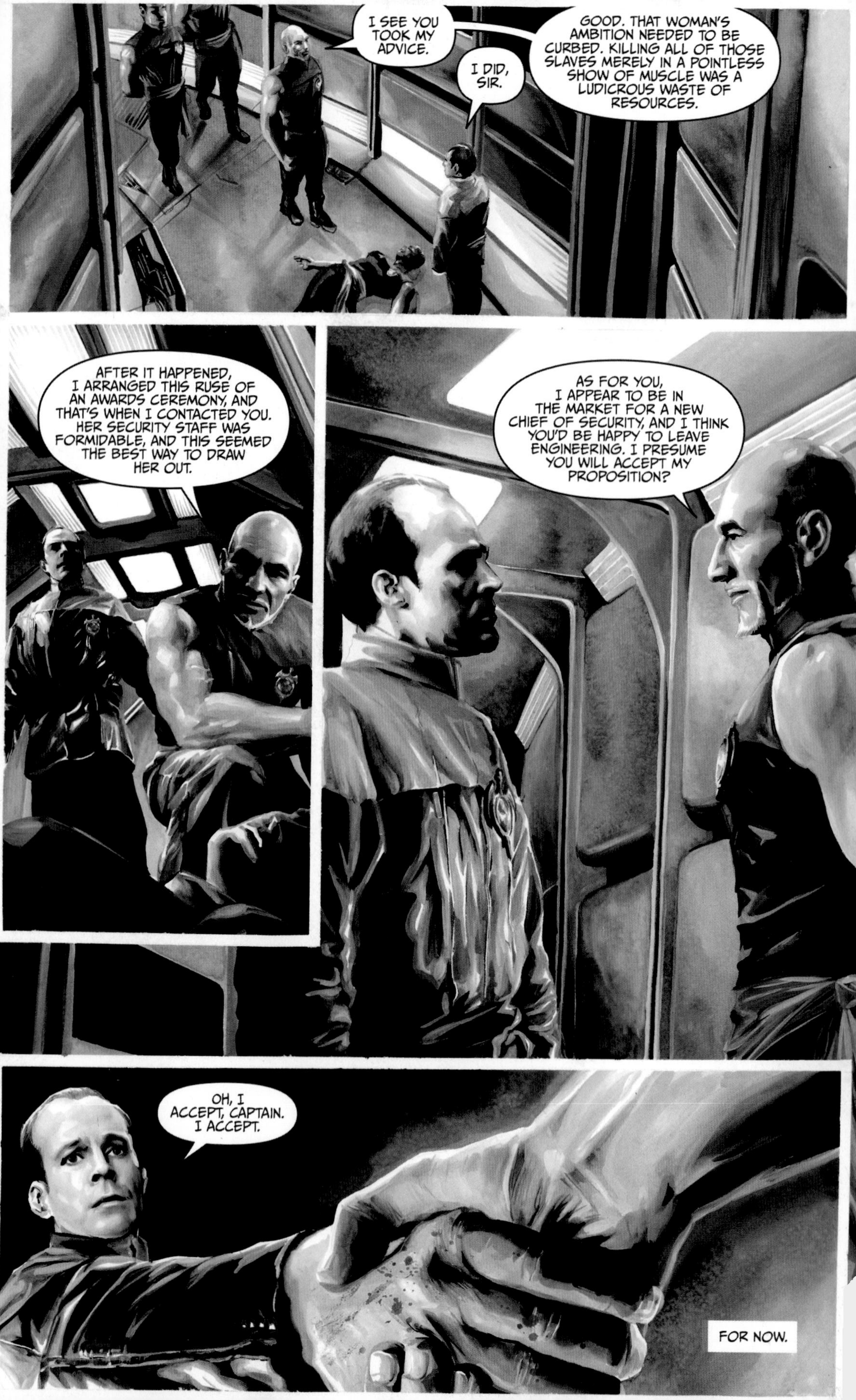
I SEE YOU TOOK MY ADVICE.
I DID, SIR.
GOOD. THAT WOMAN'S AMBITION NEEDED TO BE CURBED. KILLING ALL OF THOSE SLAVES MERELY IN A POINTLESS SHOW OF MUSCLE WAS A LUDICROUS WASTE OF RESOURCES.
AFTER IT HAPPENED, I ARRANGED THIS RUSE OF AN AWARDS CEREMONY, AND THAT'S WHEN I CONTACTED YOU. HER SECURITY STAFF WAS FORMIDABLE, AND THIS SEEMED THE BEST WAY TO DRAW HER OUT.
AS FOR YOU, I APPEAR TO BE IN THE MARKET FOR A NEW CHIEF OF SECURITY, AND I THINK YOU'D BE HAPPY TO LEAVE ENGINEERING. I PRESUME YOU WILL ACCEPT MY PROPOSITION?
OH, I ACCEPT, CAPTAIN. I ACCEPT.
FOR NOW.

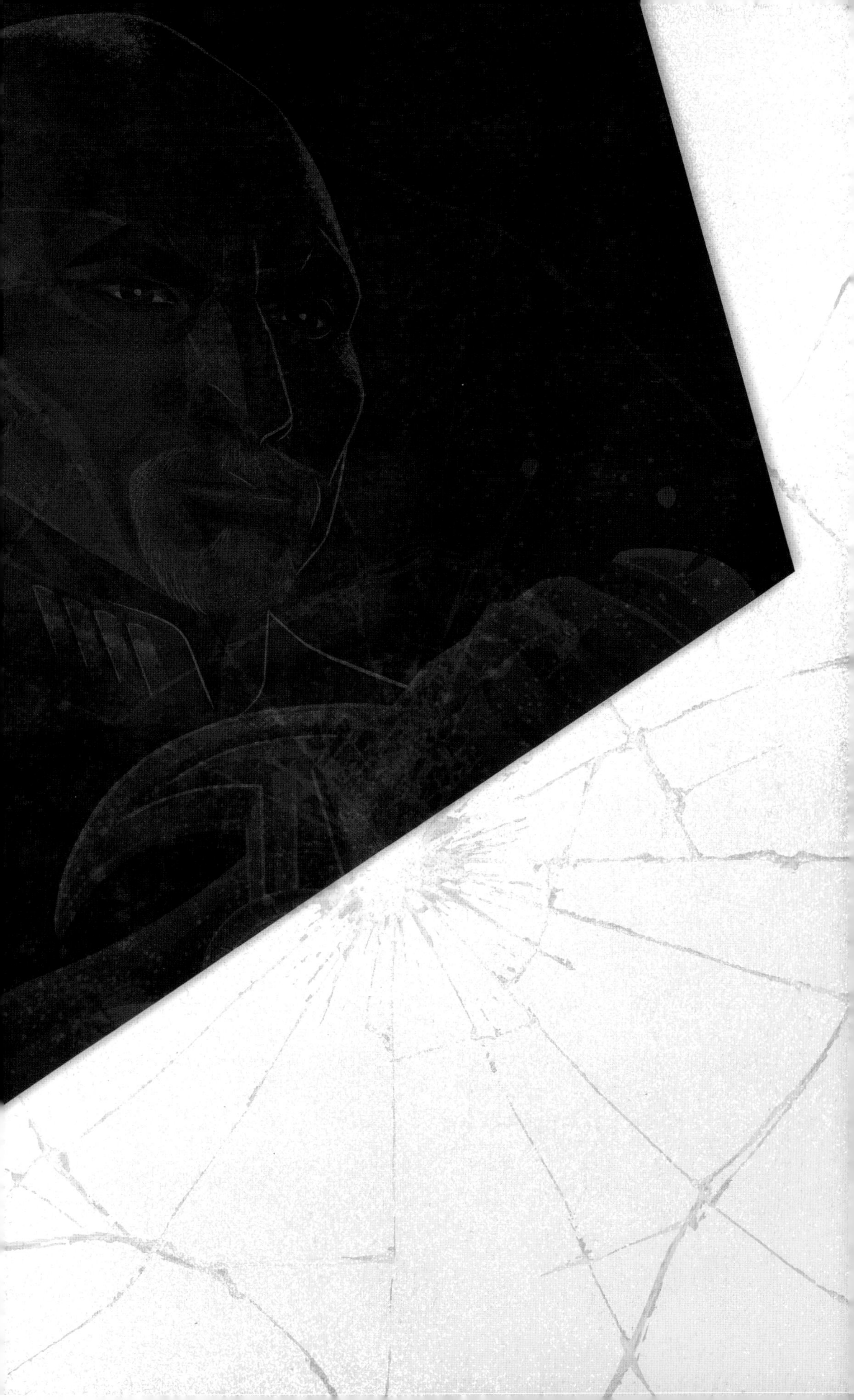

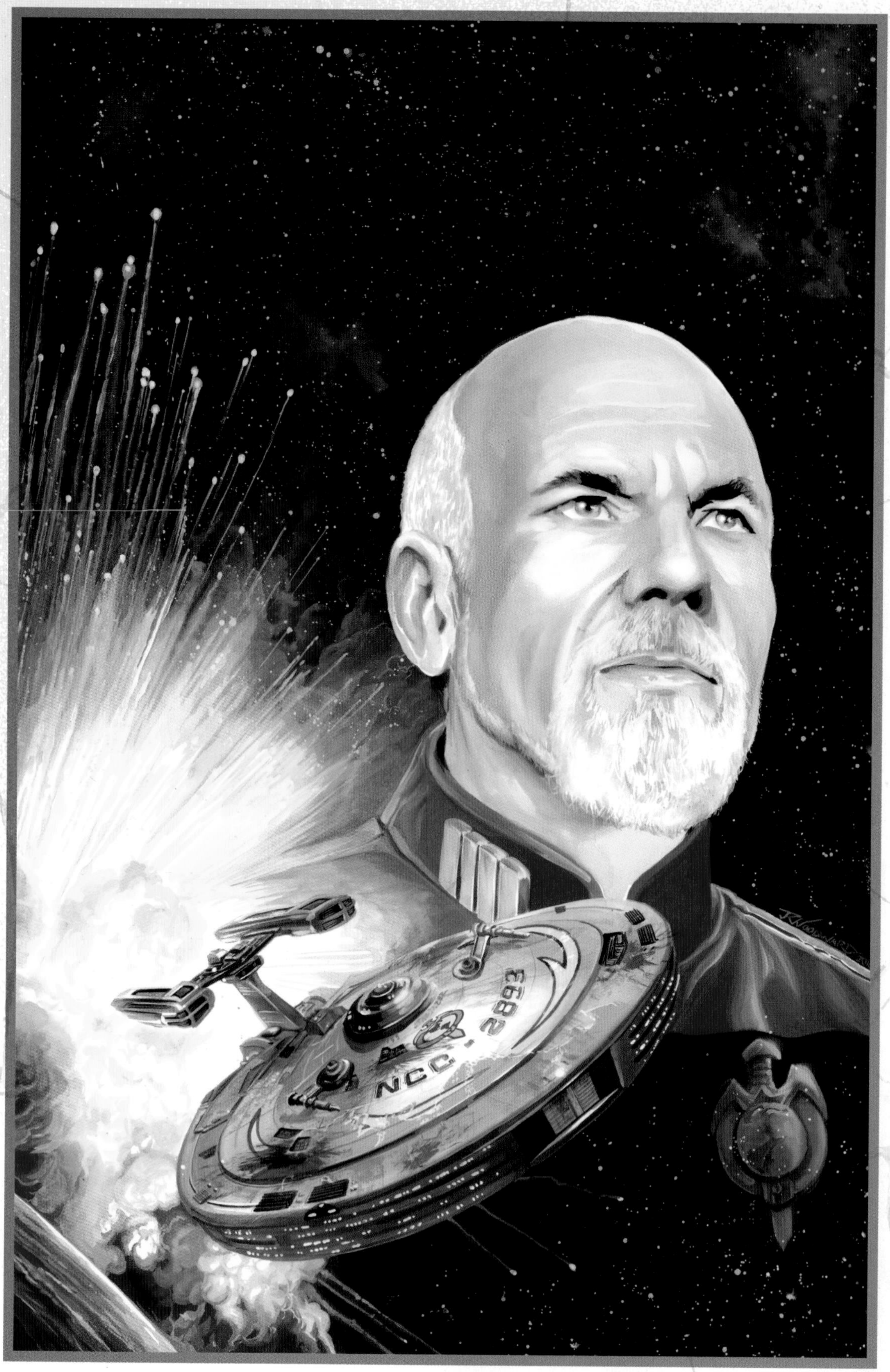
NCC-2893

ART BY
J.K. WOODWARD

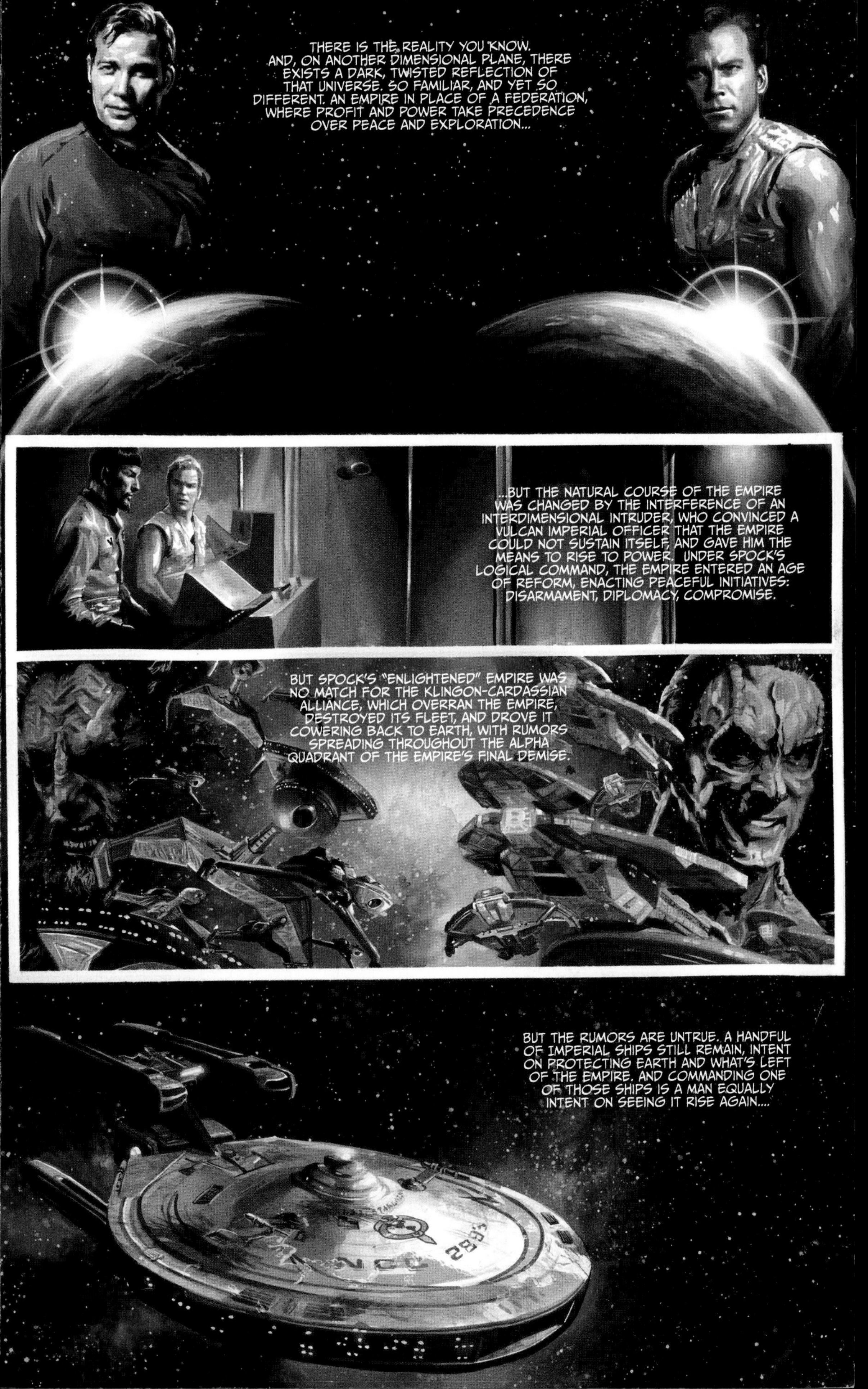
THERE IS THE REALITY YOU KNOW. AND, ON ANOTHER DIMENSIONAL PLANE, THERE EXISTS A DARK, TWISTED REFLECTION OF THAT UNIVERSE. SO FAMILIAR, AND YET SO DIFFERENT. AN EMPIRE IN PLACE OF A FEDERATION, WHERE PROFIT AND POWER TAKE PRECEDENCE OVER PEACE AND EXPLORATION...
...BUT THE NATURAL COURSE OF THE EMPIRE WAS CHANGED BY THE INTERFERENCE OF AN INTERDIMENSIONAL INTRUDER, WHO CONVINCED A VULCAN IMPERIAL OFFICER THAT THE EMPIRE COULD NOT SUSTAIN ITSELF, AND GAVE HIM THE MEANS TO RISE TO POWER. UNDER SPOCK'S LOGICAL COMMAND, THE EMPIRE ENTERED AN AGE OF REFORM, ENACTING PEACEFUL INITIATIVES: DISARMAMENT, DIPLOMACY, COMPROMISE.
BUT SPOCK'S "ENLIGHTENED" EMPIRE WAS NO MATCH FOR THE KLINGON-CARDASSIAN ALLIANCE, WHICH OVERRAN THE EMPIRE, DESTROYED ITS FLEET, AND DROVE IT COWERING BACK TO EARTH, WITH RUMORS SPREADING THROUGHOUT THE ALPHA QUADRANT OF THE EMPIRE'S FINAL DEMISE.
BUT THE RUMORS ARE UNTRUE. A HANDFUL OF IMPERIAL SHIPS STILL REMAIN, INTENT ON PROTECTING EARTH AND WHAT'S LEFT OF THE EMPIRE. AND COMMANDING ONE OF THOSE SHIPS IS A MAN EQUALLY INTENT ON SEEING IT RISE AGAIN....

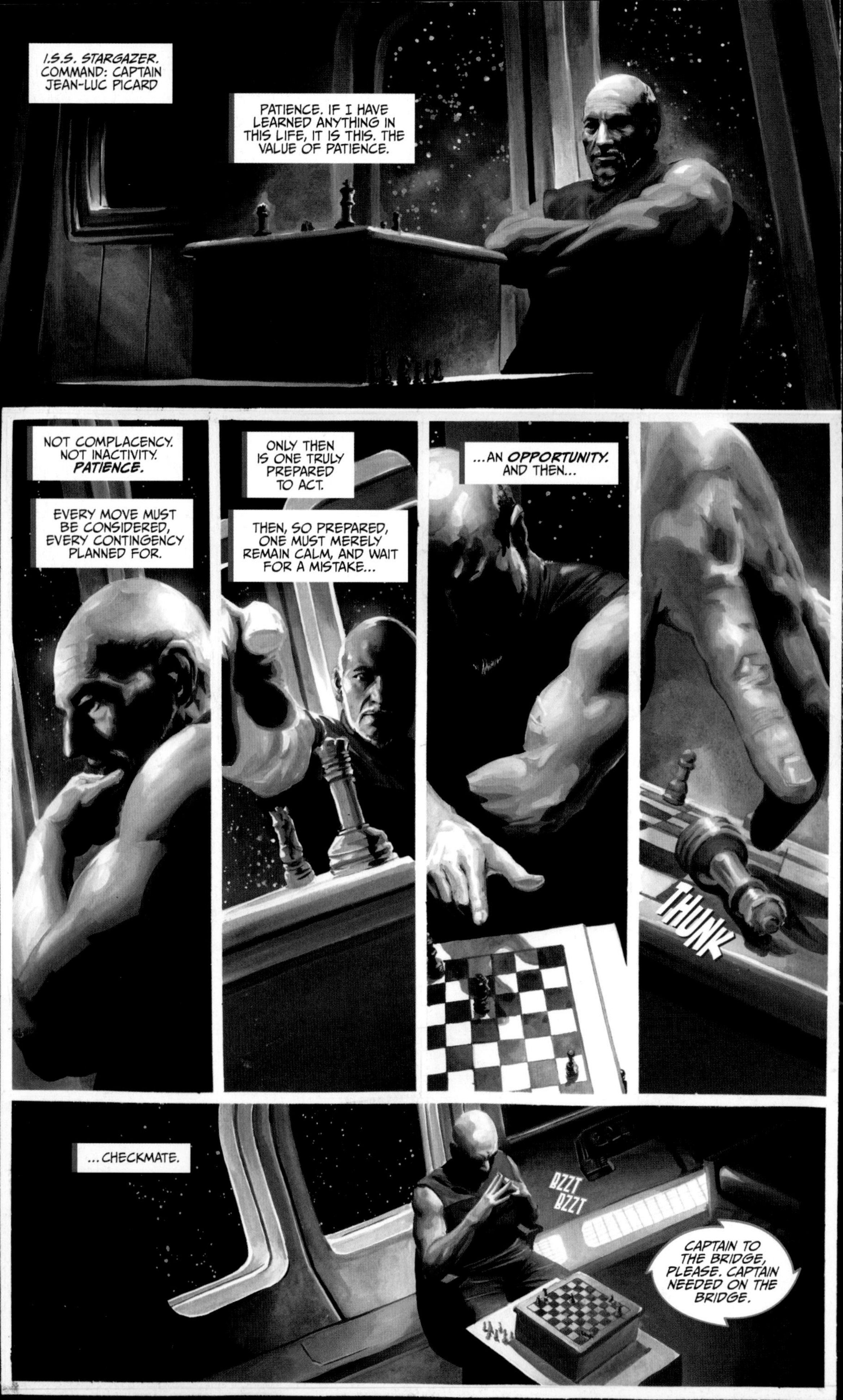
I.S.S. STARGAZER. COMMAND: CAPTAIN JEAN-LUC PICARD
PATIENCE. IF I HAVE LEARNED ANYTHING IN THIS LIFE, IT IS THIS. THE VALUE OF PATIENCE.
NOT COMPLACENCY. NOT INACTIVITY. PATIENCE.
EVERY MOVE MUST BE CONSIDERED, EVERY CONTINGENCY PLANNED FOR.
ONLY THEN IS ONE TRULY PREPARED TO ACT.
THEN, SO PREPARED, ONE MUST MERELY REMAIN CALM, AND WAIT FOR A MISTAKE...
...AN OPPORTUNITY. AND THEN...
THUNK
...CHECKMATE.
BZZT BZZT
CAPTAIN TO THE BRIDGE, PLEASE. CAPTAIN NEEDED ON THE BRIDGE.

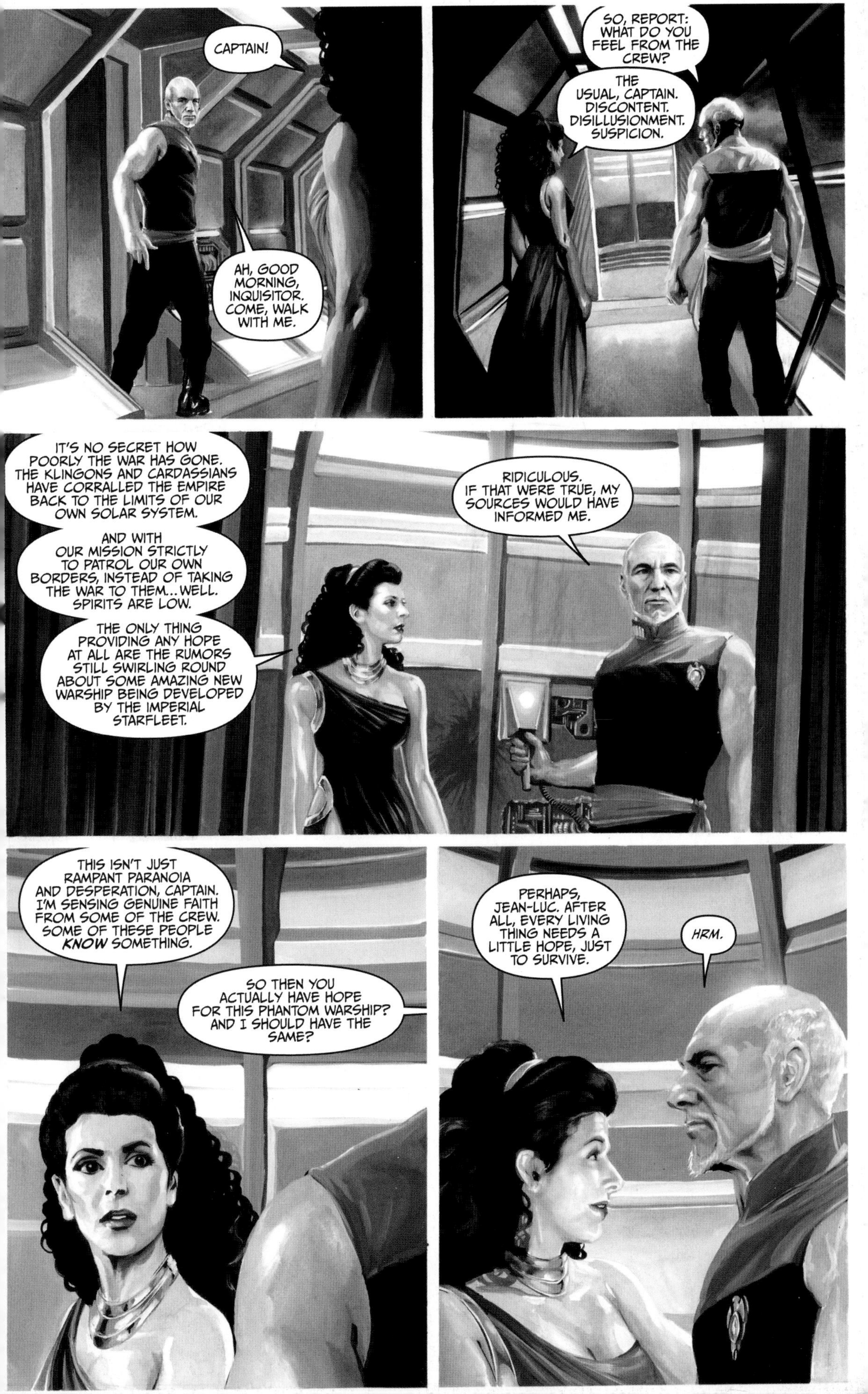
CAPTAIN!
AH, GOOD MORNING, INQUISITOR. COME, WALK WITH ME.
SO, REPORT: WHAT DO YOU FEEL FROM THE CREW?
THE USUAL, CAPTAIN. DISCONTENT. DISILLUSIONMENT. SUSPICION.
IT'S NO SECRET HOW POORLY THE WAR HAS GONE. THE KLINGONS AND CARDASSIANS HAVE CORRALLED THE EMPIRE BACK TO THE LIMITS OF OUR OWN SOLAR SYSTEM.
AND WITH OUR MISSION STRICTLY TO PATROL OUR OWN BORDERS, INSTEAD OF TAKING THE WAR TO THEM...WELL. SPIRITS ARE LOW.
THE ONLY THING PROVIDING ANY HOPE AT ALL ARE THE RUMORS STILL SWIRLING ROUND ABOUT SOME AMAZING NEW WARSHIP BEING DEVELOPED BY THE IMPERIAL STARFLEET.
RIDICULOUS. IF THAT WERE TRUE, MY SOURCES WOULD HAVE INFORMED ME.
THIS ISN'T JUST RAMPANT PARANOIA AND DESPERATION, CAPTAIN. I'M SENSING GENUINE FAITH FROM SOME OF THE CREW. SOME OF THESE PEOPLE **KNOW** SOMETHING.
SO THEN YOU ACTUALLY HAVE HOPE FOR THIS PHANTOM WARSHIP? AND I SHOULD HAVE THE SAME?
PERHAPS, JEAN-LUC. AFTER ALL, EVERY LIVING THING NEEDS A LITTLE HOPE, JUST TO SURVIVE.
HRM.

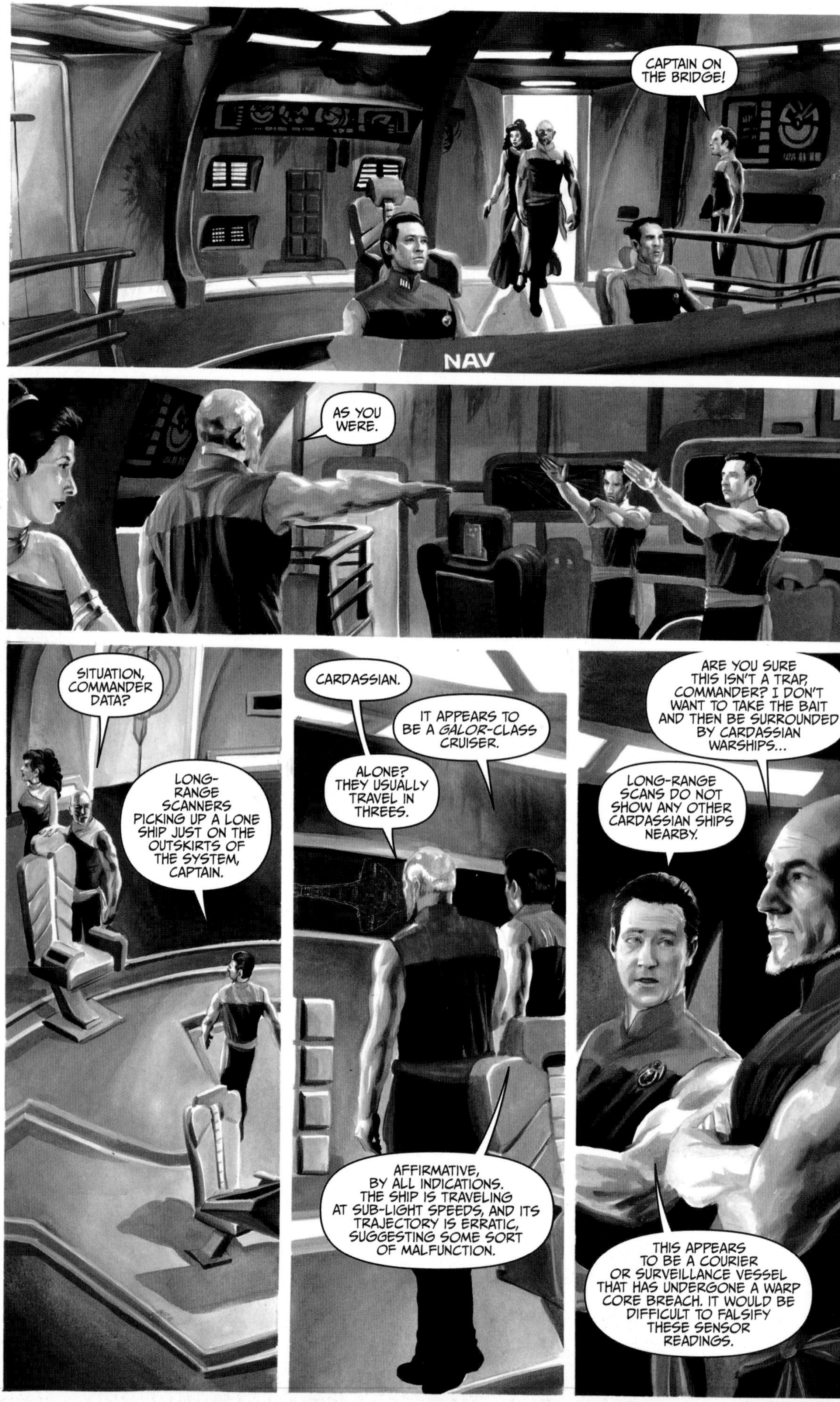
CAPTAIN ON THE BRIDGE!
NAV
AS YOU WERE.
SITUATION, COMMANDER DATA?
LONG-RANGE SCANNERS PICKING UP A LONE SHIP JUST ON THE OUTSKIRTS OF THE SYSTEM, CAPTAIN.
CARDASSIAN.
IT APPEARS TO BE A *GALOR*-CLASS CRUISER.
ALONE? THEY USUALLY TRAVEL IN THREES.
AFFIRMATIVE, BY ALL INDICATIONS. THE SHIP IS TRAVELING AT SUB-LIGHT SPEEDS, AND ITS TRAJECTORY IS ERRATIC, SUGGESTING SOME SORT OF MALFUNCTION.
ARE YOU SURE THIS ISN'T A TRAP, COMMANDER? I DON'T WANT TO TAKE THE BAIT AND THEN BE SURROUNDED BY CARDASSIAN WARSHIPS...
LONG-RANGE SCANS DO NOT SHOW ANY OTHER CARDASSIAN SHIPS NEARBY.
THIS APPEARS TO BE A COURIER OR SURVEILLANCE VESSEL THAT HAS UNDERGONE A WARP CORE BREACH. IT WOULD BE DIFFICULT TO FALSIFY THESE SENSOR READINGS.

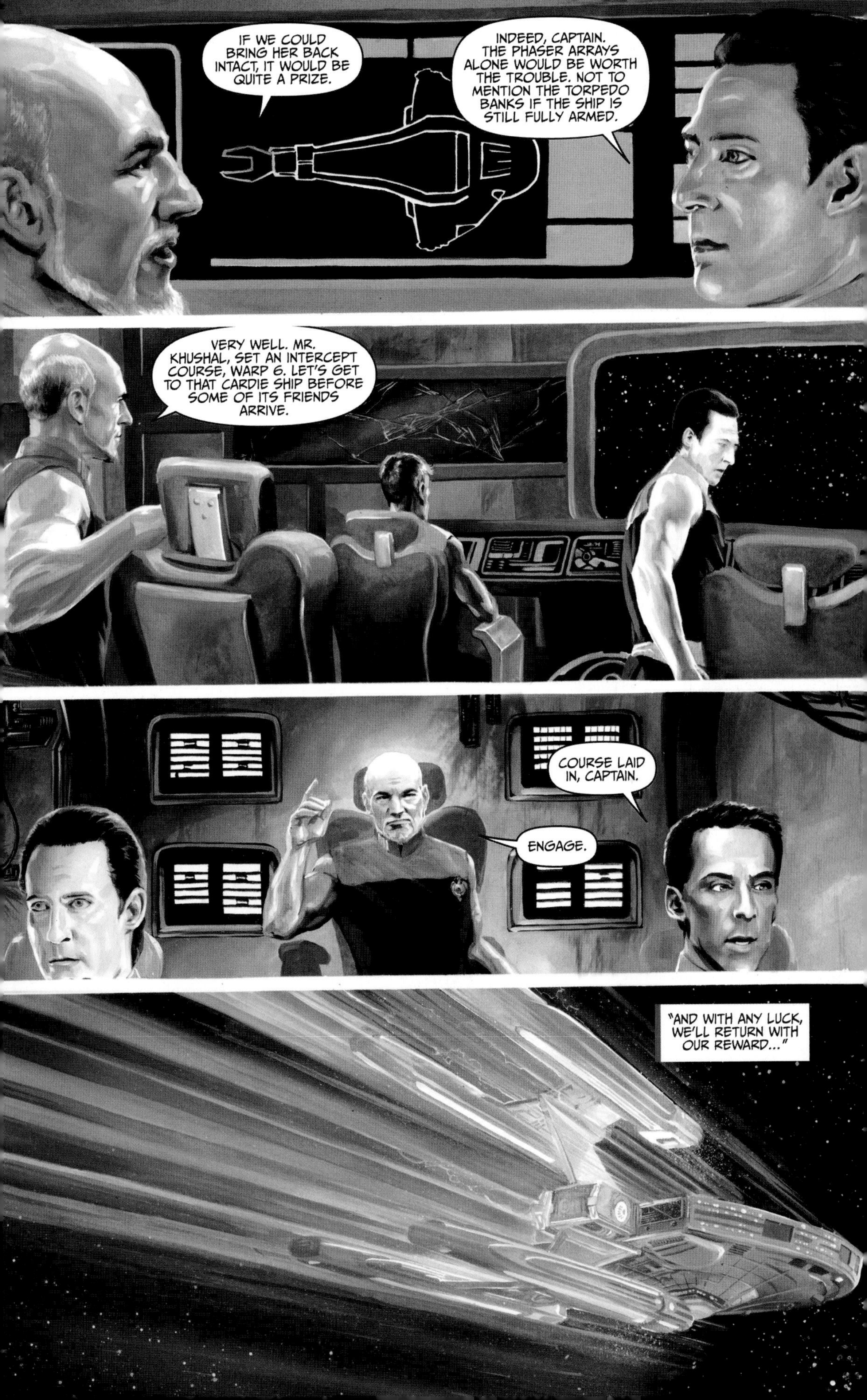
IF WE COULD BRING HER BACK INTACT, IT WOULD BE QUITE A PRIZE.
INDEED, CAPTAIN. THE PHASER ARRAYS ALONE WOULD BE WORTH THE TROUBLE. NOT TO MENTION THE TORPEDO BANKS IF THE SHIP IS STILL FULLY ARMED.
VERY WELL. MR. KHUSHAL, SET AN INTERCEPT COURSE, WARP 6. LET'S GET TO THAT CARDIE SHIP BEFORE SOME OF ITS FRIENDS ARRIVE.
COURSE LAID IN, CAPTAIN.
ENGAGE.
"AND WITH ANY LUCK, WE'LL RETURN WITH OUR REWARD..."

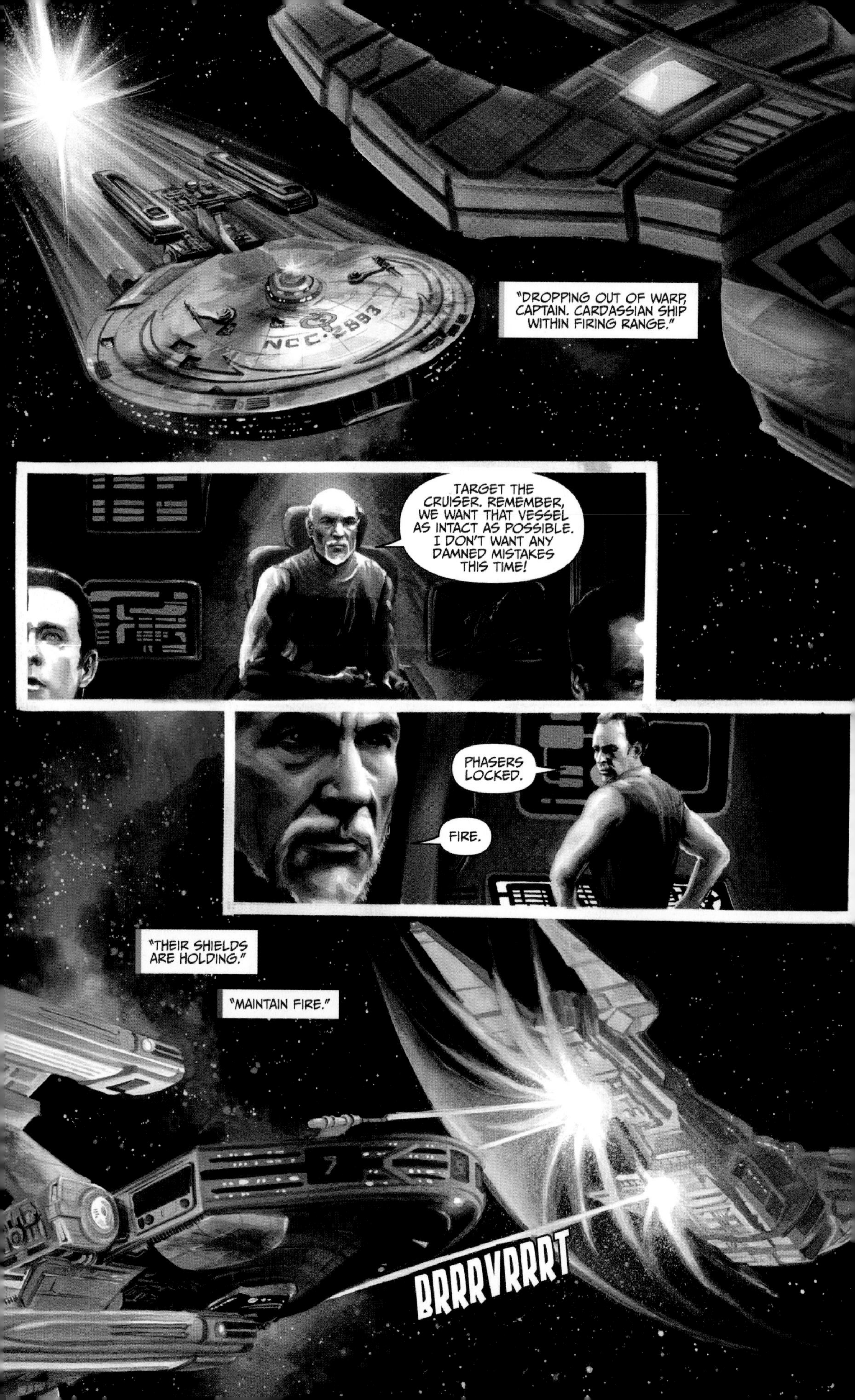
"DROPPING OUT OF WARP, CAPTAIN. CARDASSIAN SHIP WITHIN FIRING RANGE."
TARGET THE CRUISER. REMEMBER, WE WANT THAT VESSEL AS INTACT AS POSSIBLE. I DON'T WANT ANY DAMNED MISTAKES THIS TIME!
PHASERS LOCKED.
FIRE.
"THEIR SHIELDS ARE HOLDING."
"MAINTAIN FIRE."
BRRRVRRRT

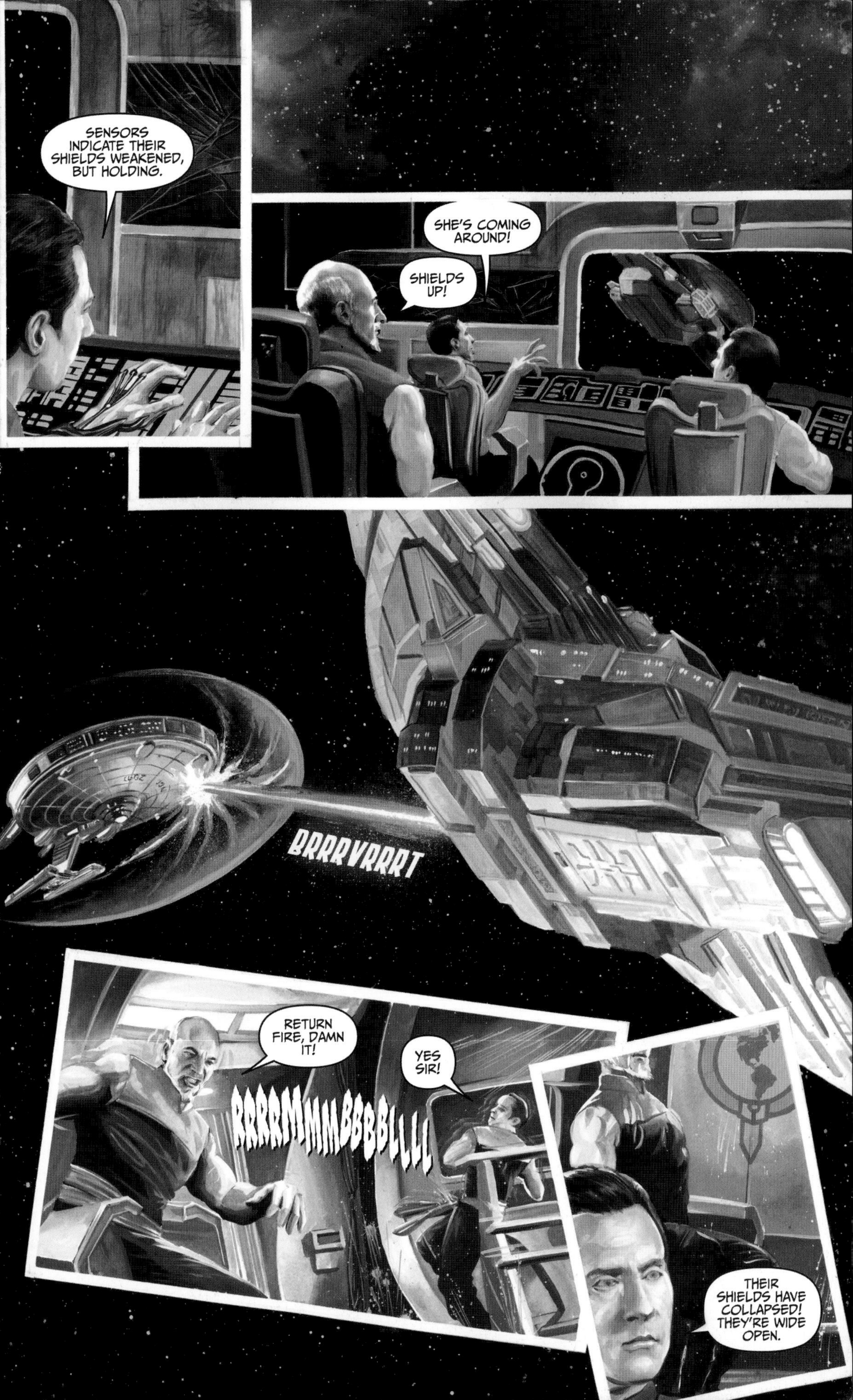
SENSORS INDICATE THEIR SHIELDS WEAKENED, BUT HOLDING.
SHE'S COMING AROUND!
SHIELDS UP!
BRRRVRRRT
RETURN FIRE, DAMN IT!
BRRRMMMMBBBBLLLL
YES SIR!
THEIR SHIELDS HAVE COLLAPSED! THEY'RE WIDE OPEN.

WE DON'T WANT THEM GOING ANYWHERE. MR. BARCLAY, CONTINUE FIRE.

THIS SHOULD KEEP THEM AROUND...

"FIRE!"

THE PRIORITY IS THE SHIP, COMMANDER, NOT THE CREW. TAKE THE SHOT.

UNDERSTOOD, CAPTAIN.

TARGETING THE SHIP'S LIFE-SUPPORT SYSTEMS AND REAR SHUTTLE BAY HATCHES. READY TO FIRE, CAPTAIN.

FIRE!

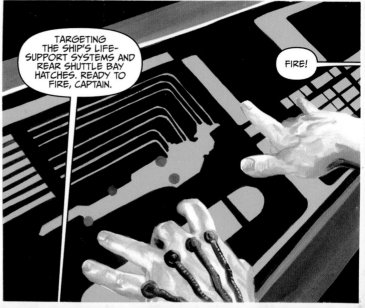

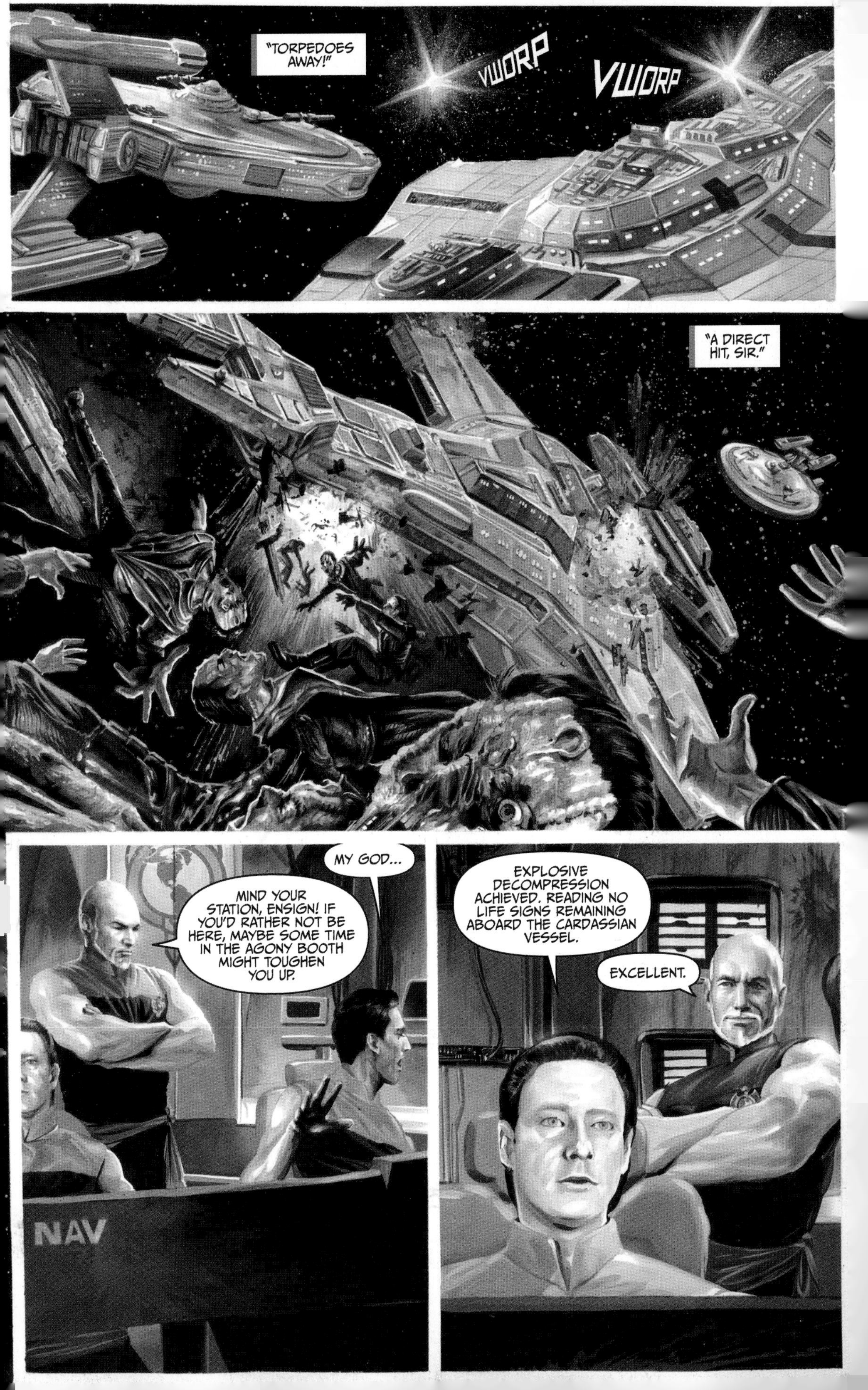

"TORPEDOES AWAY!"
VWORP
VWORP
"A DIRECT HIT, SIR."
MY GOD...
MIND YOUR STATION, ENSIGN! IF YOU'D RATHER NOT BE HERE, MAYBE SOME TIME IN THE AGONY BOOTH MIGHT TOUGHEN YOU UP.
NAV
EXPLOSIVE DECOMPRESSION ACHIEVED. READING NO LIFE SIGNS REMAINING ABOARD THE CARDASSIAN VESSEL.
EXCELLENT.

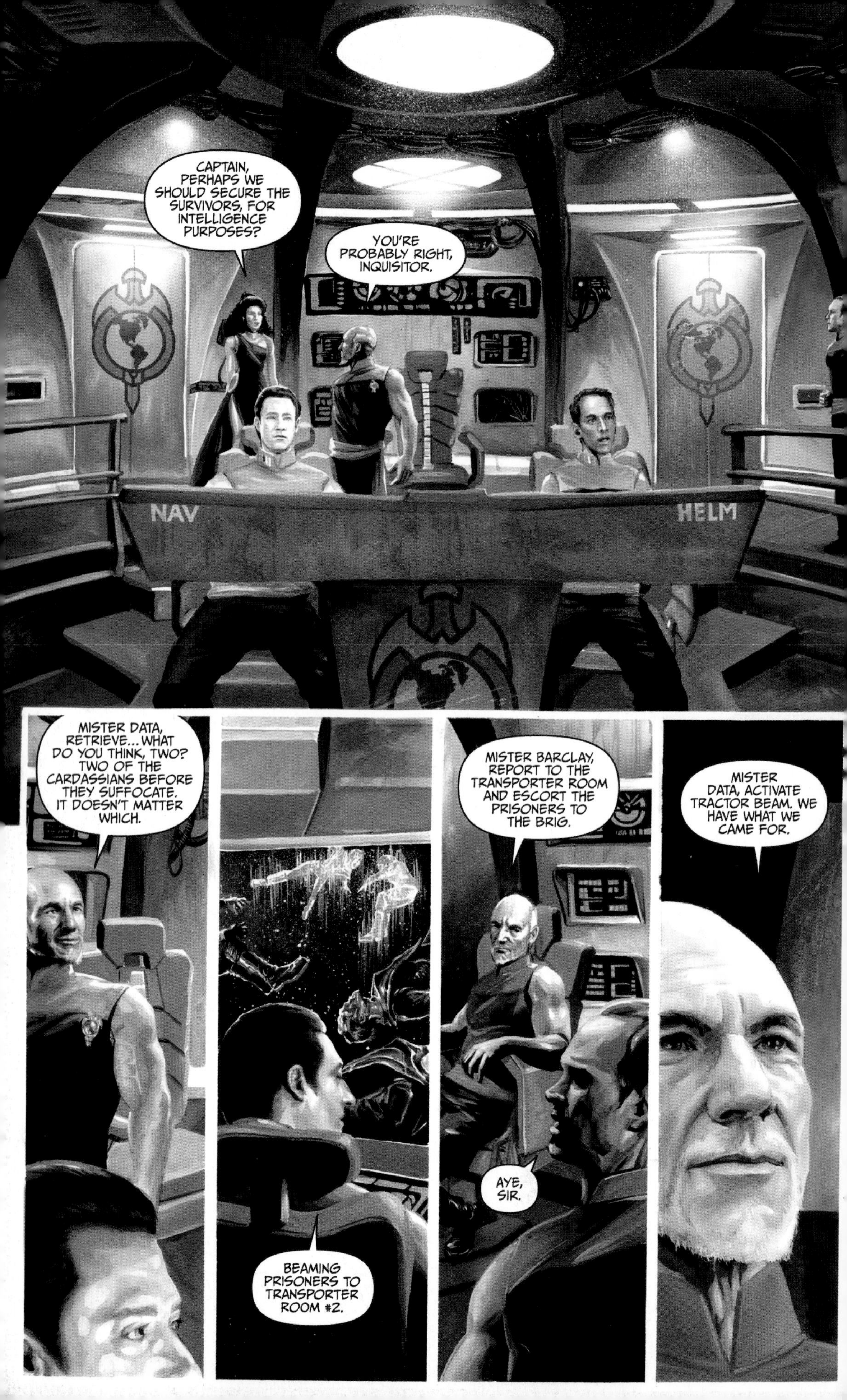
CAPTAIN, PERHAPS WE SHOULD SECURE THE SURVIVORS, FOR INTELLIGENCE PURPOSES?
YOU'RE PROBABLY RIGHT, INQUISITOR.
NAV
HELM
MISTER DATA, RETRIEVE... WHAT DO YOU THINK, TWO? TWO OF THE CARDASSIANS BEFORE THEY SUFFOCATE. IT DOESN'T MATTER WHICH.
BEAMING PRISONERS TO TRANSPORTER ROOM #2.
MISTER BARCLAY, REPORT TO THE TRANSPORTER ROOM AND ESCORT THE PRISONERS TO THE BRIG.
AYE, SIR.
MISTER DATA, ACTIVATE TRACTOR BEAM. WE HAVE WHAT WE CAME FOR.

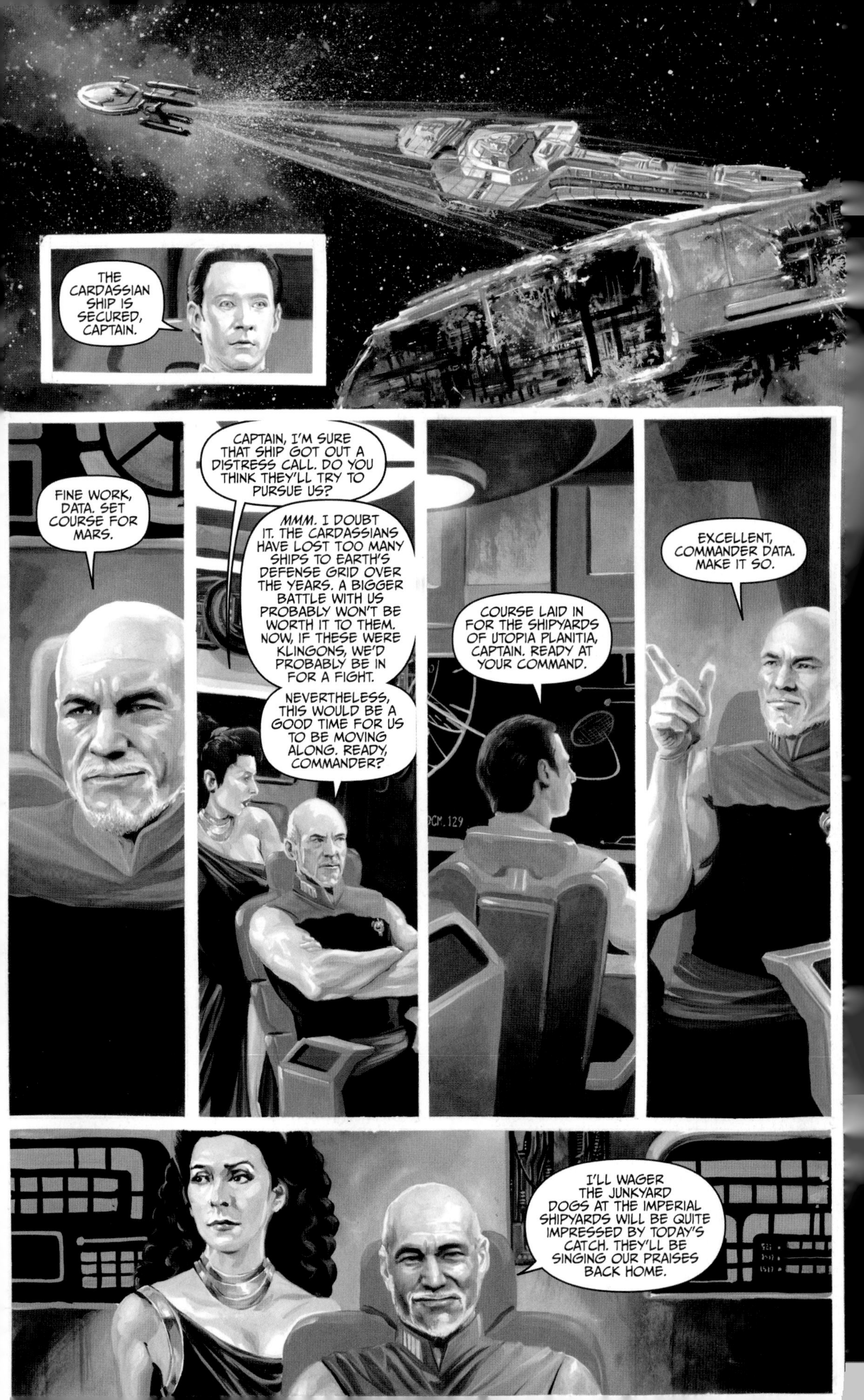
THE CARDASSIAN SHIP IS SECURED, CAPTAIN.
FINE WORK, DATA. SET COURSE FOR MARS.
CAPTAIN, I'M SURE THAT SHIP GOT OUT A DISTRESS CALL. DO YOU THINK THEY'LL TRY TO PURSUE US?
MMM. I DOUBT IT. THE CARDASSIANS HAVE LOST TOO MANY SHIPS TO EARTH'S DEFENSE GRID OVER THE YEARS. A BIGGER BATTLE WITH US PROBABLY WON'T BE WORTH IT TO THEM. NOW, IF THESE WERE KLINGONS, WE'D PROBABLY BE IN FOR A FIGHT.
NEVERTHELESS, THIS WOULD BE A GOOD TIME FOR US TO BE MOVING ALONG. READY, COMMANDER?
COURSE LAID IN FOR THE SHIPYARDS OF UTOPIA PLANITIA, CAPTAIN. READY AT YOUR COMMAND.
EXCELLENT, COMMANDER DATA. MAKE IT SO.
I'LL WAGER THE JUNKYARD DOGS AT THE IMPERIAL SHIPYARDS WILL BE QUITE IMPRESSED BY TODAY'S CATCH. THEY'LL BE SINGING OUR PRAISES BACK HOME.

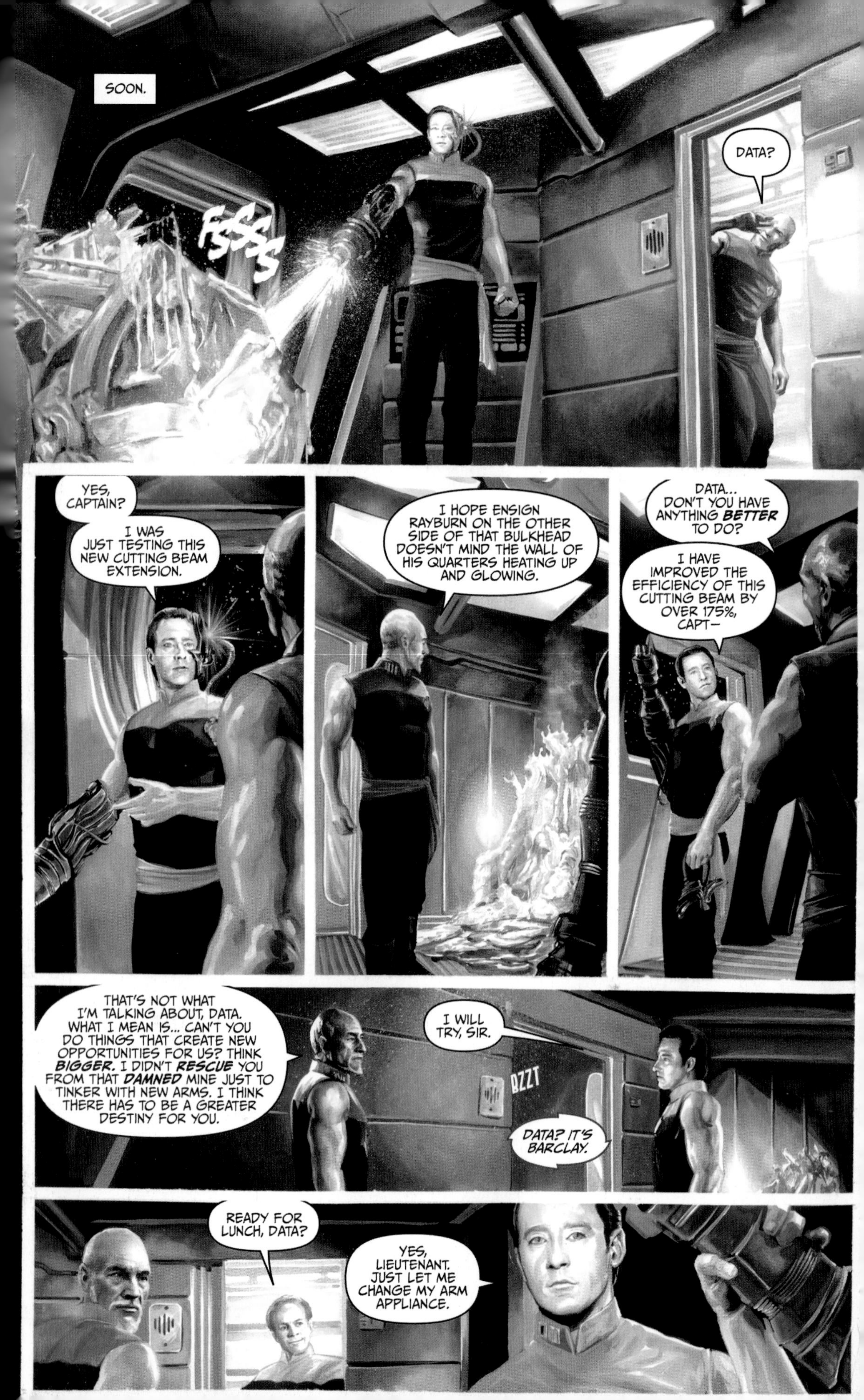
SOON.
FSSSS
DATA?
YES, CAPTAIN?
I WAS JUST TESTING THIS NEW CUTTING BEAM EXTENSION.
I HOPE ENSIGN RAYBURN ON THE OTHER SIDE OF THAT BULKHEAD DOESN'T MIND THE WALL OF HIS QUARTERS HEATING UP AND GLOWING.
DATA... DON'T YOU HAVE ANYTHING **BETTER** TO DO?
I HAVE IMPROVED THE EFFICIENCY OF THIS CUTTING BEAM BY OVER 175%, CAPT—
THAT'S NOT WHAT I'M TALKING ABOUT, DATA. WHAT I MEAN IS... CAN'T YOU DO THINGS THAT CREATE NEW OPPORTUNITIES FOR US? THINK **BIGGER.** I DIDN'T **RESCUE** YOU FROM THAT **DAMNED** MINE JUST TO TINKER WITH NEW ARMS. I THINK THERE HAS TO BE A GREATER DESTINY FOR YOU.
I WILL TRY, SIR.
BZZT
DATA? IT'S BARCLAY.
READY FOR LUNCH, DATA?
YES, LIEUTENANT. JUST LET ME CHANGE MY ARM APPLIANCE.

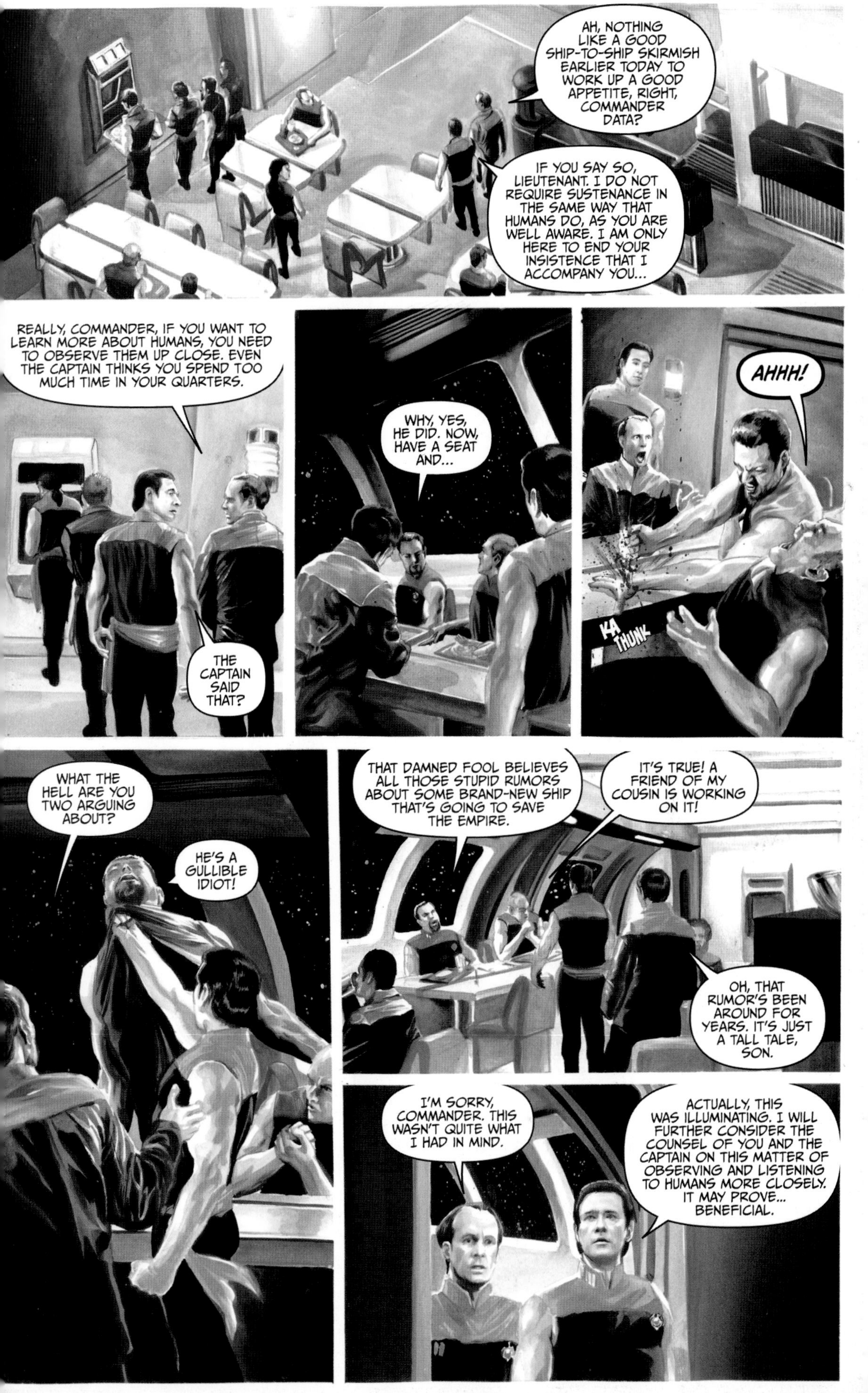
AH, NOTHING LIKE A GOOD SHIP-TO-SHIP SKIRMISH EARLIER TODAY TO WORK UP A GOOD APPETITE, RIGHT, COMMANDER DATA?
IF YOU SAY SO, LIEUTENANT. I DO NOT REQUIRE SUSTENANCE IN THE SAME WAY THAT HUMANS DO, AS YOU ARE WELL AWARE. I AM ONLY HERE TO END YOUR INSISTENCE THAT I ACCOMPANY YOU...
REALLY, COMMANDER, IF YOU WANT TO LEARN MORE ABOUT HUMANS, YOU NEED TO OBSERVE THEM UP CLOSE. EVEN THE CAPTAIN THINKS YOU SPEND TOO MUCH TIME IN YOUR QUARTERS.
THE CAPTAIN SAID THAT?
WHY, YES, HE DID. NOW, HAVE A SEAT AND...
AHHH!
KA THUNK
WHAT THE HELL ARE YOU TWO ARGUING ABOUT?
HE'S A GULLIBLE IDIOT!
THAT DAMNED FOOL BELIEVES ALL THOSE STUPID RUMORS ABOUT SOME BRAND-NEW SHIP THAT'S GOING TO SAVE THE EMPIRE.
IT'S TRUE! A FRIEND OF MY COUSIN IS WORKING ON IT!
OH, THAT RUMOR'S BEEN AROUND FOR YEARS. IT'S JUST A TALL TALE, SON.
I'M SORRY, COMMANDER. THIS WASN'T QUITE WHAT I HAD IN MIND.
ACTUALLY, THIS WAS ILLUMINATING. I WILL FURTHER CONSIDER THE COUNSEL OF YOU AND THE CAPTAIN ON THIS MATTER OF OBSERVING AND LISTENING TO HUMANS MORE CLOSELY. IT MAY PROVE... BENEFICIAL.

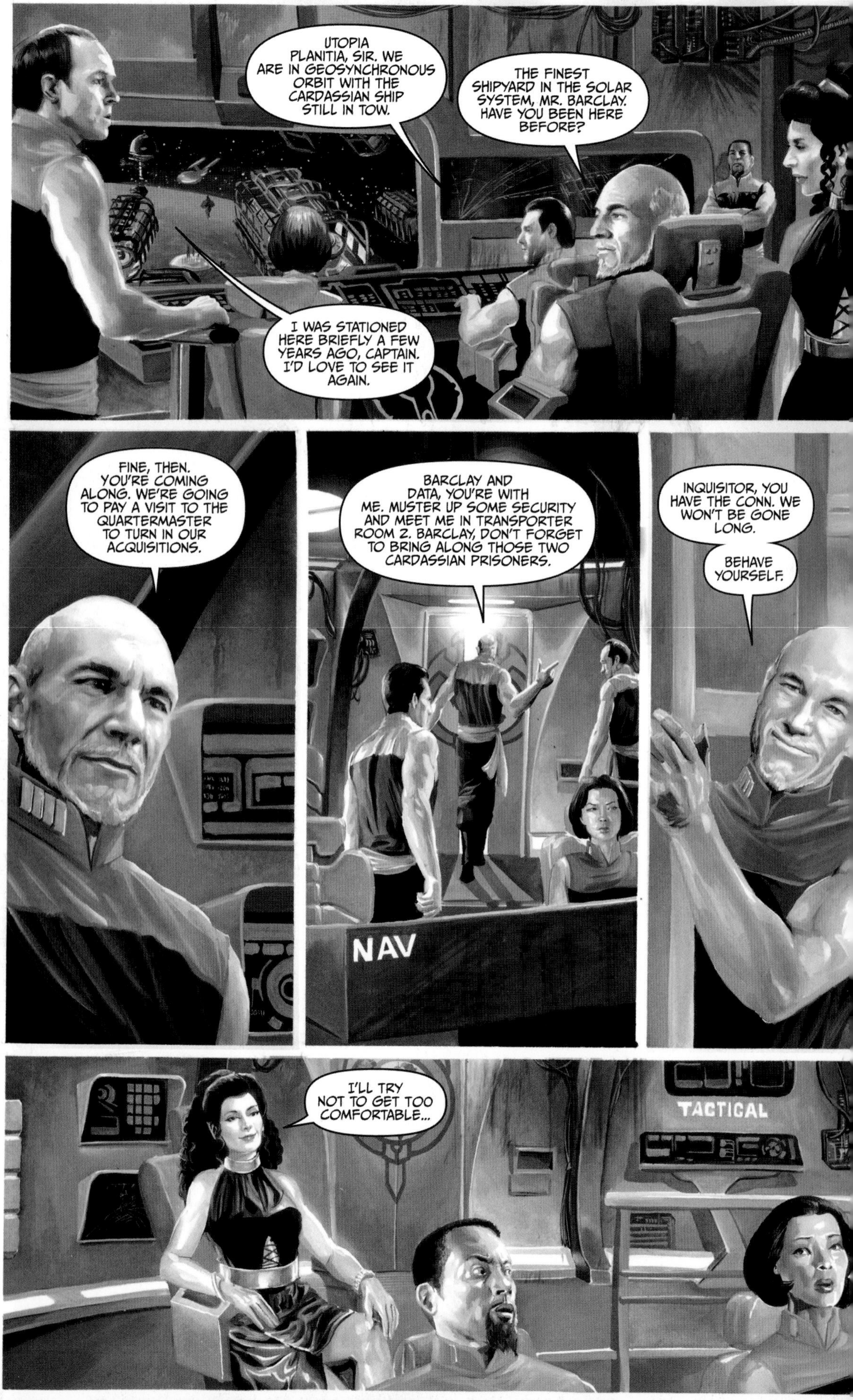
UTOPIA PLANITIA, SIR. WE ARE IN GEOSYNCHRONOUS ORBIT WITH THE CARDASSIAN SHIP STILL IN TOW.
THE FINEST SHIPYARD IN THE SOLAR SYSTEM, MR. BARCLAY. HAVE YOU BEEN HERE BEFORE?
I WAS STATIONED HERE BRIEFLY A FEW YEARS AGO, CAPTAIN. I'D LOVE TO SEE IT AGAIN.
FINE, THEN. YOU'RE COMING ALONG. WE'RE GOING TO PAY A VISIT TO THE QUARTERMASTER TO TURN IN OUR ACQUISITIONS.
BARCLAY AND DATA, YOU'RE WITH ME. MUSTER UP SOME SECURITY AND MEET ME IN TRANSPORTER ROOM 2. BARCLAY, DON'T FORGET TO BRING ALONG THOSE TWO CARDASSIAN PRISONERS.
NAV
INQUISITOR, YOU HAVE THE CONN. WE WON'T BE GONE LONG.
BEHAVE YOURSELF.
I'LL TRY NOT TO GET TOO COMFORTABLE...
TACTICAL

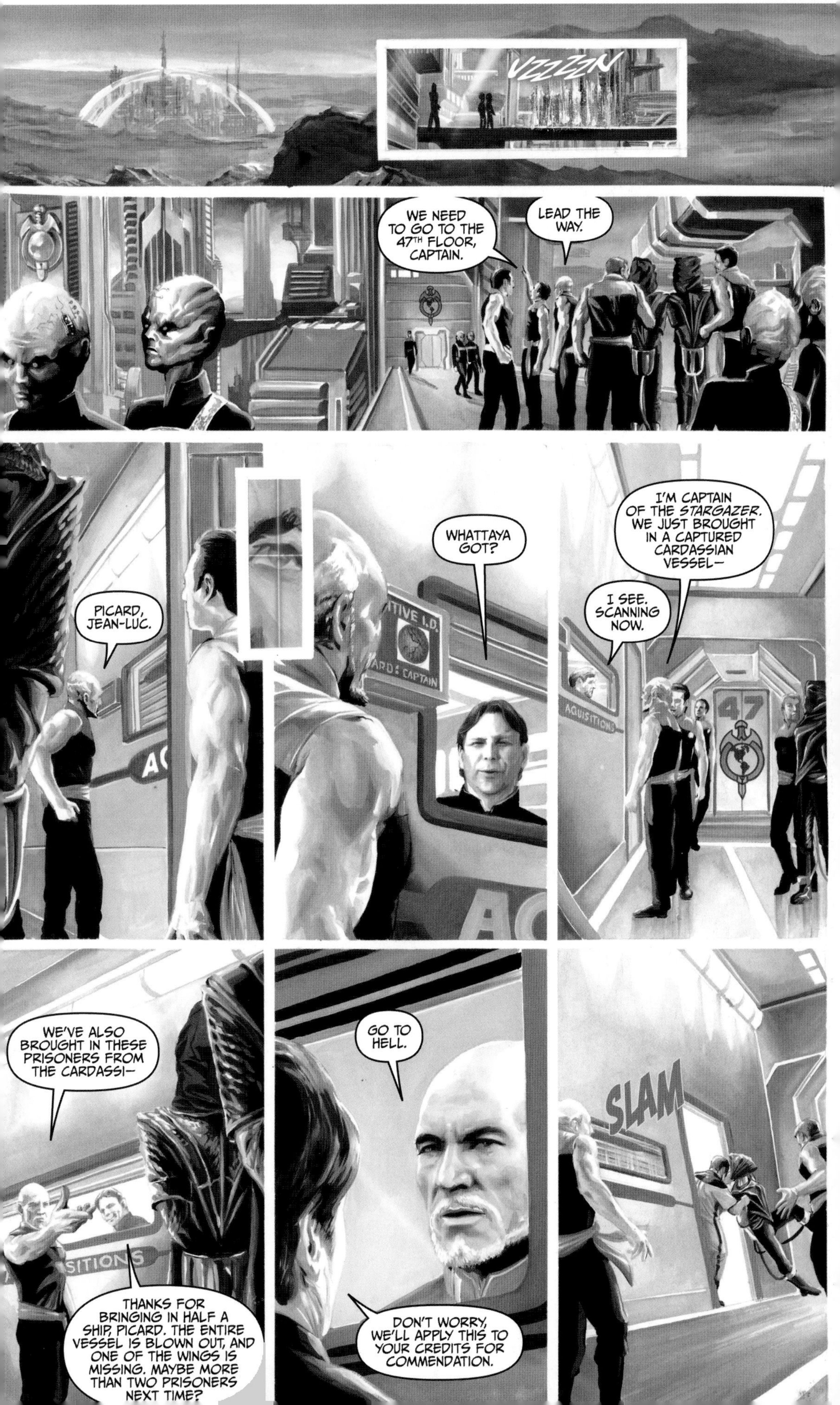
VZZZZN
WE NEED TO GO TO THE 47TH FLOOR, CAPTAIN.
LEAD THE WAY.
PICARD, JEAN-LUC.
WHATTAYA GOT?
I'M CAPTAIN OF THE STARGAZER. WE JUST BROUGHT IN A CAPTURED CARDASSIAN VESSEL—
I SEE. SCANNING NOW.
ACQUISITIONS
47
WE'VE ALSO BROUGHT IN THESE PRISONERS FROM THE CARDASSI—
THANKS FOR BRINGING IN HALF A SHIP, PICARD. THE ENTIRE VESSEL IS BLOWN OUT, AND ONE OF THE WINGS IS MISSING. MAYBE MORE THAN TWO PRISONERS NEXT TIME?
GO TO HELL.
DON'T WORRY, WE'LL APPLY THIS TO YOUR CREDITS FOR COMMENDATION.
SLAM

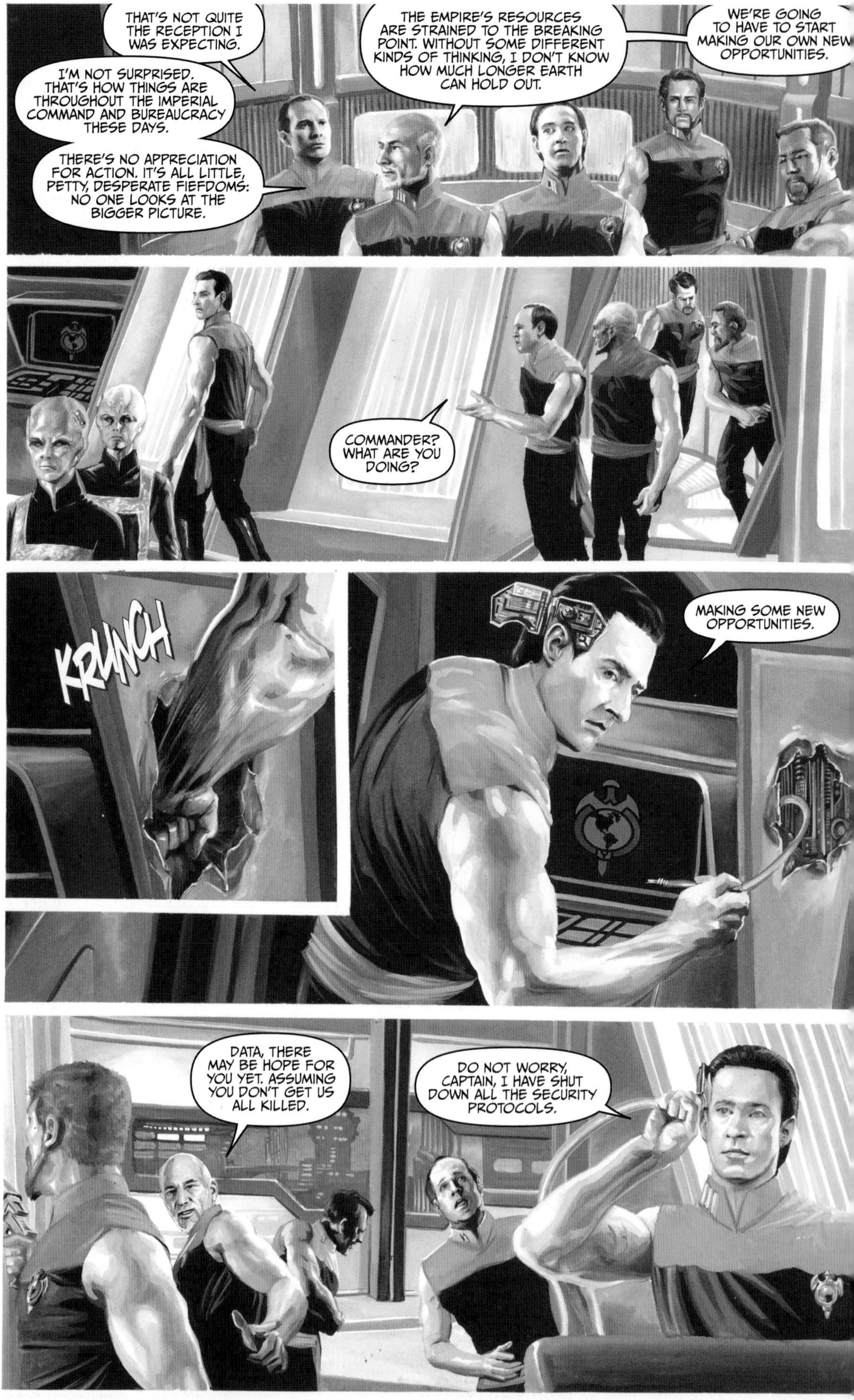
THAT'S NOT QUITE THE RECEPTION I WAS EXPECTING.
I'M NOT SURPRISED. THAT'S HOW THINGS ARE THROUGHOUT THE IMPERIAL COMMAND AND BUREAUCRACY THESE DAYS.
THERE'S NO APPRECIATION FOR ACTION. IT'S ALL LITTLE, PETTY, DESPERATE FIEFDOMS: NO ONE LOOKS AT THE BIGGER PICTURE.
THE EMPIRE'S RESOURCES ARE STRAINED TO THE BREAKING POINT. WITHOUT SOME DIFFERENT KINDS OF THINKING, I DON'T KNOW HOW MUCH LONGER EARTH CAN HOLD OUT.
WE'RE GOING TO HAVE TO START MAKING OUR OWN NEW OPPORTUNITIES.
COMMANDER? WHAT ARE YOU DOING?
KRUNCH
MAKING SOME NEW OPPORTUNITIES.
DATA, THERE MAY BE HOPE FOR YOU YET. ASSUMING YOU DON'T GET US ALL KILLED.
DO NOT WORRY, CAPTAIN, I HAVE SHUT DOWN ALL THE SECURITY PROTOCOLS.

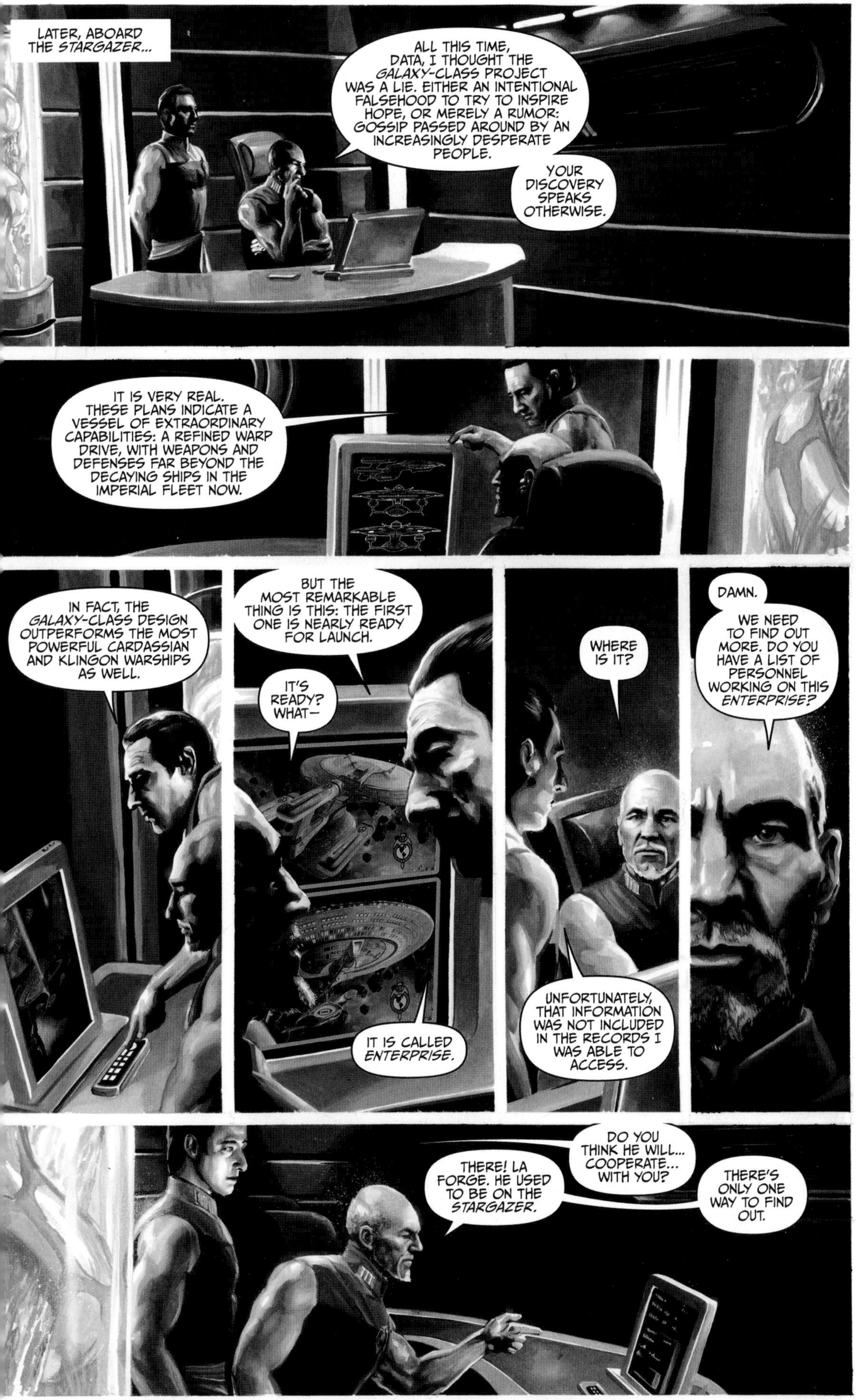
LATER, ABOARD THE *STARGAZER*...
ALL THIS TIME, DATA, I THOUGHT THE *GALAXY*-CLASS PROJECT WAS A LIE. EITHER AN INTENTIONAL FALSEHOOD TO TRY TO INSPIRE HOPE, OR MERELY A RUMOR: GOSSIP PASSED AROUND BY AN INCREASINGLY DESPERATE PEOPLE.
YOUR DISCOVERY SPEAKS OTHERWISE.
IT IS VERY REAL. THESE PLANS INDICATE A VESSEL OF EXTRAORDINARY CAPABILITIES: A REFINED WARP DRIVE, WITH WEAPONS AND DEFENSES FAR BEYOND THE DECAYING SHIPS IN THE IMPERIAL FLEET NOW.
IN FACT, THE *GALAXY*-CLASS DESIGN OUTPERFORMS THE MOST POWERFUL CARDASSIAN AND KLINGON WARSHIPS AS WELL.
BUT THE MOST REMARKABLE THING IS THIS: THE FIRST ONE IS NEARLY READY FOR LAUNCH.
IT'S READY? WHAT—
IT IS CALLED *ENTERPRISE*.
WHERE IS IT?
UNFORTUNATELY, THAT INFORMATION WAS NOT INCLUDED IN THE RECORDS I WAS ABLE TO ACCESS.
DAMN.
WE NEED TO FIND OUT MORE. DO YOU HAVE A LIST OF PERSONNEL WORKING ON THIS *ENTERPRISE*?
THERE! LA FORGE. HE USED TO BE ON THE *STARGAZER*.
DO YOU THINK HE WILL... COOPERATE... WITH YOU?
THERE'S ONLY ONE WAY TO FIND OUT.

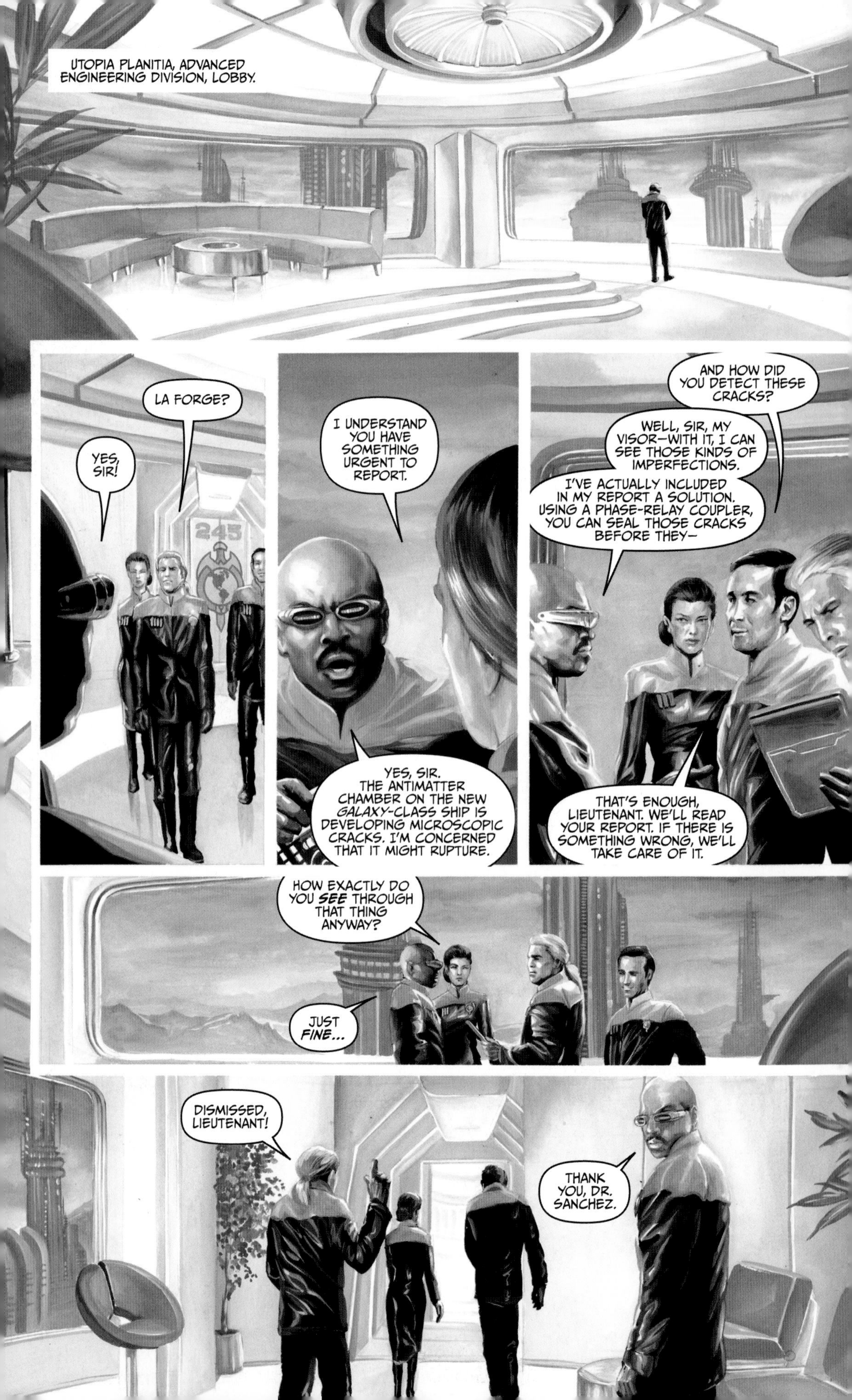
UTOPIA PLANITIA, ADVANCED ENGINEERING DIVISION, LOBBY.
LA FORGE?
YES, SIR!
245
I UNDERSTAND YOU HAVE SOMETHING URGENT TO REPORT.
YES, SIR. THE ANTIMATTER CHAMBER ON THE NEW *GALAXY*-CLASS SHIP IS DEVELOPING MICROSCOPIC CRACKS. I'M CONCERNED THAT IT MIGHT RUPTURE.
AND HOW DID YOU DETECT THESE CRACKS?
WELL, SIR, MY VISOR—WITH IT, I CAN SEE THOSE KINDS OF IMPERFECTIONS.
I'VE ACTUALLY INCLUDED IN MY REPORT A SOLUTION. USING A PHASE-RELAY COUPLER, YOU CAN SEAL THOSE CRACKS BEFORE THEY—
THAT'S ENOUGH, LIEUTENANT. WE'LL READ YOUR REPORT. IF THERE IS SOMETHING WRONG, WE'LL TAKE CARE OF IT.
HOW EXACTLY DO YOU ***SEE*** THROUGH THAT THING ANYWAY?
JUST ***FINE...***
DISMISSED, LIEUTENANT!
THANK YOU, DR. SANCHEZ.

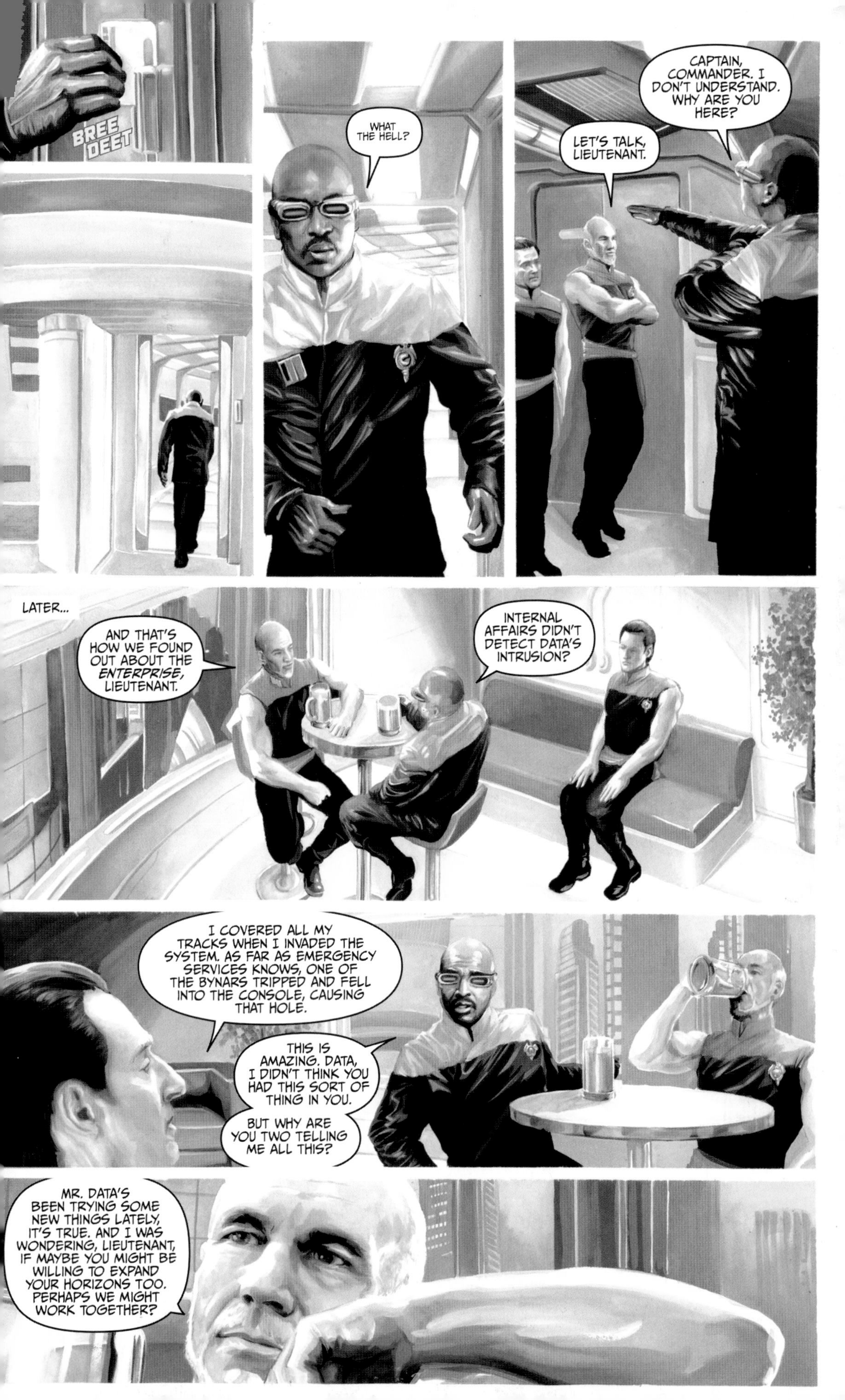
BREE DEET
WHAT THE HELL?
CAPTAIN, COMMANDER. I DON'T UNDERSTAND. WHY ARE YOU HERE?
LET'S TALK, LIEUTENANT.
LATER...
AND THAT'S HOW WE FOUND OUT ABOUT THE *ENTERPRISE,* LIEUTENANT.
INTERNAL AFFAIRS DIDN'T DETECT DATA'S INTRUSION?
I COVERED ALL MY TRACKS WHEN I INVADED THE SYSTEM. AS FAR AS EMERGENCY SERVICES KNOWS, ONE OF THE BYNARS TRIPPED AND FELL INTO THE CONSOLE, CAUSING THAT HOLE.
THIS IS AMAZING. DATA, I DIDN'T THINK YOU HAD THIS SORT OF THING IN YOU.
BUT WHY ARE YOU TWO TELLING ME ALL THIS?
MR. DATA'S BEEN TRYING SOME NEW THINGS LATELY, IT'S TRUE. AND I WAS WONDERING, LIEUTENANT, IF MAYBE YOU MIGHT BE WILLING TO EXPAND YOUR HORIZONS TOO. PERHAPS WE MIGHT WORK TOGETHER?

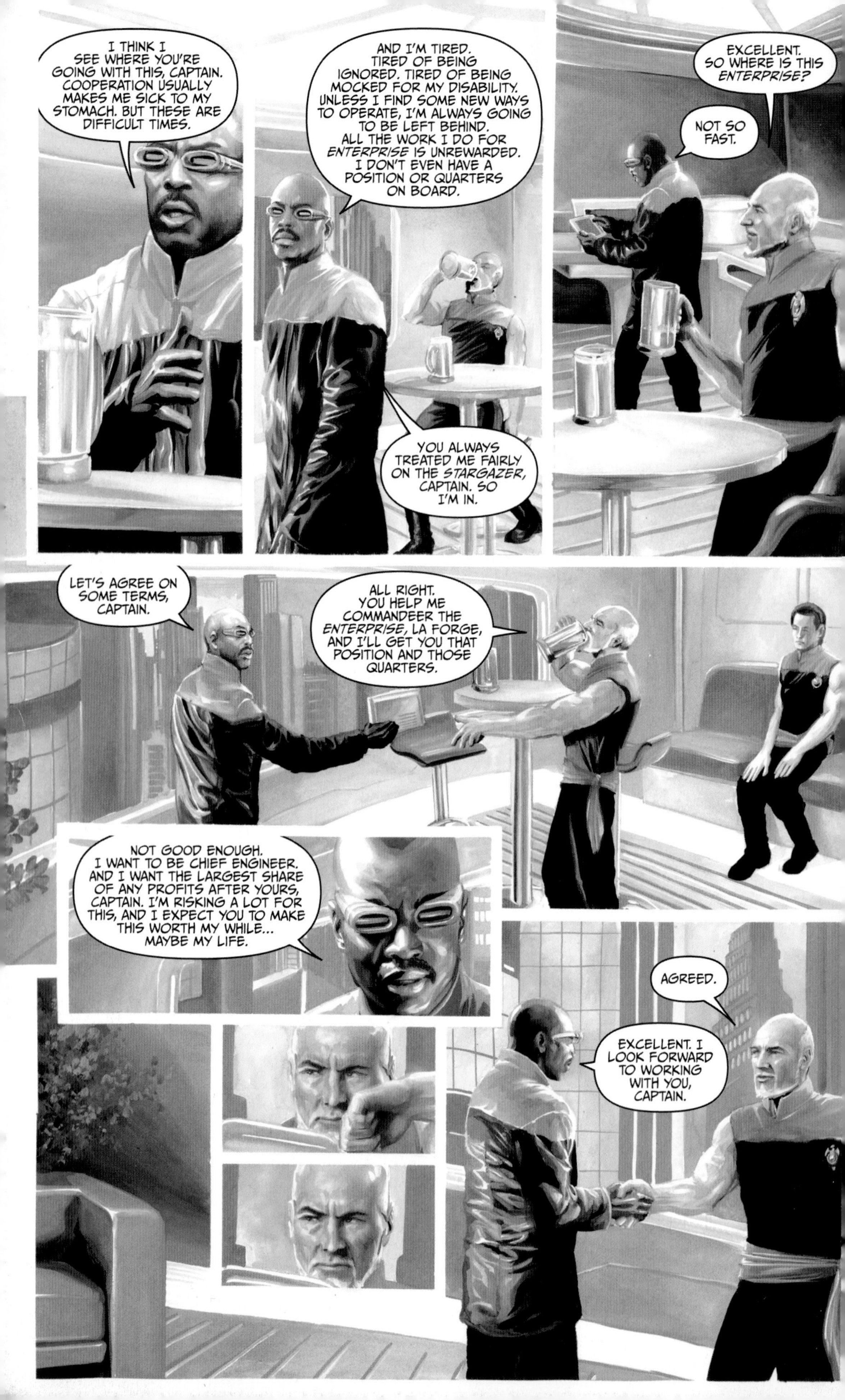
I THINK I SEE WHERE YOU'RE GOING WITH THIS, CAPTAIN. COOPERATION USUALLY MAKES ME SICK TO MY STOMACH. BUT THESE ARE DIFFICULT TIMES.
AND I'M TIRED. TIRED OF BEING IGNORED. TIRED OF BEING MOCKED FOR MY DISABILITY. UNLESS I FIND SOME NEW WAYS TO OPERATE, I'M ALWAYS GOING TO BE LEFT BEHIND. ALL THE WORK I DO FOR ENTERPRISE IS UNREWARDED. I DON'T EVEN HAVE A POSITION OR QUARTERS ON BOARD.
YOU ALWAYS TREATED ME FAIRLY ON THE STARGAZER, CAPTAIN. SO I'M IN.
EXCELLENT. SO WHERE IS THIS ENTERPRISE?
NOT SO FAST.
LET'S AGREE ON SOME TERMS, CAPTAIN.
ALL RIGHT. YOU HELP ME COMMANDEER THE ENTERPRISE, LA FORGE, AND I'LL GET YOU THAT POSITION AND THOSE QUARTERS.
NOT GOOD ENOUGH. I WANT TO BE CHIEF ENGINEER. AND I WANT THE LARGEST SHARE OF ANY PROFITS AFTER YOURS, CAPTAIN. I'M RISKING A LOT FOR THIS, AND I EXPECT YOU TO MAKE THIS WORTH MY WHILE... MAYBE MY LIFE.
AGREED.
EXCELLENT. I LOOK FORWARD TO WORKING WITH YOU, CAPTAIN.

NOW, WHERE IS THIS DAMNED SHIP?

FOLLOW ME.

IT'S RIGHT... THERE.

NONSENSE. WE WOULD HAVE SEEN IT FROM ORBIT. AND THERE'S NO WAY THAT THEY'D BUILD THAT SHIP IN SUCH AN OBVIOUS PLACE AS UTOPIA PLANITIA. LA FORGE, IF YOU'RE STRINGING ME ALONG...

IT'S COVERED WITH A CLOAKING NET. IT TOOK MONTHS TO ACQUIRE AND ADAPT THE SIX KLINGON CLOAKING DEVICES THEY NEEDED TO MAKE THIS WORK.

THE CLOAKING NET ISN'T PERFECT, THOUGH...THERE'S A HOLE IN THE BOTTOM. BUT ONLY A FEW OF US KNOW EXACTLY WHERE TO LOOK.

MARS' ATMOSPHERE IS PRETTY THIN. YOU'LL GET A GOOD VIEW.

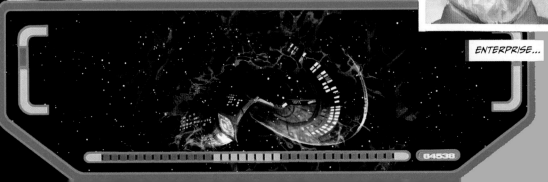

ENTERPRISE...

84538

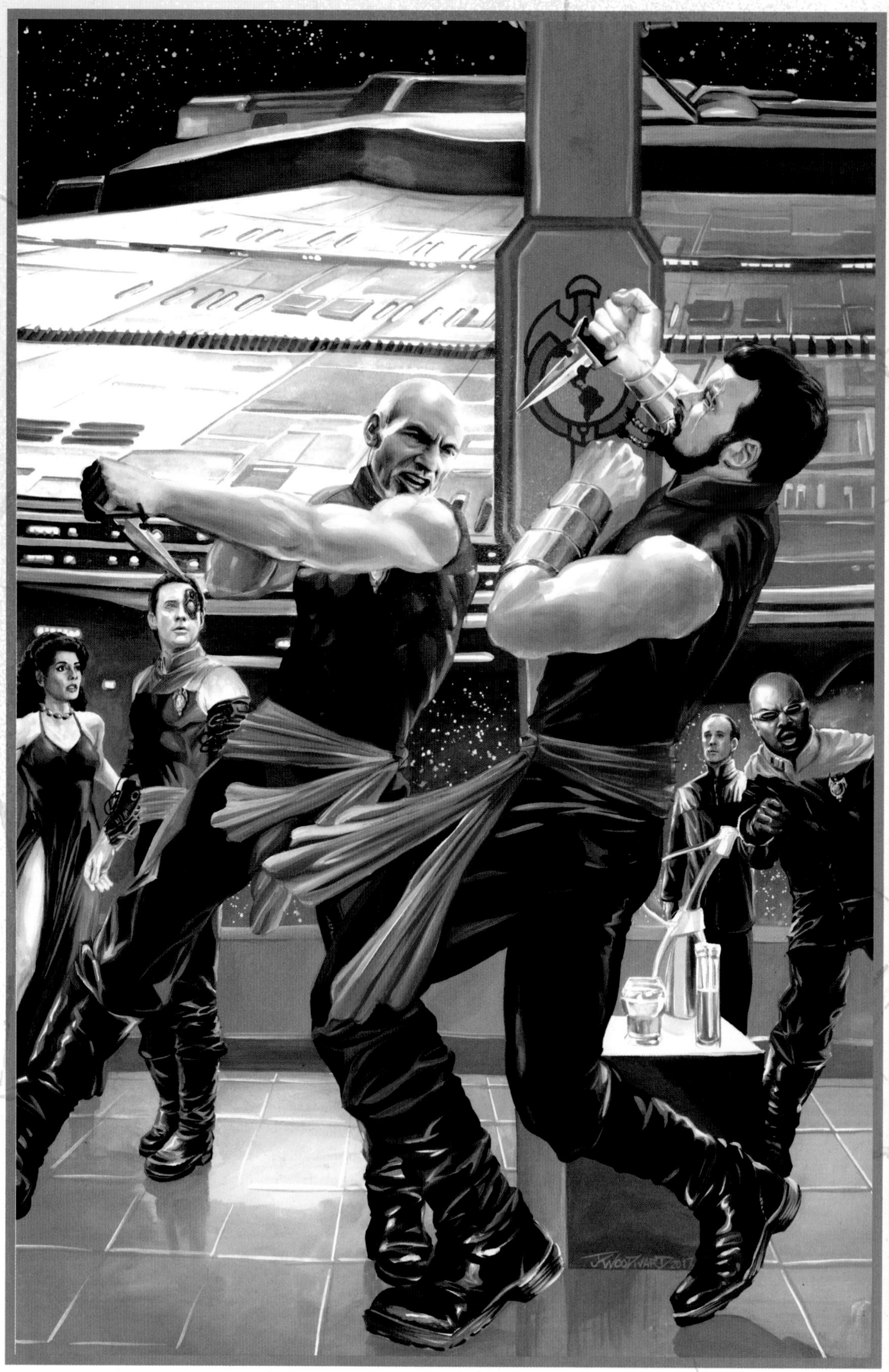

ART BY
J.K. WOODWARD

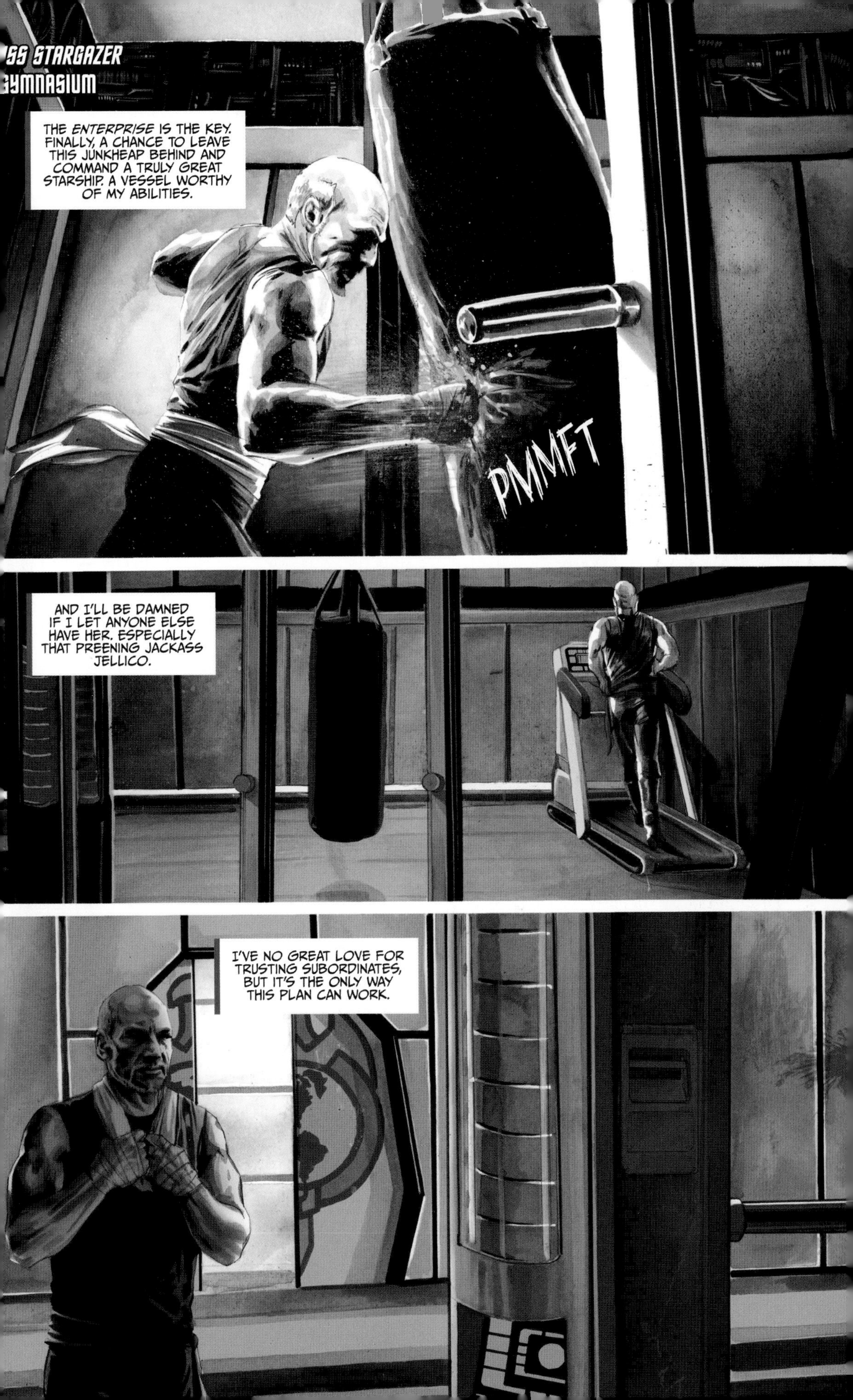
SS STARGAZER
GYMNASIUM
THE *ENTERPRISE* IS THE KEY. FINALLY, A CHANCE TO LEAVE THIS JUNKHEAP BEHIND AND COMMAND A TRULY GREAT STARSHIP. A VESSEL WORTHY OF MY ABILITIES.
PMMFT
AND I'LL BE DAMNED IF I LET ANYONE ELSE HAVE HER. ESPECIALLY THAT PREENING JACKASS JELLICO.
I'VE NO GREAT LOVE FOR TRUSTING SUBORDINATES, BUT IT'S THE ONLY WAY THIS PLAN CAN WORK.

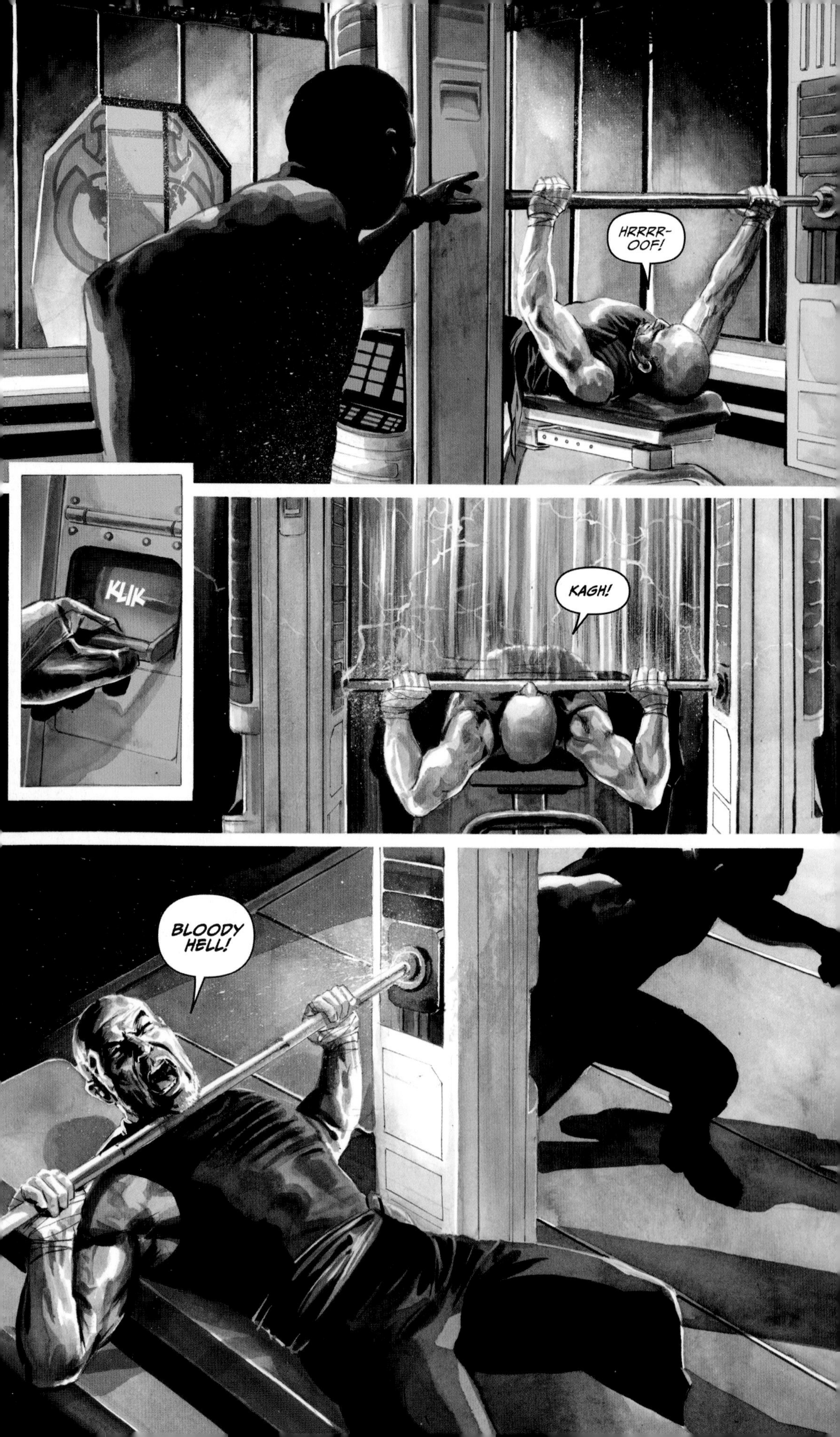
HRRRR-
OOF!
KLIK
KAGH!
BLOODY
HELL!

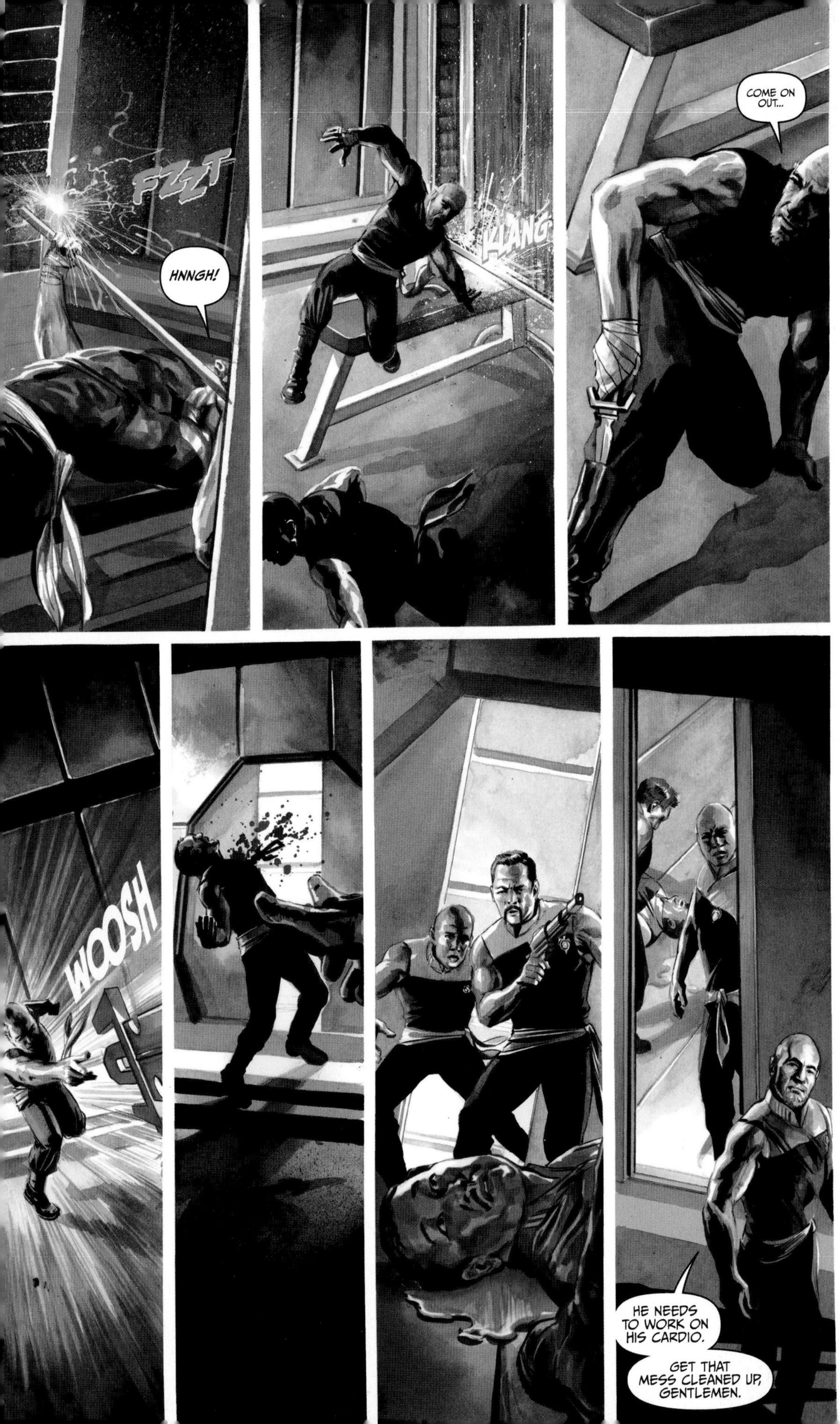
FZZT
HNNGH!
KLANG
COME ON OUT...
WOOSH
HE NEEDS TO WORK ON HIS CARDIO.
GET THAT MESS CLEANED UP, GENTLEMEN.

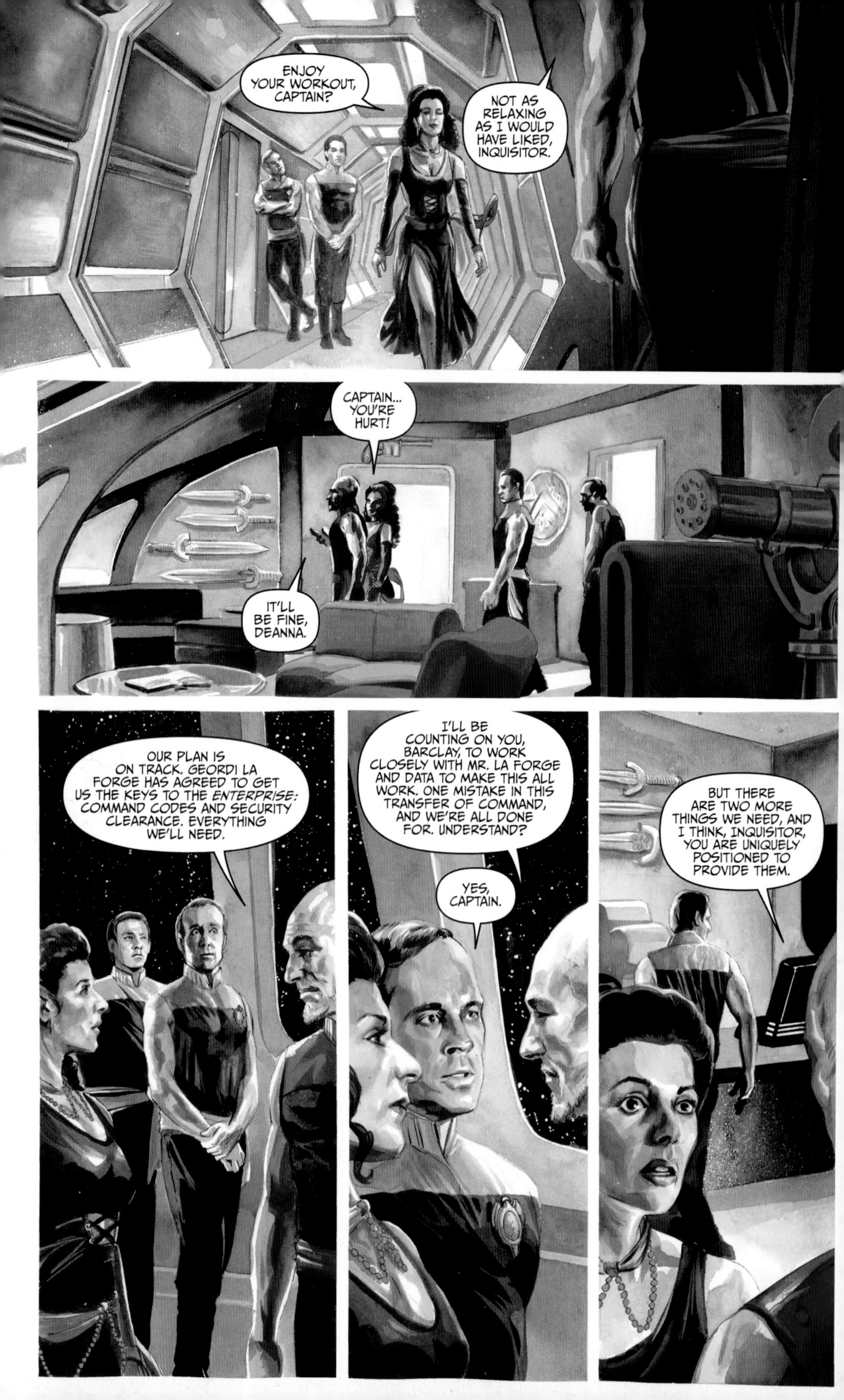
ENJOY YOUR WORKOUT, CAPTAIN?
NOT AS RELAXING AS I WOULD HAVE LIKED, INQUISITOR.
CAPTAIN... YOU'RE HURT!
IT'LL BE FINE, DEANNA.
OUR PLAN IS ON TRACK. GEORDI LA FORGE HAS AGREED TO GET US THE KEYS TO THE *ENTERPRISE:* COMMAND CODES AND SECURITY CLEARANCE. EVERYTHING WE'LL NEED.
I'LL BE COUNTING ON YOU, BARCLAY, TO WORK CLOSELY WITH MR. LA FORGE AND DATA TO MAKE THIS ALL WORK. ONE MISTAKE IN THIS TRANSFER OF COMMAND, AND WE'RE ALL DONE FOR. UNDERSTAND?
YES, CAPTAIN.
BUT THERE ARE TWO MORE THINGS WE NEED, AND I THINK, INQUISITOR, YOU ARE UNIQUELY POSITIONED TO PROVIDE THEM.

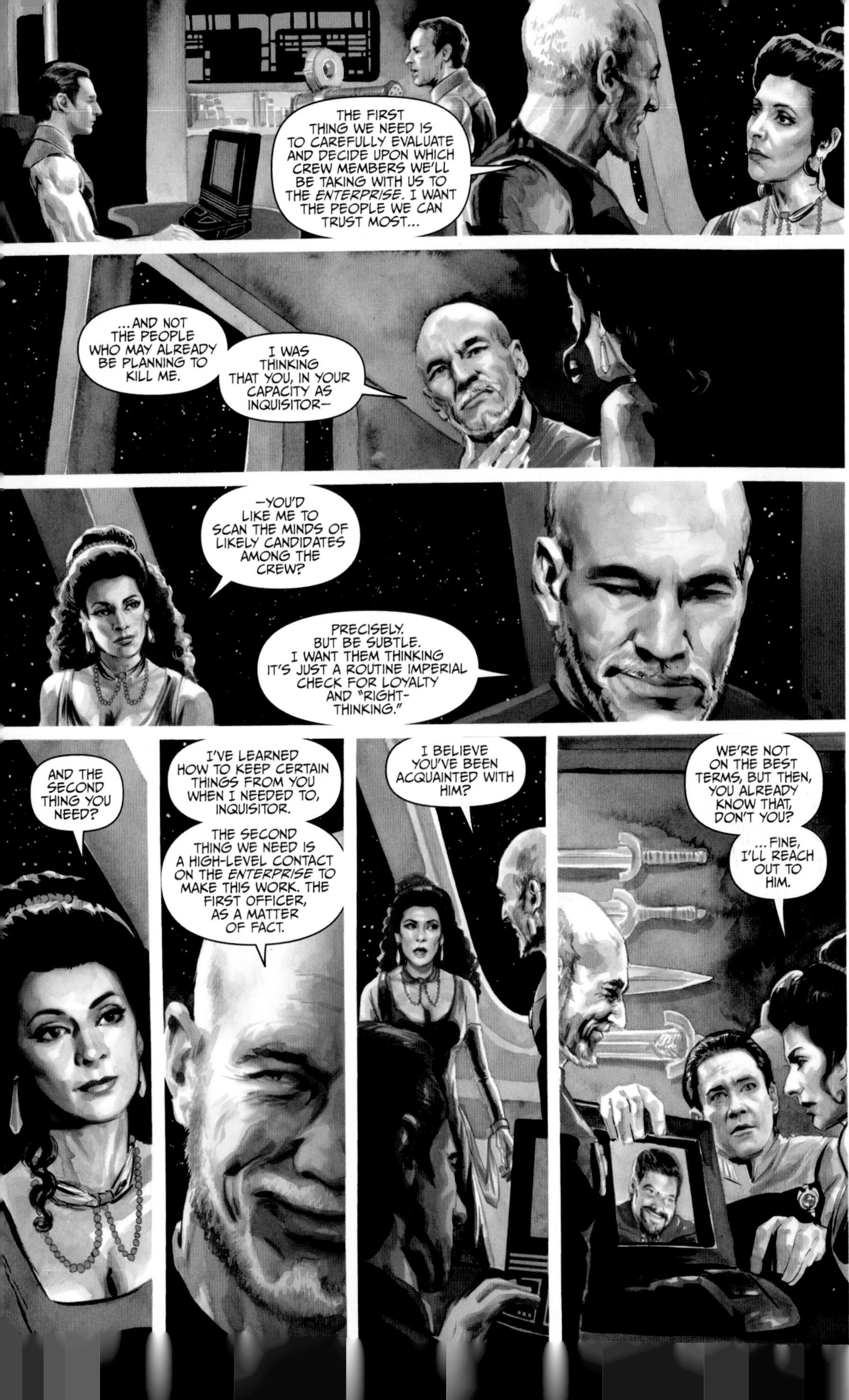

THE FIRST THING WE NEED IS TO CAREFULLY EVALUATE AND DECIDE UPON WHICH CREW MEMBERS WE'LL BE TAKING WITH US TO THE *ENTERPRISE*. I WANT THE PEOPLE WE CAN TRUST MOST...
...AND NOT THE PEOPLE WHO MAY ALREADY BE PLANNING TO KILL ME.
I WAS THINKING THAT YOU, IN YOUR CAPACITY AS INQUISITOR—
—YOU'D LIKE ME TO SCAN THE MINDS OF LIKELY CANDIDATES AMONG THE CREW?
PRECISELY. BUT BE SUBTLE. I WANT THEM THINKING IT'S JUST A ROUTINE IMPERIAL CHECK FOR LOYALTY AND "RIGHT-THINKING."
AND THE SECOND THING YOU NEED?
I'VE LEARNED HOW TO KEEP CERTAIN THINGS FROM YOU WHEN I NEEDED TO, INQUISITOR.
THE SECOND THING WE NEED IS A HIGH-LEVEL CONTACT ON THE *ENTERPRISE* TO MAKE THIS WORK. THE FIRST OFFICER, AS A MATTER OF FACT.
I BELIEVE YOU'VE BEEN ACQUAINTED WITH HIM?
WE'RE NOT ON THE BEST TERMS, BUT THEN, YOU ALREADY KNOW THAT, DON'T YOU?
...FINE, I'LL REACH OUT TO HIM.

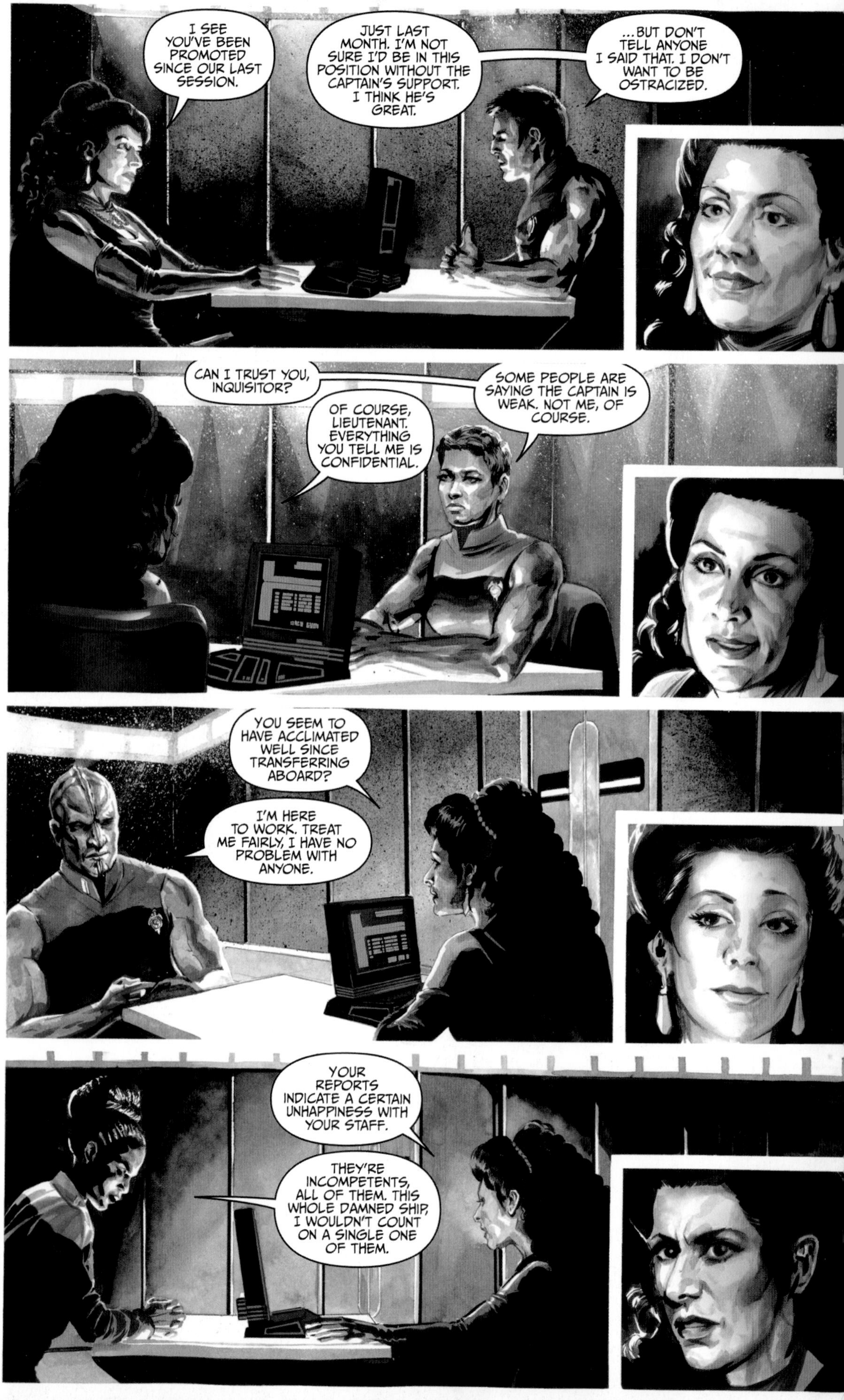
I SEE YOU'VE BEEN PROMOTED SINCE OUR LAST SESSION.
JUST LAST MONTH. I'M NOT SURE I'D BE IN THIS POSITION WITHOUT THE CAPTAIN'S SUPPORT. I THINK HE'S GREAT.
...BUT DON'T TELL ANYONE I SAID THAT. I DON'T WANT TO BE OSTRACIZED.
CAN I TRUST YOU, INQUISITOR?
OF COURSE, LIEUTENANT. EVERYTHING YOU TELL ME IS CONFIDENTIAL.
SOME PEOPLE ARE SAYING THE CAPTAIN IS WEAK. NOT ME, OF COURSE.
YOU SEEM TO HAVE ACCLIMATED WELL SINCE TRANSFERRING ABOARD?
I'M HERE TO WORK. TREAT ME FAIRLY, I HAVE NO PROBLEM WITH ANYONE.
YOUR REPORTS INDICATE A CERTAIN UNHAPPINESS WITH YOUR STAFF.
THEY'RE INCOMPETENTS, ALL OF THEM. THIS WHOLE DAMNED SHIP, I WOULDN'T COUNT ON A SINGLE ONE OF THEM.

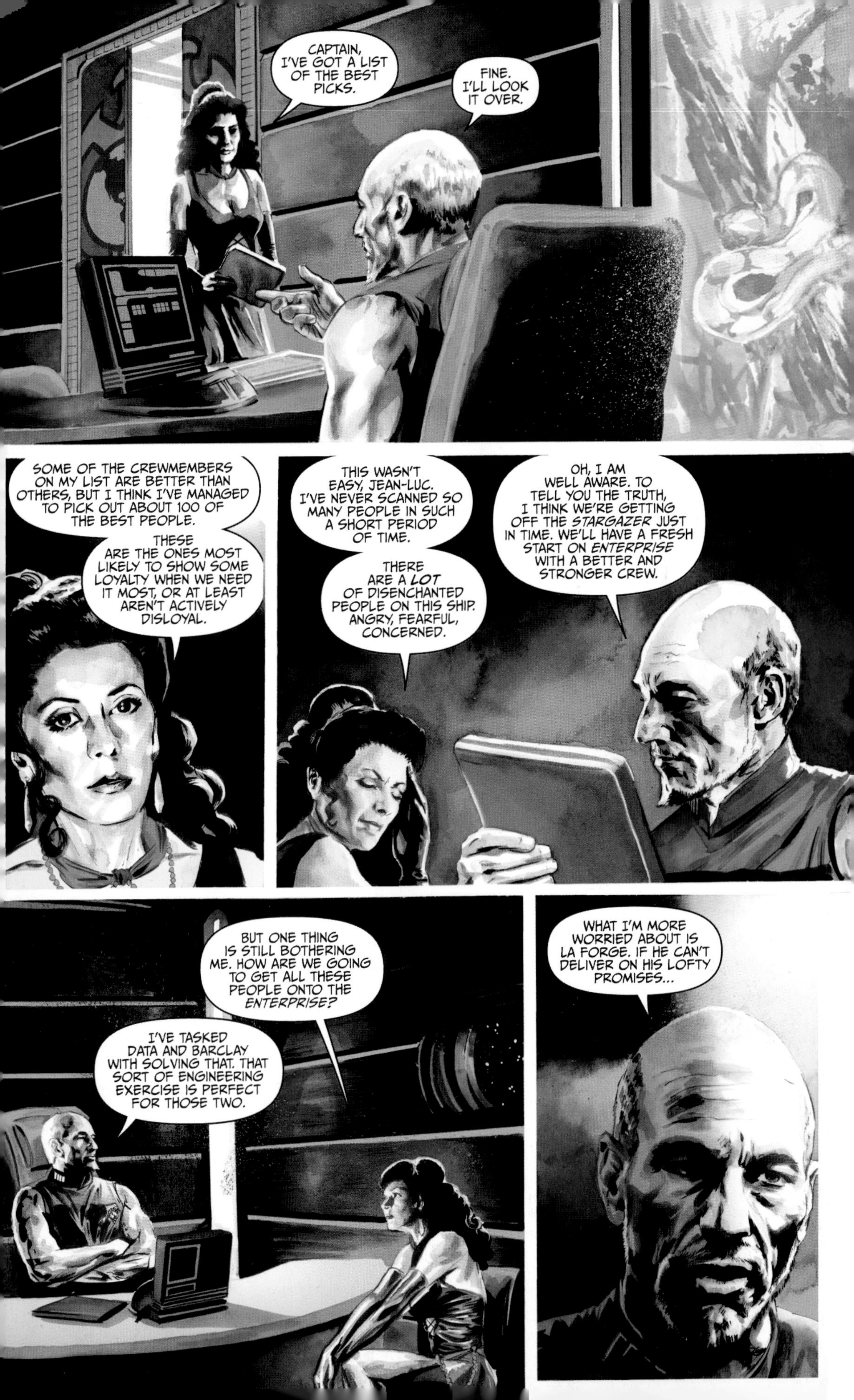
CAPTAIN, I'VE GOT A LIST OF THE BEST PICKS.
FINE. I'LL LOOK IT OVER.
SOME OF THE CREWMEMBERS ON MY LIST ARE BETTER THAN OTHERS, BUT I THINK I'VE MANAGED TO PICK OUT ABOUT 100 OF THE BEST PEOPLE.
THESE ARE THE ONES MOST LIKELY TO SHOW SOME LOYALTY WHEN WE NEED IT MOST, OR AT LEAST AREN'T ACTIVELY DISLOYAL.
THIS WASN'T EASY, JEAN-LUC. I'VE NEVER SCANNED SO MANY PEOPLE IN SUCH A SHORT PERIOD OF TIME.
THERE ARE A *LOT* OF DISENCHANTED PEOPLE ON THIS SHIP. ANGRY, FEARFUL, CONCERNED.
OH, I AM WELL AWARE. TO TELL YOU THE TRUTH, I THINK WE'RE GETTING OFF THE *STARGAZER* JUST IN TIME. WE'LL HAVE A FRESH START ON *ENTERPRISE* WITH A BETTER AND STRONGER CREW.
BUT ONE THING IS STILL BOTHERING ME. HOW ARE WE GOING TO GET ALL THESE PEOPLE ONTO THE *ENTERPRISE*?
I'VE TASKED DATA AND BARCLAY WITH SOLVING THAT. THAT SORT OF ENGINEERING EXERCISE IS PERFECT FOR THOSE TWO.
WHAT I'M MORE WORRIED ABOUT IS LA FORGE. IF HE CAN'T DELIVER ON HIS LOFTY PROMISES...

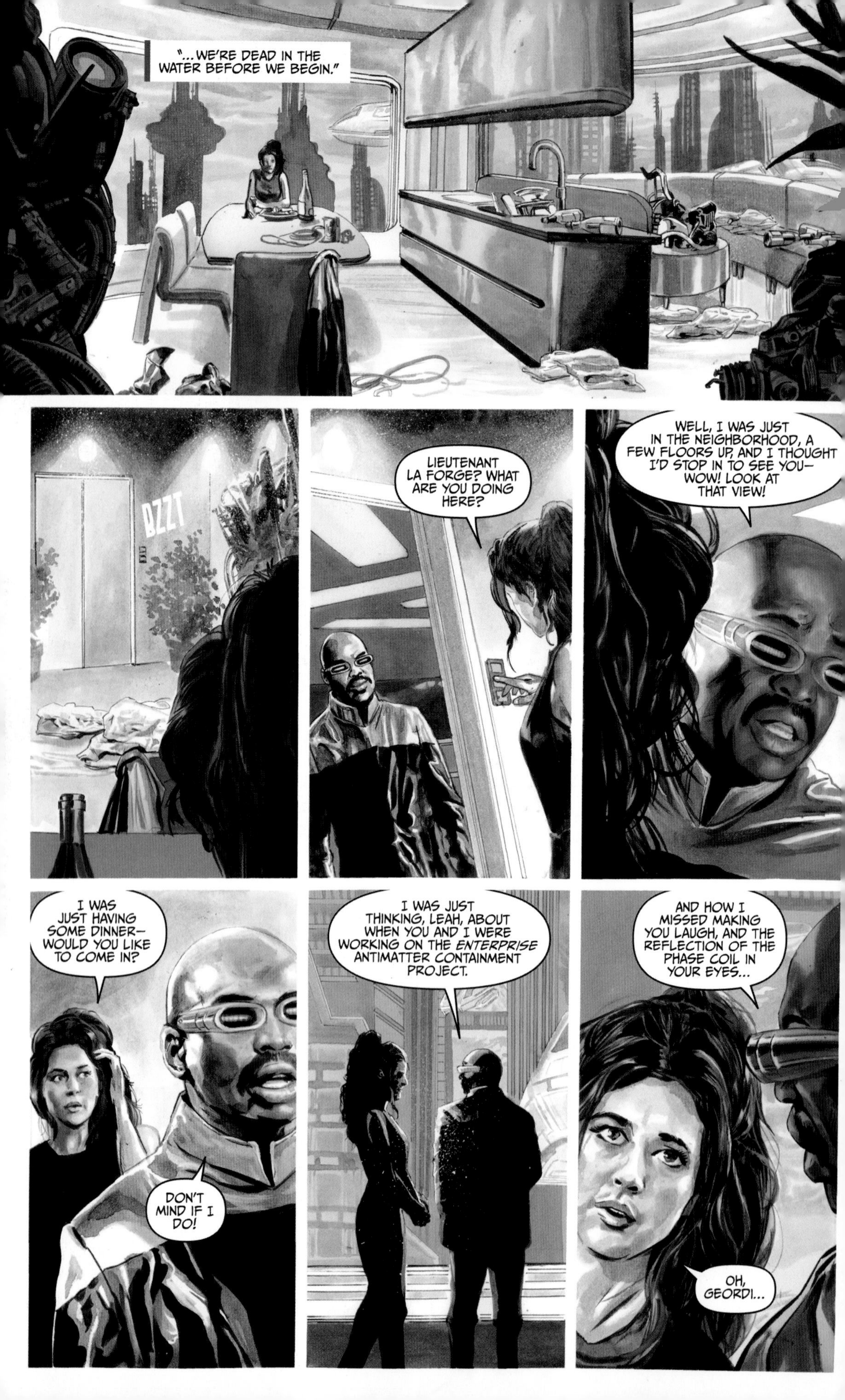
"...WE'RE DEAD IN THE WATER BEFORE WE BEGIN."
BZZT
LIEUTENANT LA FORGE? WHAT ARE YOU DOING HERE?
WELL, I WAS JUST IN THE NEIGHBORHOOD, A FEW FLOORS UP, AND I THOUGHT I'D STOP IN TO SEE YOU— WOW! LOOK AT THAT VIEW!
I WAS JUST HAVING SOME DINNER— WOULD YOU LIKE TO COME IN?
DON'T MIND IF I DO!
I WAS JUST THINKING, LEAH, ABOUT WHEN YOU AND I WERE WORKING ON THE *ENTERPRISE* ANTIMATTER CONTAINMENT PROJECT.
AND HOW I MISSED MAKING YOU LAUGH, AND THE REFLECTION OF THE PHASE COIL IN YOUR EYES...
OH, GEORDI...

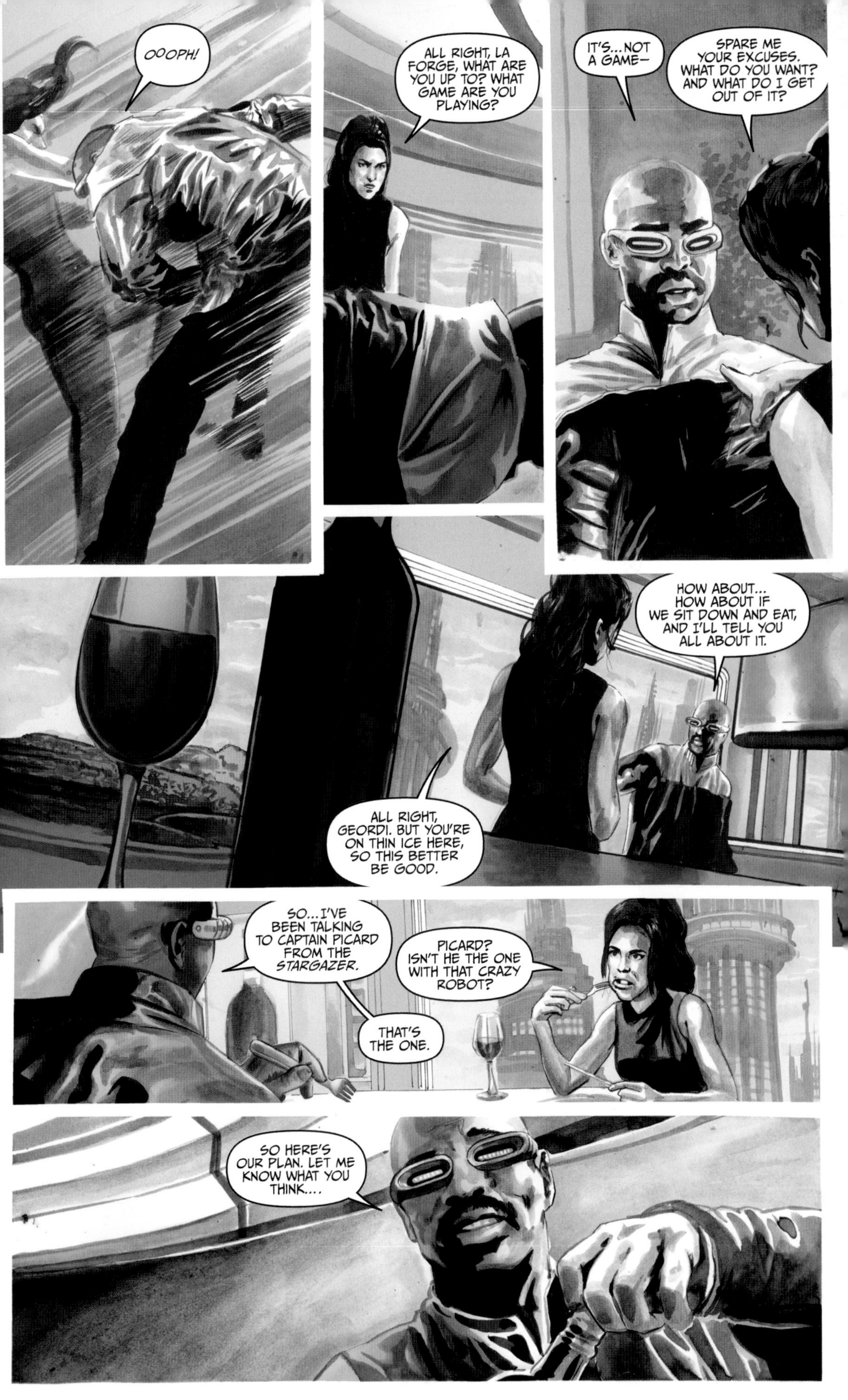
OOOPH!
ALL RIGHT, LA FORGE, WHAT ARE YOU UP TO? WHAT GAME ARE YOU PLAYING?
IT'S...NOT A GAME—
SPARE ME YOUR EXCUSES. WHAT DO YOU WANT? AND WHAT DO I GET OUT OF IT?
HOW ABOUT... HOW ABOUT IF WE SIT DOWN AND EAT, AND I'LL TELL YOU ALL ABOUT IT.
ALL RIGHT, GEORDI. BUT YOU'RE ON THIN ICE HERE, SO THIS BETTER BE GOOD.
SO...I'VE BEEN TALKING TO CAPTAIN PICARD FROM THE STARGAZER.
PICARD? ISN'T HE THE ONE WITH THAT CRAZY ROBOT?
THAT'S THE ONE.
SO HERE'S OUR PLAN. LET ME KNOW WHAT YOU THINK....

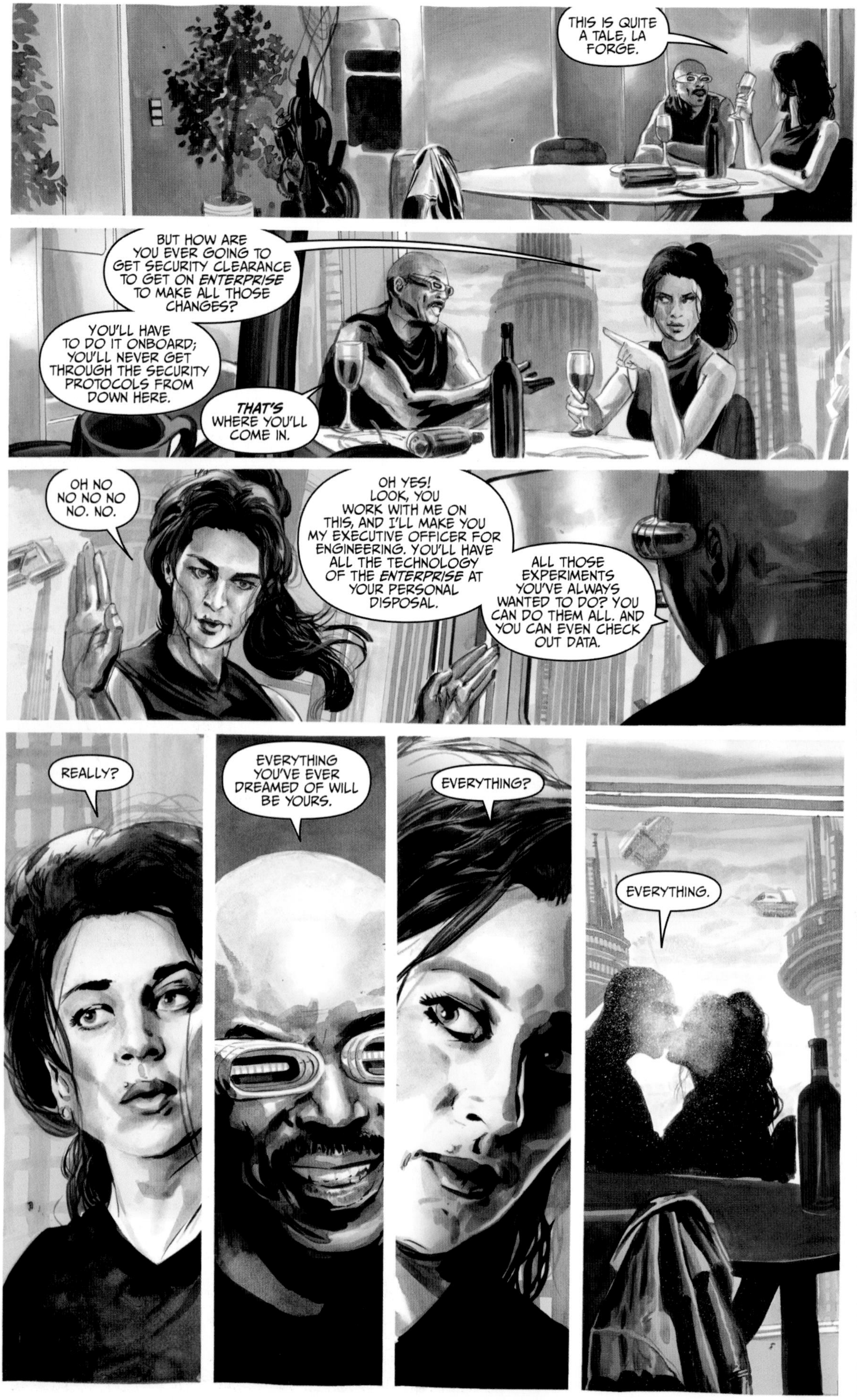
THIS IS QUITE A TALE, LA FORGE.
BUT HOW ARE YOU EVER GOING TO GET SECURITY CLEARANCE TO GET ON *ENTERPRISE* TO MAKE ALL THOSE CHANGES?
YOU'LL HAVE TO DO IT ONBOARD; YOU'LL NEVER GET THROUGH THE SECURITY PROTOCOLS FROM DOWN HERE.
THAT'S WHERE YOU'LL COME IN.
OH NO NO NO NO NO. NO.
OH YES! LOOK, YOU WORK WITH ME ON THIS, AND I'LL MAKE YOU MY EXECUTIVE OFFICER FOR ENGINEERING. YOU'LL HAVE ALL THE TECHNOLOGY OF THE *ENTERPRISE* AT YOUR PERSONAL DISPOSAL.
ALL THOSE EXPERIMENTS YOU'VE ALWAYS WANTED TO DO? YOU CAN DO THEM ALL. AND YOU CAN EVEN CHECK OUT DATA.
REALLY?
EVERYTHING YOU'VE EVER DREAMED OF WILL BE YOURS.
EVERYTHING?
EVERYTHING.

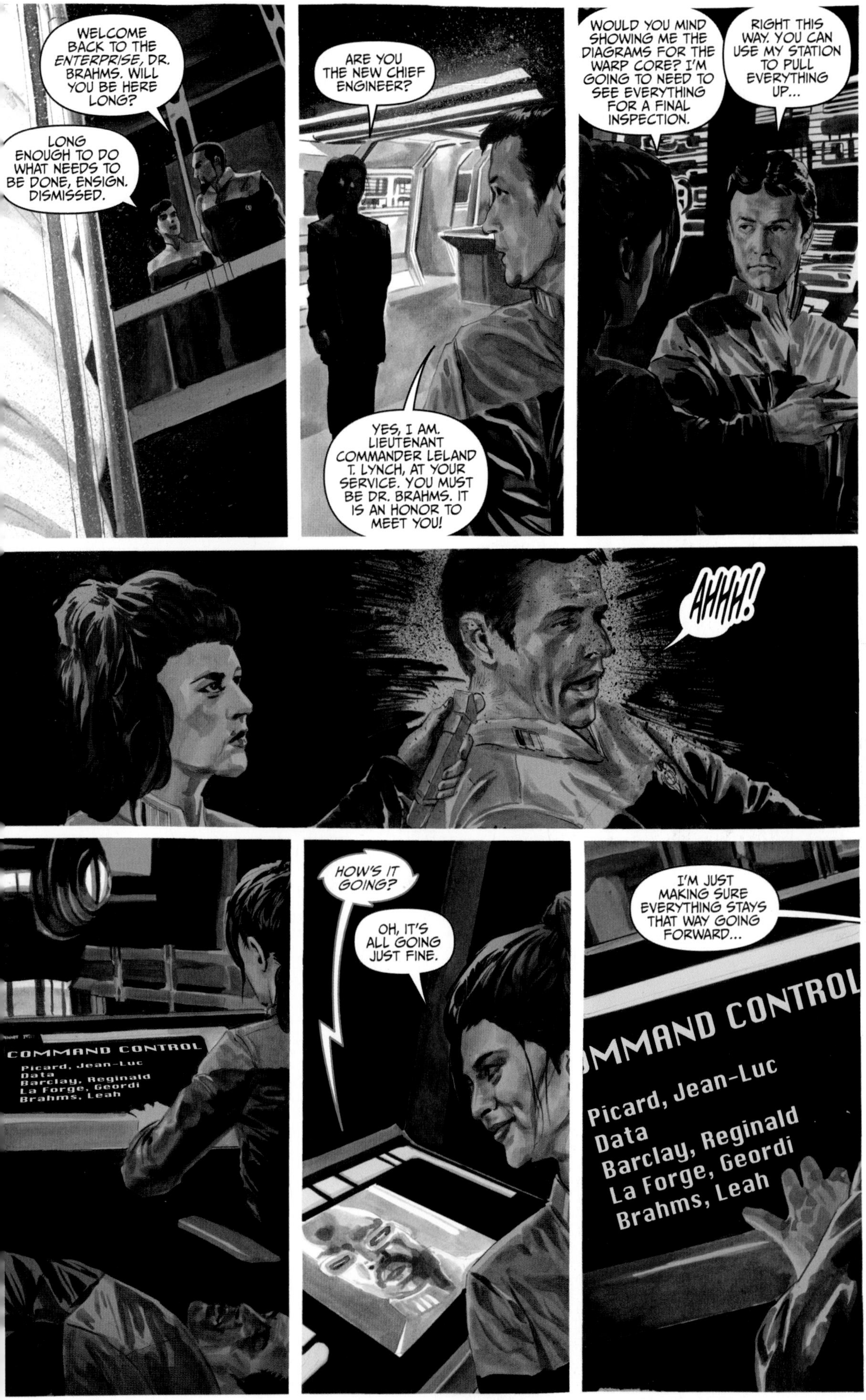
WELCOME BACK TO THE *ENTERPRISE*, DR. BRAHMS. WILL YOU BE HERE LONG?
LONG ENOUGH TO DO WHAT NEEDS TO BE DONE, ENSIGN. DISMISSED.
ARE YOU THE NEW CHIEF ENGINEER?
YES, I AM. LIEUTENANT COMMANDER LELAND T. LYNCH, AT YOUR SERVICE. YOU MUST BE DR. BRAHMS. IT IS AN HONOR TO MEET YOU!
WOULD YOU MIND SHOWING ME THE DIAGRAMS FOR THE WARP CORE? I'M GOING TO NEED TO SEE EVERYTHING FOR A FINAL INSPECTION.
RIGHT THIS WAY. YOU CAN USE MY STATION TO PULL EVERYTHING UP...
AHHH!
COMMAND CONTROL
Picard, Jean-Luc
Data
Barclay, Reginald
La Forge, Geordi
Brahms, Leah
HOW'S IT GOING?
OH, IT'S ALL GOING JUST FINE.
I'M JUST MAKING SURE EVERYTHING STAYS THAT WAY GOING FORWARD...
OMMAND CONTROL
Picard, Jean-Luc
Data
Barclay, Reginald
La Forge, Geordi
Brahms, Leah

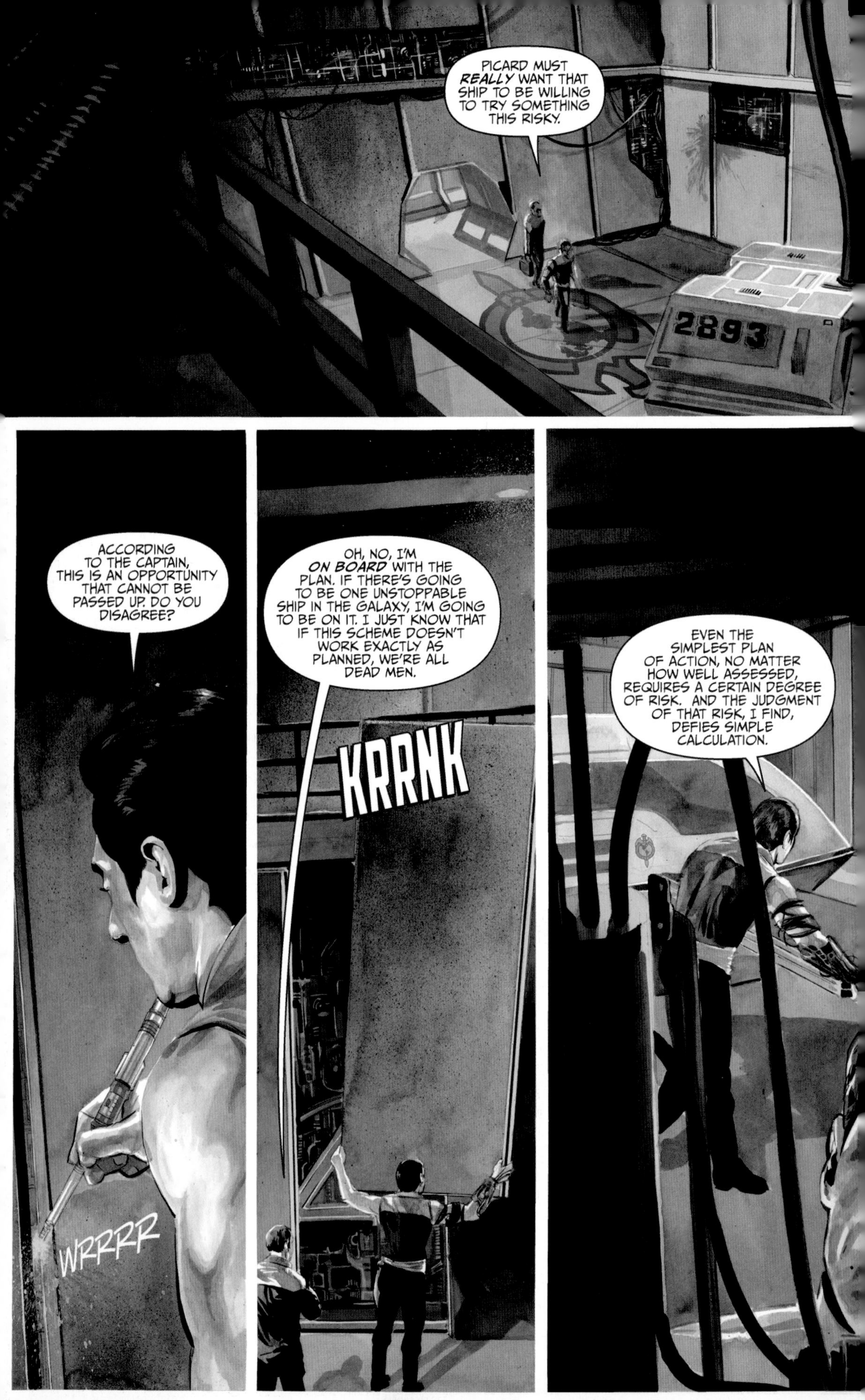
PICARD MUST *REALLY* WANT THAT SHIP TO BE WILLING TO TRY SOMETHING THIS RISKY.
2893
ACCORDING TO THE CAPTAIN, THIS IS AN OPPORTUNITY THAT CANNOT BE PASSED UP. DO YOU DISAGREE?
WRRRR
OH, NO, I'M *ON BOARD* WITH THE PLAN. IF THERE'S GOING TO BE ONE UNSTOPPABLE SHIP IN THE GALAXY, I'M GOING TO BE ON IT. I JUST KNOW THAT IF THIS SCHEME DOESN'T WORK EXACTLY AS PLANNED, WE'RE ALL DEAD MEN.
KRRNK
EVEN THE SIMPLEST PLAN OF ACTION, NO MATTER HOW WELL ASSESSED, REQUIRES A CERTAIN DEGREE OF RISK. AND THE JUDGMENT OF THAT RISK, I FIND, DEFIES SIMPLE CALCULATION.

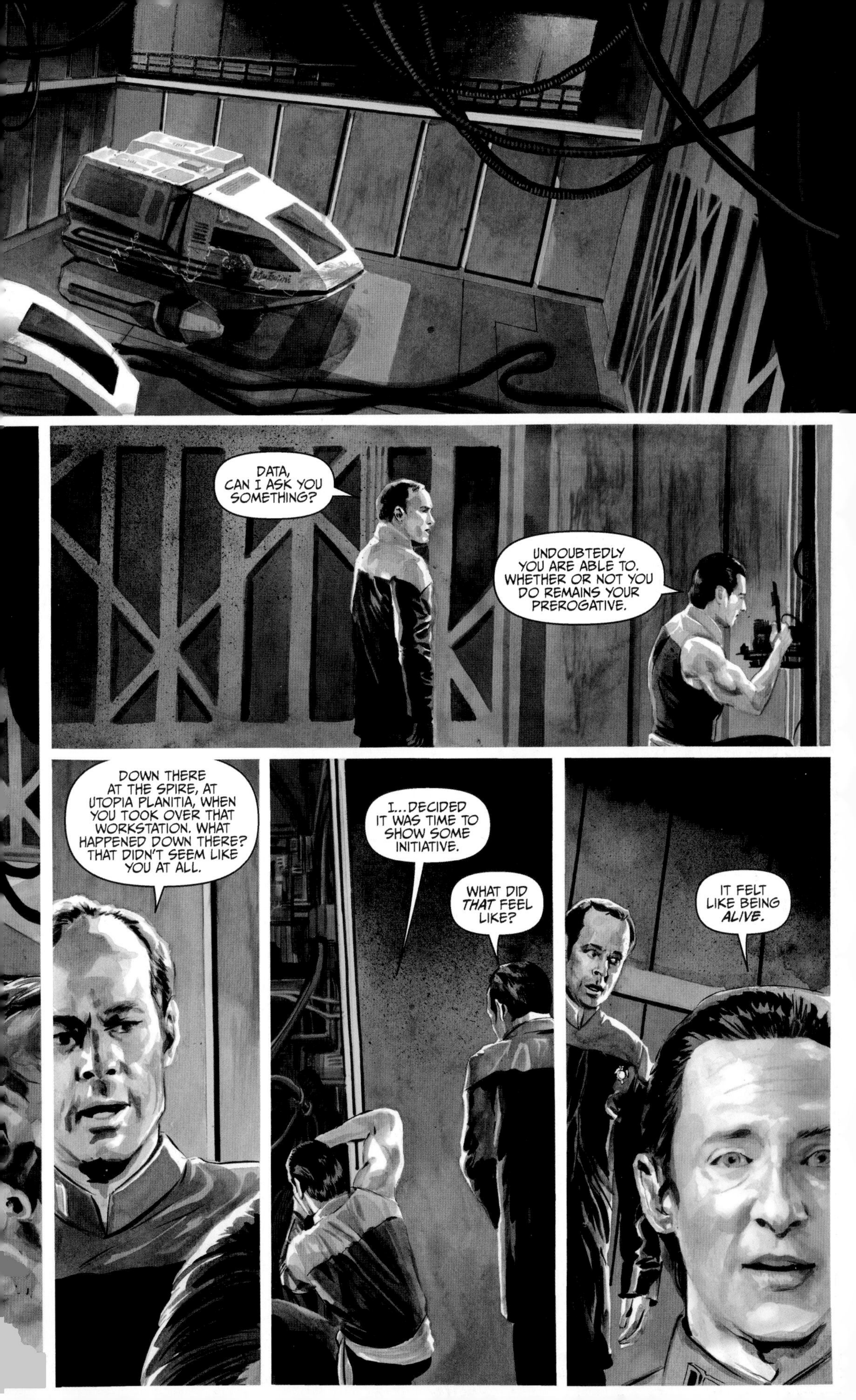
DATA, CAN I ASK YOU SOMETHING?
UNDOUBTEDLY YOU ARE ABLE TO. WHETHER OR NOT YOU DO REMAINS YOUR PREROGATIVE.
DOWN THERE AT THE SPIRE, AT UTOPIA PLANITIA, WHEN YOU TOOK OVER THAT WORKSTATION. WHAT HAPPENED DOWN THERE? THAT DIDN'T SEEM LIKE YOU AT ALL.
I...DECIDED IT WAS TIME TO SHOW SOME INITIATIVE.
WHAT DID *THAT* FEEL LIKE?
IT FELT LIKE BEING *ALIVE*.

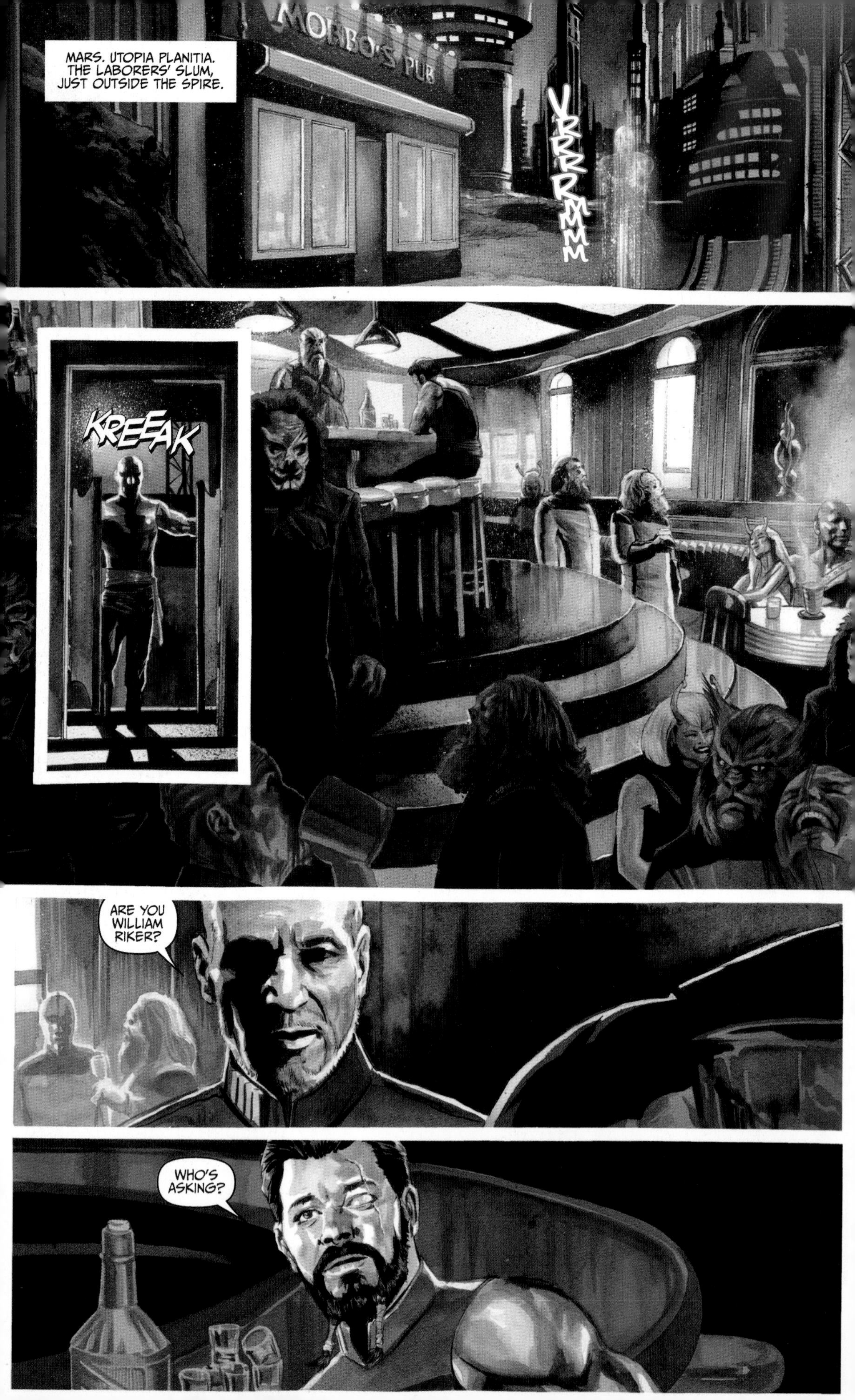
MORBO'S PUB
MARS. UTOPIA PLANITIA. THE LABORERS' SLUM, JUST OUTSIDE THE SPIRE.
VRRRRMMM
KREEAK
ARE YOU WILLIAM RIKER?
WHO'S ASKING?

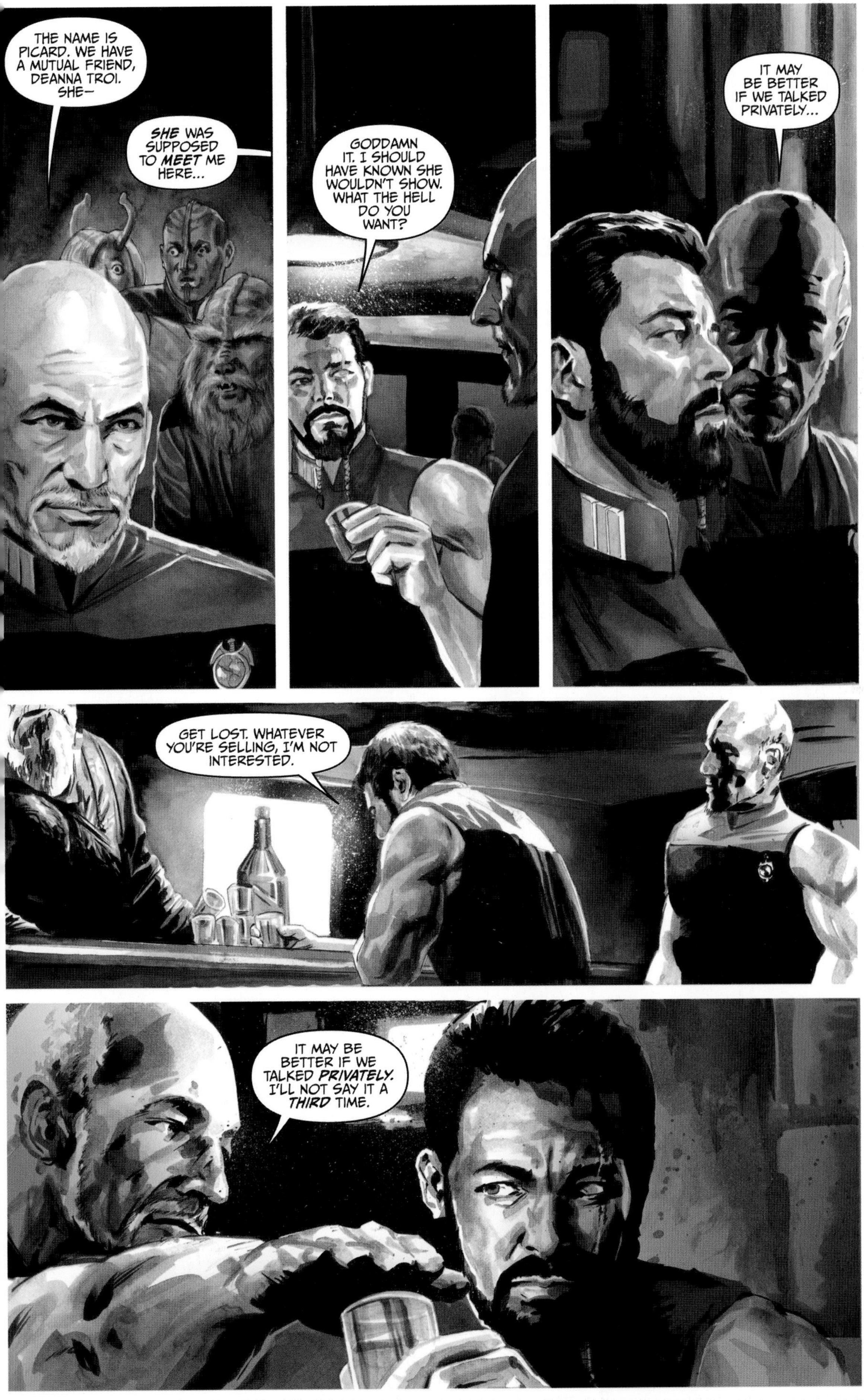
THE NAME IS PICARD. WE HAVE A MUTUAL FRIEND, DEANNA TROI. SHE–
SHE WAS SUPPOSED TO MEET ME HERE...
GODDAMN IT. I SHOULD HAVE KNOWN SHE WOULDN'T SHOW. WHAT THE HELL DO YOU WANT?
IT MAY BE BETTER IF WE TALKED PRIVATELY...
GET LOST. WHATEVER YOU'RE SELLING, I'M NOT INTERESTED.
IT MAY BE BETTER IF WE TALKED PRIVATELY. I'LL NOT SAY IT A THIRD TIME.

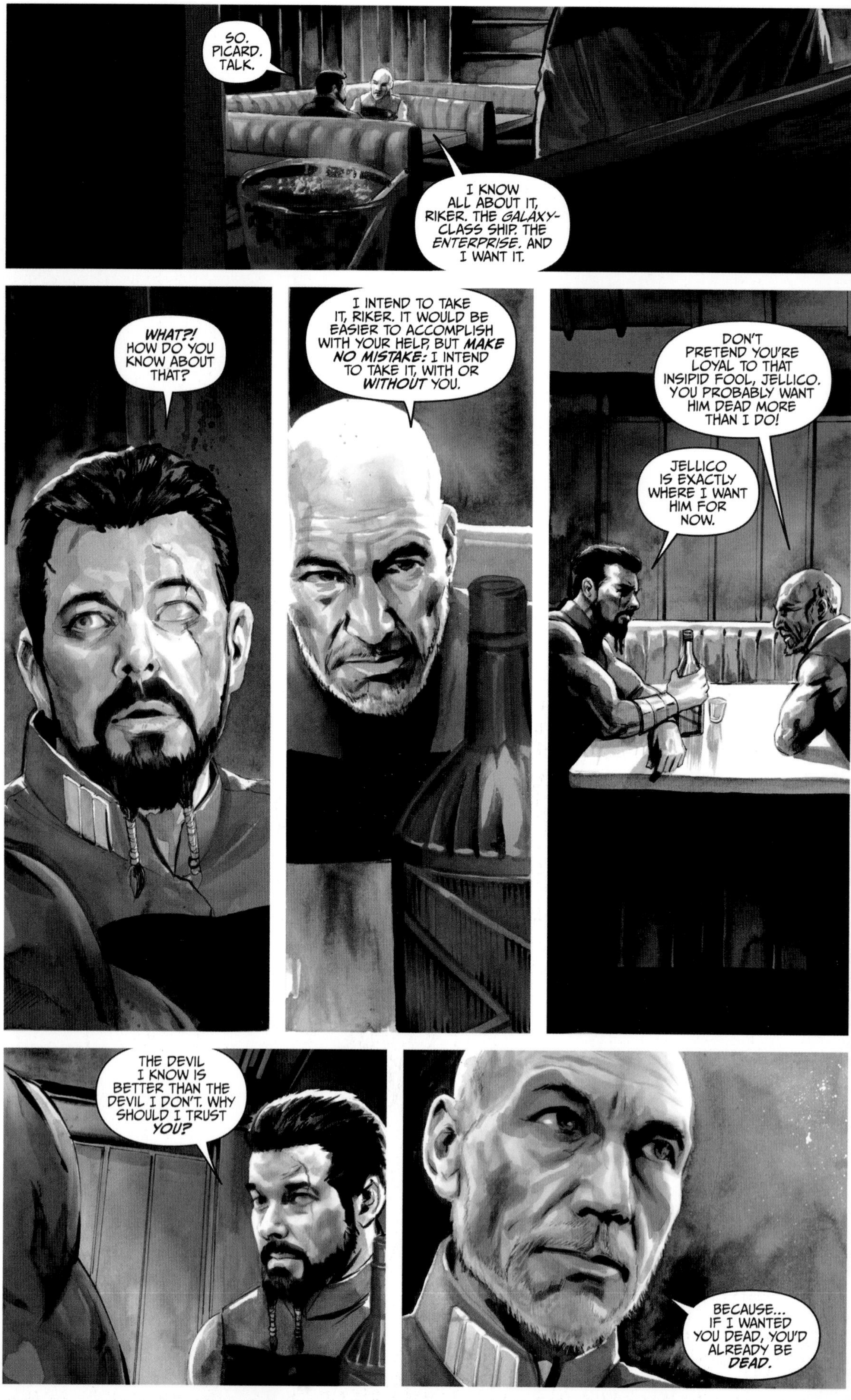
SO. PICARD. TALK.
I KNOW ALL ABOUT IT, RIKER. THE *GALAXY*-CLASS SHIP. THE *ENTERPRISE*. AND I WANT IT.
WHAT?! HOW DO YOU KNOW ABOUT THAT?
I INTEND TO TAKE IT, RIKER. IT WOULD BE EASIER TO ACCOMPLISH WITH YOUR HELP, BUT ***MAKE NO MISTAKE:*** I INTEND TO TAKE IT, WITH OR ***WITHOUT*** YOU.
DON'T PRETEND YOU'RE LOYAL TO THAT INSIPID FOOL, JELLICO. YOU PROBABLY WANT HIM DEAD MORE THAN I DO!
JELLICO IS EXACTLY WHERE I WANT HIM FOR NOW.
THE DEVIL I KNOW IS BETTER THAN THE DEVIL I DON'T. WHY SHOULD I TRUST ***YOU?***
BECAUSE... IF I WANTED YOU DEAD, YOU'D ALREADY BE ***DEAD.***

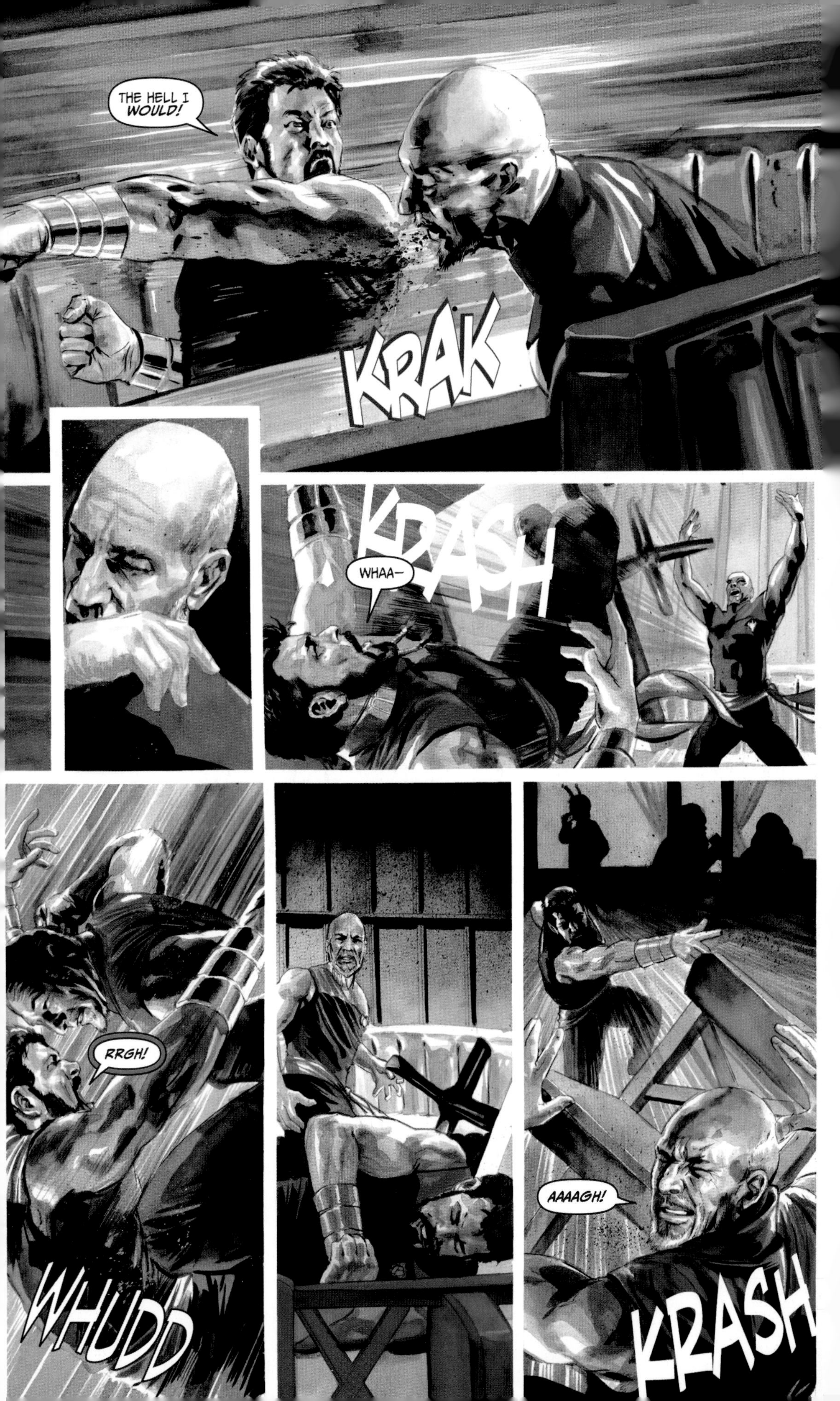

THE HELL I WOULD!
KRAK
KRASH
WHAA–
RRGH!
WHUDD
AAAAGH!
KRASH

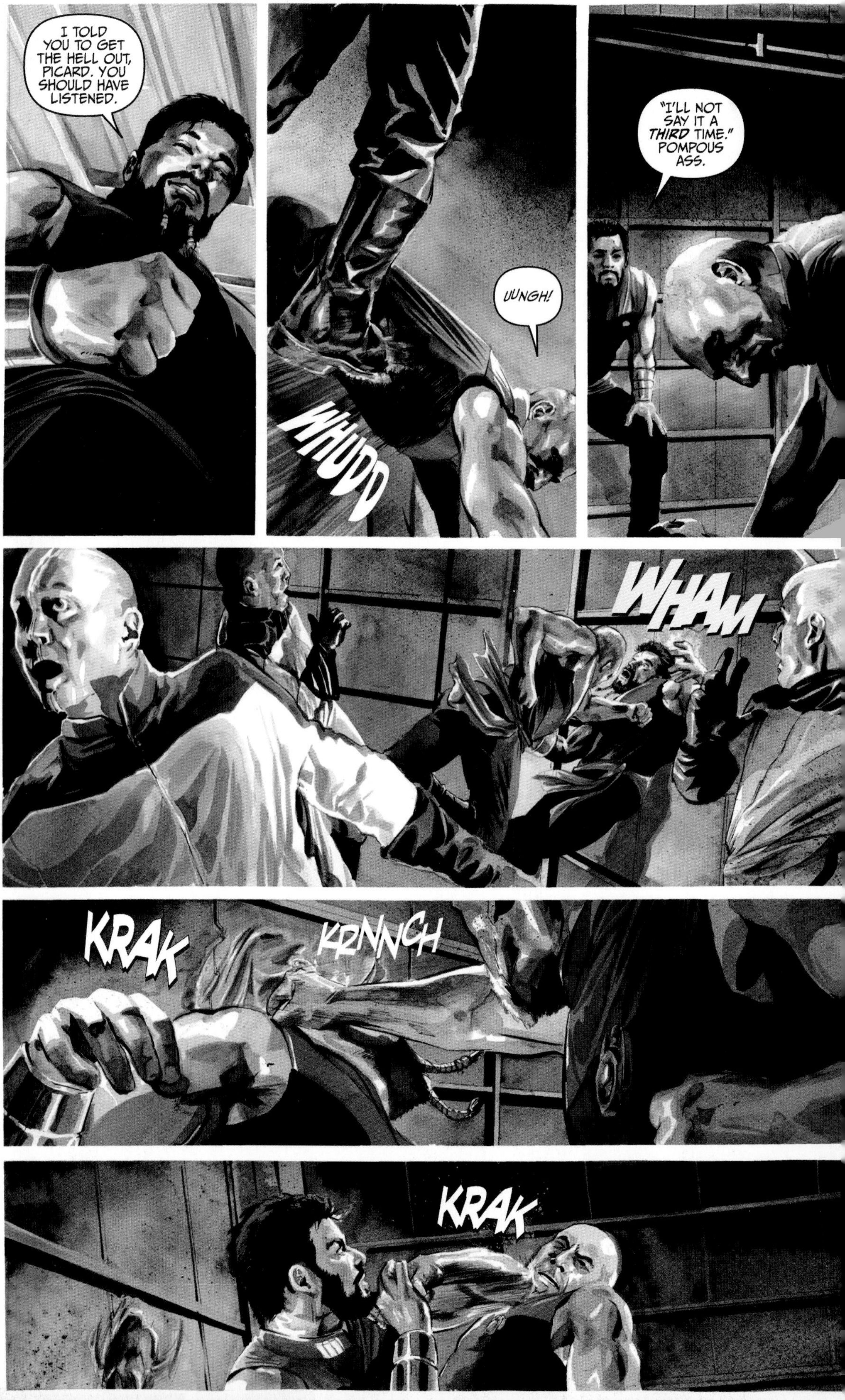
I TOLD YOU TO GET THE HELL OUT, PICARD. YOU SHOULD HAVE LISTENED.
UUNGH!
WHUDD
"I'LL NOT SAY IT A *THIRD* TIME." POMPOUS ASS.
WHAM
KRAK
KRNNCH
KRAK

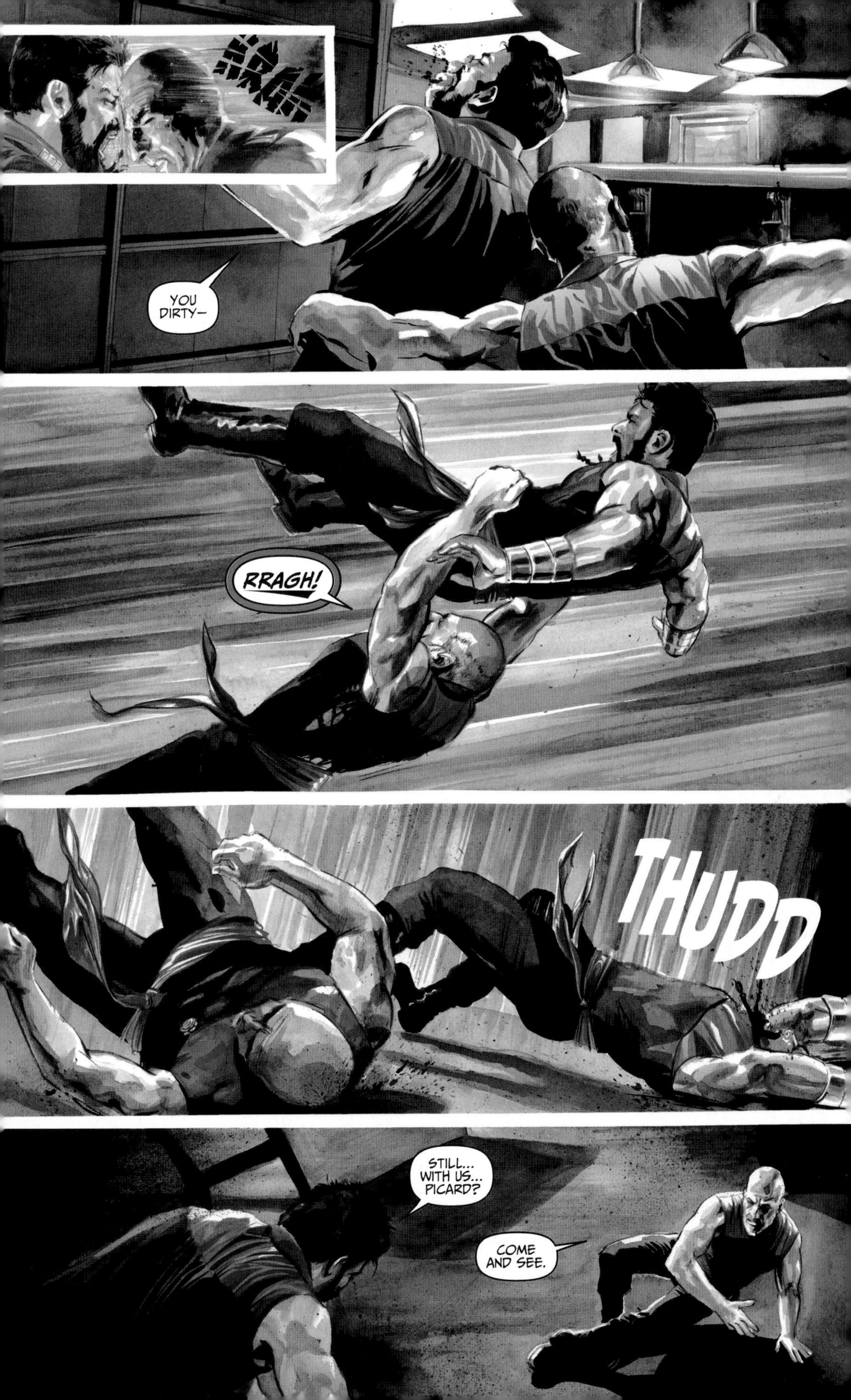

YOU DIRTY—
RRAGH!
THUDD
STILL... WITH US... PICARD?
COME AND SEE.

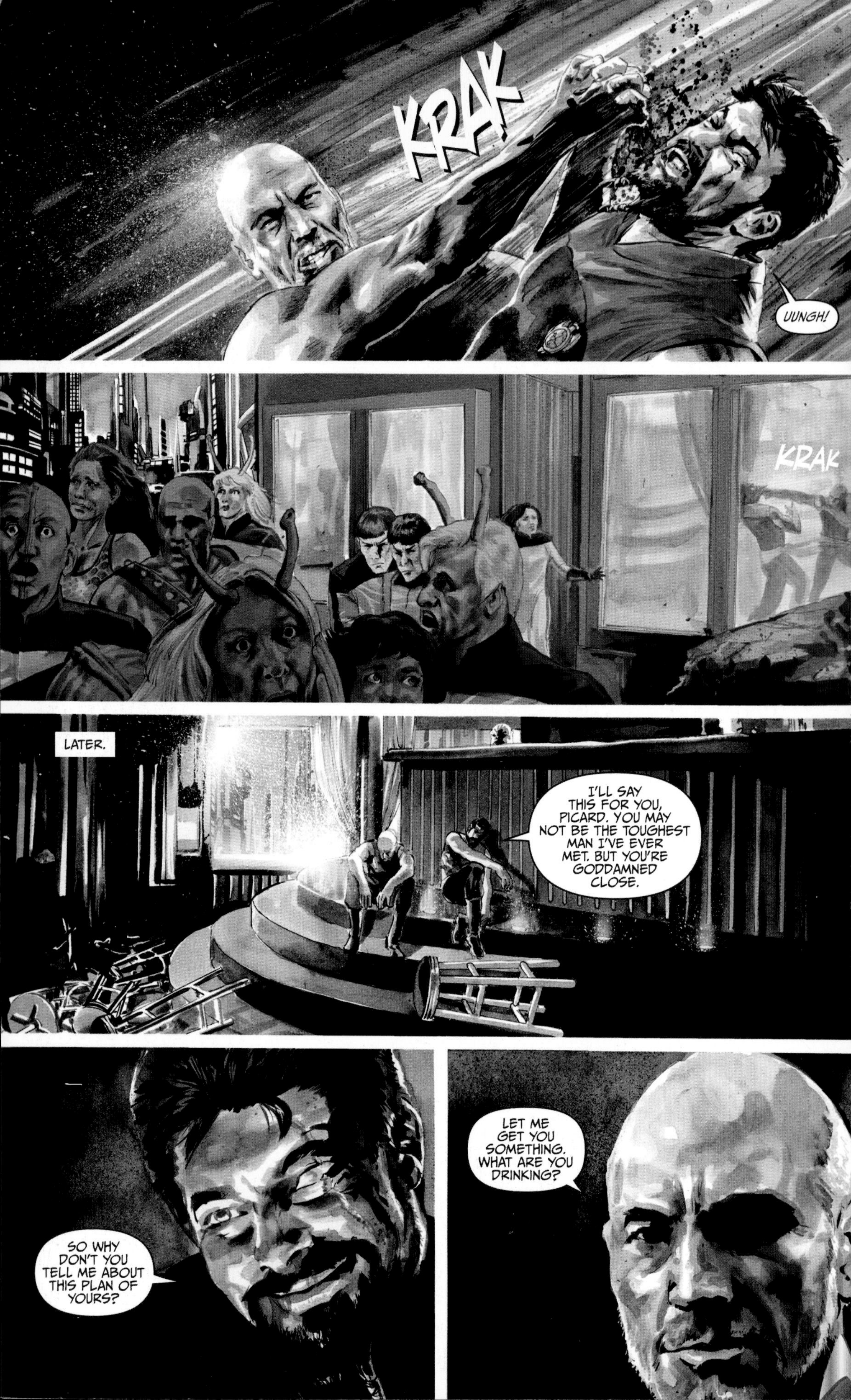
KRAK
UUNGH!
KRAK
LATER.
I'LL SAY THIS FOR YOU, PICARD. YOU MAY NOT BE THE TOUGHEST MAN I'VE EVER MET. BUT YOU'RE GODDAMNED CLOSE.
SO WHY DON'T YOU TELL ME ABOUT THIS PLAN OF YOURS?
LET ME GET YOU SOMETHING. WHAT ARE YOU DRINKING?

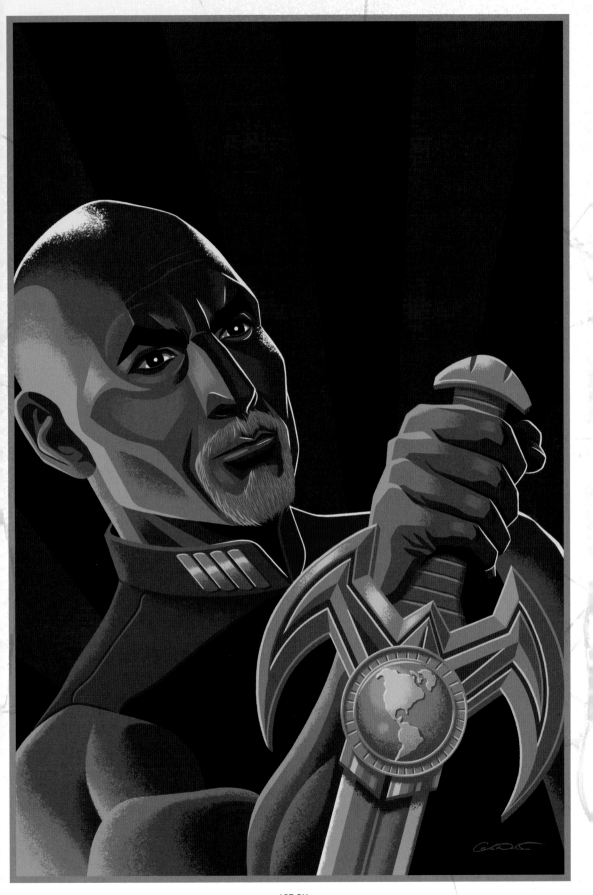

ART BY
GEORGE CALTSOUDAS

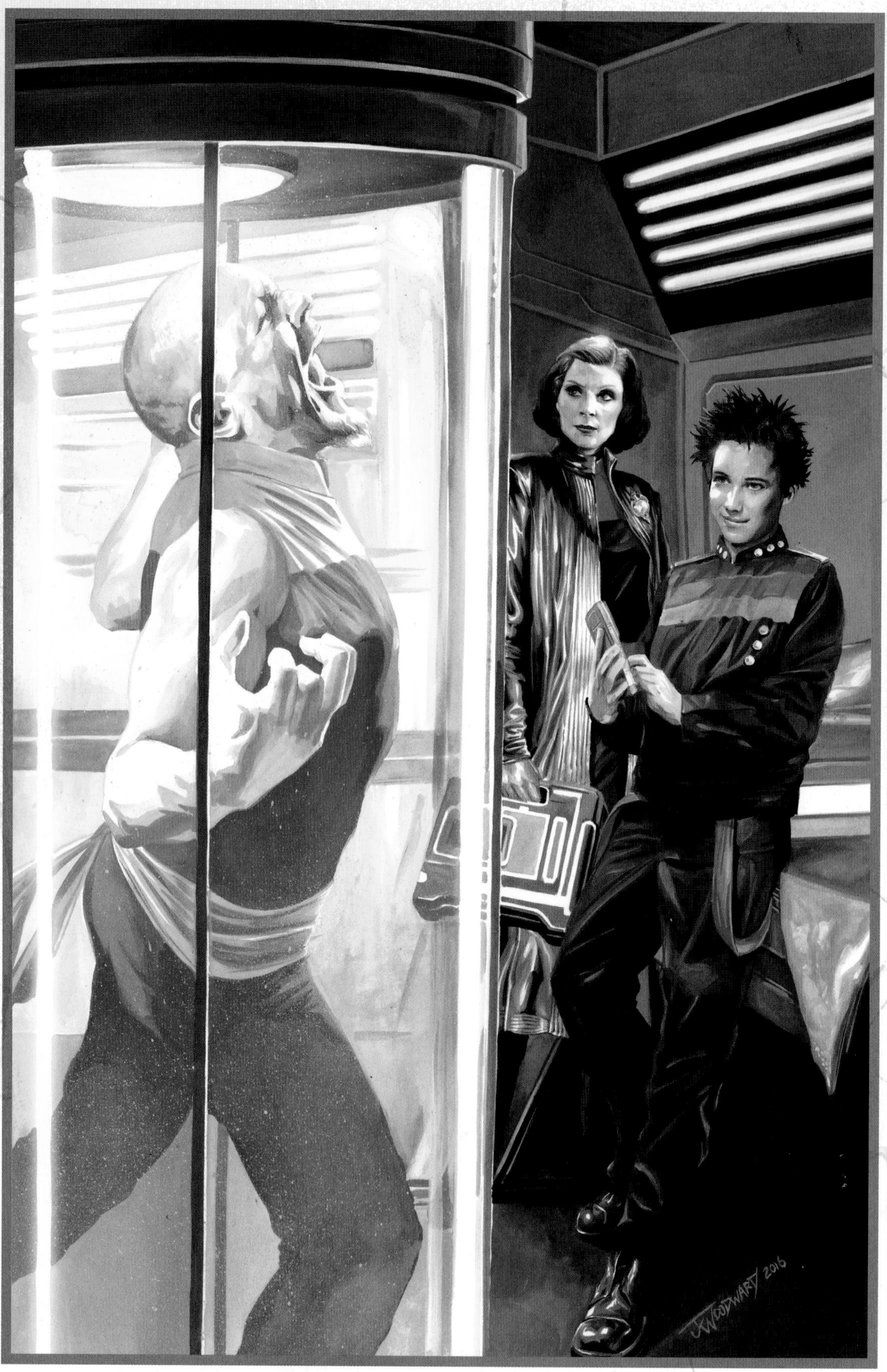

ART BY
J.K. WOODWARD

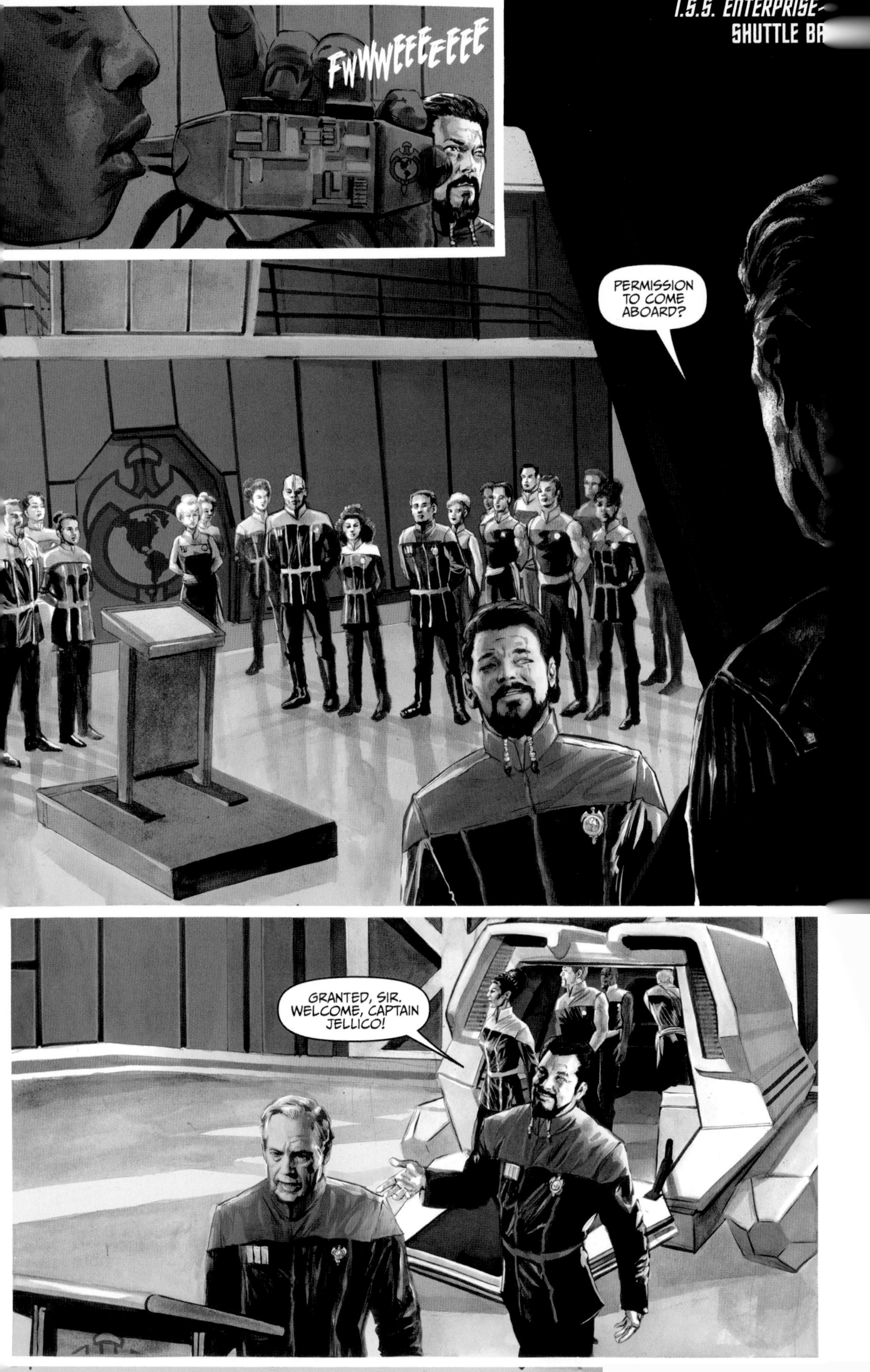
I.S.S. ENTERPRISE-
SHUTTLE BA
FWWWEEEEEEE
PERMISSION TO COME ABOARD?
GRANTED, SIR. WELCOME, CAPTAIN JELLICO!

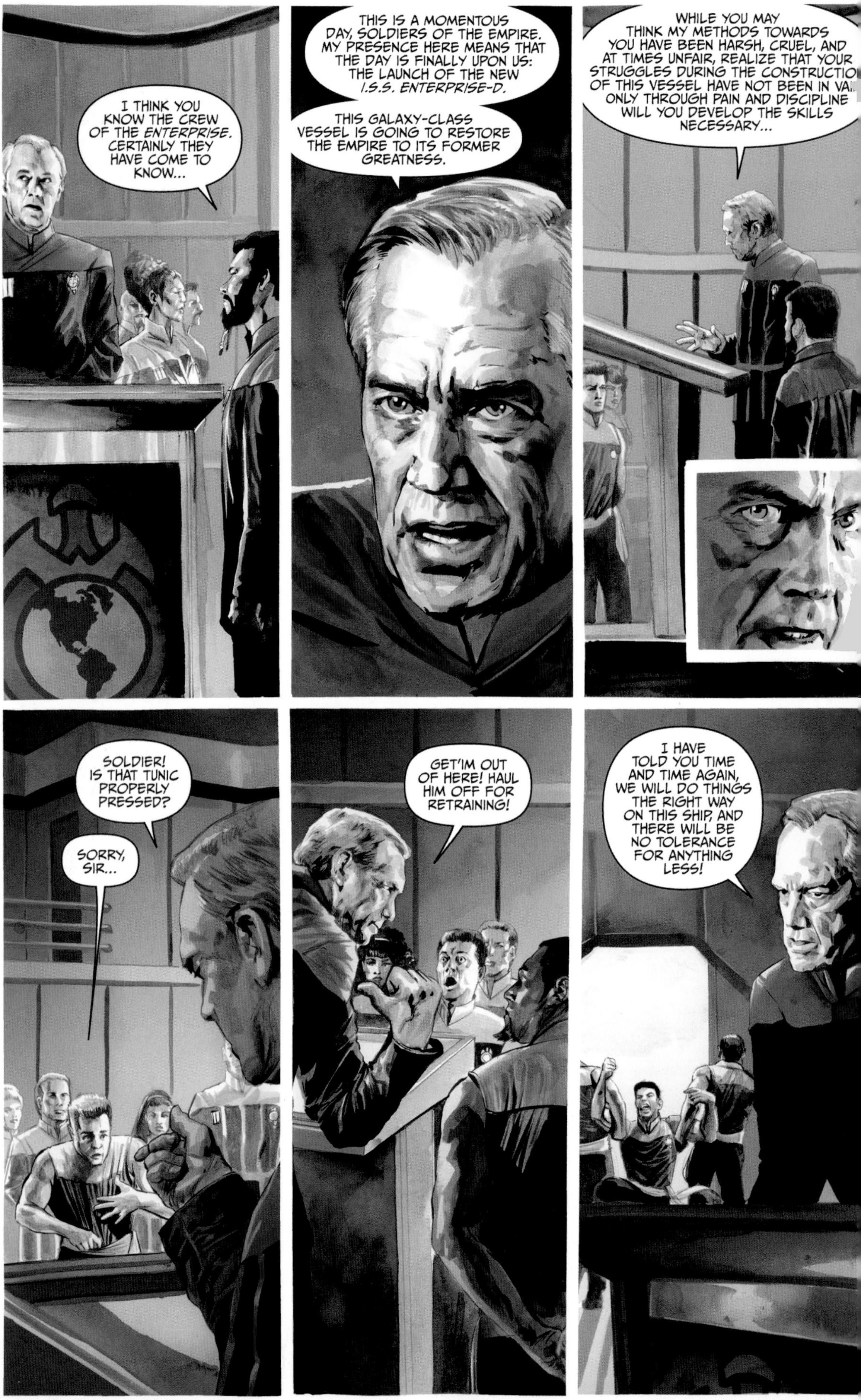
I THINK YOU KNOW THE CREW OF THE *ENTERPRISE*. CERTAINLY THEY HAVE COME TO KNOW...
THIS IS A MOMENTOUS DAY, SOLDIERS OF THE EMPIRE. MY PRESENCE HERE MEANS THAT THE DAY IS FINALLY UPON US: THE LAUNCH OF THE NEW *I.S.S. ENTERPRISE-D.*
THIS GALAXY-CLASS VESSEL IS GOING TO RESTORE THE EMPIRE TO ITS FORMER GREATNESS.
WHILE YOU MAY THINK MY METHODS TOWARDS YOU HAVE BEEN HARSH, CRUEL, AND AT TIMES UNFAIR, REALIZE THAT YOUR STRUGGLES DURING THE CONSTRUCTIO OF THIS VESSEL HAVE NOT BEEN IN VA ONLY THROUGH PAIN AND DISCIPLINE WILL YOU DEVELOP THE SKILLS NECESSARY...
SOLDIER! IS THAT TUNIC PROPERLY PRESSED?
SORRY, SIR...
GET'IM OUT OF HERE! HAUL HIM OFF FOR RETRAINING!
I HAVE TOLD YOU TIME AND TIME AGAIN, WE WILL DO THINGS THE RIGHT WAY ON THIS SHIP, AND THERE WILL BE NO TOLERANCE FOR ANYTHING LESS!

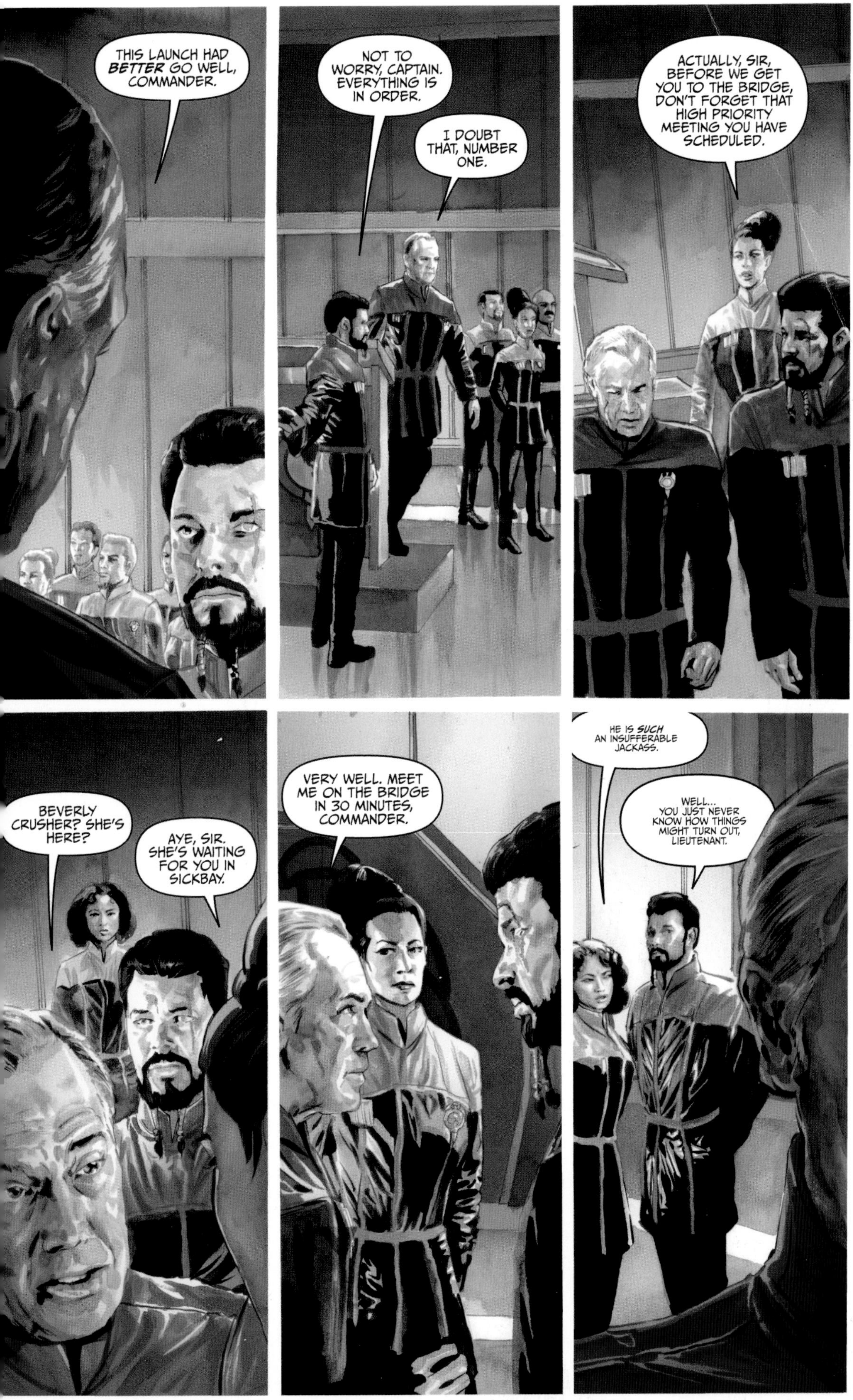
THIS LAUNCH HAD *BETTER* GO WELL, COMMANDER.
NOT TO WORRY, CAPTAIN. EVERYTHING IS IN ORDER.
I DOUBT THAT, NUMBER ONE.
ACTUALLY, SIR, BEFORE WE GET YOU TO THE BRIDGE, DON'T FORGET THAT HIGH PRIORITY MEETING YOU HAVE SCHEDULED.
BEVERLY CRUSHER? SHE'S HERE?
AYE, SIR. SHE'S WAITING FOR YOU IN SICKBAY.
VERY WELL. MEET ME ON THE BRIDGE IN 30 MINUTES, COMMANDER.
HE IS *SUCH* AN INSUFFERABLE JACKASS.
WELL... YOU JUST NEVER KNOW HOW THINGS MIGHT TURN OUT, LIEUTENANT.

DOCTOR CRUSHER!

CAPTAIN JELLICO.

I'M GLAD YOU ACCEPTED THIS ASSIGNMENT, DOCTOR. I SPECIFICALLY REQUESTED YOU.

IT WOULD HAVE BEEN DIFFICULT TO TURN DOWN THE OPPORTUNITY TO WORK IN THE MOST WELL EQUIPPED SICKBAY IN THE FLEET.

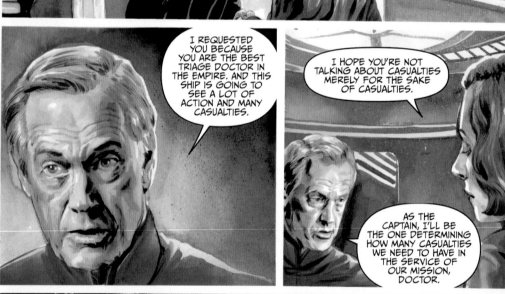

I REQUESTED YOU BECAUSE YOU ARE THE BEST TRIAGE DOCTOR IN THE EMPIRE. AND THIS SHIP IS GOING TO SEE A LOT OF ACTION AND MANY CASUALTIES.

I HOPE YOU'RE NOT TALKING ABOUT CASUALTIES MERELY FOR THE SAKE OF CASUALTIES.

AS THE CAPTAIN, I'LL BE THE ONE DETERMINING HOW MANY CASUALTIES WE NEED TO HAVE IN THE SERVICE OF OUR MISSION, DOCTOR.

YOUR JOB IS TO HEAL THEM UP AND KEEP THEM FIGHTING. IS THAT CLEAR?

YES, CAPTAIN.

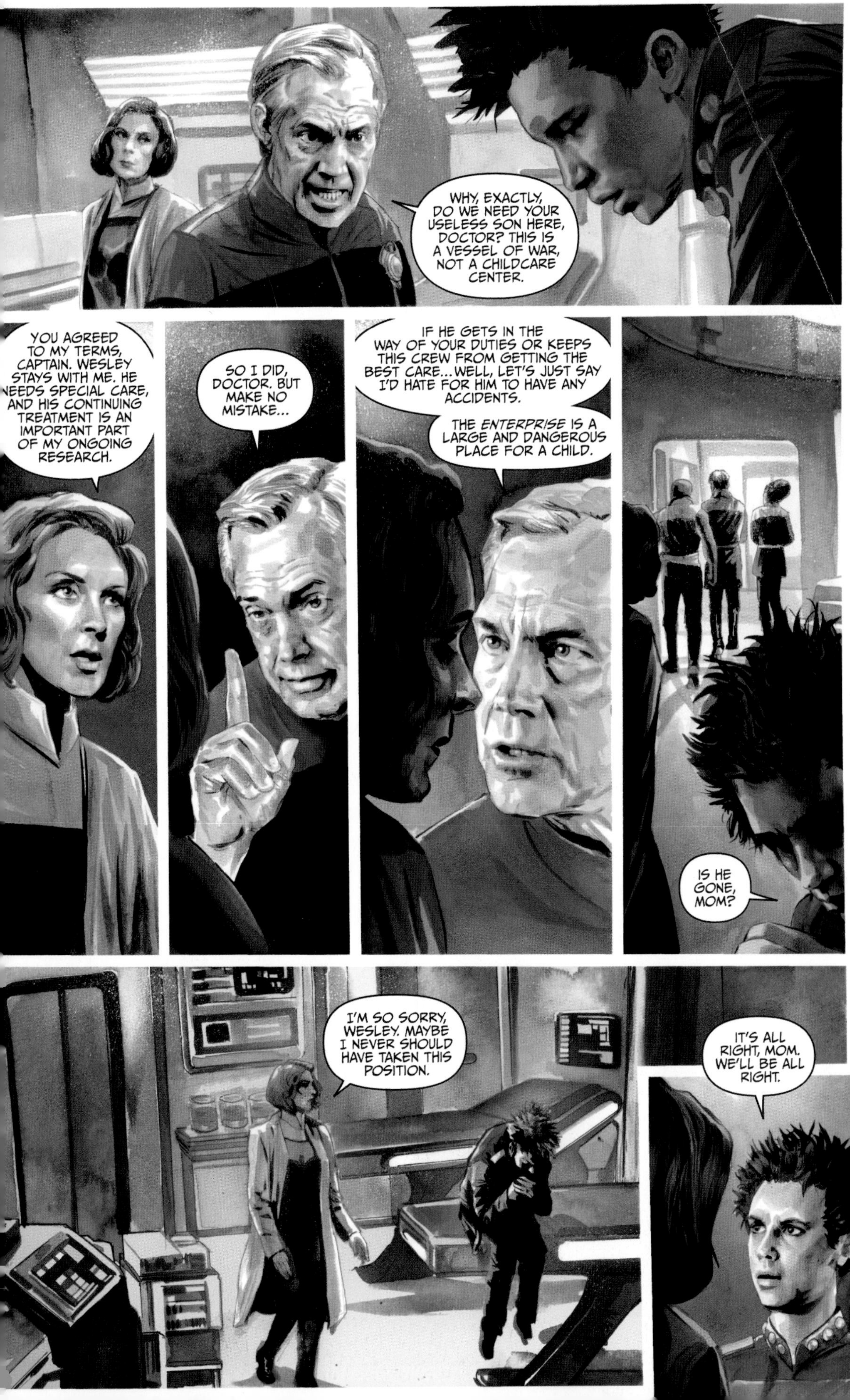
WHY, EXACTLY, DO WE NEED YOUR USELESS SON HERE, DOCTOR? THIS IS A VESSEL OF WAR, NOT A CHILDCARE CENTER.
YOU AGREED TO MY TERMS, CAPTAIN. WESLEY STAYS WITH ME. HE NEEDS SPECIAL CARE, AND HIS CONTINUING TREATMENT IS AN IMPORTANT PART OF MY ONGOING RESEARCH.
SO I DID, DOCTOR. BUT MAKE NO MISTAKE...
IF HE GETS IN THE WAY OF YOUR DUTIES OR KEEPS THIS CREW FROM GETTING THE BEST CARE...WELL, LET'S JUST SAY I'D HATE FOR HIM TO HAVE ANY ACCIDENTS.
THE *ENTERPRISE* IS A LARGE AND DANGEROUS PLACE FOR A CHILD.
IS HE GONE, MOM?
I'M SO SORRY, WESLEY. MAYBE I NEVER SHOULD HAVE TAKEN THIS POSITION.
IT'S ALL RIGHT, MOM. WE'LL BE ALL RIGHT.

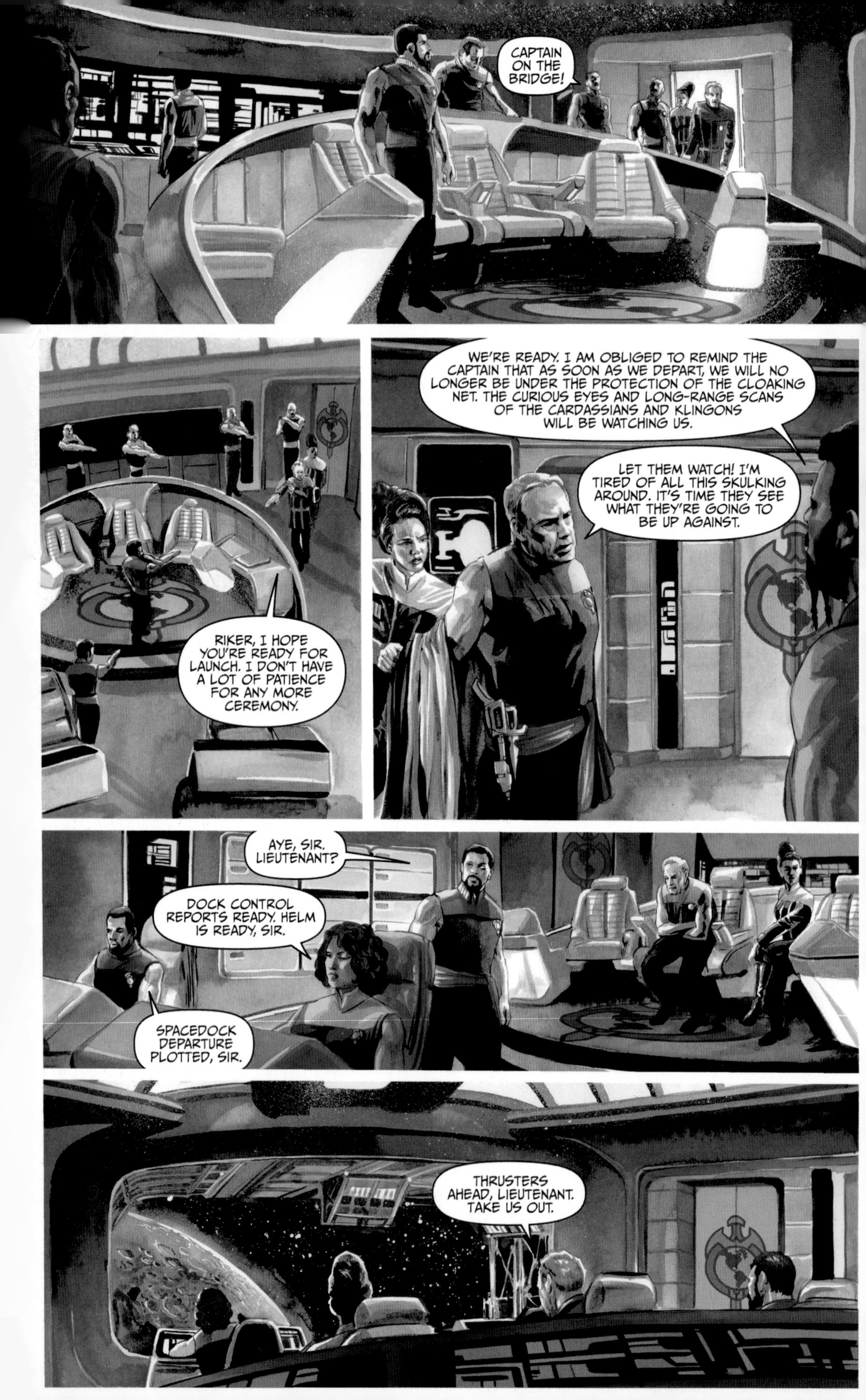
CAPTAIN ON THE BRIDGE!
RIKER, I HOPE YOU'RE READY FOR LAUNCH. I DON'T HAVE A LOT OF PATIENCE FOR ANY MORE CEREMONY.
WE'RE READY. I AM OBLIGED TO REMIND THE CAPTAIN THAT AS SOON AS WE DEPART, WE WILL NO LONGER BE UNDER THE PROTECTION OF THE CLOAKING NET. THE CURIOUS EYES AND LONG-RANGE SCANS OF THE CARDASSIANS AND KLINGONS WILL BE WATCHING US.
LET THEM WATCH! I'M TIRED OF ALL THIS SKULKING AROUND. IT'S TIME THEY SEE WHAT THEY'RE GOING TO BE UP AGAINST.
AYE, SIR. LIEUTENANT?
DOCK CONTROL REPORTS READY. HELM IS READY, SIR.
SPACEDOCK DEPARTURE PLOTTED, SIR.
THRUSTERS AHEAD, LIEUTENANT. TAKE US OUT.

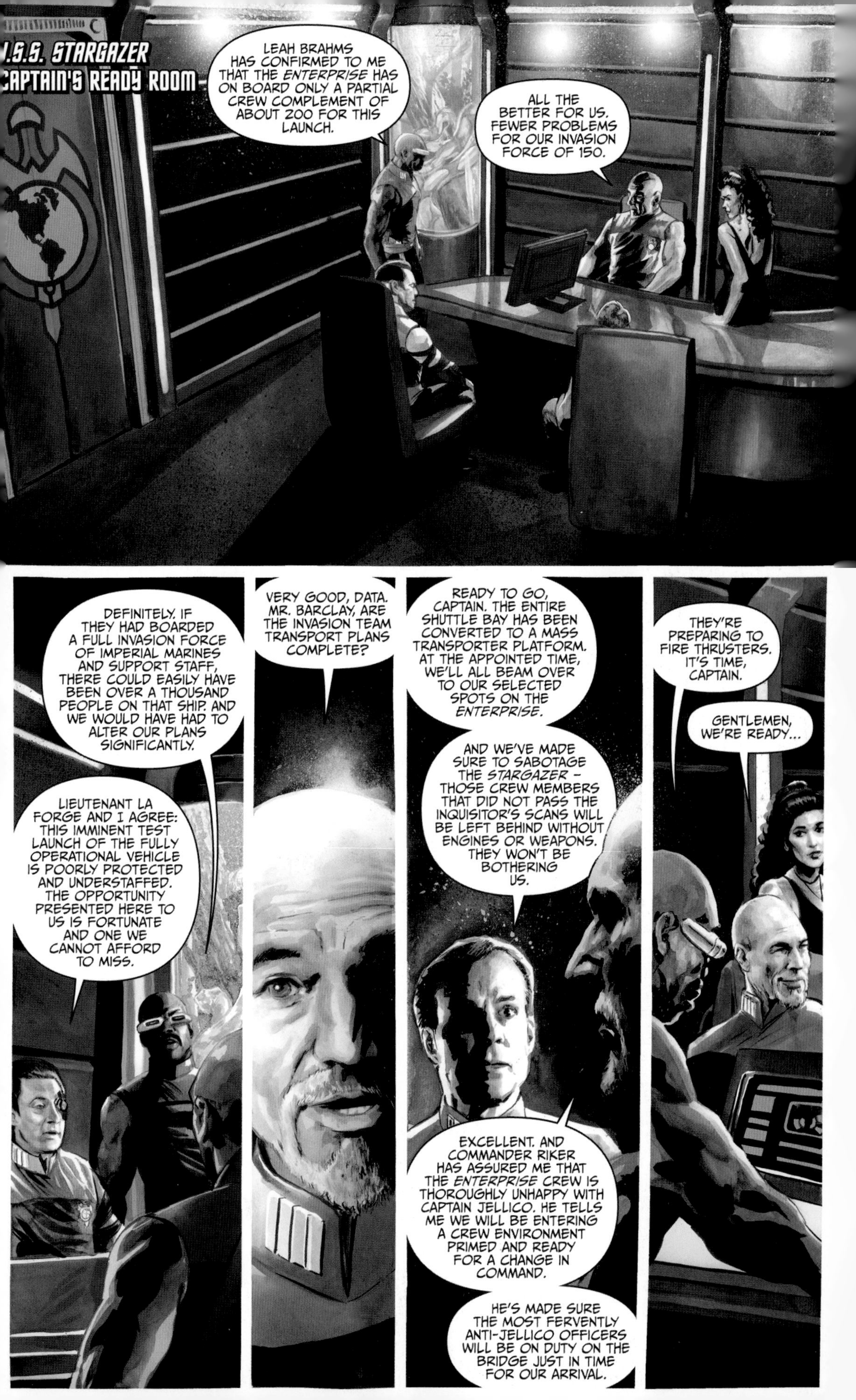
I.S.S. STARGAZER
CAPTAIN'S READY ROOM
LEAH BRAHMS HAS CONFIRMED TO ME THAT THE *ENTERPRISE* HAS ON BOARD ONLY A PARTIAL CREW COMPLEMENT OF ABOUT 200 FOR THIS LAUNCH.
ALL THE BETTER FOR US. FEWER PROBLEMS FOR OUR INVASION FORCE OF 150.
DEFINITELY. IF THEY HAD BOARDED A FULL INVASION FORCE OF IMPERIAL MARINES AND SUPPORT STAFF, THERE COULD EASILY HAVE BEEN OVER A THOUSAND PEOPLE ON THAT SHIP. AND WE WOULD HAVE HAD TO ALTER OUR PLANS SIGNIFICANTLY.
LIEUTENANT LA FORGE AND I AGREE: THIS IMMINENT TEST LAUNCH OF THE FULLY OPERATIONAL VEHICLE IS POORLY PROTECTED AND UNDERSTAFFED. THE OPPORTUNITY PRESENTED HERE TO US IS FORTUNATE AND ONE WE CANNOT AFFORD TO MISS.
VERY GOOD, DATA. MR. BARCLAY, ARE THE INVASION TEAM TRANSPORT PLANS COMPLETE?
READY TO GO, CAPTAIN. THE ENTIRE SHUTTLE BAY HAS BEEN CONVERTED TO A MASS TRANSPORTER PLATFORM. AT THE APPOINTED TIME, WE'LL ALL BEAM OVER TO OUR SELECTED SPOTS ON THE *ENTERPRISE*.
AND WE'VE MADE SURE TO SABOTAGE THE *STARGAZER* – THOSE CREW MEMBERS THAT DID NOT PASS THE INQUISITOR'S SCANS WILL BE LEFT BEHIND WITHOUT ENGINES OR WEAPONS. THEY WON'T BE BOTHERING US.
EXCELLENT. AND COMMANDER RIKER HAS ASSURED ME THAT THE *ENTERPRISE* CREW IS THOROUGHLY UNHAPPY WITH CAPTAIN JELLICO. HE TELLS ME WE WILL BE ENTERING A CREW ENVIRONMENT PRIMED AND READY FOR A CHANGE IN COMMAND.
HE'S MADE SURE THE MOST FERVENTLY ANTI-JELLICO OFFICERS WILL BE ON DUTY ON THE BRIDGE JUST IN TIME FOR OUR ARRIVAL.
THEY'RE PREPARING TO FIRE THRUSTERS. IT'S TIME, CAPTAIN.
GENTLEMEN, WE'RE READY...

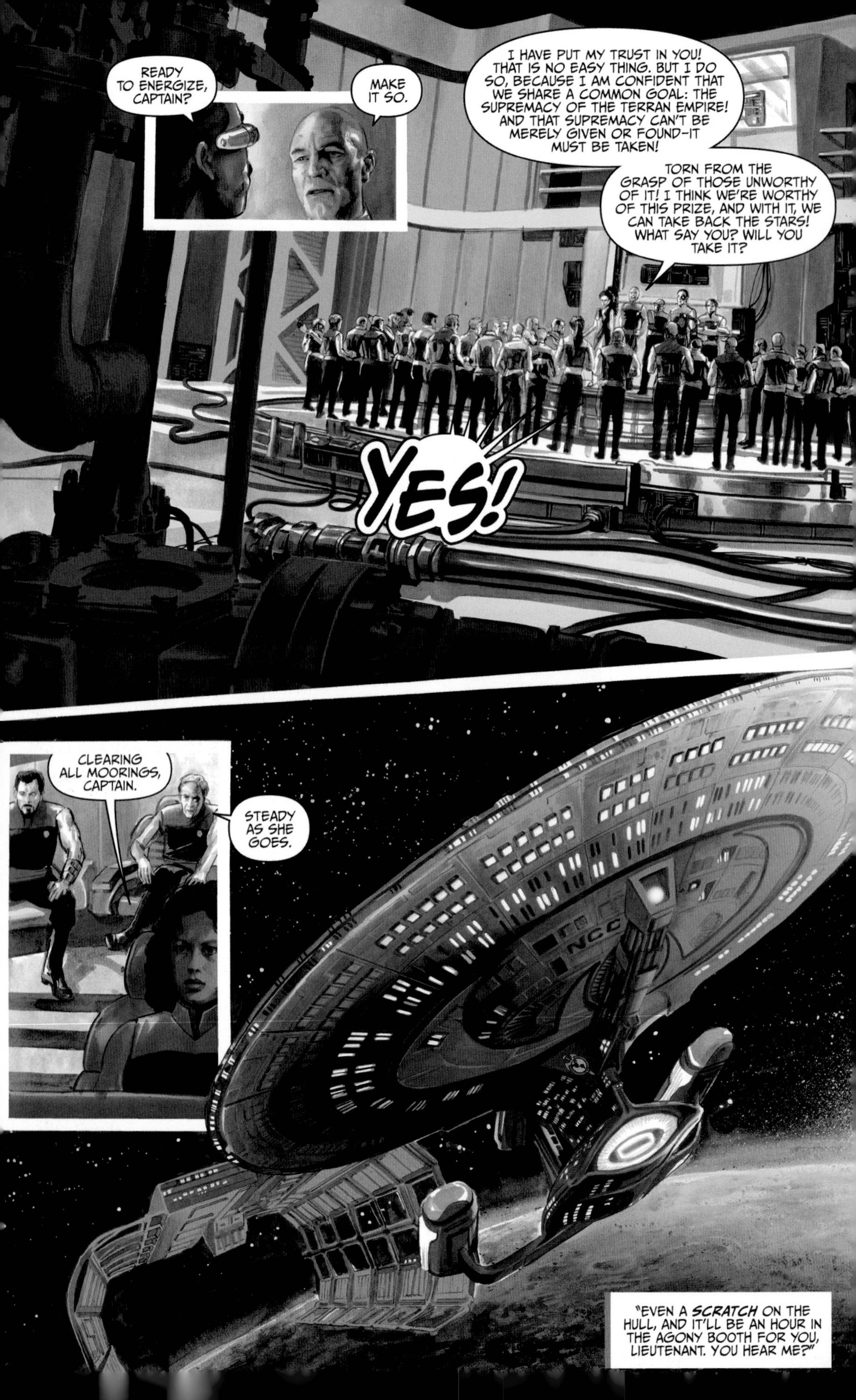
READY TO ENERGIZE, CAPTAIN?
MAKE IT SO.
I HAVE PUT MY TRUST IN YOU! THAT IS NO EASY THING. BUT I DO SO, BECAUSE I AM CONFIDENT THAT WE SHARE A COMMON GOAL: THE SUPREMACY OF THE TERRAN EMPIRE! AND THAT SUPREMACY CAN'T BE MERELY GIVEN OR FOUND–IT MUST BE TAKEN!
TORN FROM THE GRASP OF THOSE UNWORTHY OF IT! I THINK WE'RE WORTHY OF THIS PRIZE, AND WITH IT, WE CAN TAKE BACK THE STARS! WHAT SAY YOU? WILL YOU TAKE IT?
YES!
CLEARING ALL MOORINGS, CAPTAIN.
STEADY AS SHE GOES.
NCC
"EVEN A SCRATCH ON THE HULL, AND IT'LL BE AN HOUR IN THE AGONY BOOTH FOR YOU, LIEUTENANT. YOU HEAR ME?"

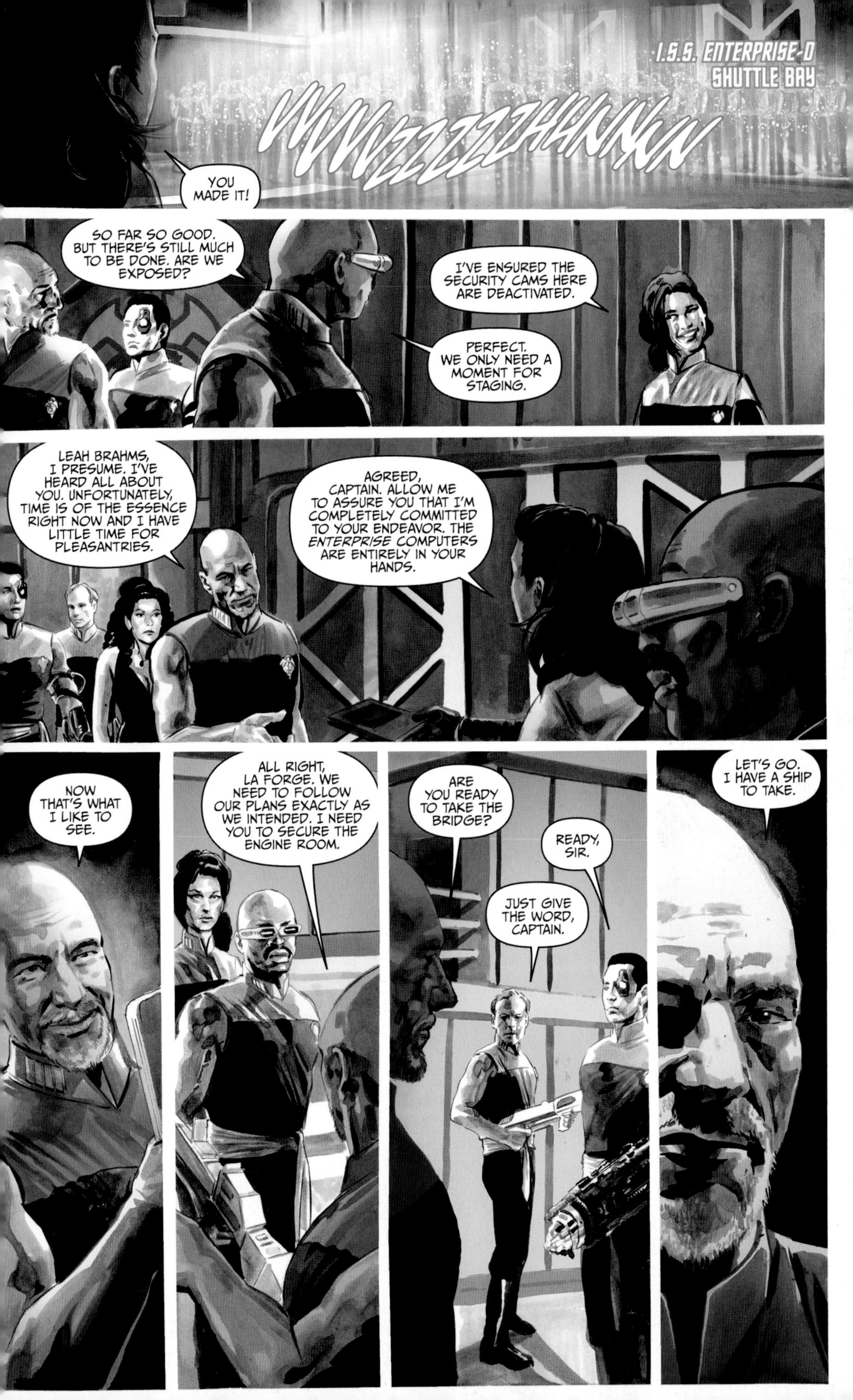
I.S.S. ENTERPRISE-D
SHUTTLE BAY
VVVVVZZZZZZHHNNNN
YOU MADE IT!
SO FAR SO GOOD. BUT THERE'S STILL MUCH TO BE DONE. ARE WE EXPOSED?
I'VE ENSURED THE SECURITY CAMS HERE ARE DEACTIVATED.
PERFECT. WE ONLY NEED A MOMENT FOR STAGING.
LEAH BRAHMS, I PRESUME. I'VE HEARD ALL ABOUT YOU. UNFORTUNATELY, TIME IS OF THE ESSENCE RIGHT NOW AND I HAVE LITTLE TIME FOR PLEASANTRIES.
AGREED, CAPTAIN. ALLOW ME TO ASSURE YOU THAT I'M COMPLETELY COMMITTED TO YOUR ENDEAVOR. THE *ENTERPRISE* COMPUTERS ARE ENTIRELY IN YOUR HANDS.
NOW THAT'S WHAT I LIKE TO SEE.
ALL RIGHT, LA FORGE. WE NEED TO FOLLOW OUR PLANS EXACTLY AS WE INTENDED. I NEED YOU TO SECURE THE ENGINE ROOM.
ARE YOU READY TO TAKE THE BRIDGE?
READY, SIR.
JUST GIVE THE WORD, CAPTAIN.
LET'S GO. I HAVE A SHIP TO TAKE.

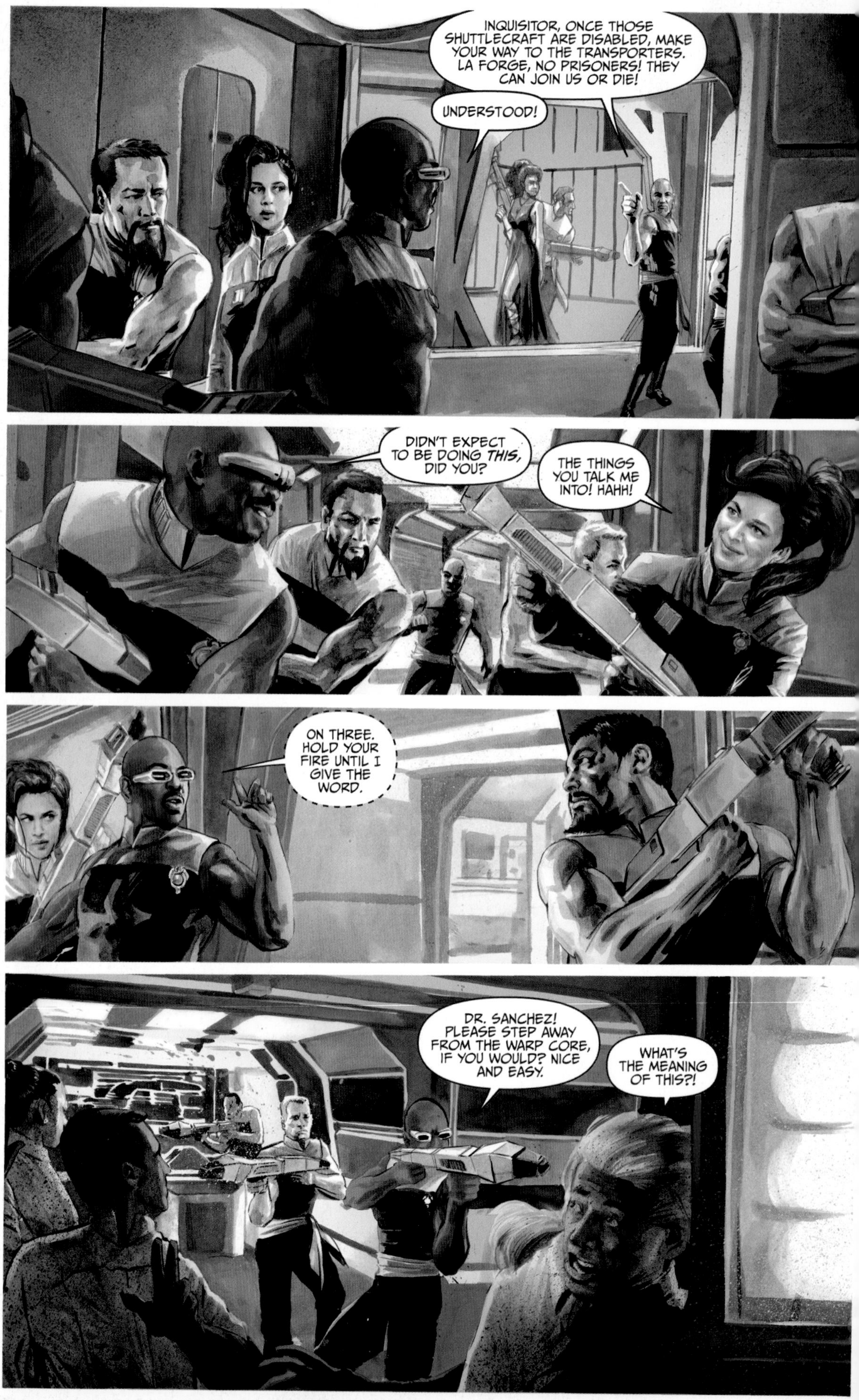
INQUISITOR, ONCE THOSE SHUTTLECRAFT ARE DISABLED, MAKE YOUR WAY TO THE TRANSPORTERS. LA FORGE, NO PRISONERS! THEY CAN JOIN US OR DIE!
UNDERSTOOD!
DIDN'T EXPECT TO BE DOING *THIS*, DID YOU?
THE THINGS YOU TALK ME INTO! HAHH!
ON THREE. HOLD YOUR FIRE UNTIL I GIVE THE WORD.
DR. SANCHEZ! PLEASE STEP AWAY FROM THE WARP CORE, IF YOU WOULD? NICE AND EASY.
WHAT'S THE MEANING OF THIS?!

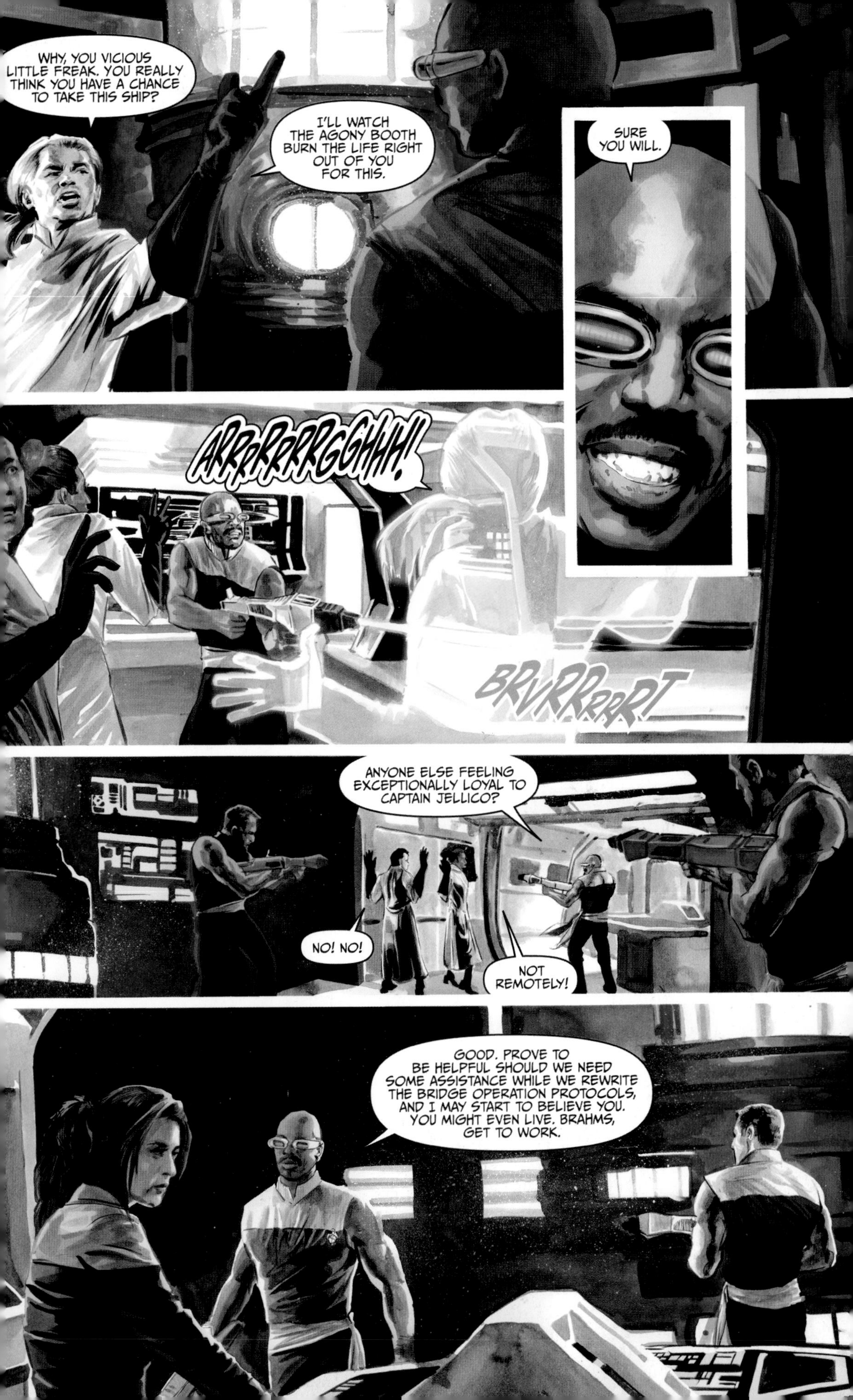
WHY, YOU VICIOUS LITTLE FREAK. YOU REALLY THINK YOU HAVE A CHANCE TO TAKE THIS SHIP?
I'LL WATCH THE AGONY BOOTH BURN THE LIFE RIGHT OUT OF YOU FOR THIS.
SURE YOU WILL.
ARRRRRRRGGHHH!
BRVRRRRRT
ANYONE ELSE FEELING EXCEPTIONALLY LOYAL TO CAPTAIN JELLICO?
NO! NO!
NOT REMOTELY!
GOOD. PROVE TO BE HELPFUL SHOULD WE NEED SOME ASSISTANCE WHILE WE REWRITE THE BRIDGE OPERATION PROTOCOLS, AND I MAY START TO BELIEVE YOU. YOU MIGHT EVEN LIVE. BRAHMS, GET TO WORK.

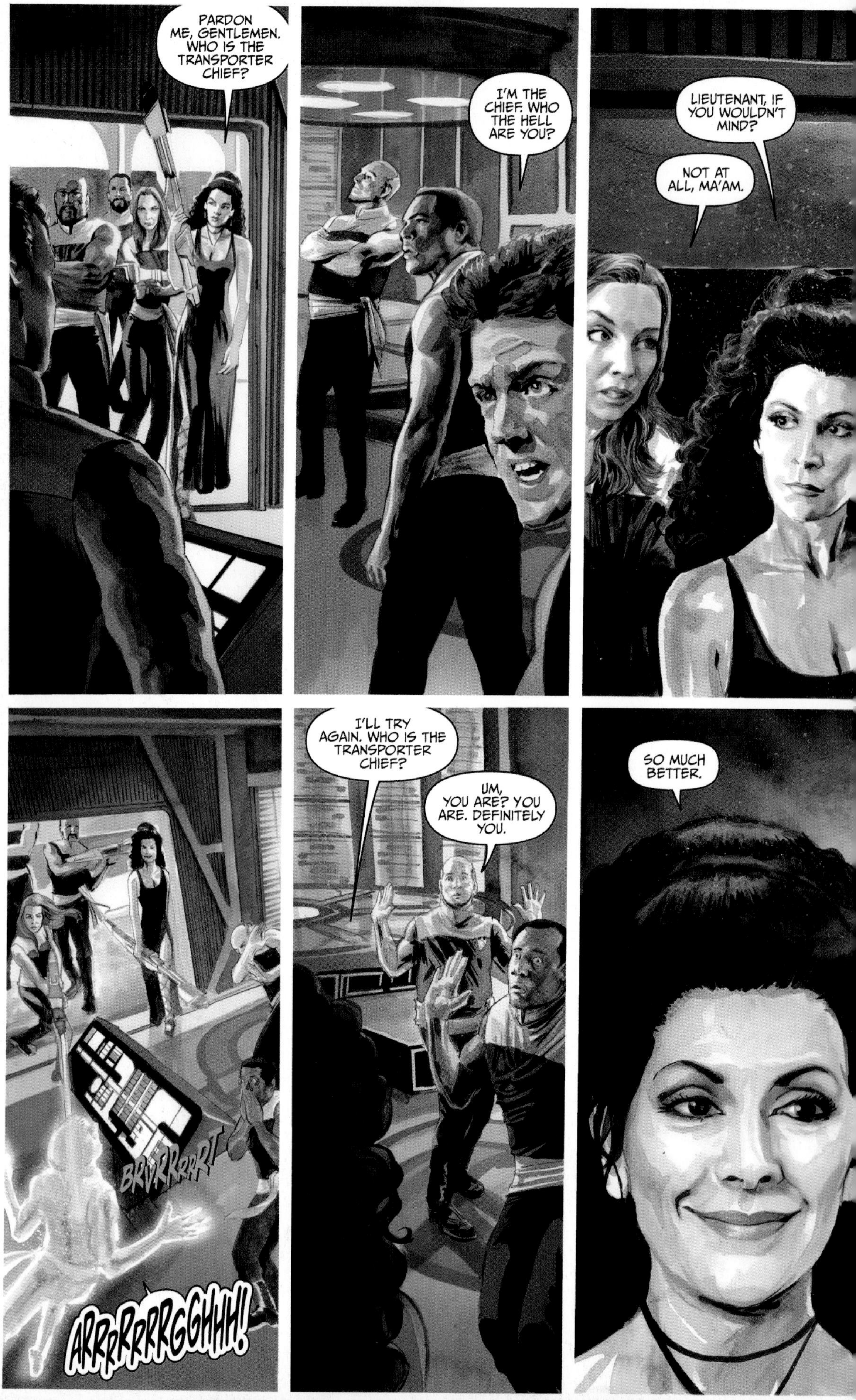
PARDON ME, GENTLEMEN. WHO IS THE TRANSPORTER CHIEF?
I'M THE CHIEF. WHO THE HELL ARE YOU?
LIEUTENANT, IF YOU WOULDN'T MIND?
NOT AT ALL, MA'AM.
BRVRRRRRT
ARRRRRRRGGHHH!
I'LL TRY AGAIN. WHO IS THE TRANSPORTER CHIEF?
UM, YOU ARE? YOU ARE. DEFINITELY YOU.
SO MUCH BETTER.

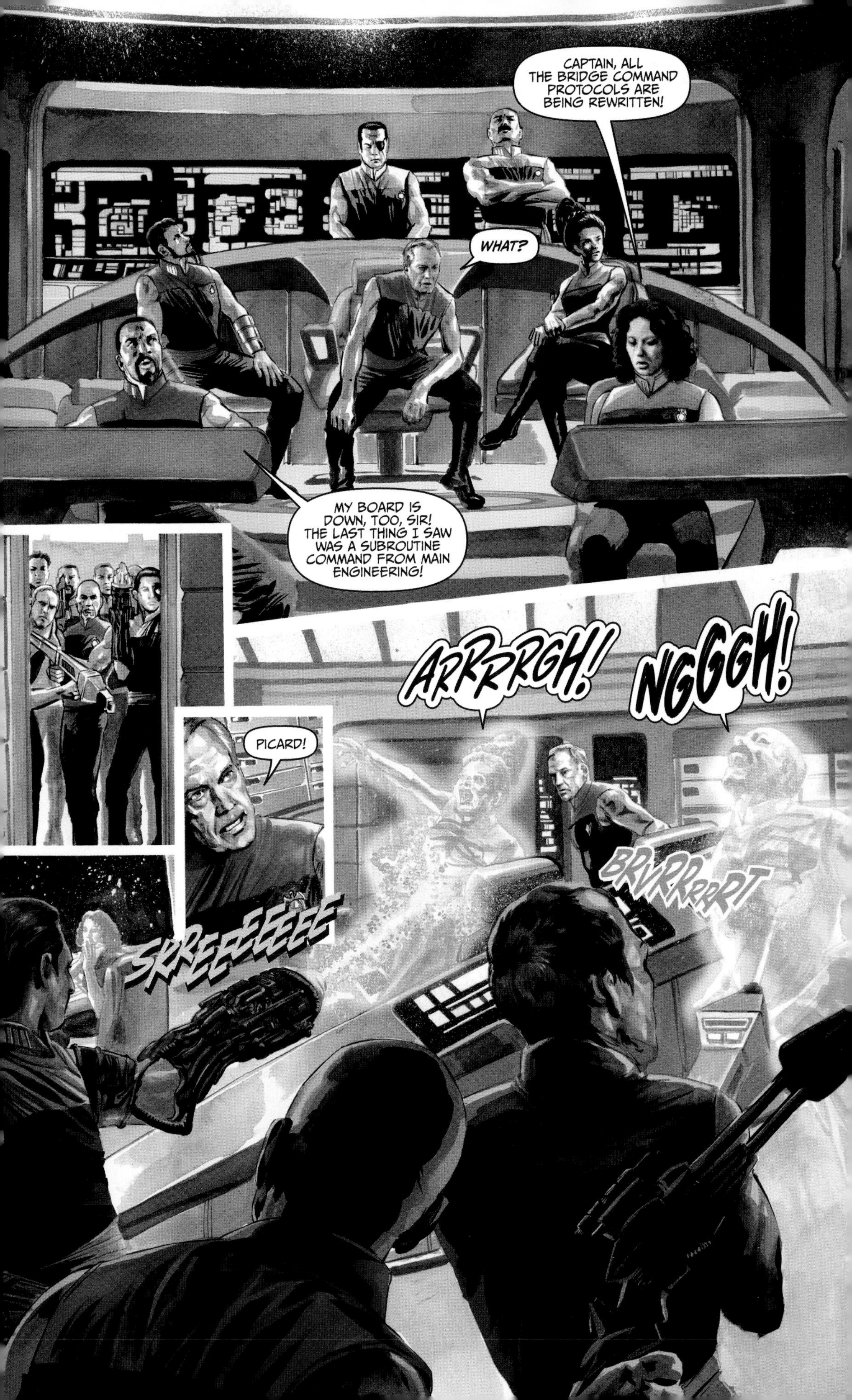
CAPTAIN, ALL THE BRIDGE COMMAND PROTOCOLS ARE BEING REWRITTEN!
WHAT?
MY BOARD IS DOWN, TOO, SIR! THE LAST THING I SAW WAS A SUBROUTINE COMMAND FROM MAIN ENGINEERING!
PICARD!
SKREEEEEEEE
ARRRRGH!
NGGGH!
BRVRRRRRT

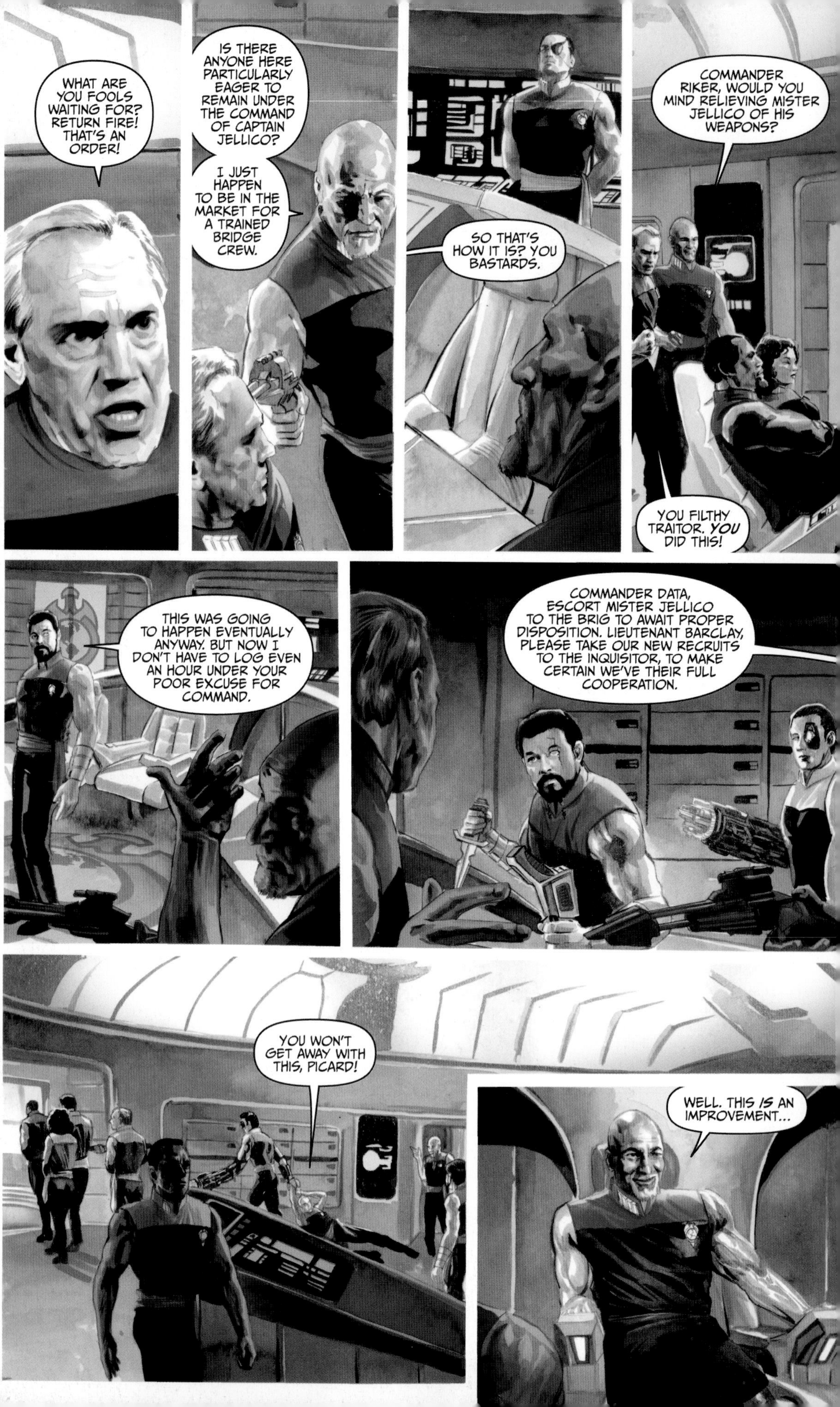
WHAT ARE YOU FOOLS WAITING FOR? RETURN FIRE! THAT'S AN ORDER!
IS THERE ANYONE HERE PARTICULARLY EAGER TO REMAIN UNDER THE COMMAND OF CAPTAIN JELLICO?
I JUST HAPPEN TO BE IN THE MARKET FOR A TRAINED BRIDGE CREW.
SO THAT'S HOW IT IS? YOU BASTARDS.
COMMANDER RIKER, WOULD YOU MIND RELIEVING MISTER JELLICO OF HIS WEAPONS?
YOU FILTHY TRAITOR. *YOU* DID THIS!
THIS WAS GOING TO HAPPEN EVENTUALLY ANYWAY. BUT NOW I DON'T HAVE TO LOG EVEN AN HOUR UNDER YOUR POOR EXCUSE FOR COMMAND.
COMMANDER DATA, ESCORT MISTER JELLICO TO THE BRIG TO AWAIT PROPER DISPOSITION. LIEUTENANT BARCLAY, PLEASE TAKE OUR NEW RECRUITS TO THE INQUISITOR, TO MAKE CERTAIN WE'VE THEIR FULL COOPERATION.
YOU WON'T GET AWAY WITH THIS, PICARD!
WELL. THIS *IS* AN IMPROVEMENT...

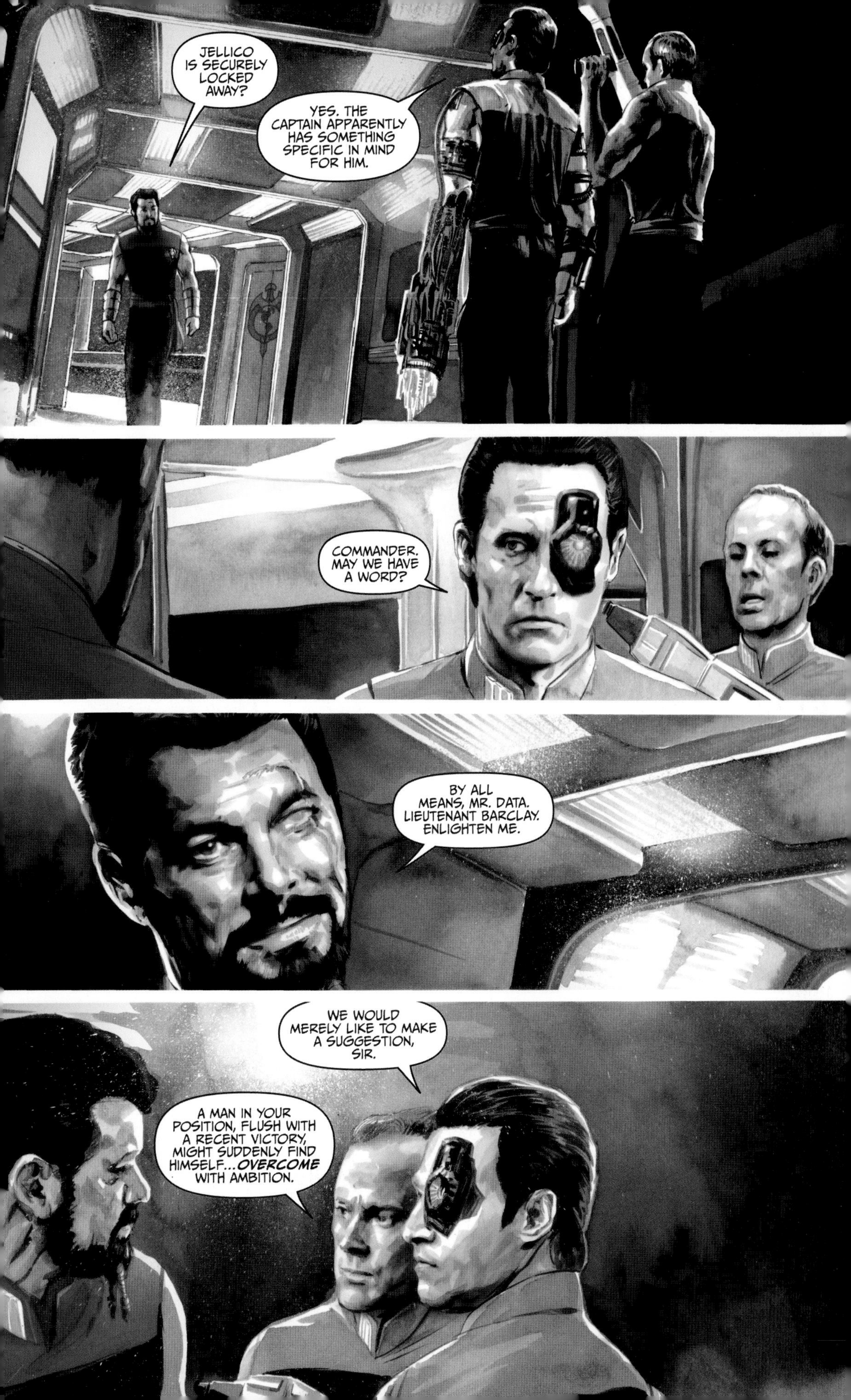
JELLICO IS SECURELY LOCKED AWAY?
YES. THE CAPTAIN APPARENTLY HAS SOMETHING SPECIFIC IN MIND FOR HIM.
COMMANDER. MAY WE HAVE A WORD?
BY ALL MEANS, MR. DATA. LIEUTENANT BARCLAY. ENLIGHTEN ME.
WE WOULD MERELY LIKE TO MAKE A SUGGESTION, SIR.
A MAN IN YOUR POSITION, FLUSH WITH A RECENT VICTORY, MIGHT SUDDENLY FIND HIMSELF...*OVERCOME* WITH AMBITION.

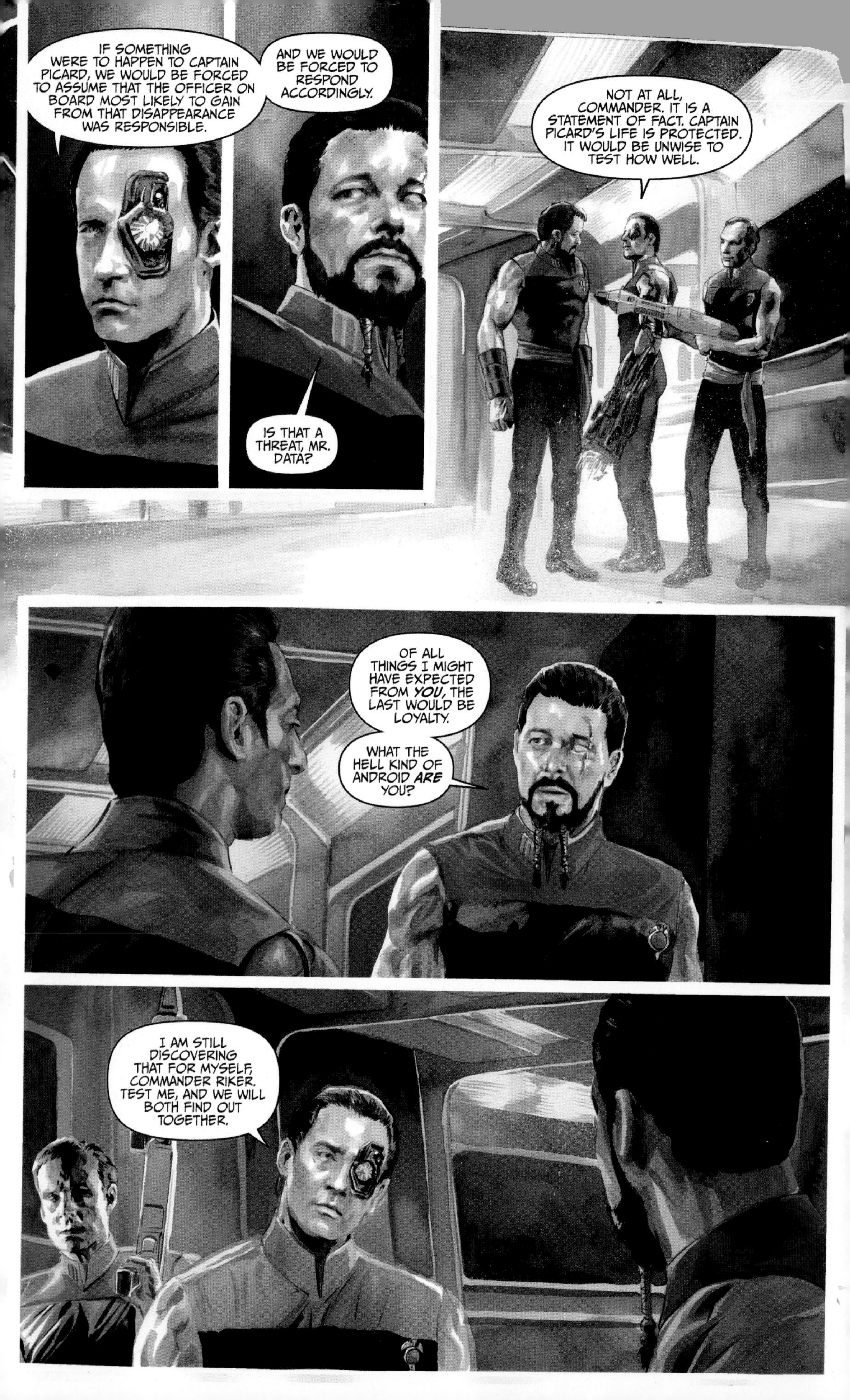
IF SOMETHING WERE TO HAPPEN TO CAPTAIN PICARD, WE WOULD BE FORCED TO ASSUME THAT THE OFFICER ON BOARD MOST LIKELY TO GAIN FROM THAT DISAPPEARANCE WAS RESPONSIBLE.
AND WE WOULD BE FORCED TO RESPOND ACCORDINGLY.
IS THAT A THREAT, MR. DATA?
NOT AT ALL, COMMANDER. IT IS A STATEMENT OF FACT. CAPTAIN PICARD'S LIFE IS PROTECTED. IT WOULD BE UNWISE TO TEST HOW WELL.
OF ALL THINGS I MIGHT HAVE EXPECTED FROM YOU, THE LAST WOULD BE LOYALTY.
WHAT THE HELL KIND OF ANDROID ARE YOU?
I AM STILL DISCOVERING THAT FOR MYSELF, COMMANDER RIKER. TEST ME, AND WE WILL BOTH FIND OUT TOGETHER.

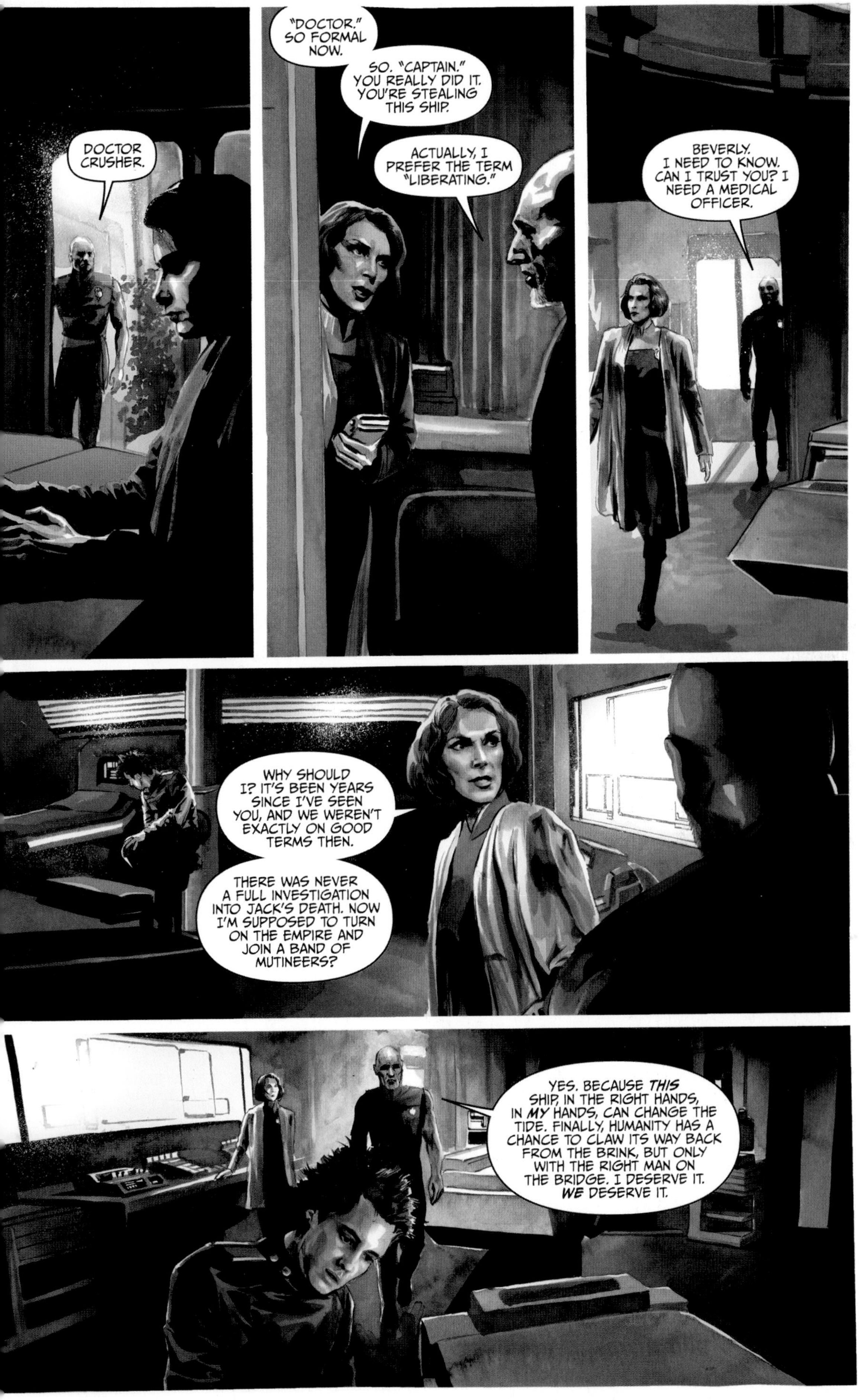
DOCTOR CRUSHER.
"DOCTOR." SO FORMAL NOW.
SO. "CAPTAIN." YOU REALLY DID IT. YOU'RE STEALING THIS SHIP.
ACTUALLY, I PREFER THE TERM "LIBERATING."
BEVERLY. I NEED TO KNOW. CAN I TRUST YOU? I NEED A MEDICAL OFFICER.
WHY SHOULD I? IT'S BEEN YEARS SINCE I'VE SEEN YOU, AND WE WEREN'T EXACTLY ON GOOD TERMS THEN.
THERE WAS NEVER A FULL INVESTIGATION INTO JACK'S DEATH. NOW I'M SUPPOSED TO TURN ON THE EMPIRE AND JOIN A BAND OF MUTINEERS?
YES. BECAUSE *THIS* SHIP, IN THE RIGHT HANDS, IN *MY* HANDS, CAN CHANGE THE TIDE. FINALLY, HUMANITY HAS A CHANCE TO CLAW ITS WAY BACK FROM THE BRINK, BUT ONLY WITH THE RIGHT MAN ON THE BRIDGE. I DESERVE IT. *WE* DESERVE IT.

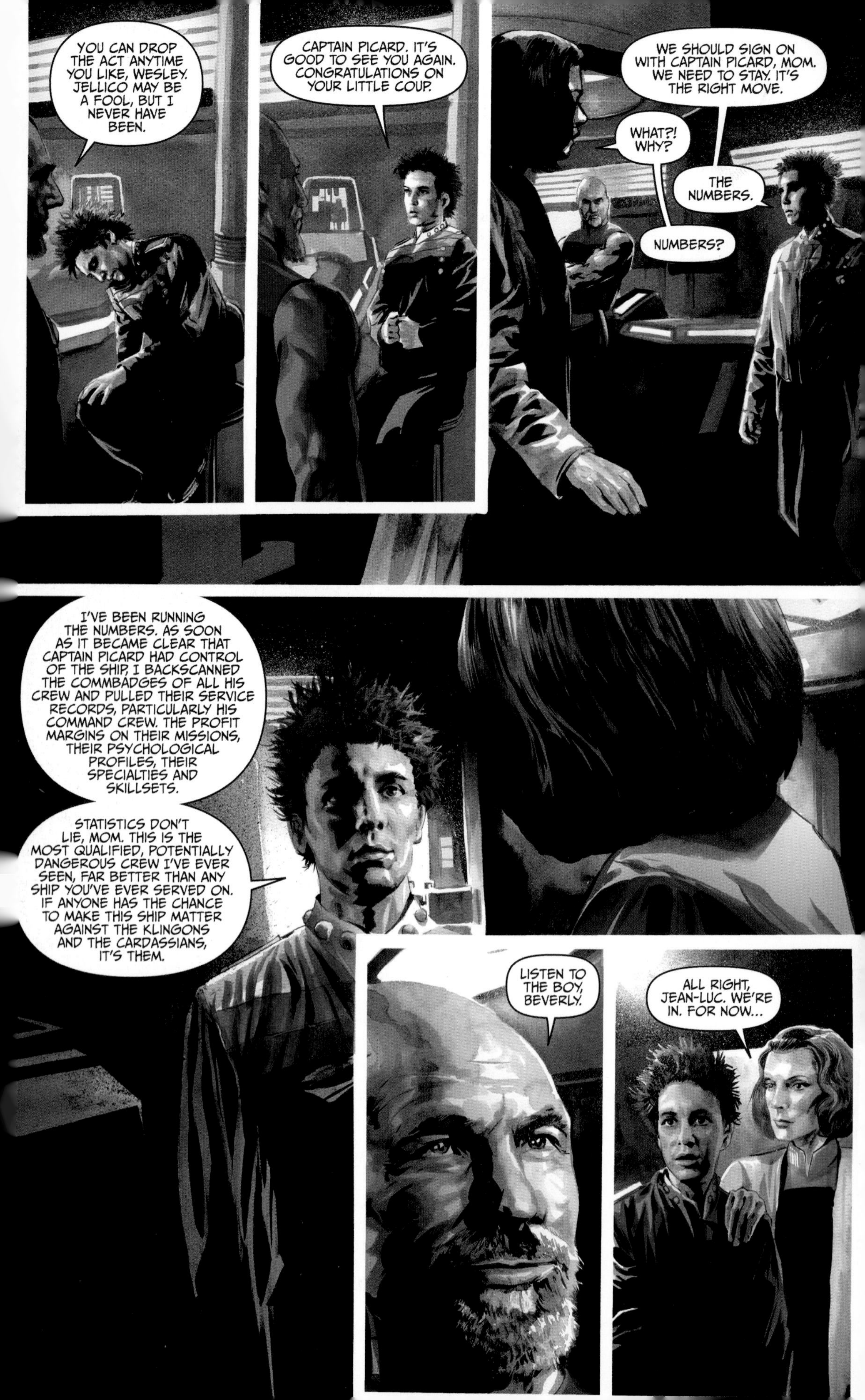
YOU CAN DROP THE ACT ANYTIME YOU LIKE, WESLEY. JELLICO MAY BE A FOOL, BUT I NEVER HAVE BEEN.
CAPTAIN PICARD. IT'S GOOD TO SEE YOU AGAIN. CONGRATULATIONS ON YOUR LITTLE COUP.
WE SHOULD SIGN ON WITH CAPTAIN PICARD, MOM. WE NEED TO STAY. IT'S THE RIGHT MOVE.
WHAT?! WHY?
THE NUMBERS.
NUMBERS?
I'VE BEEN RUNNING THE NUMBERS. AS SOON AS IT BECAME CLEAR THAT CAPTAIN PICARD HAD CONTROL OF THE SHIP, I BACKSCANNED THE COMMBADGES OF ALL HIS CREW AND PULLED THEIR SERVICE RECORDS, PARTICULARLY HIS COMMAND CREW. THE PROFIT MARGINS ON THEIR MISSIONS, THEIR PSYCHOLOGICAL PROFILES, THEIR SPECIALTIES AND SKILLSETS.
STATISTICS DON'T LIE, MOM. THIS IS THE MOST QUALIFIED, POTENTIALLY DANGEROUS CREW I'VE EVER SEEN, FAR BETTER THAN ANY SHIP YOU'VE EVER SERVED ON. IF ANYONE HAS THE CHANCE TO MAKE THIS SHIP MATTER AGAINST THE KLINGONS AND THE CARDASSIANS, IT'S THEM.
LISTEN TO THE BOY, BEVERLY.
ALL RIGHT, JEAN-LUC. WE'RE IN. FOR NOW...

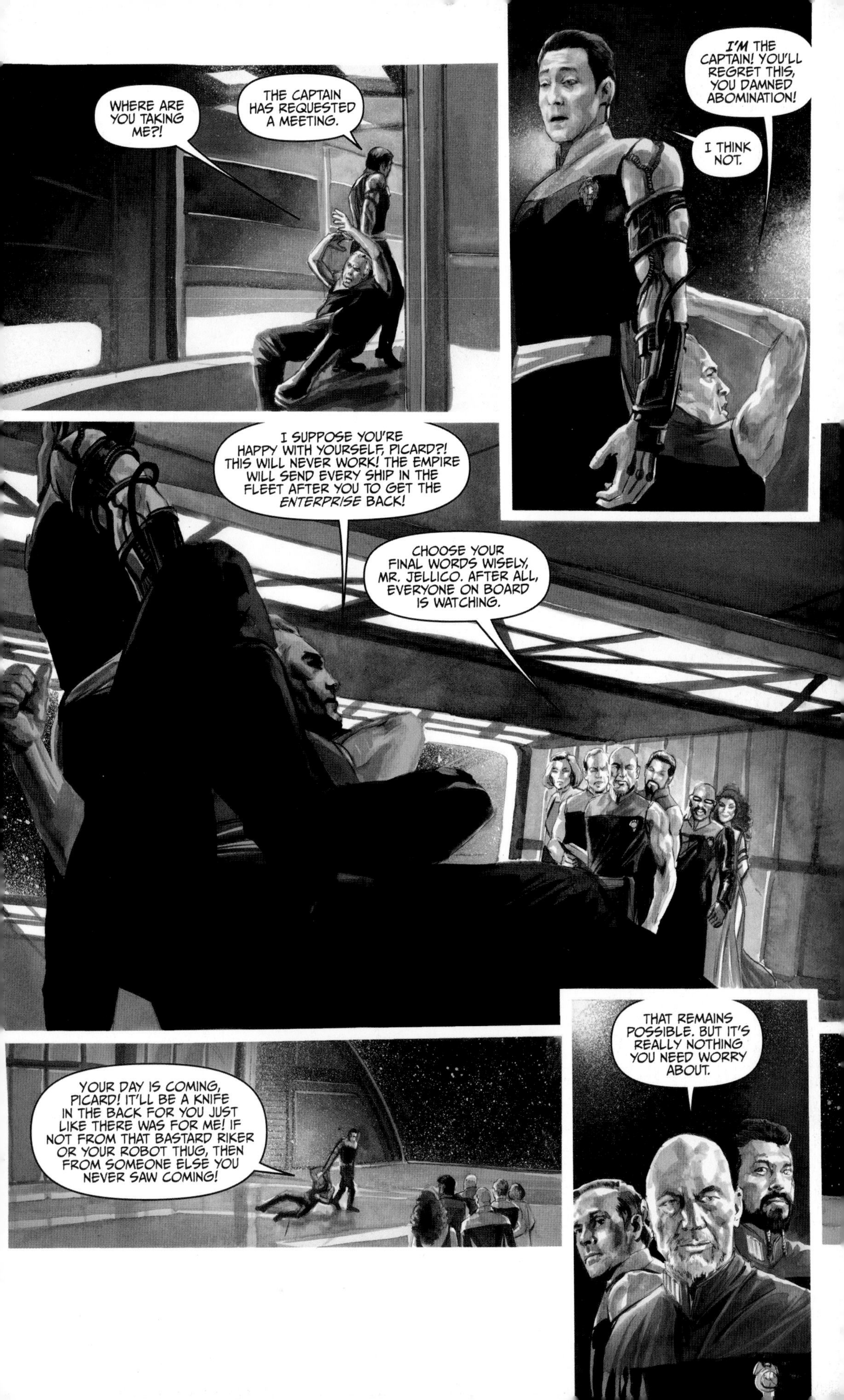
WHERE ARE YOU TAKING ME?!
THE CAPTAIN HAS REQUESTED A MEETING.
I'M THE CAPTAIN! YOU'LL REGRET THIS, YOU DAMNED ABOMINATION!
I THINK NOT.
I SUPPOSE YOU'RE HAPPY WITH YOURSELF, PICARD?! THIS WILL NEVER WORK! THE EMPIRE WILL SEND EVERY SHIP IN THE FLEET AFTER YOU TO GET THE ENTERPRISE BACK!
CHOOSE YOUR FINAL WORDS WISELY, MR. JELLICO. AFTER ALL, EVERYONE ON BOARD IS WATCHING.
YOUR DAY IS COMING, PICARD! IT'LL BE A KNIFE IN THE BACK FOR YOU JUST LIKE THERE WAS FOR ME! IF NOT FROM THAT BASTARD RIKER OR YOUR ROBOT THUG, THEN FROM SOMEONE ELSE YOU NEVER SAW COMING!
THAT REMAINS POSSIBLE. BUT IT'S REALLY NOTHING YOU NEED WORRY ABOUT.

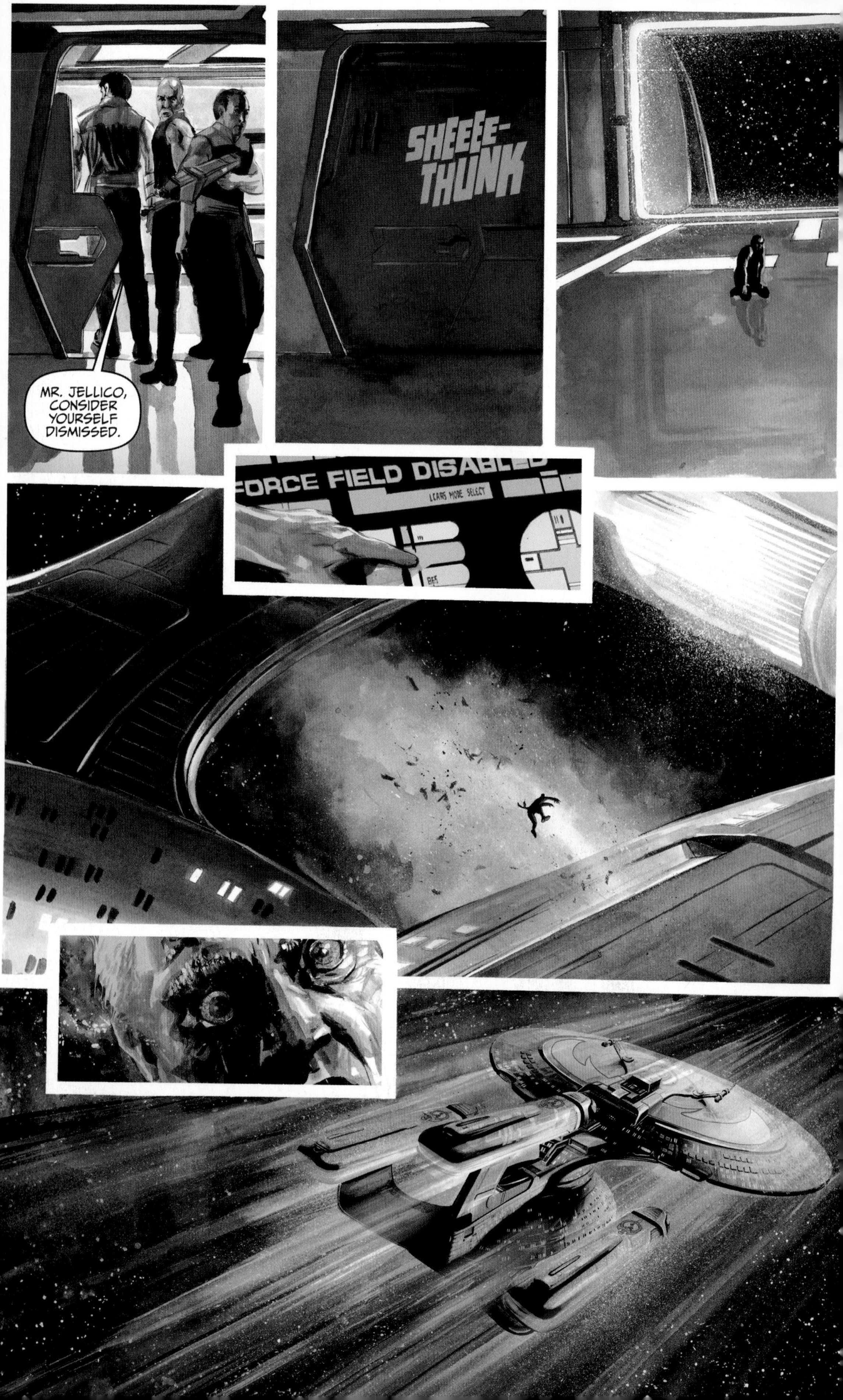
MR. JELLICO, CONSIDER YOURSELF DISMISSED.
SHEEEE-
THUNK
FORCE FIELD DISABLED
LCARS MODE SELECT

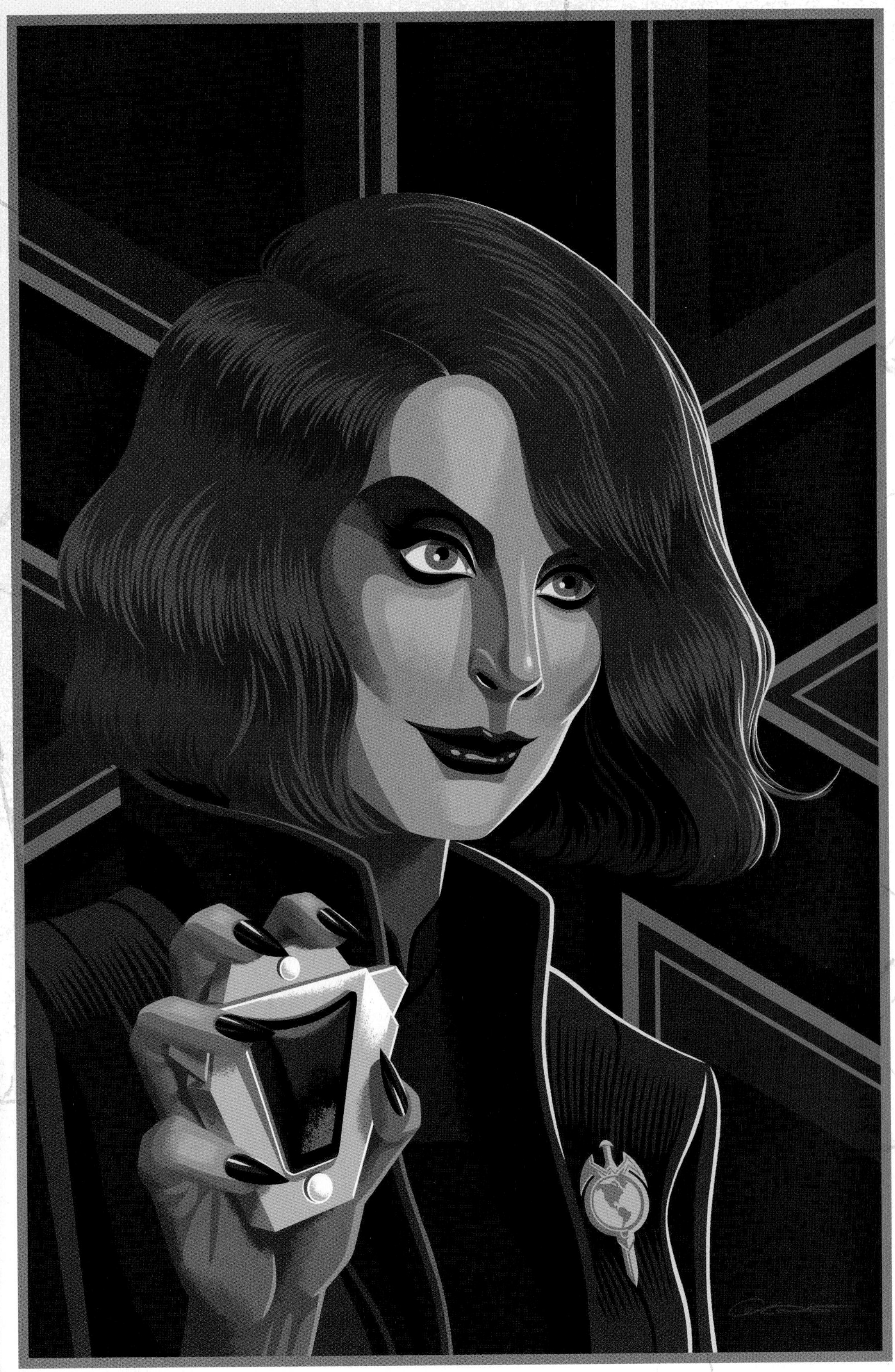

ART BY
GEORGE CALTSOUDAS

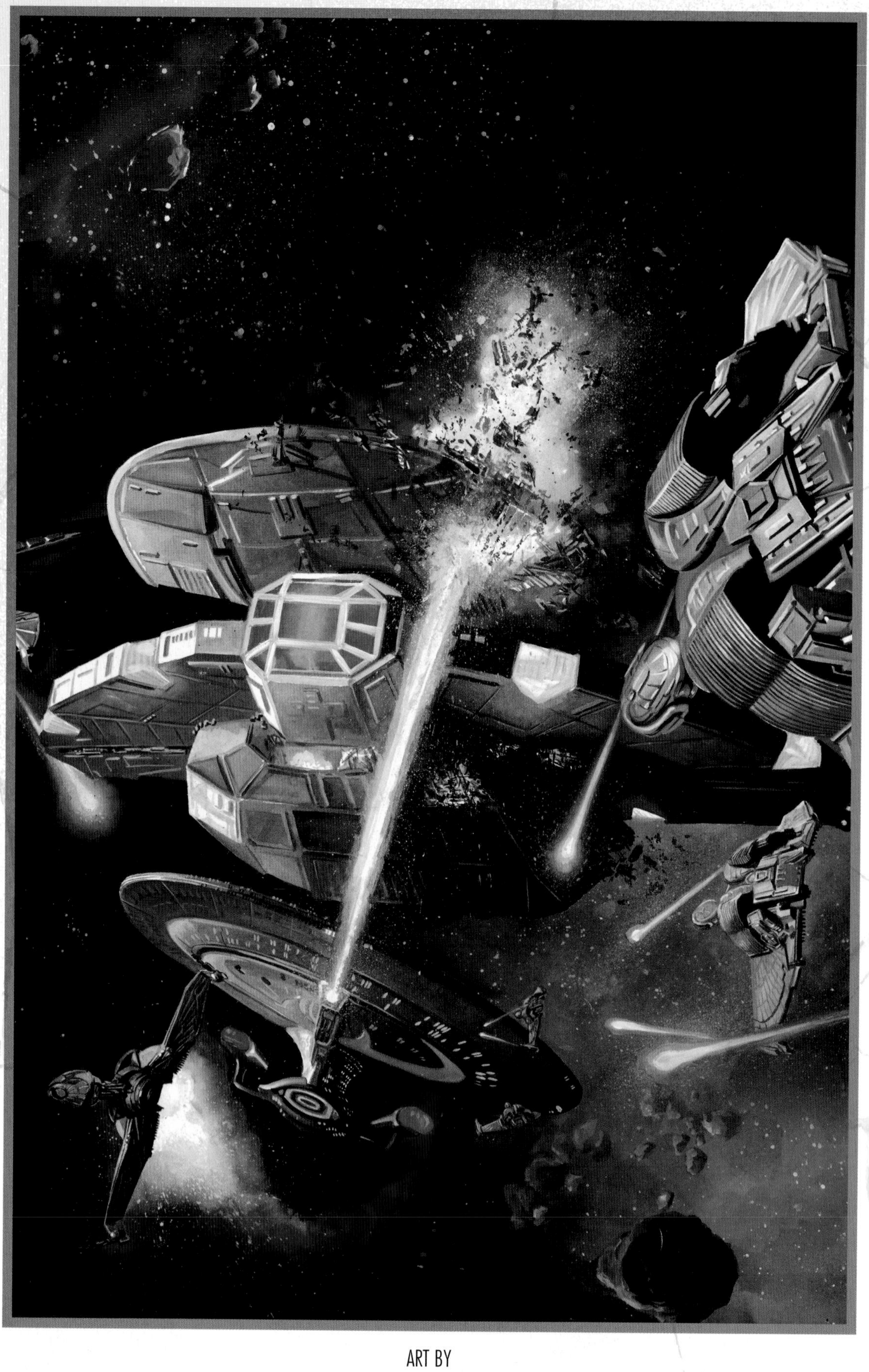

ART BY
J.K. WOODWARD

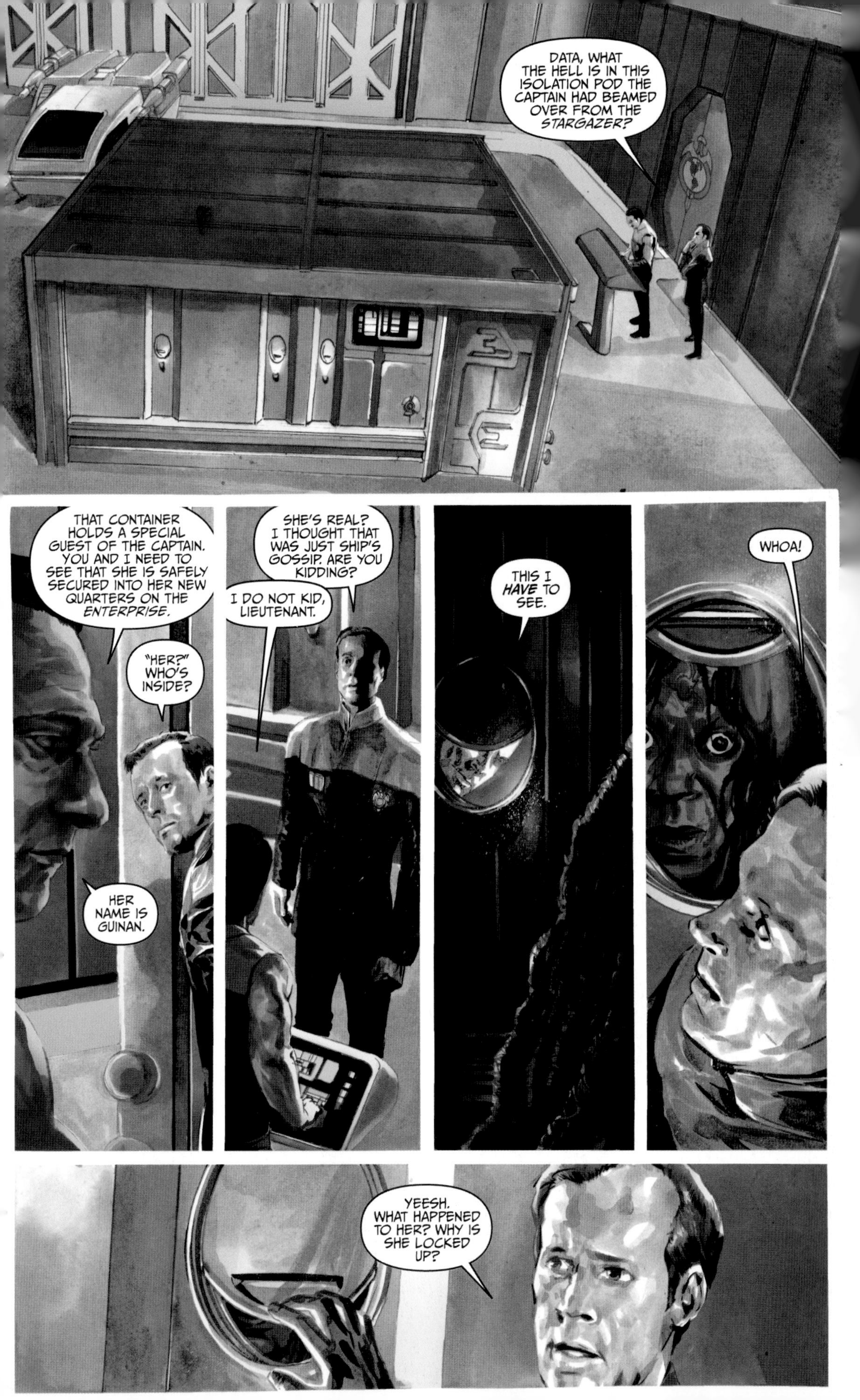
DATA, WHAT THE HELL IS IN THIS ISOLATION POD THE CAPTAIN HAD BEAMED OVER FROM THE *STARGAZER?*
THAT CONTAINER HOLDS A SPECIAL GUEST OF THE CAPTAIN. YOU AND I NEED TO SEE THAT SHE IS SAFELY SECURED INTO HER NEW QUARTERS ON THE *ENTERPRISE.*
"HER?" WHO'S INSIDE?
HER NAME IS GUINAN.
SHE'S REAL? I THOUGHT THAT WAS JUST SHIP'S GOSSIP. ARE YOU KIDDING?
I DO NOT KID, LIEUTENANT.
THIS I ***HAVE*** TO SEE.
WHOA!
YEESH. WHAT HAPPENED TO HER? WHY IS SHE LOCKED UP?

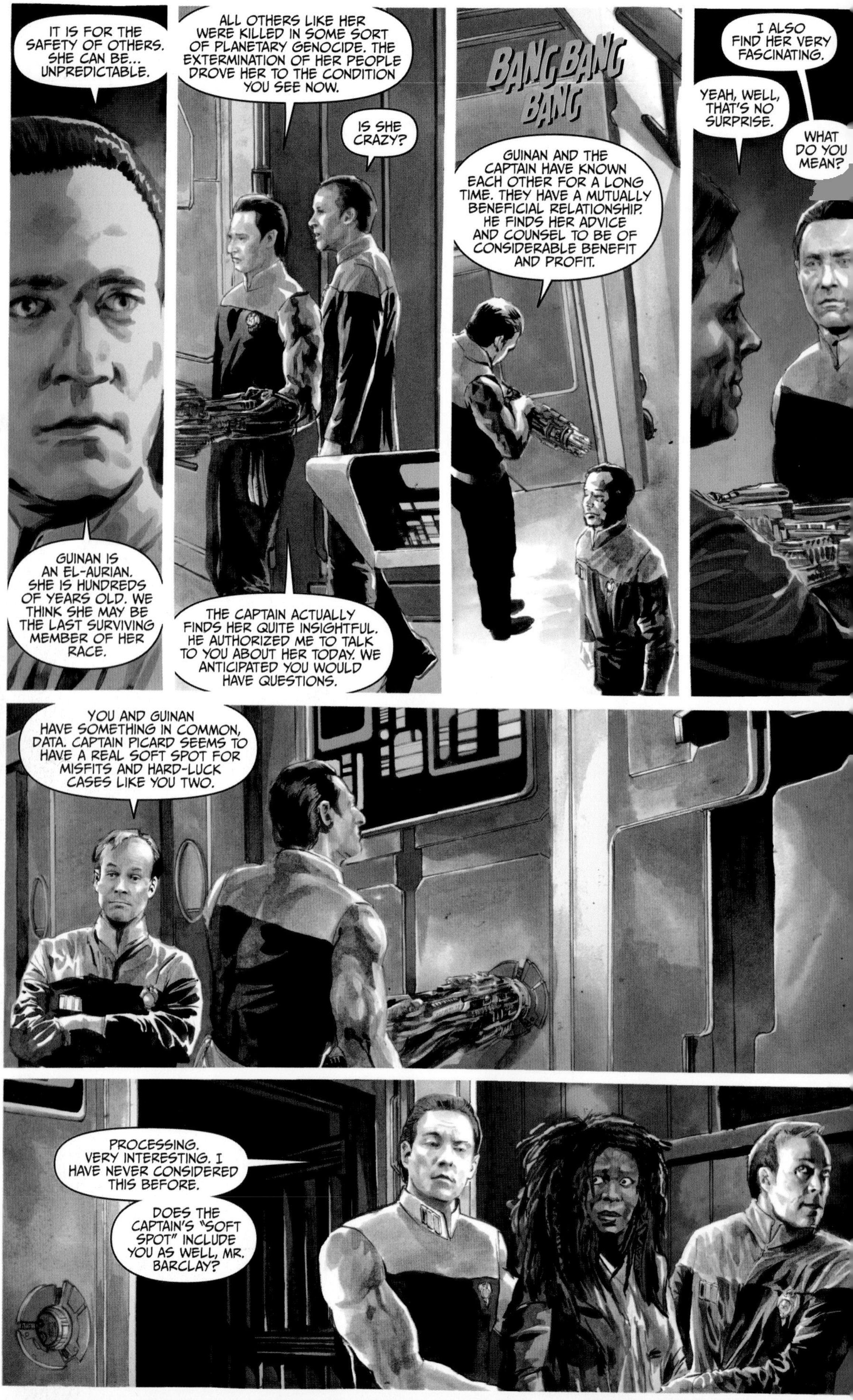
IT IS FOR THE SAFETY OF OTHERS. SHE CAN BE... UNPREDICTABLE.
GUINAN IS AN EL-AURIAN. SHE IS HUNDREDS OF YEARS OLD. WE THINK SHE MAY BE THE LAST SURVIVING MEMBER OF HER RACE.
ALL OTHERS LIKE HER WERE KILLED IN SOME SORT OF PLANETARY GENOCIDE. THE EXTERMINATION OF HER PEOPLE DROVE HER TO THE CONDITION YOU SEE NOW.
IS SHE CRAZY?
THE CAPTAIN ACTUALLY FINDS HER QUITE INSIGHTFUL. HE AUTHORIZED ME TO TALK TO YOU ABOUT HER TODAY. WE ANTICIPATED YOU WOULD HAVE QUESTIONS.
BANG BANG BANG
GUINAN AND THE CAPTAIN HAVE KNOWN EACH OTHER FOR A LONG TIME. THEY HAVE A MUTUALLY BENEFICIAL RELATIONSHIP. HE FINDS HER ADVICE AND COUNSEL TO BE OF CONSIDERABLE BENEFIT AND PROFIT.
I ALSO FIND HER VERY FASCINATING.
YEAH, WELL, THAT'S NO SURPRISE.
WHAT DO YOU MEAN?
YOU AND GUINAN HAVE SOMETHING IN COMMON, DATA. CAPTAIN PICARD SEEMS TO HAVE A REAL SOFT SPOT FOR MISFITS AND HARD-LUCK CASES LIKE YOU TWO.
PROCESSING. VERY INTERESTING. I HAVE NEVER CONSIDERED THIS BEFORE.
DOES THE CAPTAIN'S "SOFT SPOT" INCLUDE YOU AS WELL, MR. BARCLAY?

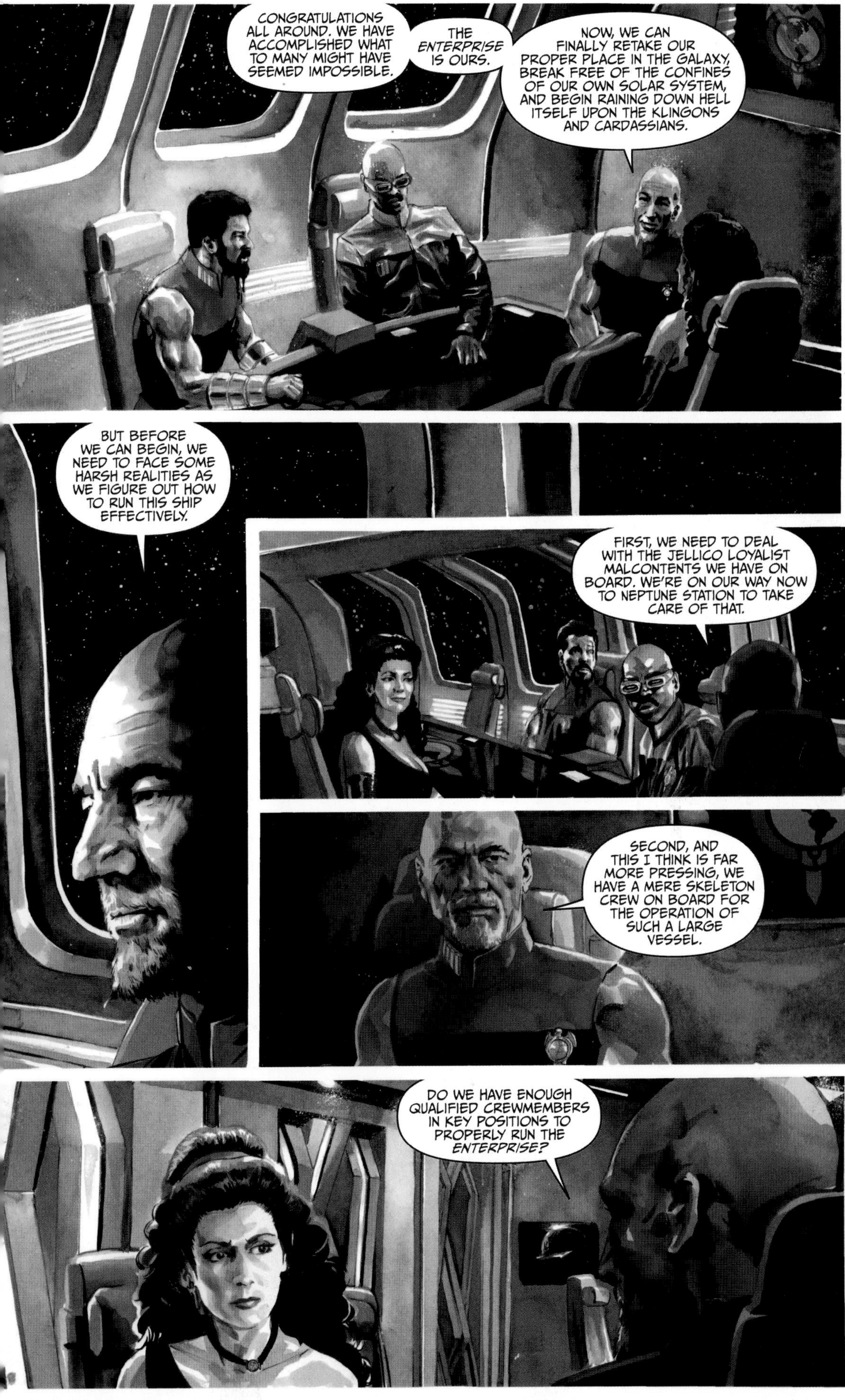
CONGRATULATIONS ALL AROUND. WE HAVE ACCOMPLISHED WHAT TO MANY MIGHT HAVE SEEMED IMPOSSIBLE.
THE *ENTERPRISE* IS OURS.
NOW, WE CAN FINALLY RETAKE OUR PROPER PLACE IN THE GALAXY, BREAK FREE OF THE CONFINES OF OUR OWN SOLAR SYSTEM, AND BEGIN RAINING DOWN HELL ITSELF UPON THE KLINGONS AND CARDASSIANS.
BUT BEFORE WE CAN BEGIN, WE NEED TO FACE SOME HARSH REALITIES AS WE FIGURE OUT HOW TO RUN THIS SHIP EFFECTIVELY.
FIRST, WE NEED TO DEAL WITH THE JELLICO LOYALIST MALCONTENTS WE HAVE ON BOARD. WE'RE ON OUR WAY NOW TO NEPTUNE STATION TO TAKE CARE OF THAT.
SECOND, AND THIS I THINK IS FAR MORE PRESSING, WE HAVE A MERE SKELETON CREW ON BOARD FOR THE OPERATION OF SUCH A LARGE VESSEL.
DO WE HAVE ENOUGH QUALIFIED CREWMEMBERS IN KEY POSITIONS TO PROPERLY RUN THE *ENTERPRISE*?

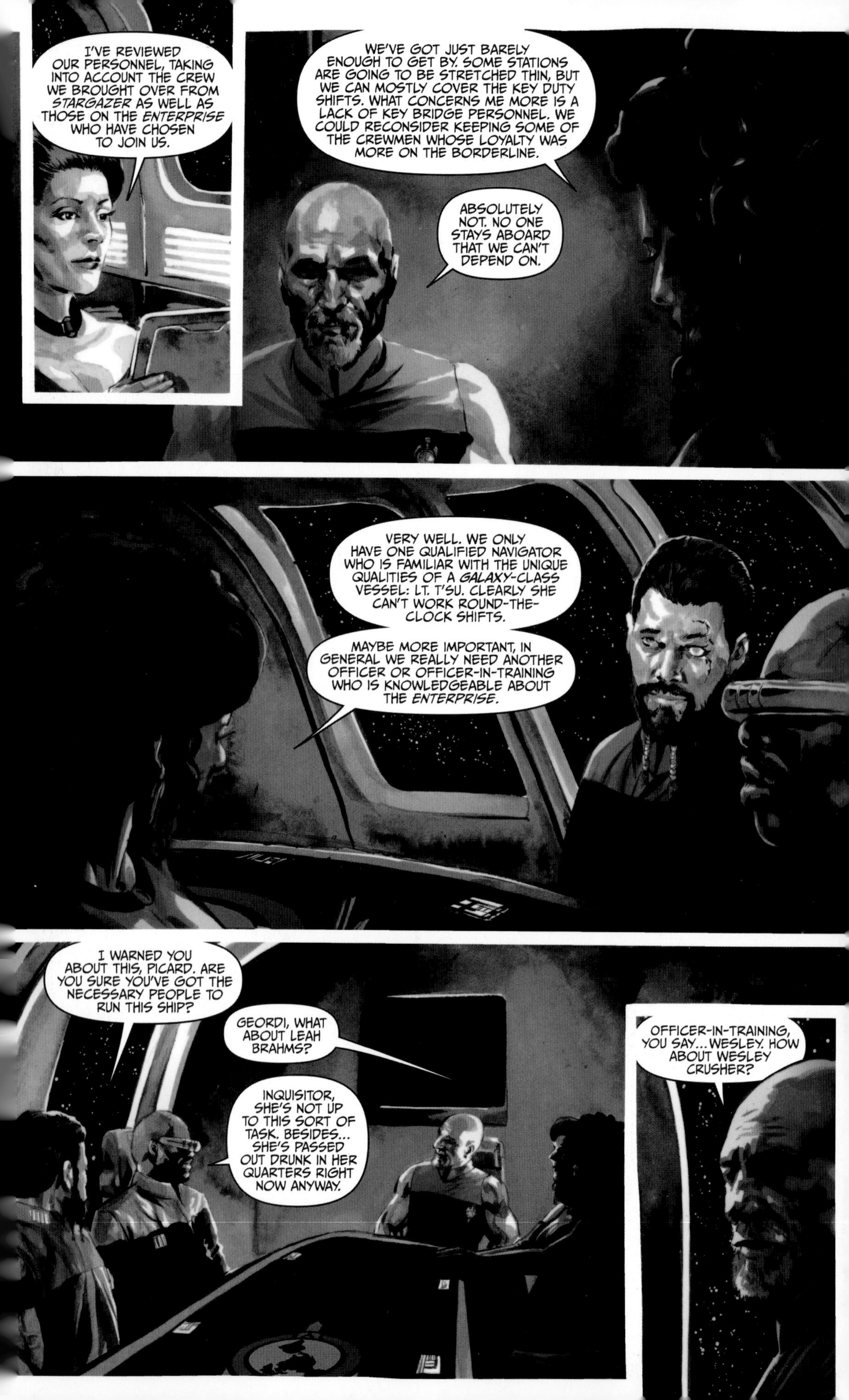
I'VE REVIEWED OUR PERSONNEL, TAKING INTO ACCOUNT THE CREW WE BROUGHT OVER FROM *STARGAZER* AS WELL AS THOSE ON THE *ENTERPRISE* WHO HAVE CHOSEN TO JOIN US.
WE'VE GOT JUST BARELY ENOUGH TO GET BY. SOME STATIONS ARE GOING TO BE STRETCHED THIN, BUT WE CAN MOSTLY COVER THE KEY DUTY SHIFTS. WHAT CONCERNS ME MORE IS A LACK OF KEY BRIDGE PERSONNEL. WE COULD RECONSIDER KEEPING SOME OF THE CREWMEN WHOSE LOYALTY WAS MORE ON THE BORDERLINE.
ABSOLUTELY NOT. NO ONE STAYS ABOARD THAT WE CAN'T DEPEND ON.
VERY WELL. WE ONLY HAVE ONE QUALIFIED NAVIGATOR WHO IS FAMILIAR WITH THE UNIQUE QUALITIES OF A *GALAXY*-CLASS VESSEL: LT. T'SU. CLEARLY SHE CAN'T WORK ROUND-THE-CLOCK SHIFTS.
MAYBE MORE IMPORTANT, IN GENERAL WE REALLY NEED ANOTHER OFFICER OR OFFICER-IN-TRAINING WHO IS KNOWLEDGEABLE ABOUT THE *ENTERPRISE.*
I WARNED YOU ABOUT THIS, PICARD. ARE YOU SURE YOU'VE GOT THE NECESSARY PEOPLE TO RUN THIS SHIP?
GEORDI, WHAT ABOUT LEAH BRAHMS?
INQUISITOR, SHE'S NOT UP TO THIS SORT OF TASK. BESIDES... SHE'S PASSED OUT DRUNK IN HER QUARTERS RIGHT NOW ANYWAY.
OFFICER-IN-TRAINING, YOU SAY... WESLEY. HOW ABOUT WESLEY CRUSHER?

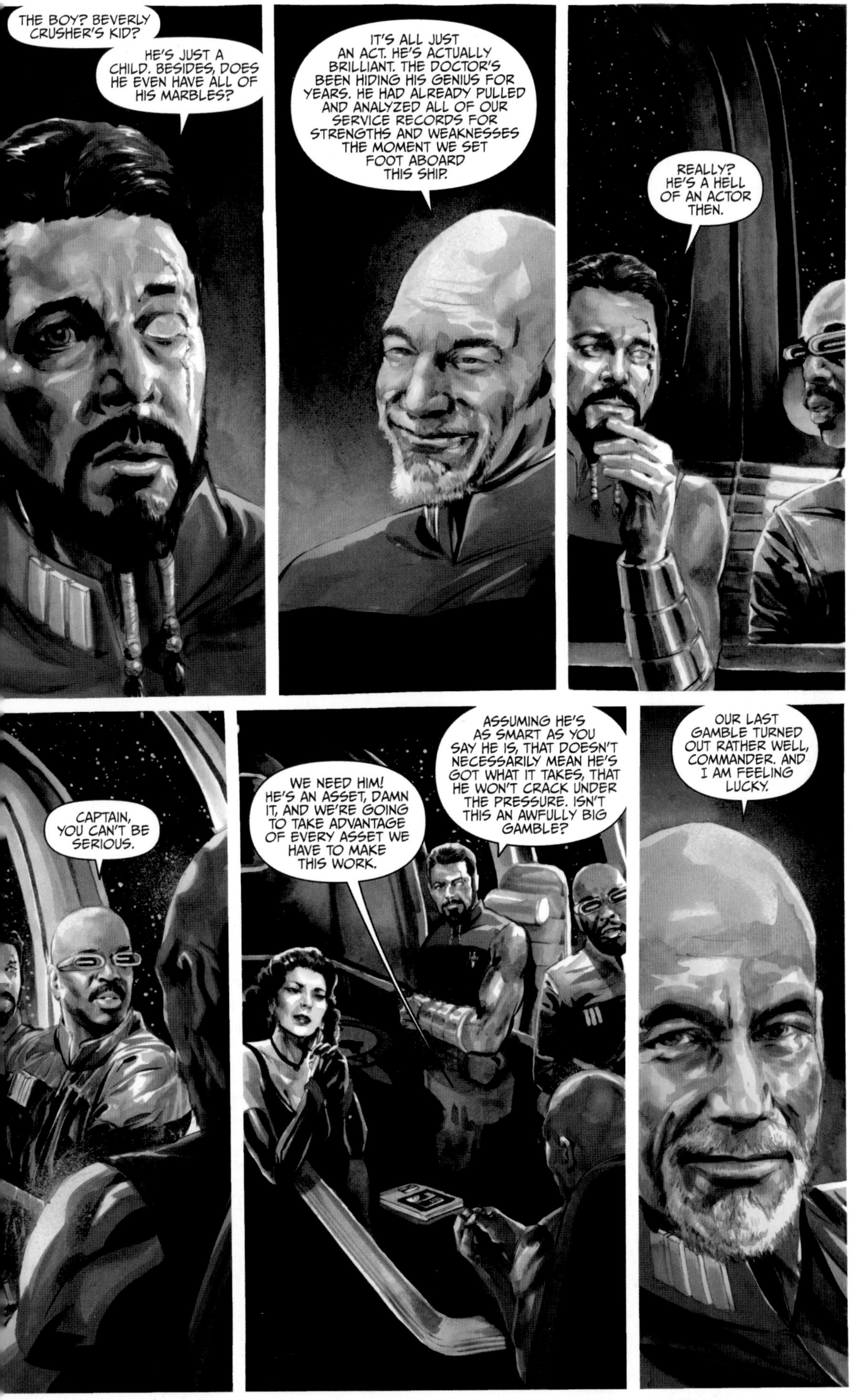

THE BOY? BEVERLY CRUSHER'S KID?
HE'S JUST A CHILD. BESIDES, DOES HE EVEN HAVE ALL OF HIS MARBLES?
IT'S ALL JUST AN ACT. HE'S ACTUALLY BRILLIANT. THE DOCTOR'S BEEN HIDING HIS GENIUS FOR YEARS. HE HAD ALREADY PULLED AND ANALYZED ALL OF OUR SERVICE RECORDS FOR STRENGTHS AND WEAKNESSES THE MOMENT WE SET FOOT ABOARD THIS SHIP.
REALLY? HE'S A HELL OF AN ACTOR THEN.
CAPTAIN, YOU CAN'T BE SERIOUS.
WE NEED HIM! HE'S AN ASSET, DAMN IT, AND WE'RE GOING TO TAKE ADVANTAGE OF EVERY ASSET WE HAVE TO MAKE THIS WORK.
ASSUMING HE'S AS SMART AS YOU SAY HE IS, THAT DOESN'T NECESSARILY MEAN HE'S GOT WHAT IT TAKES, THAT HE WON'T CRACK UNDER THE PRESSURE. ISN'T THIS AN AWFULLY BIG GAMBLE?
OUR LAST GAMBLE TURNED OUT RATHER WELL, COMMANDER. AND I AM FEELING LUCKY.

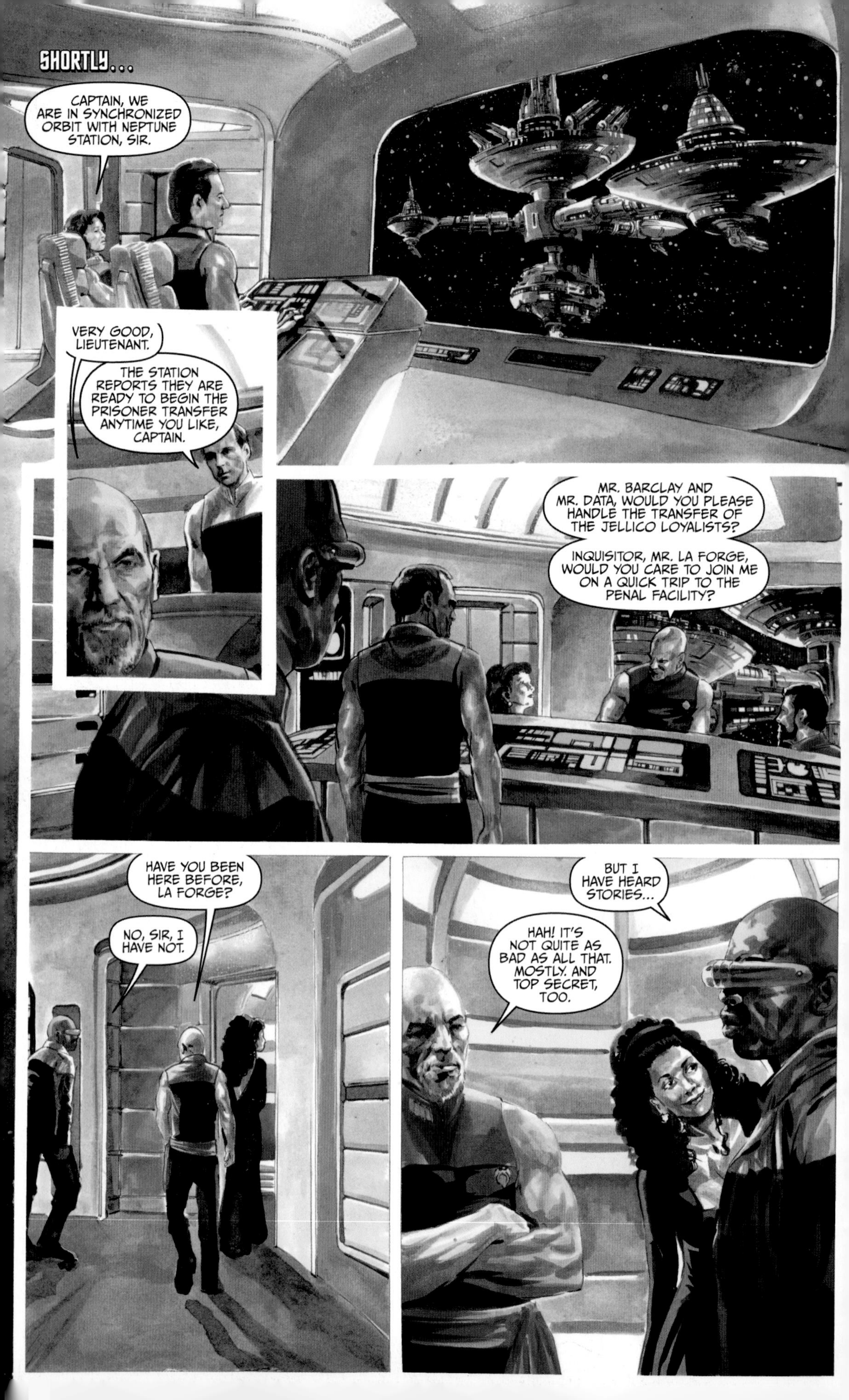
SHORTLY...
CAPTAIN, WE ARE IN SYNCHRONIZED ORBIT WITH NEPTUNE STATION, SIR.
VERY GOOD, LIEUTENANT.
THE STATION REPORTS THEY ARE READY TO BEGIN THE PRISONER TRANSFER ANYTIME YOU LIKE, CAPTAIN.
MR. BARCLAY AND MR. DATA, WOULD YOU PLEASE HANDLE THE TRANSFER OF THE JELLICO LOYALISTS?
INQUISITOR, MR. LA FORGE, WOULD YOU CARE TO JOIN ME ON A QUICK TRIP TO THE PENAL FACILITY?
HAVE YOU BEEN HERE BEFORE, LA FORGE?
NO, SIR, I HAVE NOT.
BUT I HAVE HEARD STORIES...
HAH! IT'S NOT QUITE AS BAD AS ALL THAT. MOSTLY. AND TOP SECRET, TOO.

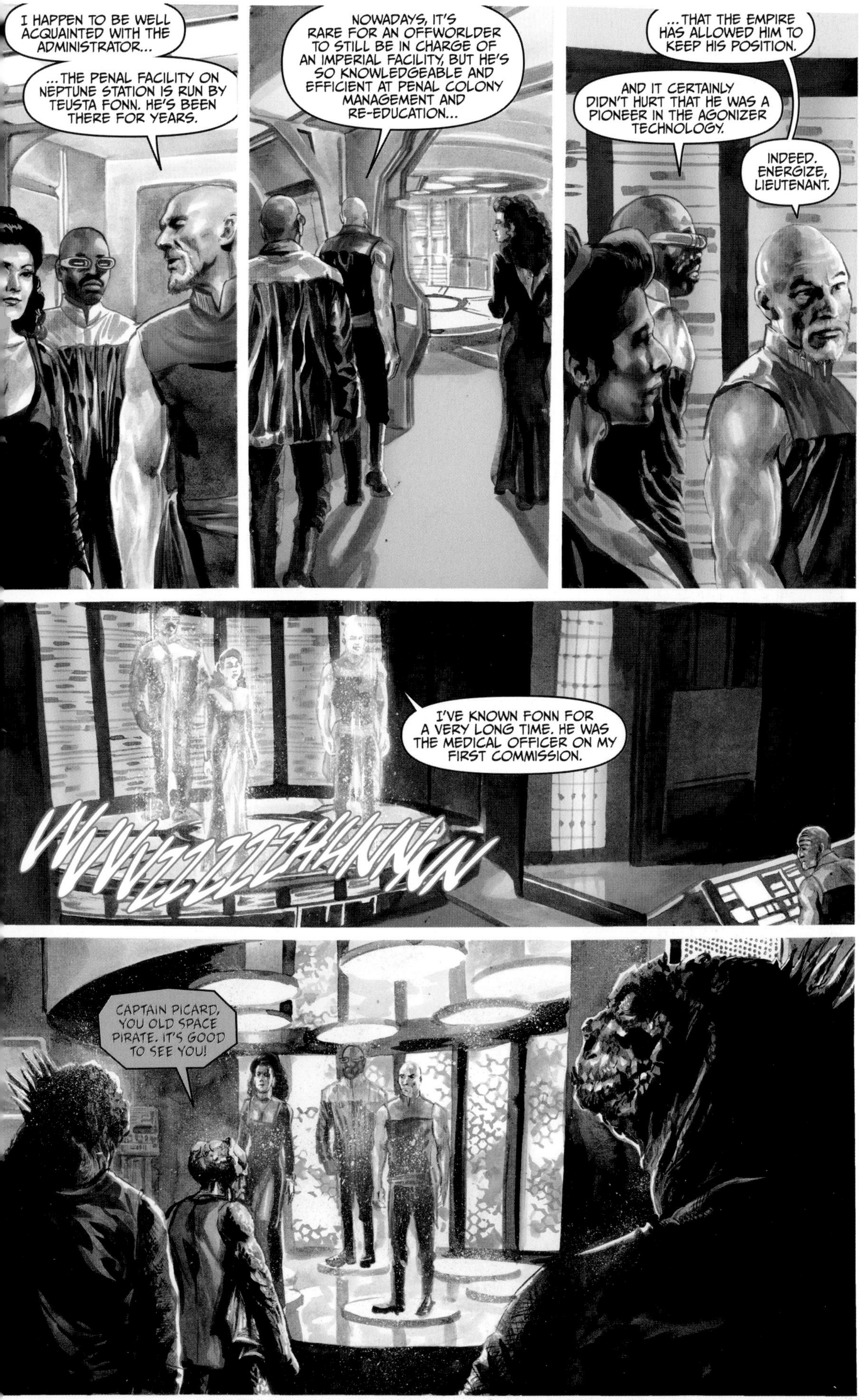
I HAPPEN TO BE WELL ACQUAINTED WITH THE ADMINISTRATOR...
...THE PENAL FACILITY ON NEPTUNE STATION IS RUN BY TEUSTA FONN. HE'S BEEN THERE FOR YEARS.
NOWADAYS, IT'S RARE FOR AN OFFWORLDER TO STILL BE IN CHARGE OF AN IMPERIAL FACILITY, BUT HE'S SO KNOWLEDGEABLE AND EFFICIENT AT PENAL COLONY MANAGEMENT AND RE-EDUCATION...
...THAT THE EMPIRE HAS ALLOWED HIM TO KEEP HIS POSITION.
AND IT CERTAINLY DIDN'T HURT THAT HE WAS A PIONEER IN THE AGONIZER TECHNOLOGY.
INDEED. ENERGIZE, LIEUTENANT.
I'VE KNOWN FONN FOR A VERY LONG TIME. HE WAS THE MEDICAL OFFICER ON MY FIRST COMMISSION.
VVVVVZZZZZHHNNNN
CAPTAIN PICARD, YOU OLD SPACE PIRATE. IT'S GOOD TO SEE YOU!

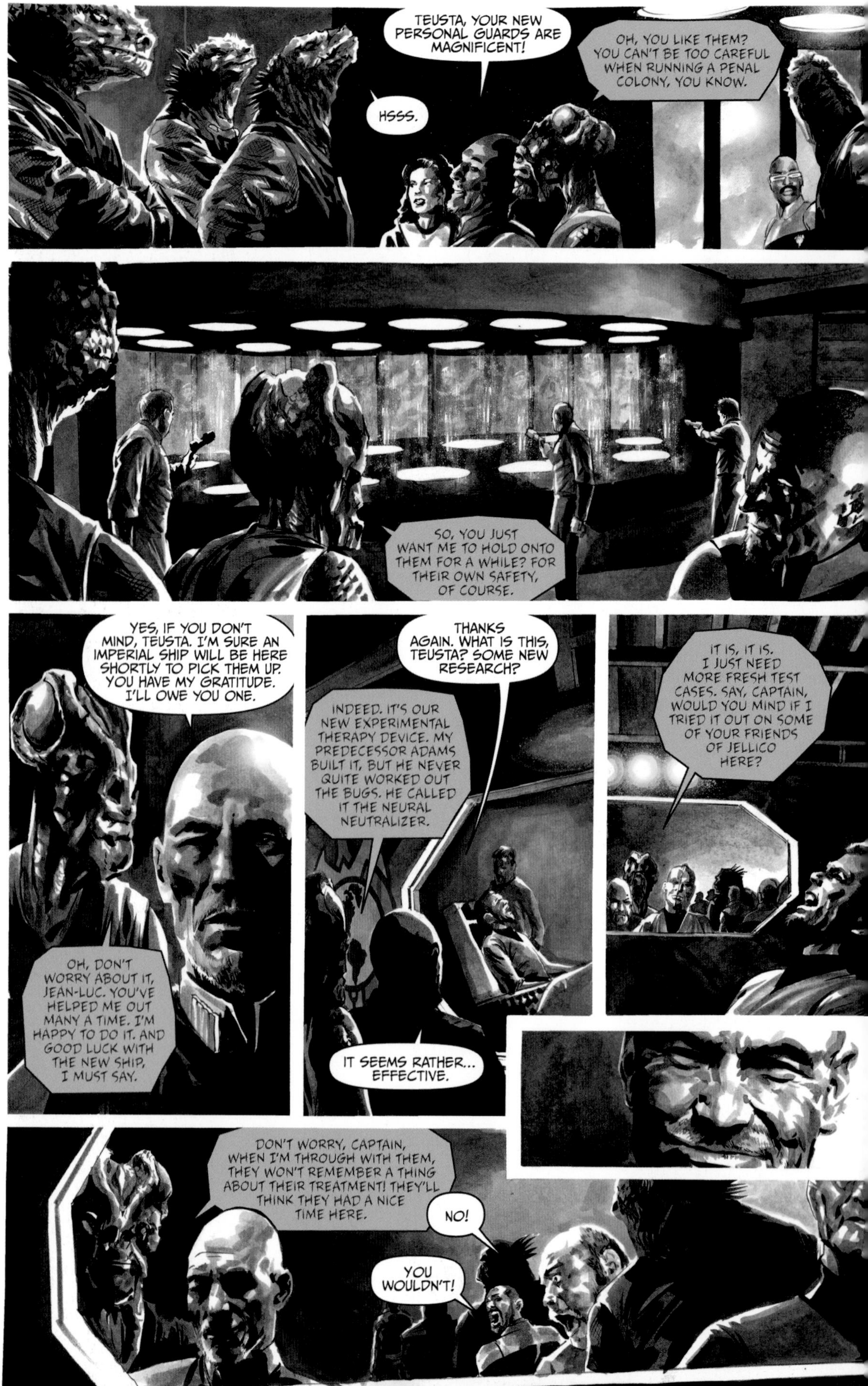
TEUSTA, YOUR NEW PERSONAL GUARDS ARE MAGNIFICENT!
HSSS.
OH, YOU LIKE THEM? YOU CAN'T BE TOO CAREFUL WHEN RUNNING A PENAL COLONY, YOU KNOW.
SO, YOU JUST WANT ME TO HOLD ONTO THEM FOR A WHILE? FOR THEIR OWN SAFETY, OF COURSE.
YES, IF YOU DON'T MIND, TEUSTA. I'M SURE AN IMPERIAL SHIP WILL BE HERE SHORTLY TO PICK THEM UP. YOU HAVE MY GRATITUDE. I'LL OWE YOU ONE.
OH, DON'T WORRY ABOUT IT, JEAN-LUC. YOU'VE HELPED ME OUT MANY A TIME. I'M HAPPY TO DO IT. AND GOOD LUCK WITH THE NEW SHIP, I MUST SAY.
THANKS AGAIN. WHAT IS THIS, TEUSTA? SOME NEW RESEARCH?
INDEED. IT'S OUR NEW EXPERIMENTAL THERAPY DEVICE. MY PREDECESSOR ADAMS BUILT IT, BUT HE NEVER QUITE WORKED OUT THE BUGS. HE CALLED IT THE NEURAL NEUTRALIZER.
IT SEEMS RATHER... EFFECTIVE.
IT IS, IT IS. I JUST NEED MORE FRESH TEST CASES. SAY, CAPTAIN, WOULD YOU MIND IF I TRIED IT OUT ON SOME OF YOUR FRIENDS OF JELLICO HERE?
DON'T WORRY, CAPTAIN, WHEN I'M THROUGH WITH THEM, THEY WON'T REMEMBER A THING ABOUT THEIR TREATMENT! THEY'LL THINK THEY HAD A NICE TIME HERE.
NO!
YOU WOULDN'T!

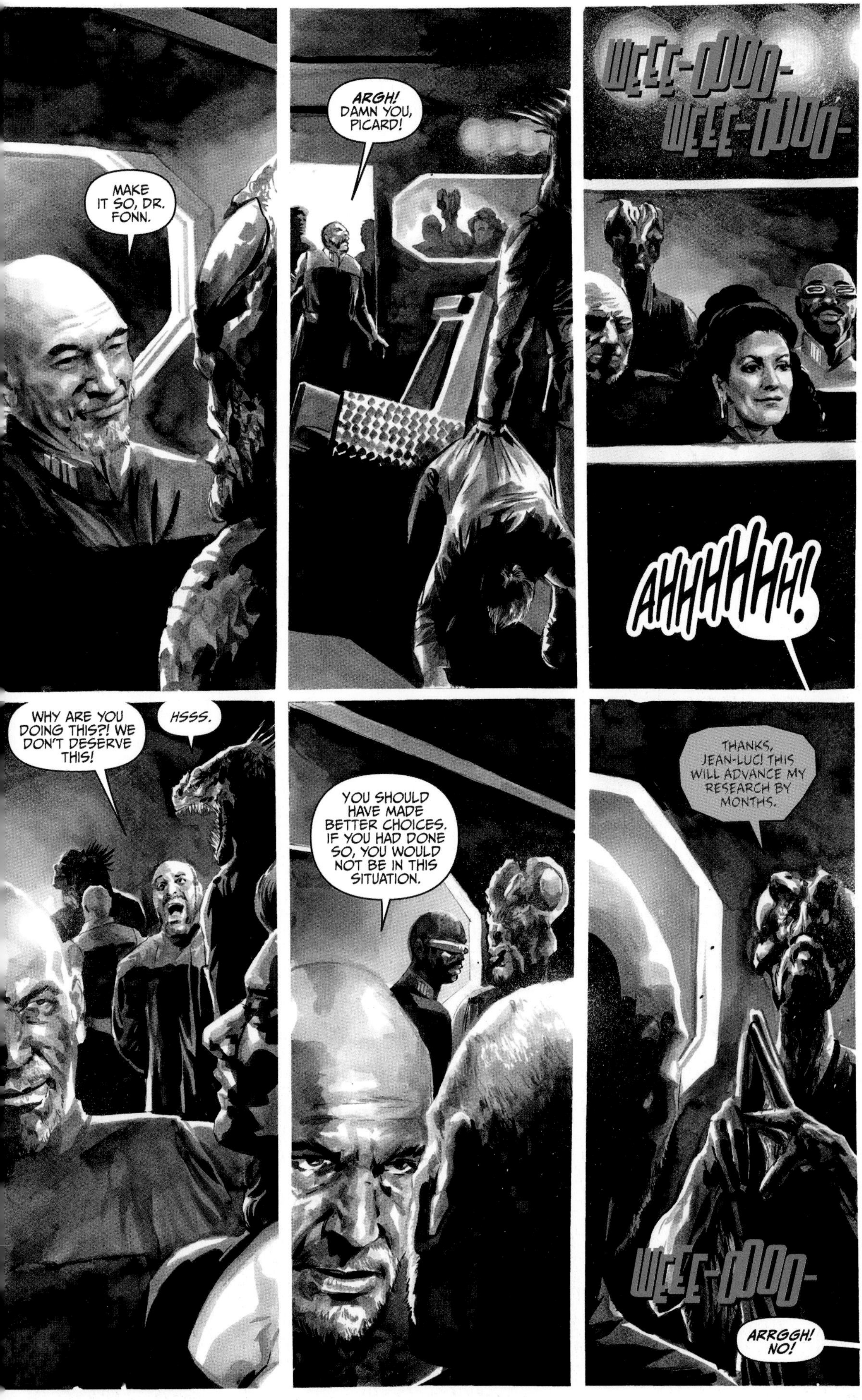
MAKE IT SO, DR. FONN.
ARGH! DAMN YOU, PICARD!
WEEE-OOOO-
WEEE-OOOO-
AHHHHHH!
WHY ARE YOU DOING THIS?! WE DON'T DESERVE THIS!
HSSS.
YOU SHOULD HAVE MADE BETTER CHOICES. IF YOU HAD DONE SO, YOU WOULD NOT BE IN THIS SITUATION.
THANKS, JEAN-LUC! THIS WILL ADVANCE MY RESEARCH BY MONTHS.
WEEE-OOOO-
ARRGGH! NO!

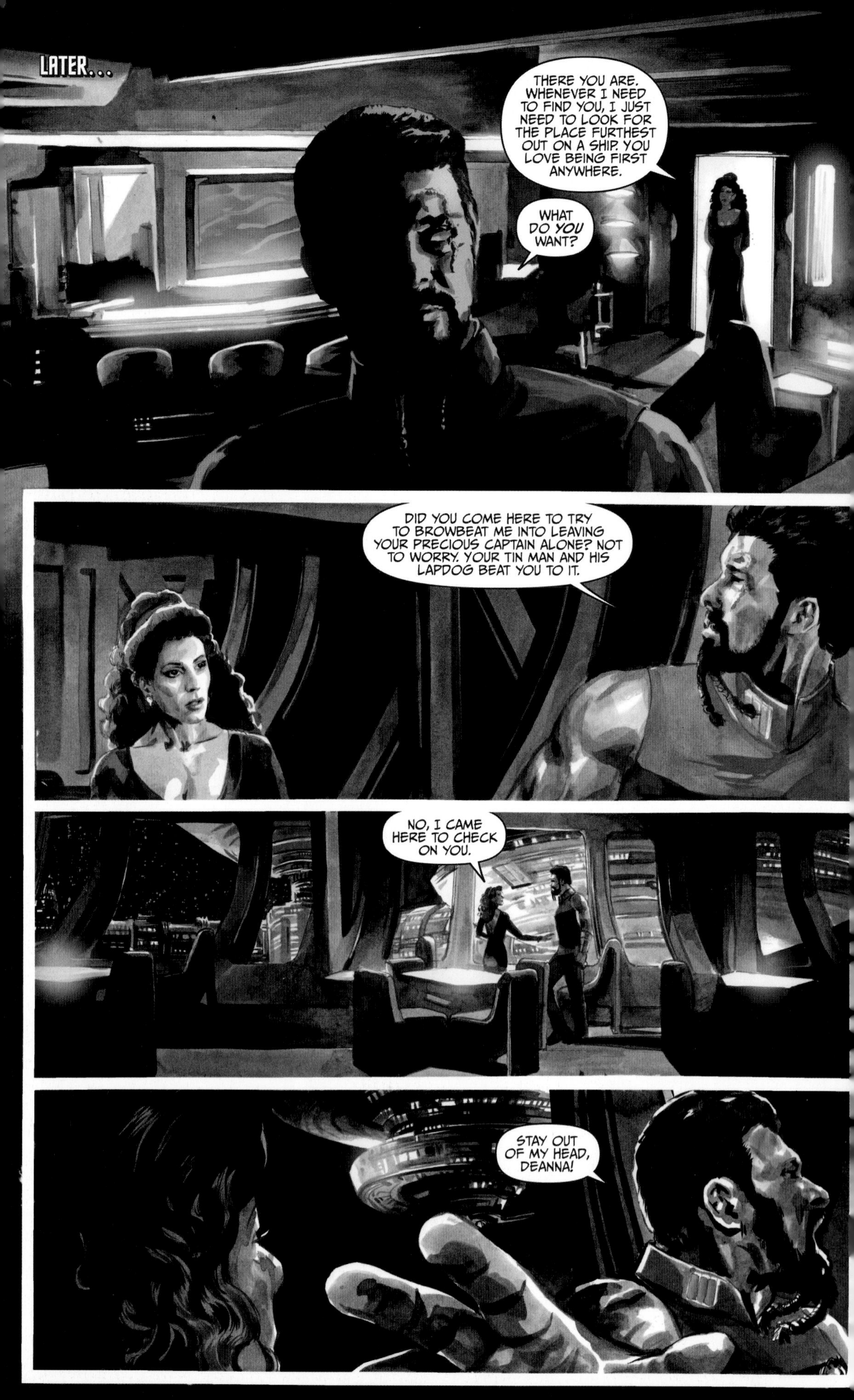
LATER...
THERE YOU ARE. WHENEVER I NEED TO FIND YOU, I JUST NEED TO LOOK FOR THE PLACE FURTHEST OUT ON A SHIP. YOU LOVE BEING FIRST ANYWHERE.
WHAT DO *YOU* WANT?
DID YOU COME HERE TO TRY TO BROWBEAT ME INTO LEAVING YOUR PRECIOUS CAPTAIN ALONE? NOT TO WORRY. YOUR TIN MAN AND HIS LAPDOG BEAT YOU TO IT.
NO, I CAME HERE TO CHECK ON YOU.
STAY OUT OF MY HEAD, DEANNA!

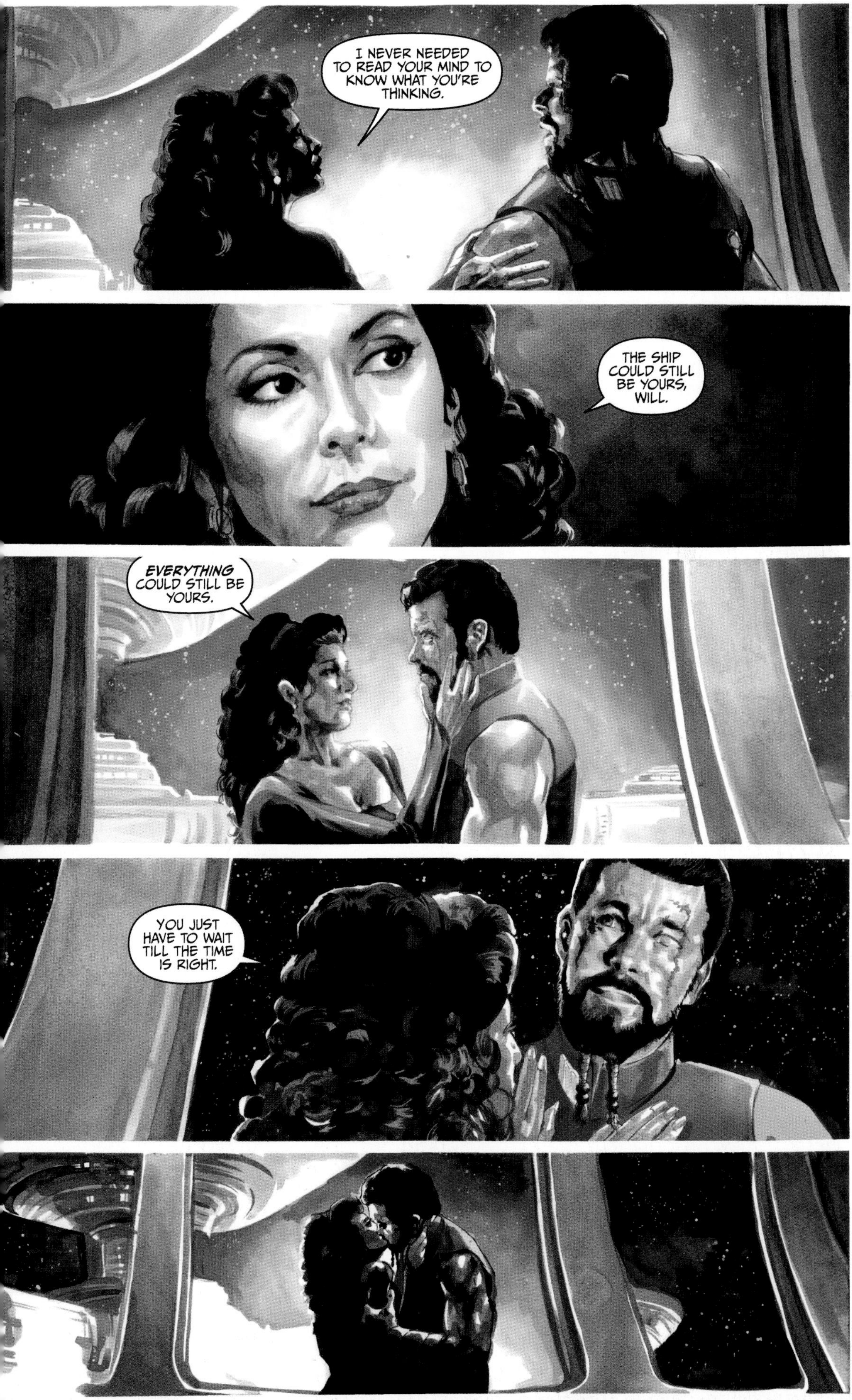
I NEVER NEEDED TO READ YOUR MIND TO KNOW WHAT YOU'RE THINKING.
THE SHIP COULD STILL BE YOURS, WILL.
EVERYTHING COULD STILL BE YOURS.
YOU JUST HAVE TO WAIT TILL THE TIME IS RIGHT.

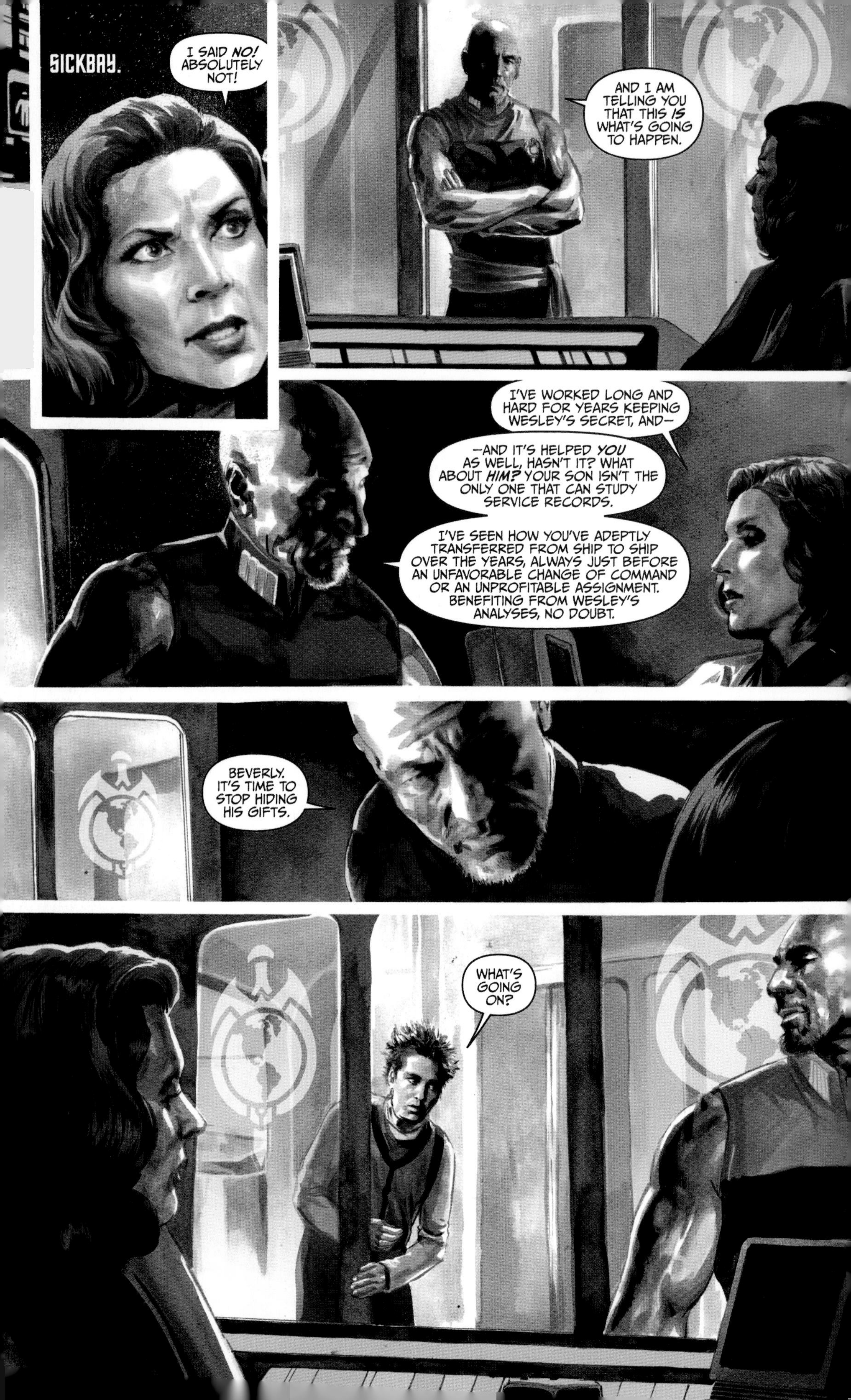
SICKBAY.
I SAID NO! ABSOLUTELY NOT!
AND I AM TELLING YOU THAT THIS IS WHAT'S GOING TO HAPPEN.
I'VE WORKED LONG AND HARD FOR YEARS KEEPING WESLEY'S SECRET, AND—
—AND IT'S HELPED YOU AS WELL, HASN'T IT? WHAT ABOUT HIM? YOUR SON ISN'T THE ONLY ONE THAT CAN STUDY SERVICE RECORDS.
I'VE SEEN HOW YOU'VE ADEPTLY TRANSFERRED FROM SHIP TO SHIP OVER THE YEARS, ALWAYS JUST BEFORE AN UNFAVORABLE CHANGE OF COMMAND OR AN UNPROFITABLE ASSIGNMENT. BENEFITING FROM WESLEY'S ANALYSES, NO DOUBT.
BEVERLY. IT'S TIME TO STOP HIDING HIS GIFTS.
WHAT'S GOING ON?

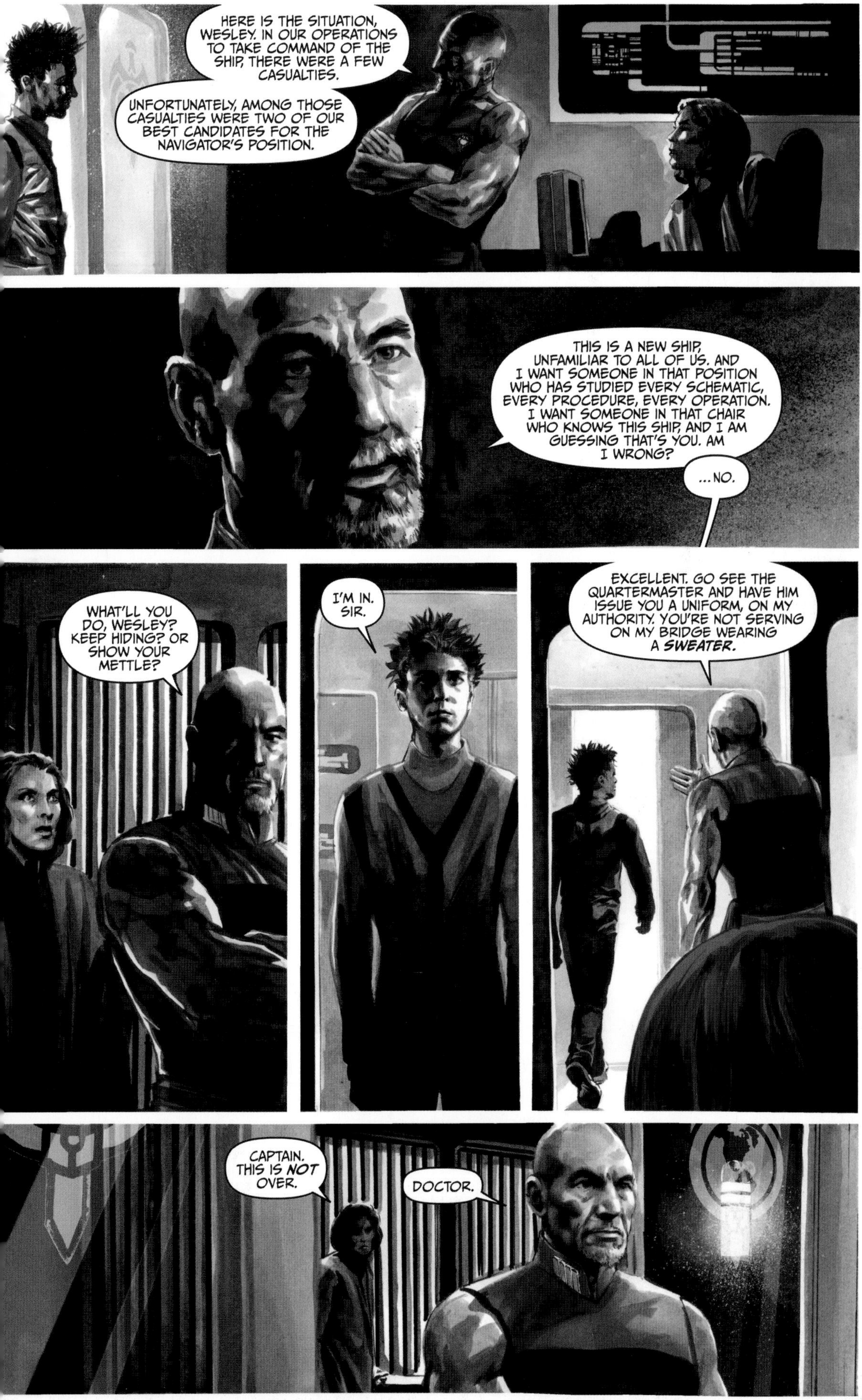
HERE IS THE SITUATION, WESLEY. IN OUR OPERATIONS TO TAKE COMMAND OF THE SHIP, THERE WERE A FEW CASUALTIES.
UNFORTUNATELY, AMONG THOSE CASUALTIES WERE TWO OF OUR BEST CANDIDATES FOR THE NAVIGATOR'S POSITION.
THIS IS A NEW SHIP, UNFAMILIAR TO ALL OF US. AND I WANT SOMEONE IN THAT POSITION WHO HAS STUDIED EVERY SCHEMATIC, EVERY PROCEDURE, EVERY OPERATION. I WANT SOMEONE IN THAT CHAIR WHO KNOWS THIS SHIP, AND I AM GUESSING THAT'S YOU. AM I WRONG?
...NO.
WHAT'LL YOU DO, WESLEY? KEEP HIDING? OR SHOW YOUR METTLE?
I'M IN. SIR.
EXCELLENT. GO SEE THE QUARTERMASTER AND HAVE HIM ISSUE YOU A UNIFORM, ON MY AUTHORITY. YOU'RE NOT SERVING ON MY BRIDGE WEARING A ***SWEATER.***
CAPTAIN. THIS IS ***NOT*** OVER.
DOCTOR.

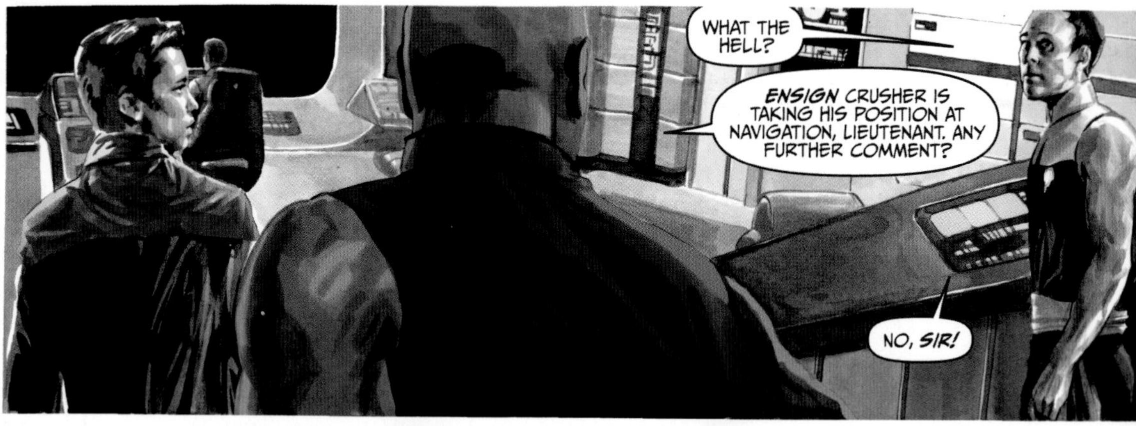
WHAT THE HELL?
ENSIGN CRUSHER IS TAKING HIS POSITION AT NAVIGATION, LIEUTENANT. ANY FURTHER COMMENT?
NO, SIR!

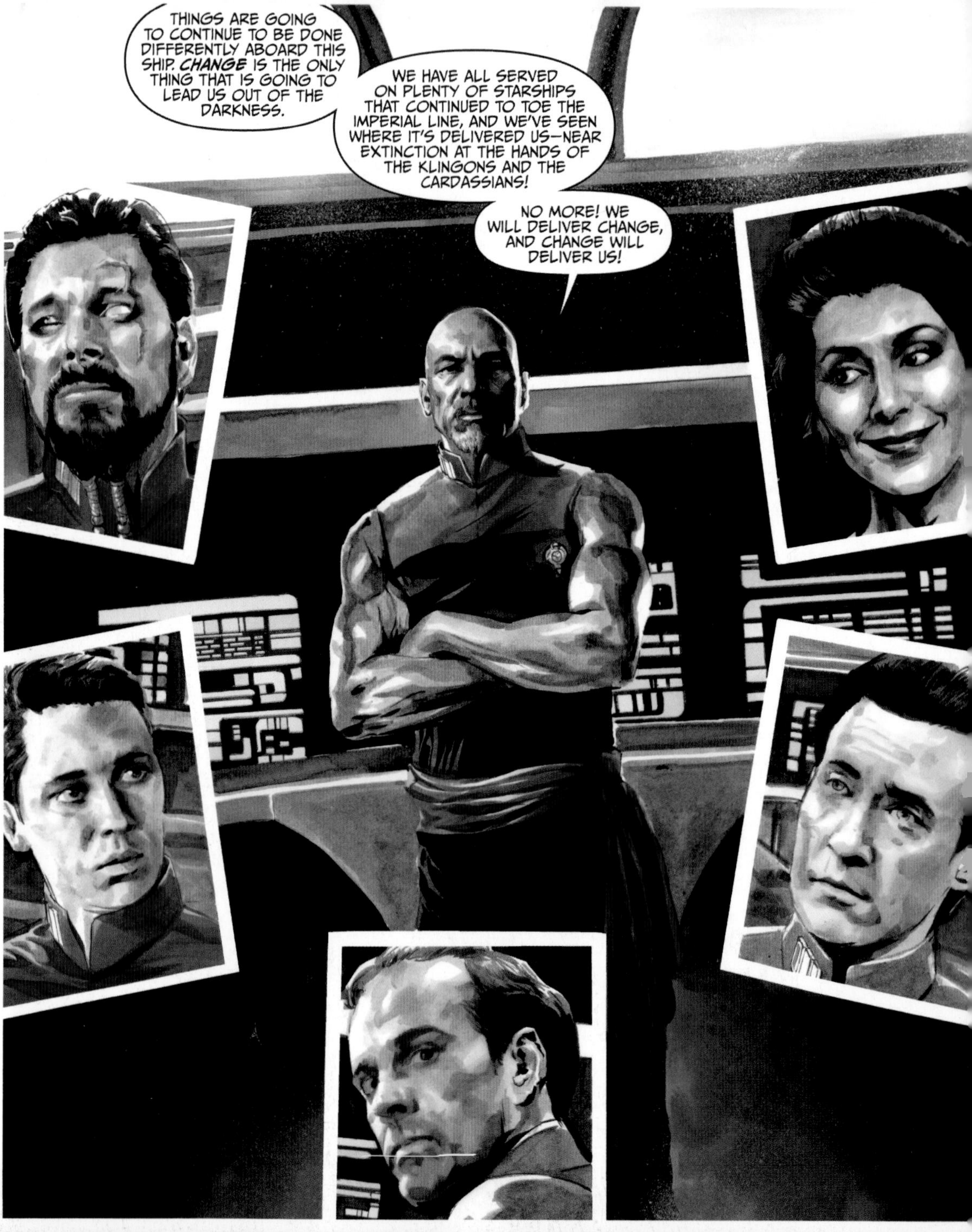
THINGS ARE GOING TO CONTINUE TO BE DONE DIFFERENTLY ABOARD THIS SHIP. CHANGE IS THE ONLY THING THAT IS GOING TO LEAD US OUT OF THE DARKNESS.
WE HAVE ALL SERVED ON PLENTY OF STARSHIPS THAT CONTINUED TO TOE THE IMPERIAL LINE, AND WE'VE SEEN WHERE IT'S DELIVERED US—NEAR EXTINCTION AT THE HANDS OF THE KLINGONS AND THE CARDASSIANS!
NO MORE! WE WILL DELIVER CHANGE, AND CHANGE WILL DELIVER US!

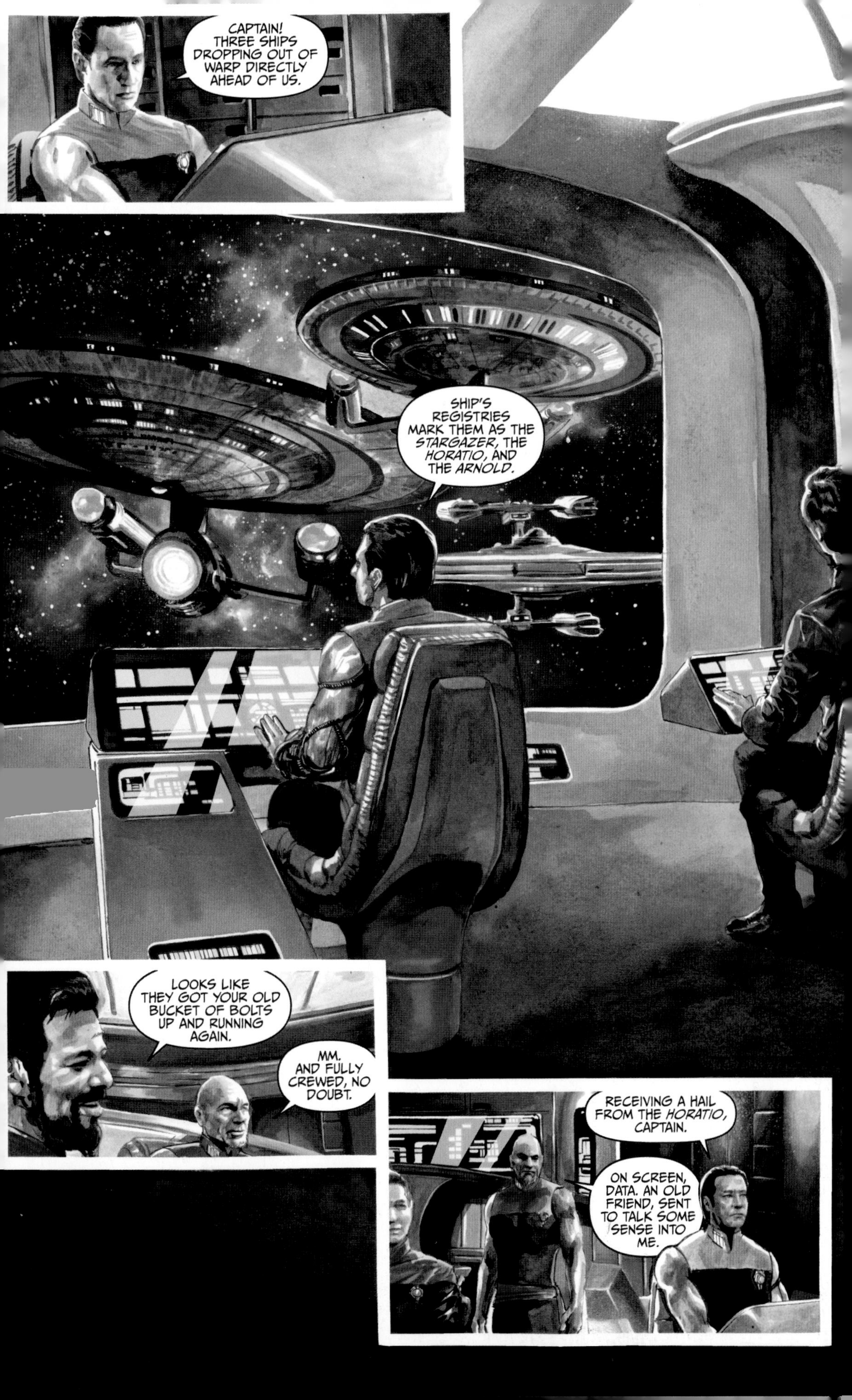
CAPTAIN! THREE SHIPS DROPPING OUT OF WARP DIRECTLY AHEAD OF US.
SHIP'S REGISTRIES MARK THEM AS THE *STARGAZER*, THE *HORATIO*, AND THE *ARNOLD*.
LOOKS LIKE THEY GOT YOUR OLD BUCKET OF BOLTS UP AND RUNNING AGAIN.
MM. AND FULLY CREWED, NO DOUBT.
RECEIVING A HAIL FROM THE *HORATIO*, CAPTAIN.
ON SCREEN, DATA. AN OLD FRIEND, SENT TO TALK SOME SENSE INTO ME.

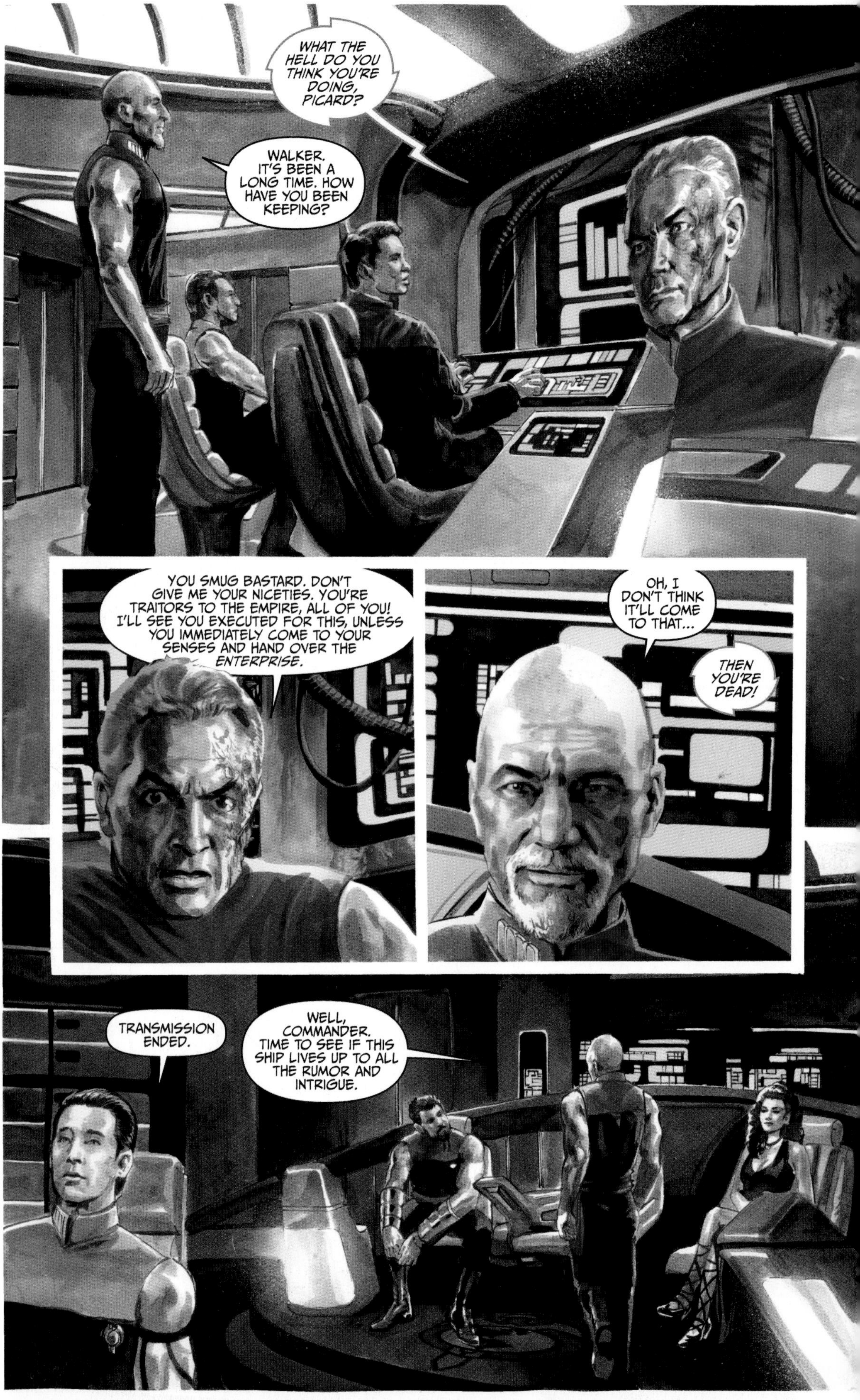
WHAT THE HELL DO YOU THINK YOU'RE DOING, PICARD?
WALKER. IT'S BEEN A LONG TIME. HOW HAVE YOU BEEN KEEPING?
YOU SMUG BASTARD. DON'T GIVE ME YOUR NICETIES. YOU'RE TRAITORS TO THE EMPIRE, ALL OF YOU! I'LL SEE YOU EXECUTED FOR THIS, UNLESS YOU IMMEDIATELY COME TO YOUR SENSES AND HAND OVER THE *ENTERPRISE*.
OH, I DON'T THINK IT'LL COME TO THAT...
THEN YOU'RE DEAD!
TRANSMISSION ENDED.
WELL, COMMANDER. TIME TO SEE IF THIS SHIP LIVES UP TO ALL THE RUMOR AND INTRIGUE.

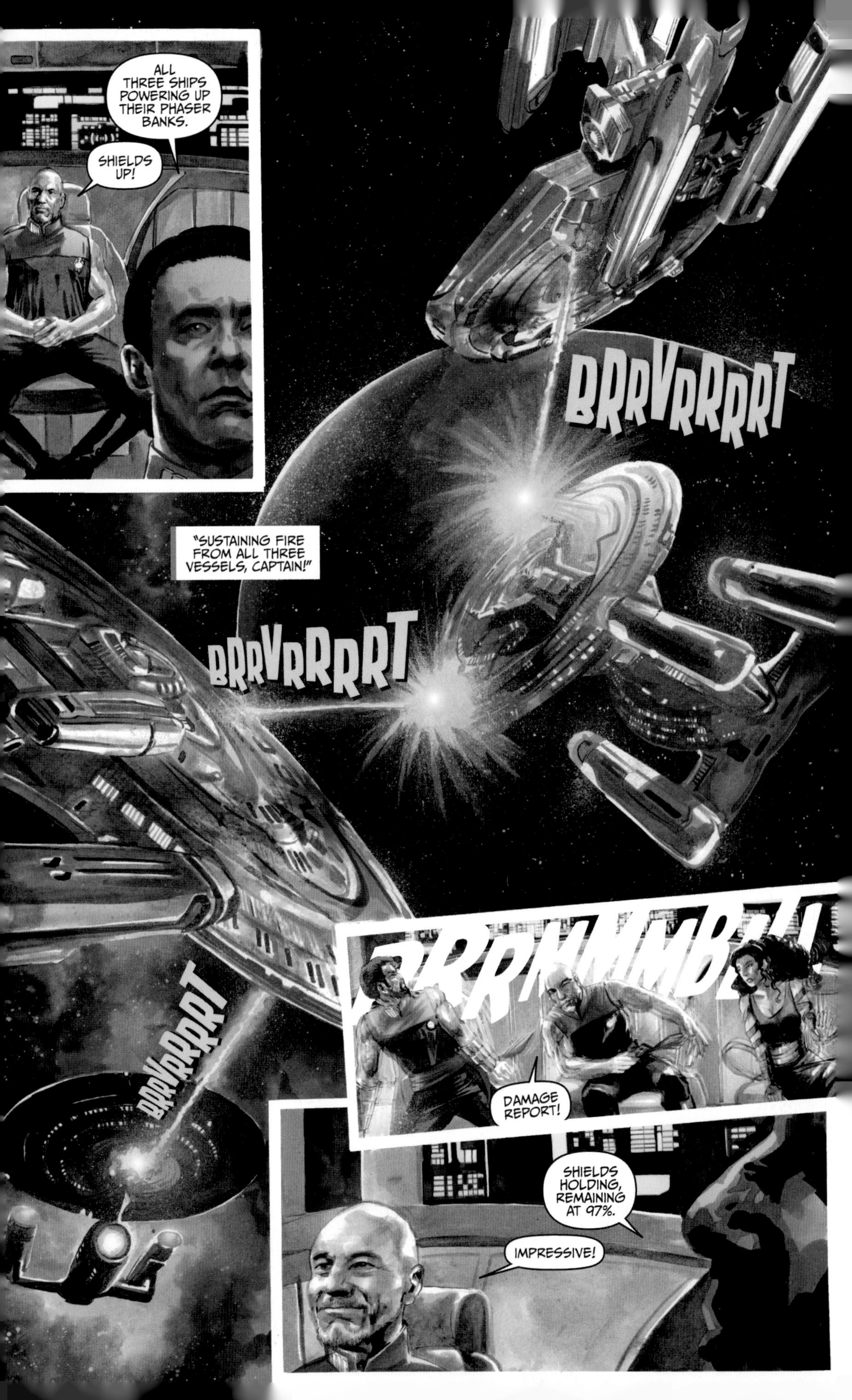

ALL THREE SHIPS POWERING UP THEIR PHASER BANKS.
SHIELDS UP!
BRRVRRRRT
"SUSTAINING FIRE FROM ALL THREE VESSELS, CAPTAIN!"
BRRVRRRRT
BRRVRRRRT
DAMAGE REPORT!
SHIELDS HOLDING, REMAINING AT 97%.
IMPRESSIVE!

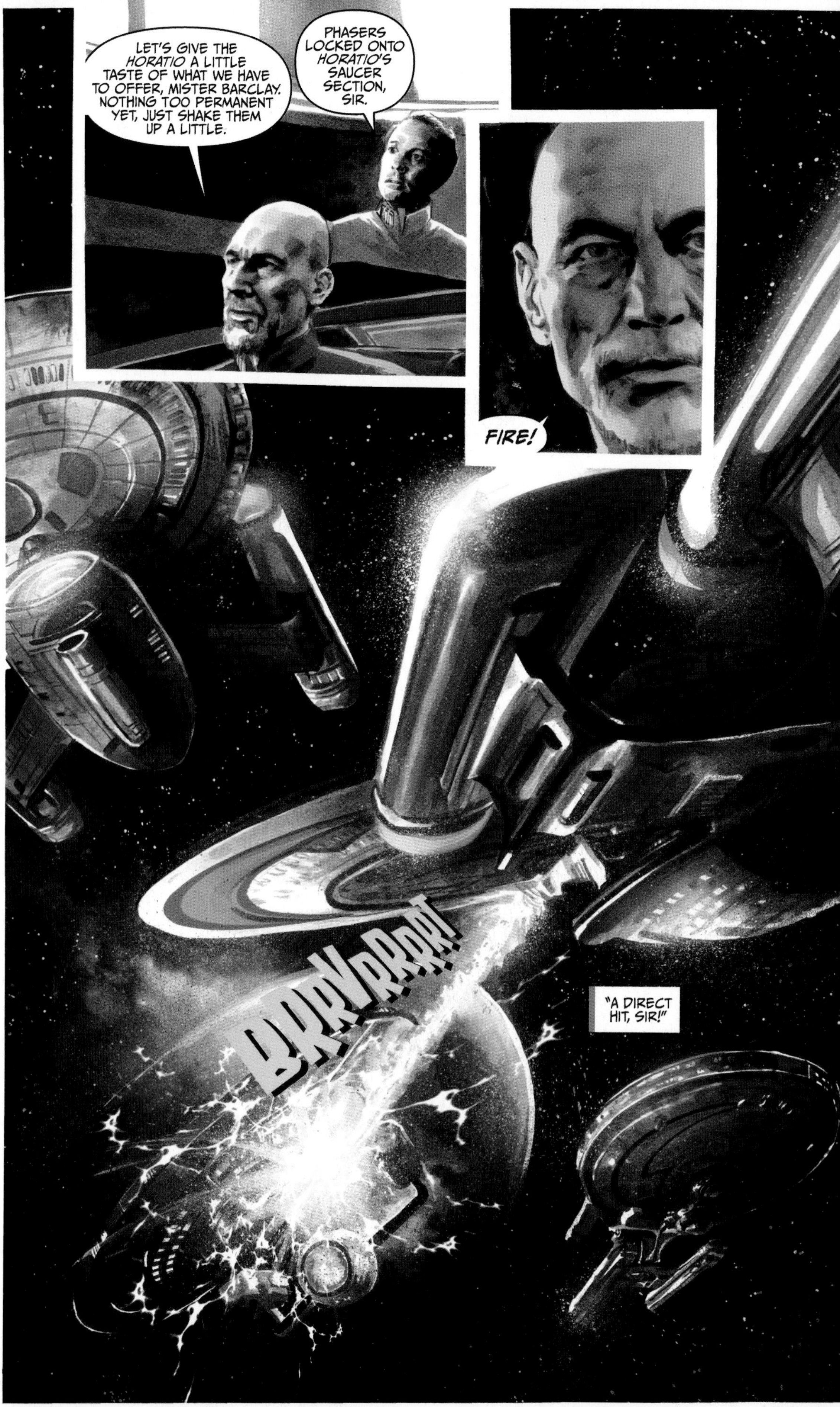
LET'S GIVE THE *HORATIO* A LITTLE TASTE OF WHAT WE HAVE TO OFFER, MISTER BARCLAY. NOTHING TOO PERMANENT YET, JUST SHAKE THEM UP A LITTLE.
PHASERS LOCKED ONTO *HORATIO'S* SAUCER SECTION, SIR.
FIRE!
BRRVRRRT!
"A DIRECT HIT, SIR!"

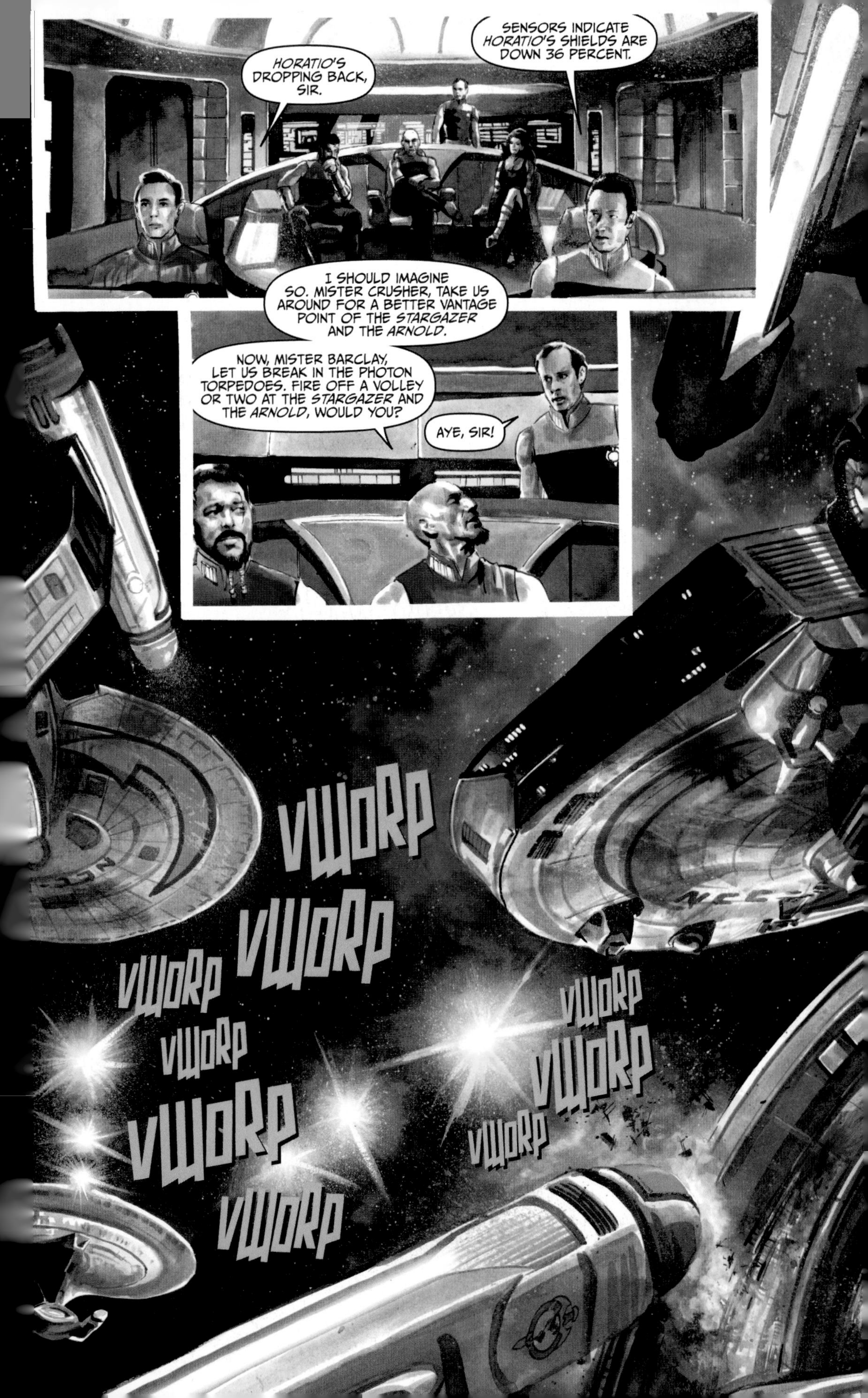
HORATIO'S DROPPING BACK, SIR.
SENSORS INDICATE HORATIO'S SHIELDS ARE DOWN 36 PERCENT.
I SHOULD IMAGINE SO. MISTER CRUSHER, TAKE US AROUND FOR A BETTER VANTAGE POINT OF THE STARGAZER AND THE ARNOLD.
NOW, MISTER BARCLAY, LET US BREAK IN THE PHOTON TORPEDOES. FIRE OFF A VOLLEY OR TWO AT THE STARGAZER AND THE ARNOLD, WOULD YOU?
AYE, SIR!
VWORP
VWORP
VWORP
VWORP
VWORP
VWORP
VWORP
VWORP
VWORP

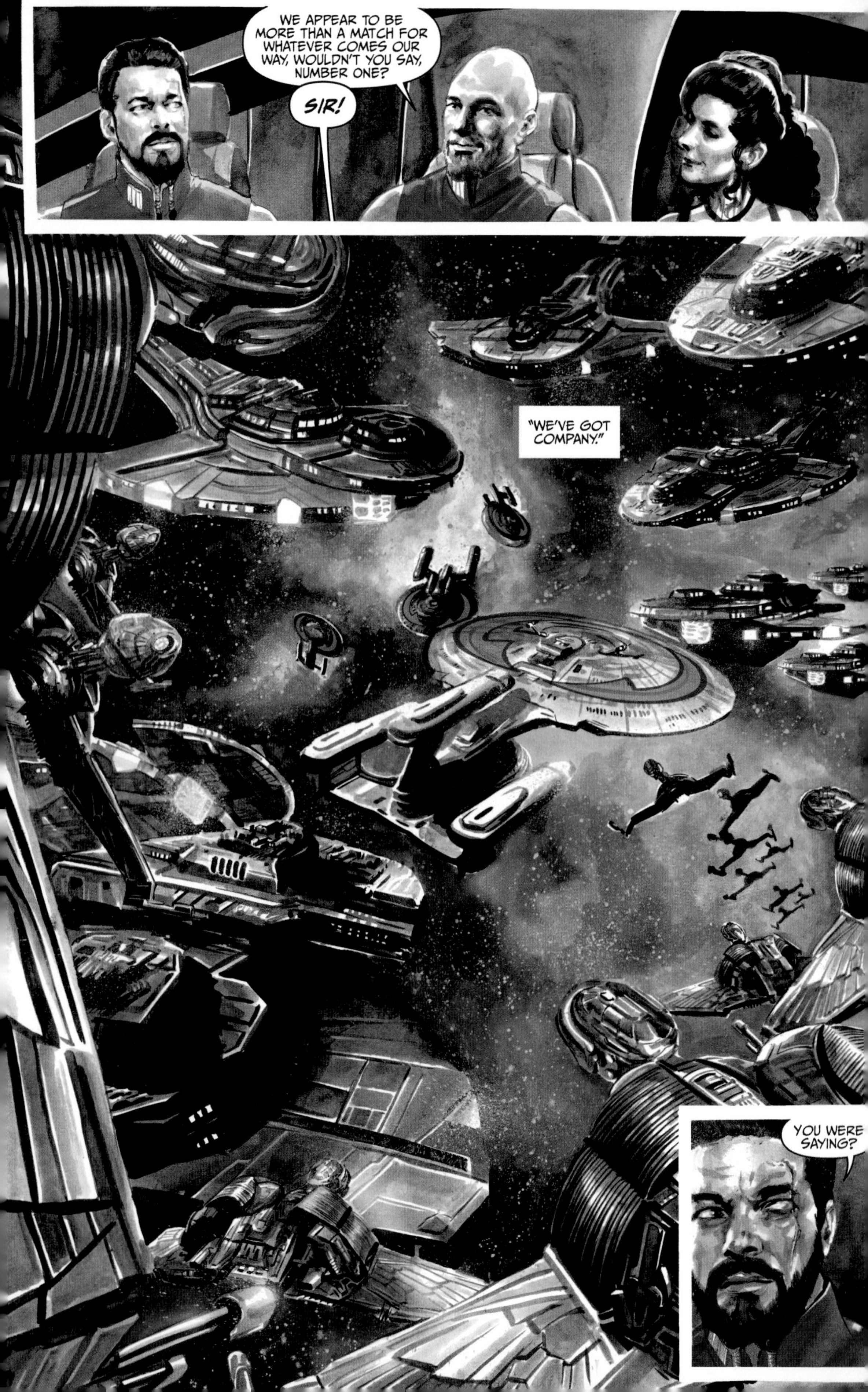
WE APPEAR TO BE MORE THAN A MATCH FOR WHATEVER COMES OUR WAY, WOULDN'T YOU SAY, NUMBER ONE?
SIR!
"WE'VE GOT COMPANY."
YOU WERE SAYING?

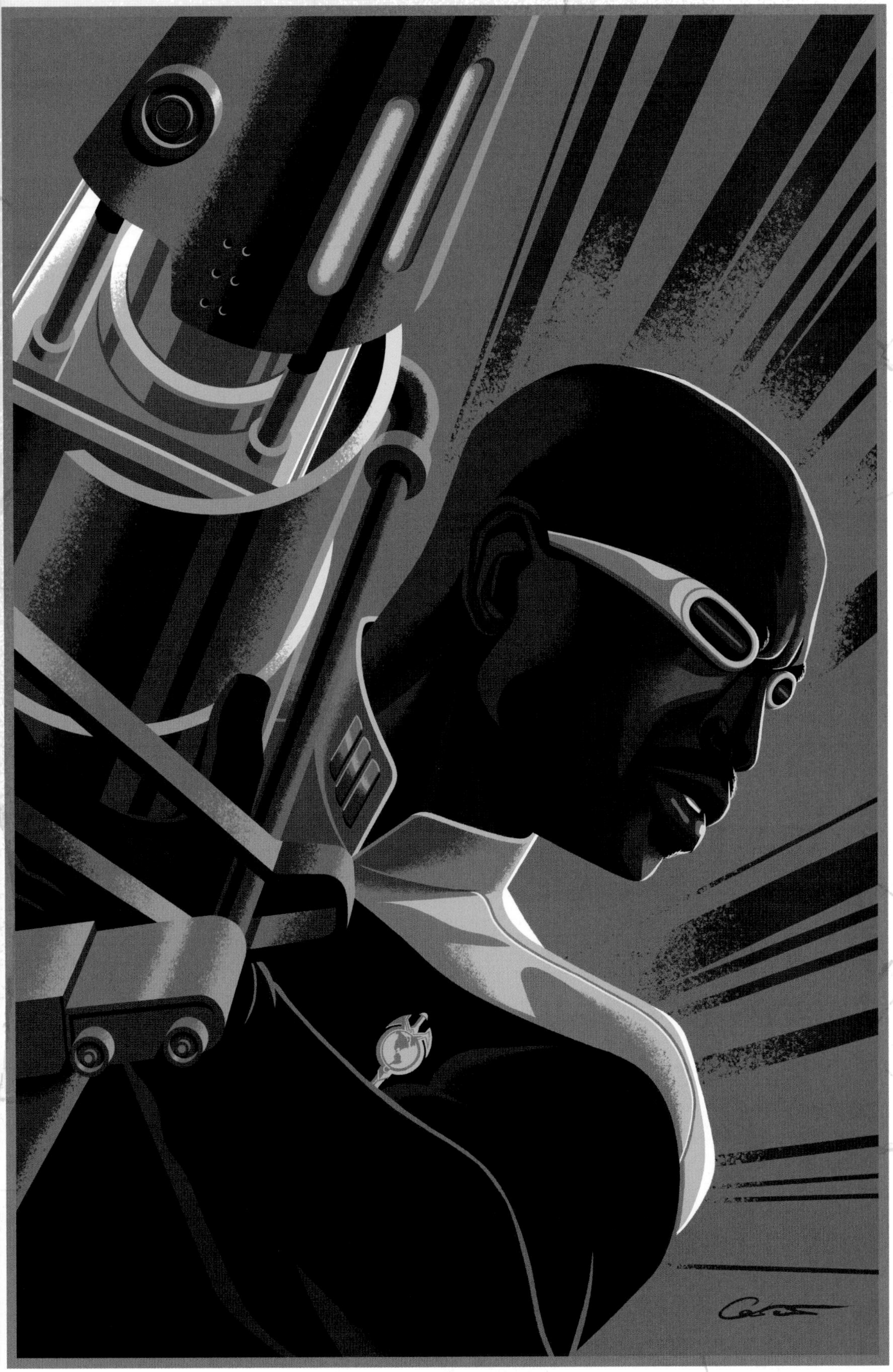

ART BY
GEORGE CALTSOUDAS

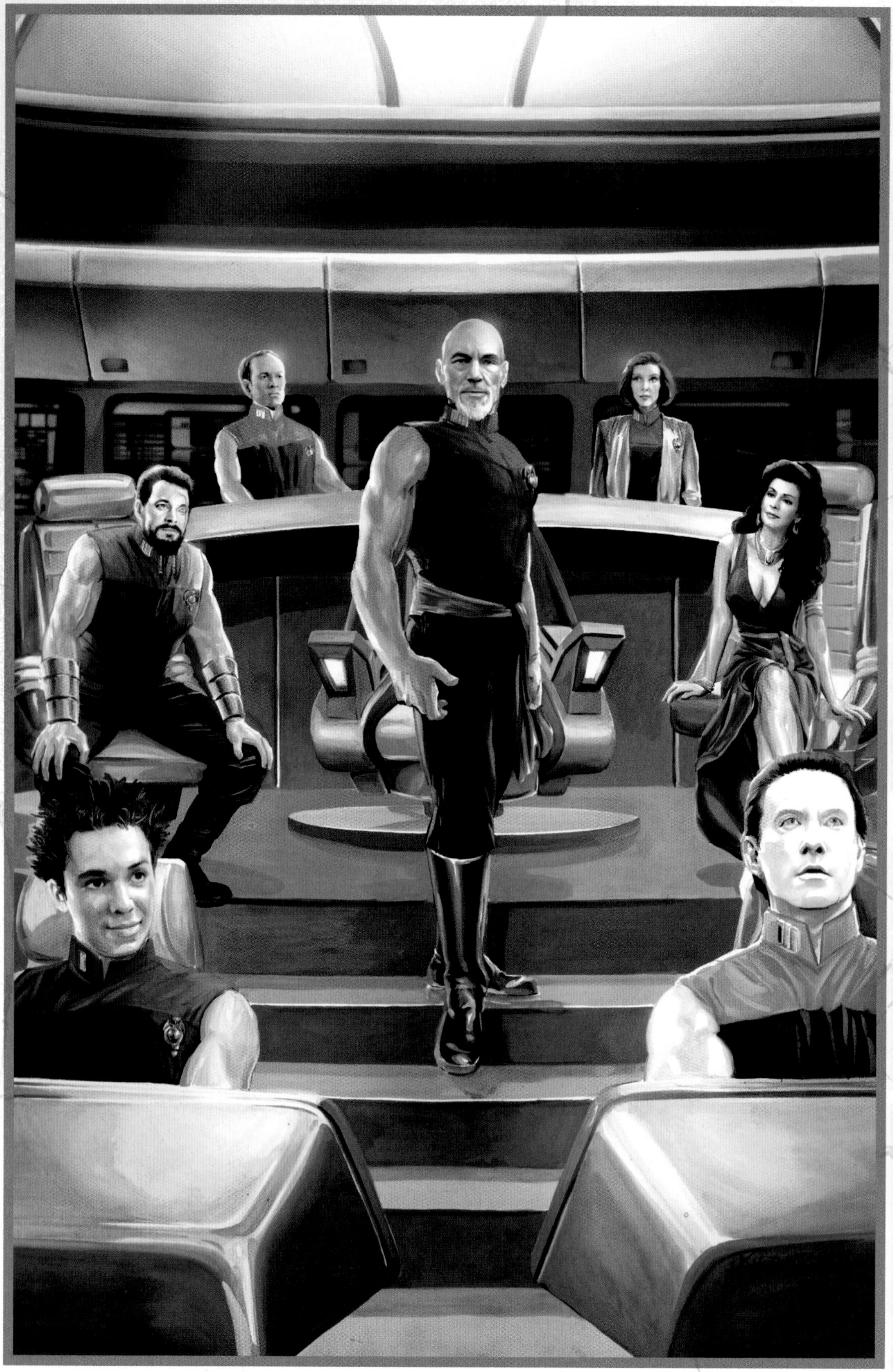

ART BY
J.K. WOODWARD

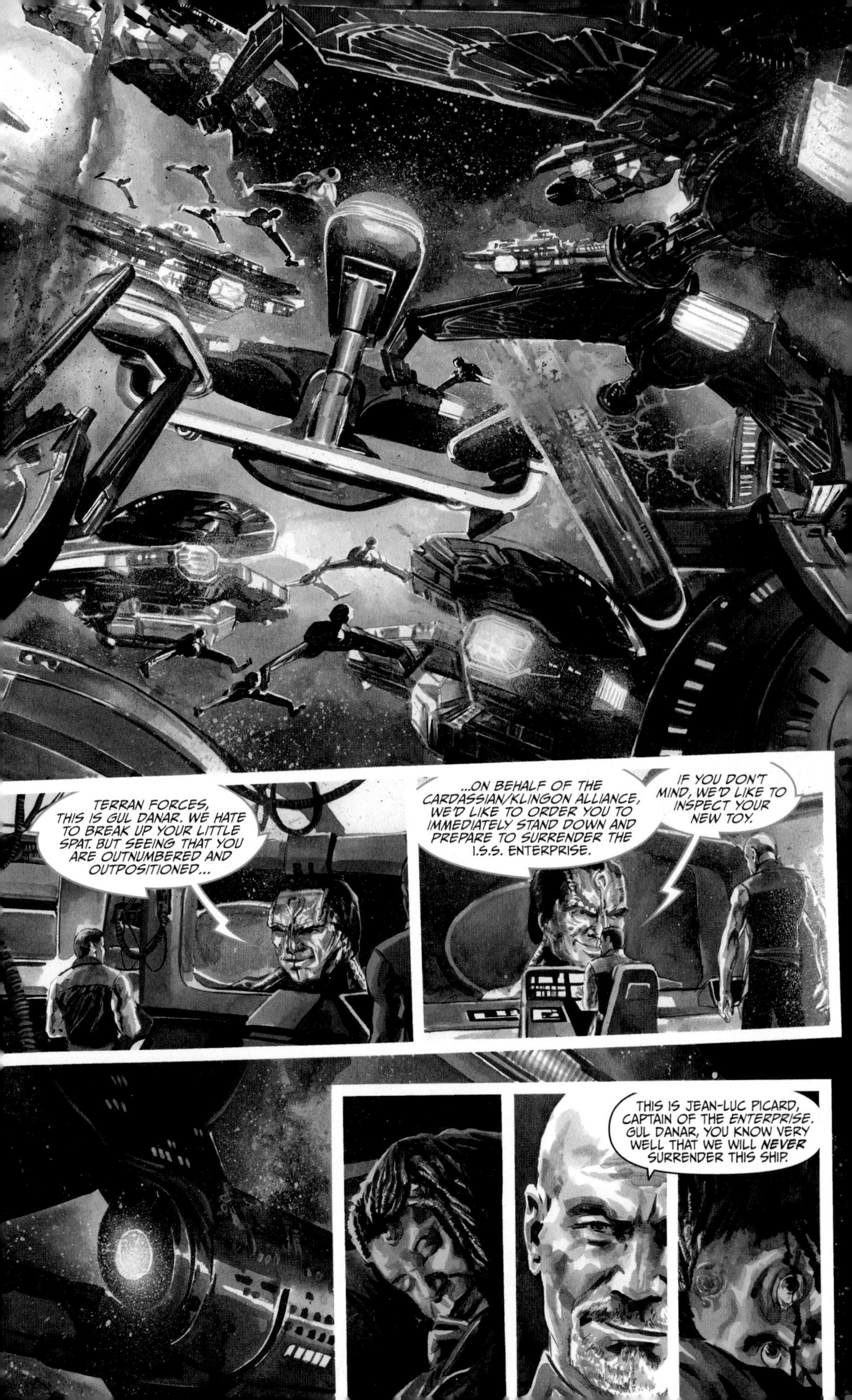
TERRAN FORCES, THIS IS GUL DANAR. WE HATE TO BREAK UP YOUR LITTLE SPAT. BUT SEEING THAT YOU ARE OUTNUMBERED AND OUTPOSITIONED...
...ON BEHALF OF THE CARDASSIAN/KLINGON ALLIANCE, WE'D LIKE TO ORDER YOU TO IMMEDIATELY STAND DOWN AND PREPARE TO SURRENDER THE I.S.S. ENTERPRISE.
IF YOU DON'T MIND, WE'D LIKE TO INSPECT YOUR NEW TOY.
THIS IS JEAN-LUC PICARD, CAPTAIN OF THE ENTERPRISE. GUL DANAR, YOU KNOW VERY WELL THAT WE WILL NEVER SURRENDER THIS SHIP.

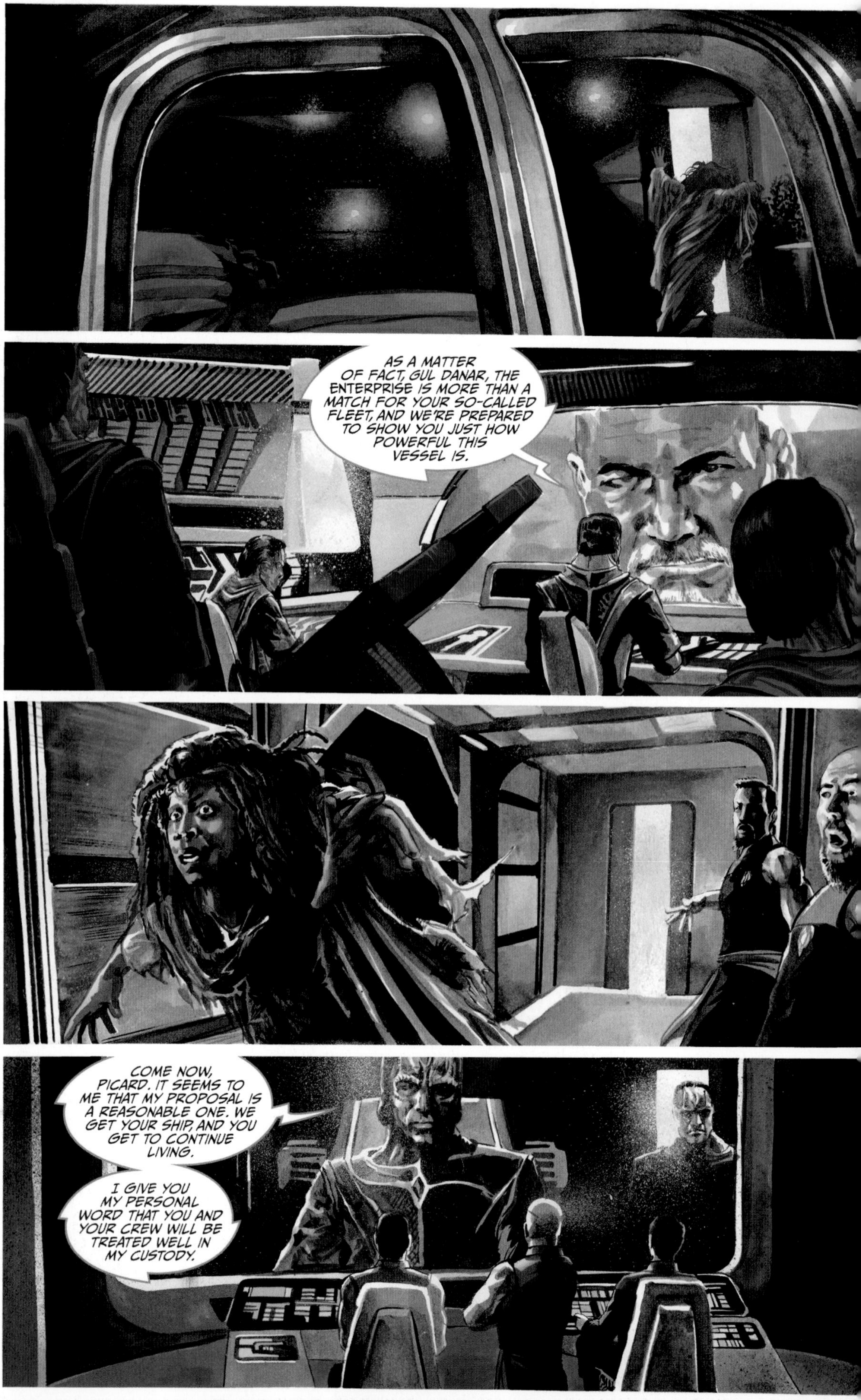
AS A MATTER OF FACT, GUL DANAR, THE ENTERPRISE IS MORE THAN A MATCH FOR YOUR SO-CALLED FLEET, AND WE'RE PREPARED TO SHOW YOU JUST HOW POWERFUL THIS VESSEL IS.
COME NOW, PICARD. IT SEEMS TO ME THAT MY PROPOSAL IS A REASONABLE ONE. WE GET YOUR SHIP, AND YOU GET TO CONTINUE LIVING.
I GIVE YOU MY PERSONAL WORD THAT YOU AND YOUR CREW WILL BE TREATED WELL IN MY CUSTODY.

OOF!

WHIAK WHIAK

I WOULD RATHER TAKE MY CHANCES IN BATTLE WITH YOU ANY DAY, CARDASSIAN.

OH, ARE YOU SO SURE ABOUT THAT, CAPTAIN? WE'VE ALREADY PREPARED A LITTLE DISPLAY FOR YOU.

EXECUTE OPERATION A, IMMEDIATELY.

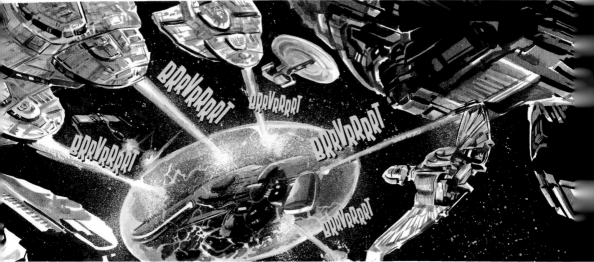

BRRVRRRRT
BRRVRRRRT
BRRVRRRRT
BRRVRRRRT
BRRVRRRRT

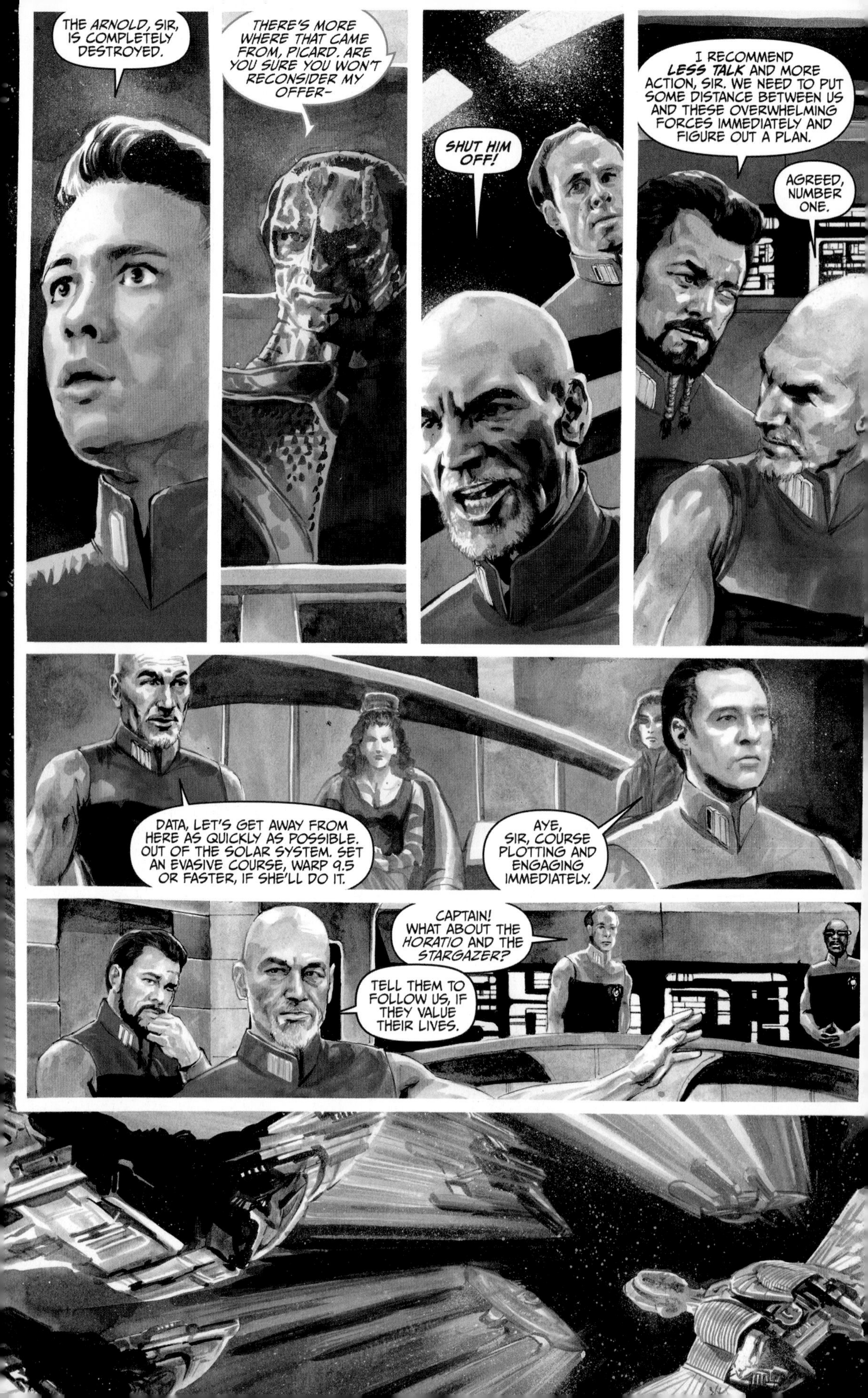
THE *ARNOLD*, SIR, IS COMPLETELY DESTROYED.
THERE'S MORE WHERE THAT CAME FROM, PICARD. ARE YOU SURE YOU WON'T RECONSIDER MY OFFER–
SHUT HIM OFF!
I RECOMMEND **LESS TALK** AND MORE ACTION, SIR. WE NEED TO PUT SOME DISTANCE BETWEEN US AND THESE OVERWHELMING FORCES IMMEDIATELY AND FIGURE OUT A PLAN.
AGREED, NUMBER ONE.
DATA, LET'S GET AWAY FROM HERE AS QUICKLY AS POSSIBLE. OUT OF THE SOLAR SYSTEM. SET AN EVASIVE COURSE, WARP 9.5 OR FASTER, IF SHE'LL DO IT.
AYE, SIR, COURSE PLOTTING AND ENGAGING IMMEDIATELY.
CAPTAIN! WHAT ABOUT THE *HORATIO* AND THE *STARGAZER*?
TELL THEM TO FOLLOW US, IF THEY VALUE THEIR LIVES.

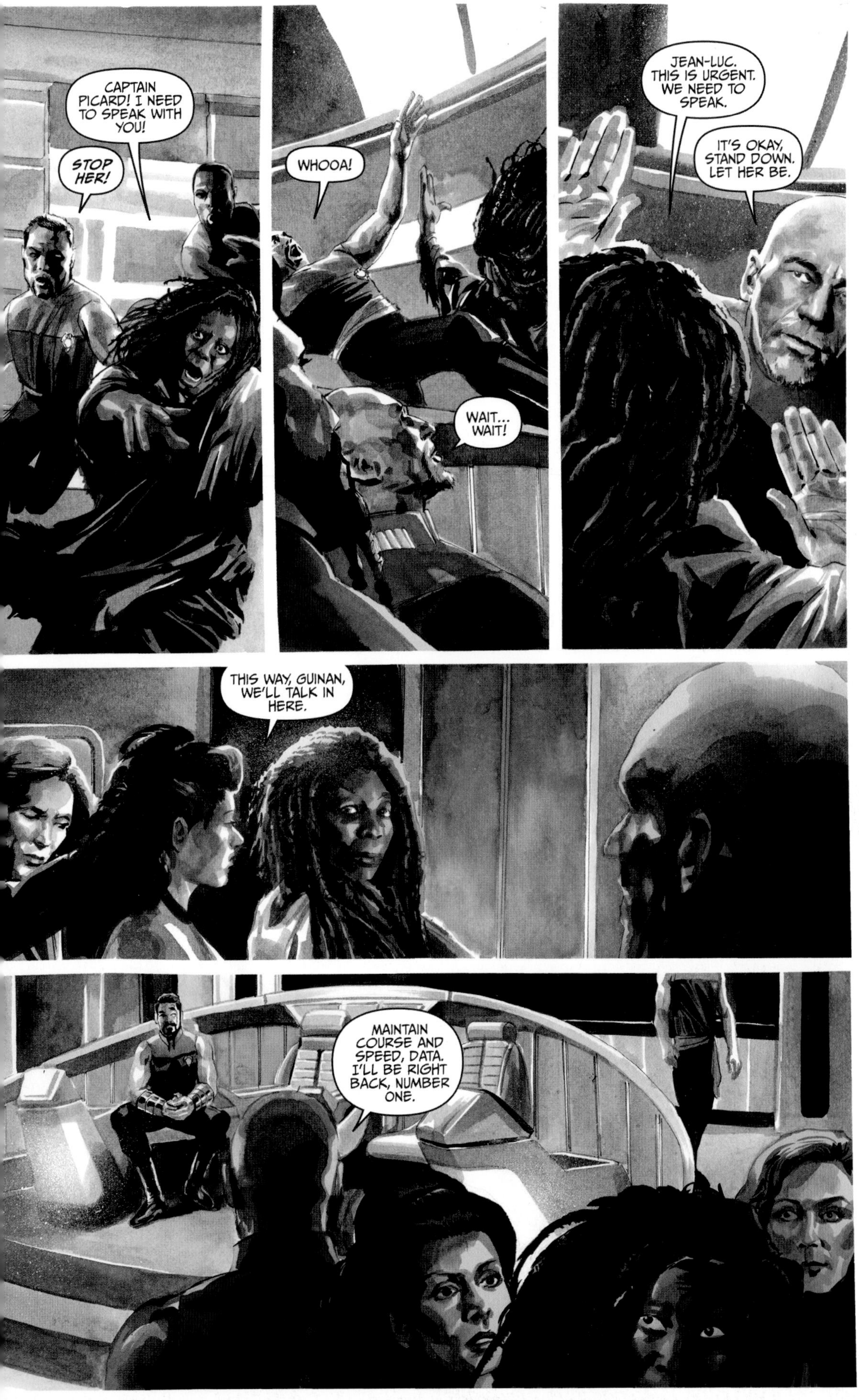
CAPTAIN PICARD! I NEED TO SPEAK WITH YOU!
STOP HER!
WHOOA!
WAIT... WAIT!
JEAN-LUC. THIS IS URGENT. WE NEED TO SPEAK.
IT'S OKAY, STAND DOWN. LET HER BE.
THIS WAY, GUINAN, WE'LL TALK IN HERE.
MAINTAIN COURSE AND SPEED, DATA. I'LL BE RIGHT BACK, NUMBER ONE.

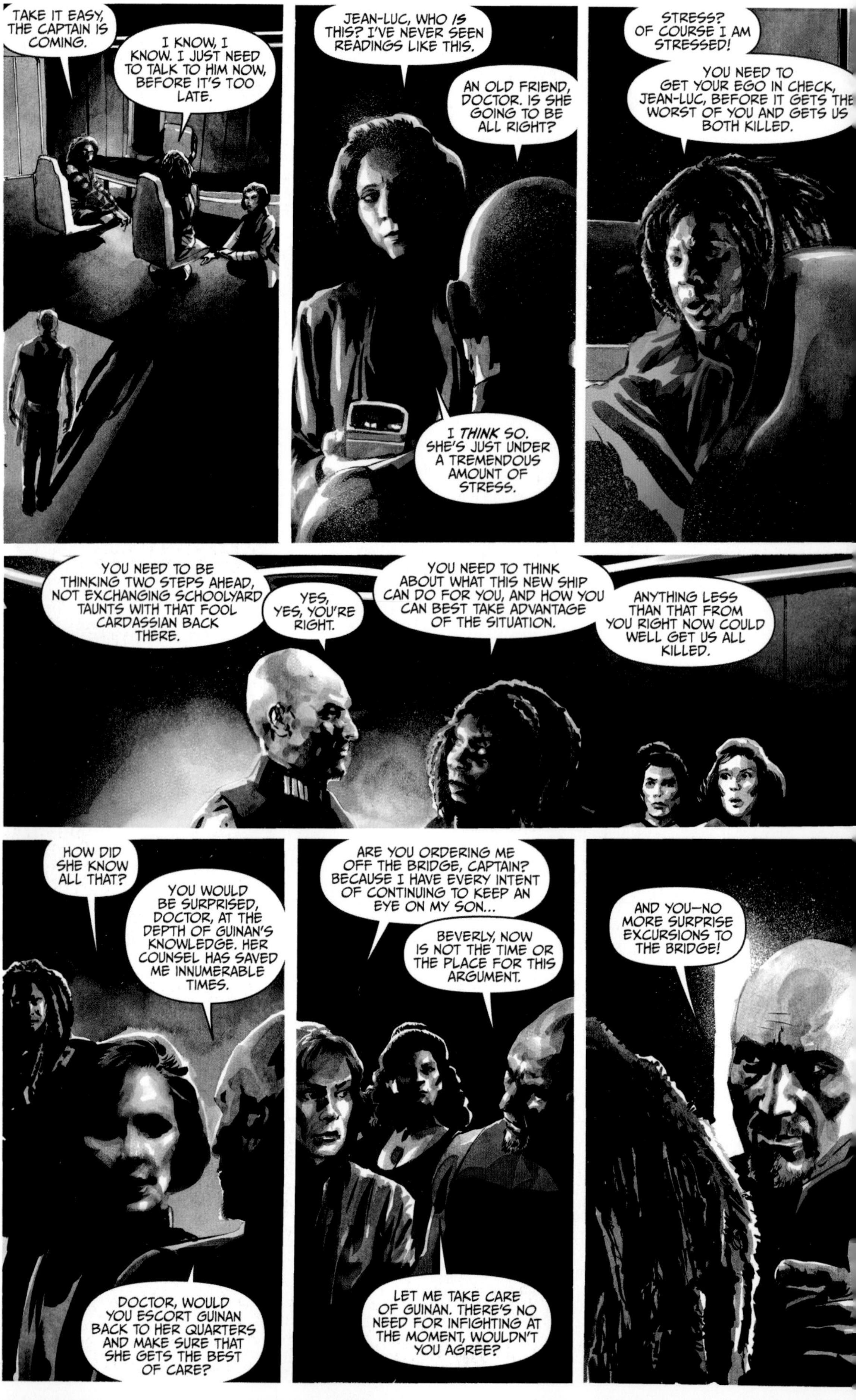
TAKE IT EASY, THE CAPTAIN IS COMING.
I KNOW. I KNOW. I JUST NEED TO TALK TO HIM NOW, BEFORE IT'S TOO LATE.
JEAN-LUC, WHO *IS* THIS? I'VE NEVER SEEN READINGS LIKE THIS.
AN OLD FRIEND, DOCTOR. IS SHE GOING TO BE ALL RIGHT?
I *THINK* SO. SHE'S JUST UNDER A TREMENDOUS AMOUNT OF STRESS.
STRESS? OF COURSE I AM STRESSED!
YOU NEED TO GET YOUR EGO IN CHECK, JEAN-LUC, BEFORE IT GETS THE WORST OF YOU AND GETS US BOTH KILLED.
YOU NEED TO BE THINKING TWO STEPS AHEAD, NOT EXCHANGING SCHOOLYARD TAUNTS WITH THAT FOOL CARDASSIAN BACK THERE.
YES, YES, YOU'RE RIGHT.
YOU NEED TO THINK ABOUT WHAT THIS NEW SHIP CAN DO FOR YOU, AND HOW YOU CAN BEST TAKE ADVANTAGE OF THE SITUATION.
ANYTHING LESS THAN THAT FROM YOU RIGHT NOW COULD WELL GET US ALL KILLED.
HOW DID SHE KNOW ALL THAT?
YOU WOULD BE SURPRISED, DOCTOR, AT THE DEPTH OF GUINAN'S KNOWLEDGE. HER COUNSEL HAS SAVED ME INNUMERABLE TIMES.
DOCTOR, WOULD YOU ESCORT GUINAN BACK TO HER QUARTERS AND MAKE SURE THAT SHE GETS THE BEST OF CARE?
ARE YOU ORDERING ME OFF THE BRIDGE, CAPTAIN? BECAUSE I HAVE EVERY INTENT OF CONTINUING TO KEEP AN EYE ON MY SON...
BEVERLY, NOW IS NOT THE TIME OR THE PLACE FOR THIS ARGUMENT.
LET ME TAKE CARE OF GUINAN. THERE'S NO NEED FOR INFIGHTING AT THE MOMENT, WOULDN'T YOU AGREE?
AND YOU—NO MORE SURPRISE EXCURSIONS TO THE BRIDGE!

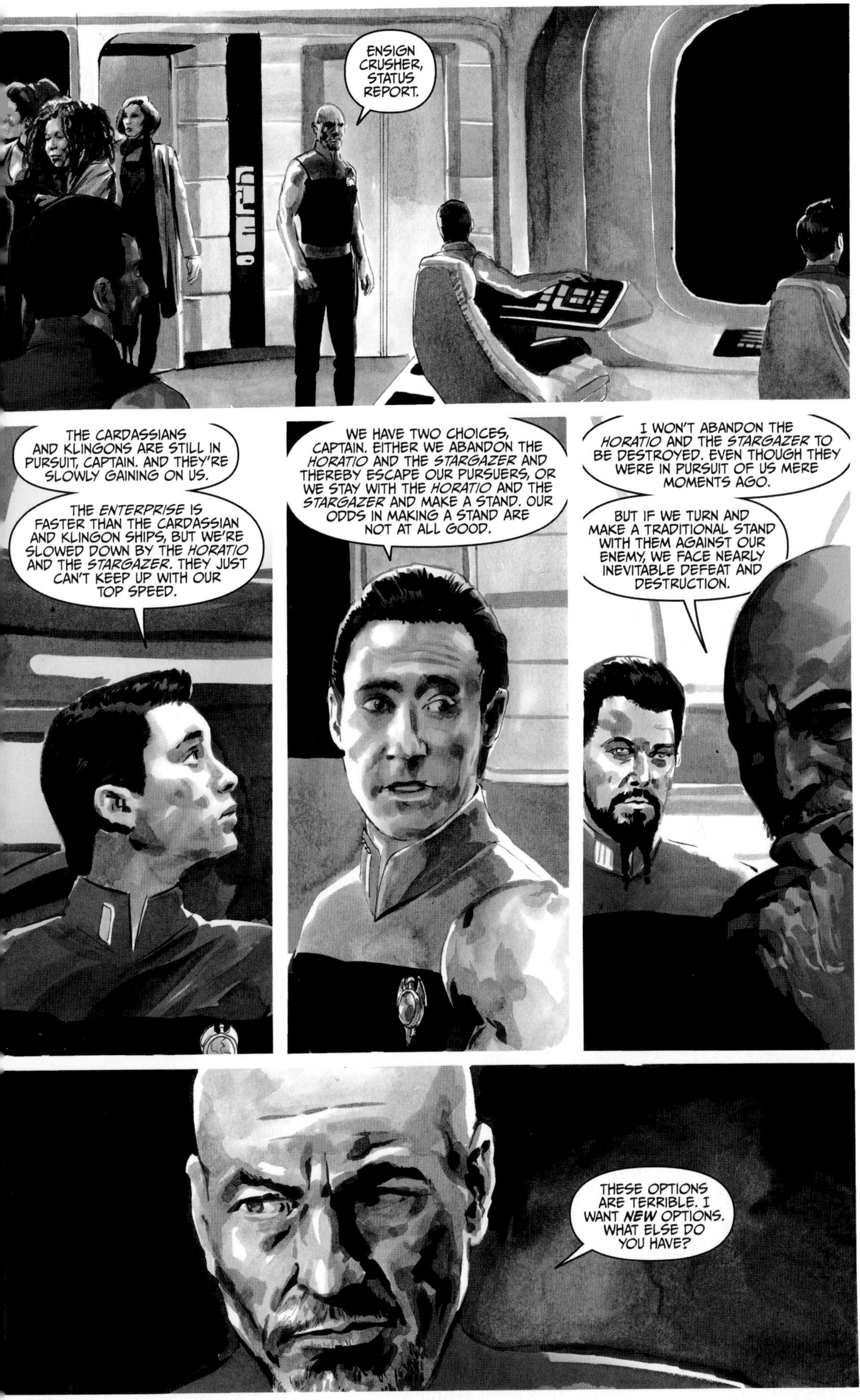
ENSIGN CRUSHER, STATUS REPORT.
THE CARDASSIANS AND KLINGONS ARE STILL IN PURSUIT, CAPTAIN. AND THEY'RE SLOWLY GAINING ON US.
THE *ENTERPRISE* IS FASTER THAN THE CARDASSIAN AND KLINGON SHIPS, BUT WE'RE SLOWED DOWN BY THE *HORATIO* AND THE *STARGAZER*. THEY JUST CAN'T KEEP UP WITH OUR TOP SPEED.
WE HAVE TWO CHOICES, CAPTAIN. EITHER WE ABANDON THE *HORATIO* AND THE *STARGAZER* AND THEREBY ESCAPE OUR PURSUERS, OR WE STAY WITH THE *HORATIO* AND THE *STARGAZER* AND MAKE A STAND. OUR ODDS IN MAKING A STAND ARE NOT AT ALL GOOD.
I WON'T ABANDON THE *HORATIO* AND THE *STARGAZER* TO BE DESTROYED. EVEN THOUGH THEY WERE IN PURSUIT OF US MERE MOMENTS AGO.
BUT IF WE TURN AND MAKE A TRADITIONAL STAND WITH THEM AGAINST OUR ENEMY, WE FACE NEARLY INEVITABLE DEFEAT AND DESTRUCTION.
THESE OPTIONS ARE TERRIBLE. I WANT ***NEW*** OPTIONS. WHAT ELSE DO YOU HAVE?

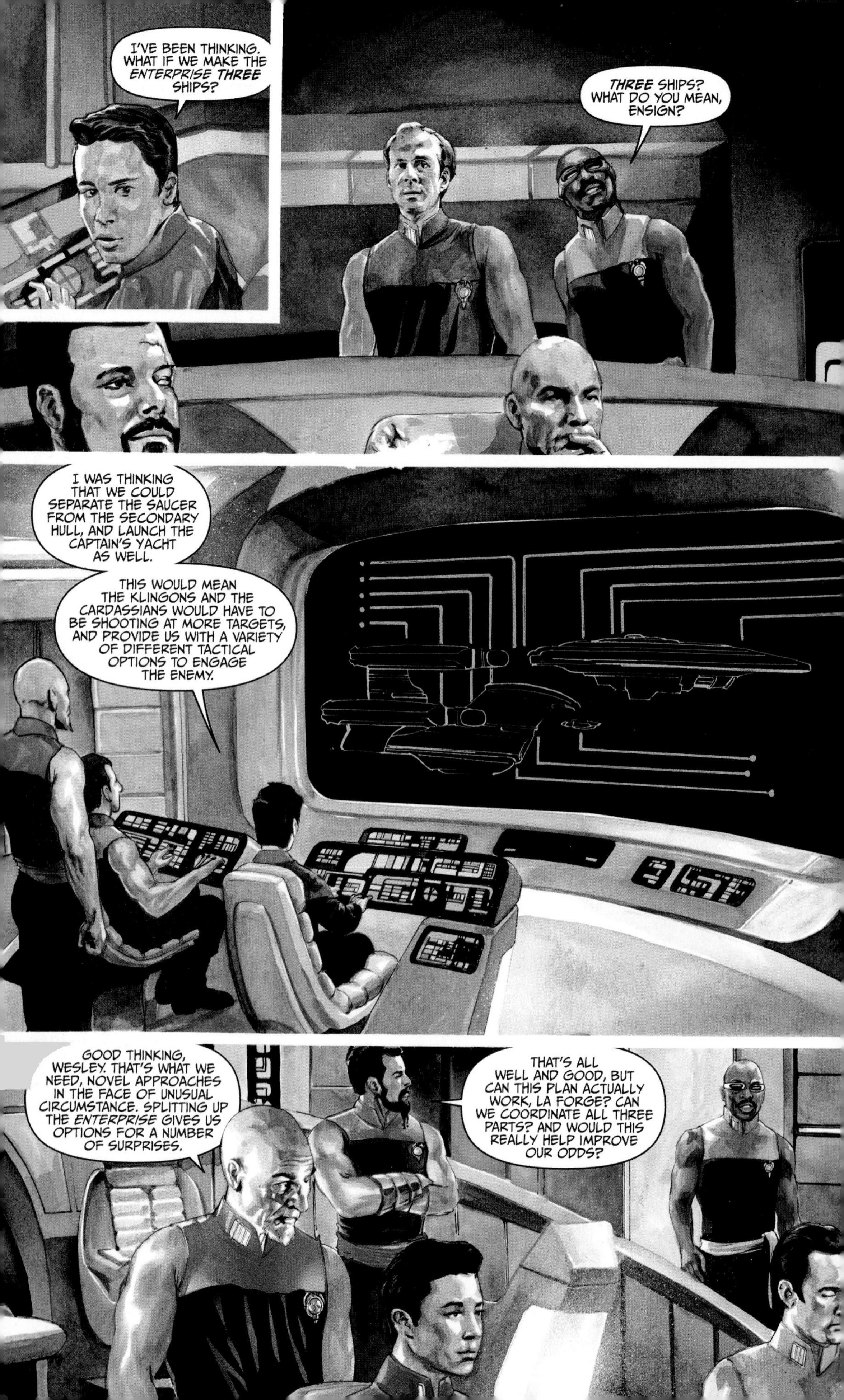
I'VE BEEN THINKING. WHAT IF WE MAKE THE *ENTERPRISE* ***THREE*** SHIPS?
THREE SHIPS? WHAT DO YOU MEAN, ENSIGN?
I WAS THINKING THAT WE COULD SEPARATE THE SAUCER FROM THE SECONDARY HULL, AND LAUNCH THE CAPTAIN'S YACHT AS WELL.
THIS WOULD MEAN THE KLINGONS AND THE CARDASSIANS WOULD HAVE TO BE SHOOTING AT MORE TARGETS, AND PROVIDE US WITH A VARIETY OF DIFFERENT TACTICAL OPTIONS TO ENGAGE THE ENEMY.
GOOD THINKING, WESLEY. THAT'S WHAT WE NEED, NOVEL APPROACHES IN THE FACE OF UNUSUAL CIRCUMSTANCE. SPLITTING UP THE *ENTERPRISE* GIVES US OPTIONS FOR A NUMBER OF SURPRISES.
THAT'S ALL WELL AND GOOD, BUT CAN THIS PLAN ACTUALLY WORK, LA FORGE? CAN WE COORDINATE ALL THREE PARTS? AND WOULD THIS REALLY HELP IMPROVE OUR ODDS?

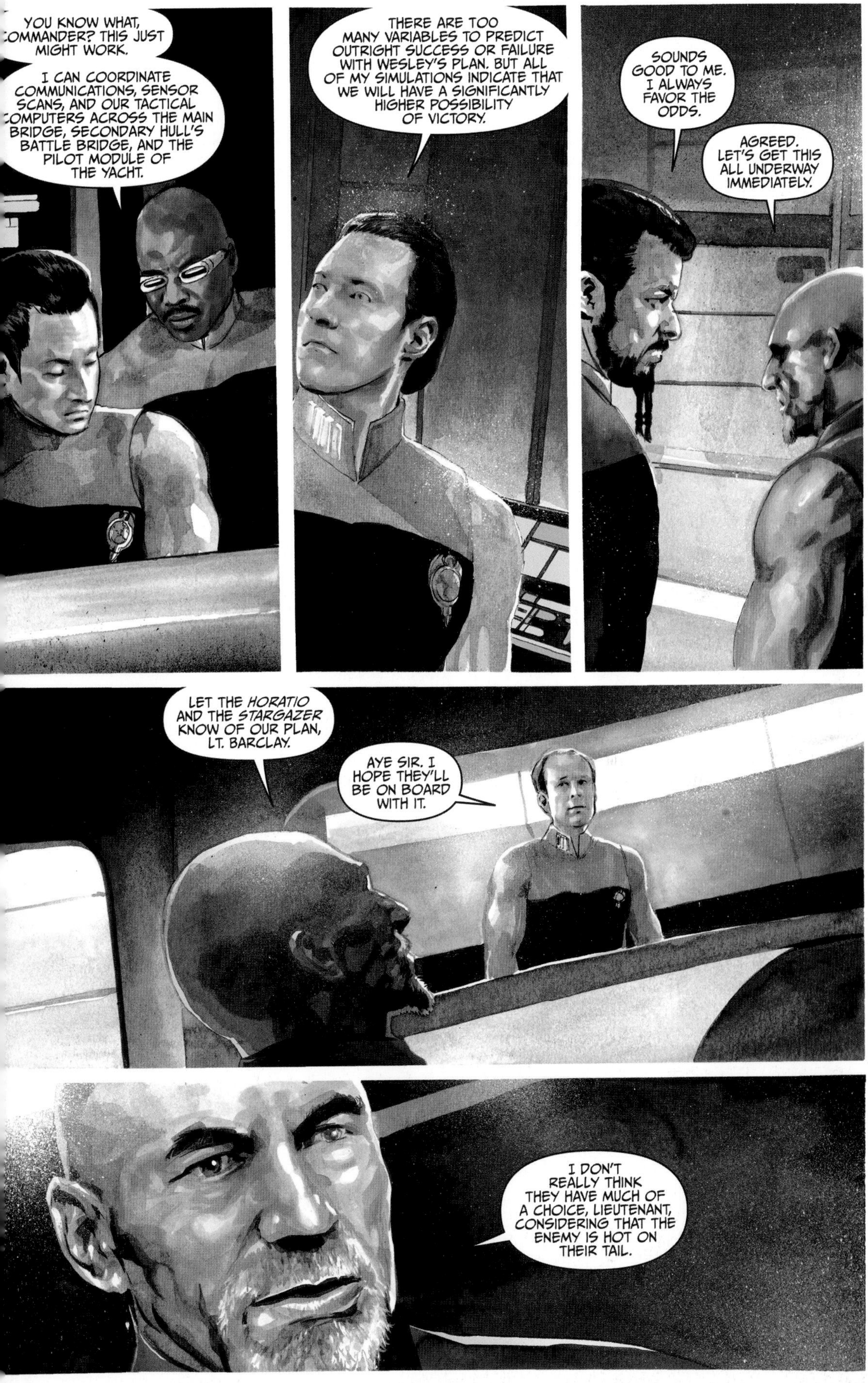

YOU KNOW WHAT, COMMANDER? THIS JUST MIGHT WORK.
I CAN COORDINATE COMMUNICATIONS, SENSOR SCANS, AND OUR TACTICAL COMPUTERS ACROSS THE MAIN BRIDGE, SECONDARY HULL'S BATTLE BRIDGE, AND THE PILOT MODULE OF THE YACHT.
THERE ARE TOO MANY VARIABLES TO PREDICT OUTRIGHT SUCCESS OR FAILURE WITH WESLEY'S PLAN. BUT ALL OF MY SIMULATIONS INDICATE THAT WE WILL HAVE A SIGNIFICANTLY HIGHER POSSIBILITY OF VICTORY.
SOUNDS GOOD TO ME. I ALWAYS FAVOR THE ODDS.
AGREED. LET'S GET THIS ALL UNDERWAY IMMEDIATELY.
LET THE *HORATIO* AND THE *STARGAZER* KNOW OF OUR PLAN, LT. BARCLAY.
AYE SIR. I HOPE THEY'LL BE ON BOARD WITH IT.
I DON'T REALLY THINK THEY HAVE MUCH OF A CHOICE, LIEUTENANT, CONSIDERING THAT THE ENEMY IS HOT ON THEIR TAIL.

NUMBER ONE, I AM THINKING...YOU SHOULD BE THE ONE IN THE CAPTAIN'S YACHT.

DAMN IT, WHY DID I KNOW YOU WERE GOING TO SAY THAT?

I'M THE FIRST OFFICER ON THIS SHIP, PICARD! I SHOULD BE COMMANDING EITHER THE SAUCER SECTION OR THE SECONDARY HULL.

HEAR ME OUT, COMMANDER.

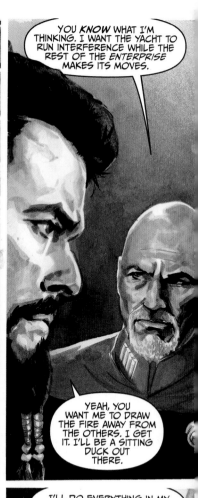

YOU *KNOW* WHAT I'M THINKING. I WANT THE YACHT TO RUN INTERFERENCE WHILE THE REST OF THE *ENTERPRISE* MAKES ITS MOVES.

YEAH, YOU WANT ME TO DRAW THE FIRE AWAY FROM THE OTHERS. I GET IT. I'LL BE A SITTING DUCK OUT THERE.

I KNOW *EXACTLY* HOW JELLICO RIGGED THAT SHIP. THE YACHT'S MORE LIKE A RECREATIONAL VEHICLE THAN A FIGHTER. AND IT'S NOT LIKE I HAVE ANY TIME TO MAKE ANY IMPROVEMENTS ON IT.

YOU KNOW DAMNED WELL YOU'RE THE BEST PILOT IN THE FLEET. IF ANYONE CAN PULL THIS OFF, IT'S YOU. IT'S A CHALLENGE, AND YOU KNOW IT.

IF I THOUGHT I HAD A BETTER CHANCE OF SUCCESS, I'D BE IN THAT SHIP MYSELF.

I'LL DO EVERYTHING IN MY POWER TO OFFER YOU COVER WHENEVER WE CAN. DO I HAVE YOUR SUPPORT ON THIS?

ALL RIGHT, PICARD. I'LL DO THIS. CONSIDERING OUR SITUATION, IT MAY WELL BE FOR THE BEST. AND I WILL ACCEPT IT AS A PERSONAL CHALLENGE.

BUT I DON'T *LIKE* IT.

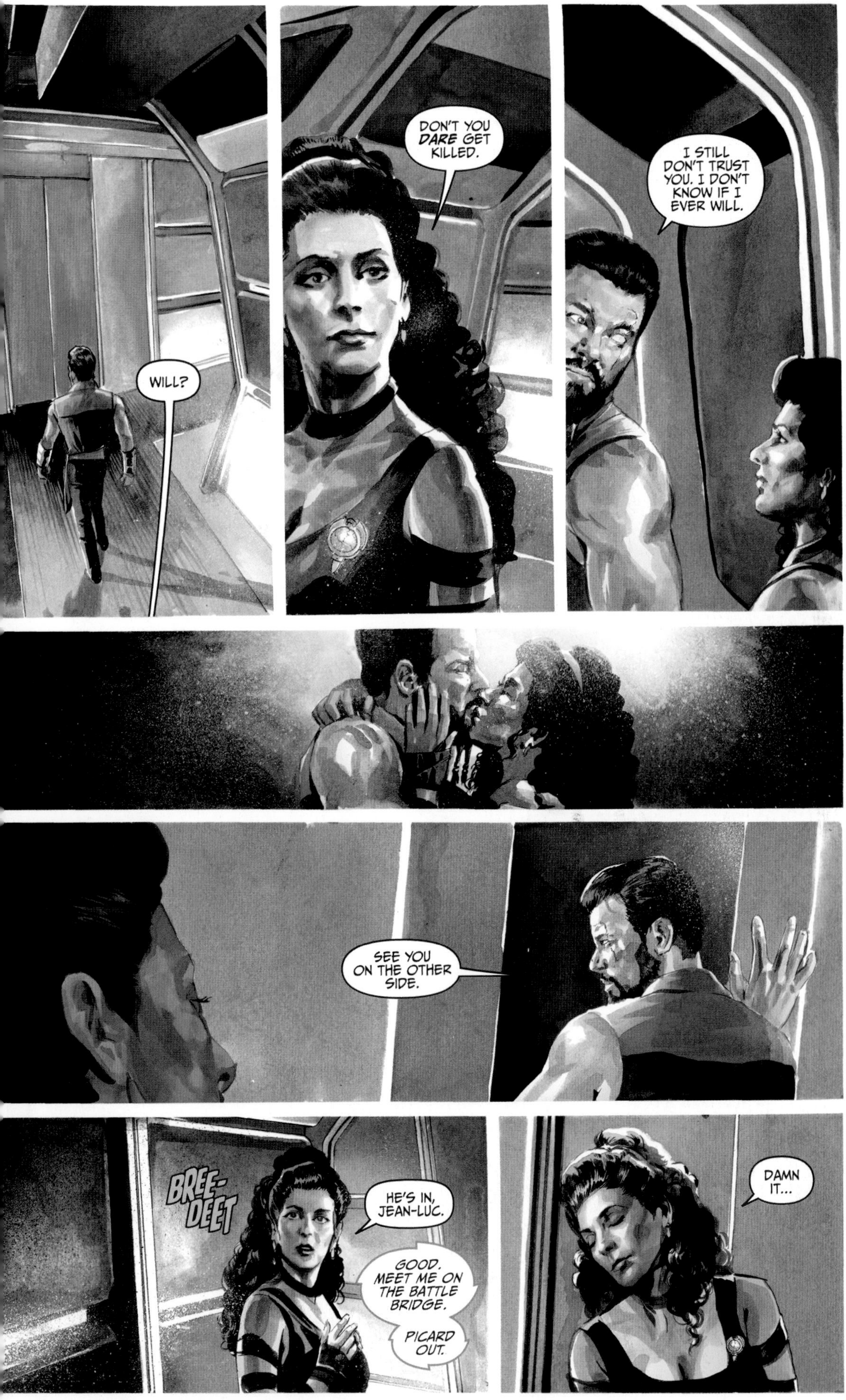
WILL?
DON'T YOU DARE GET KILLED.
I STILL DON'T TRUST YOU. I DON'T KNOW IF I EVER WILL.
SEE YOU ON THE OTHER SIDE.
BREE-DEET
HE'S IN, JEAN-LUC.
GOOD. MEET ME ON THE BATTLE BRIDGE.
PICARD OUT.
DAMN IT...

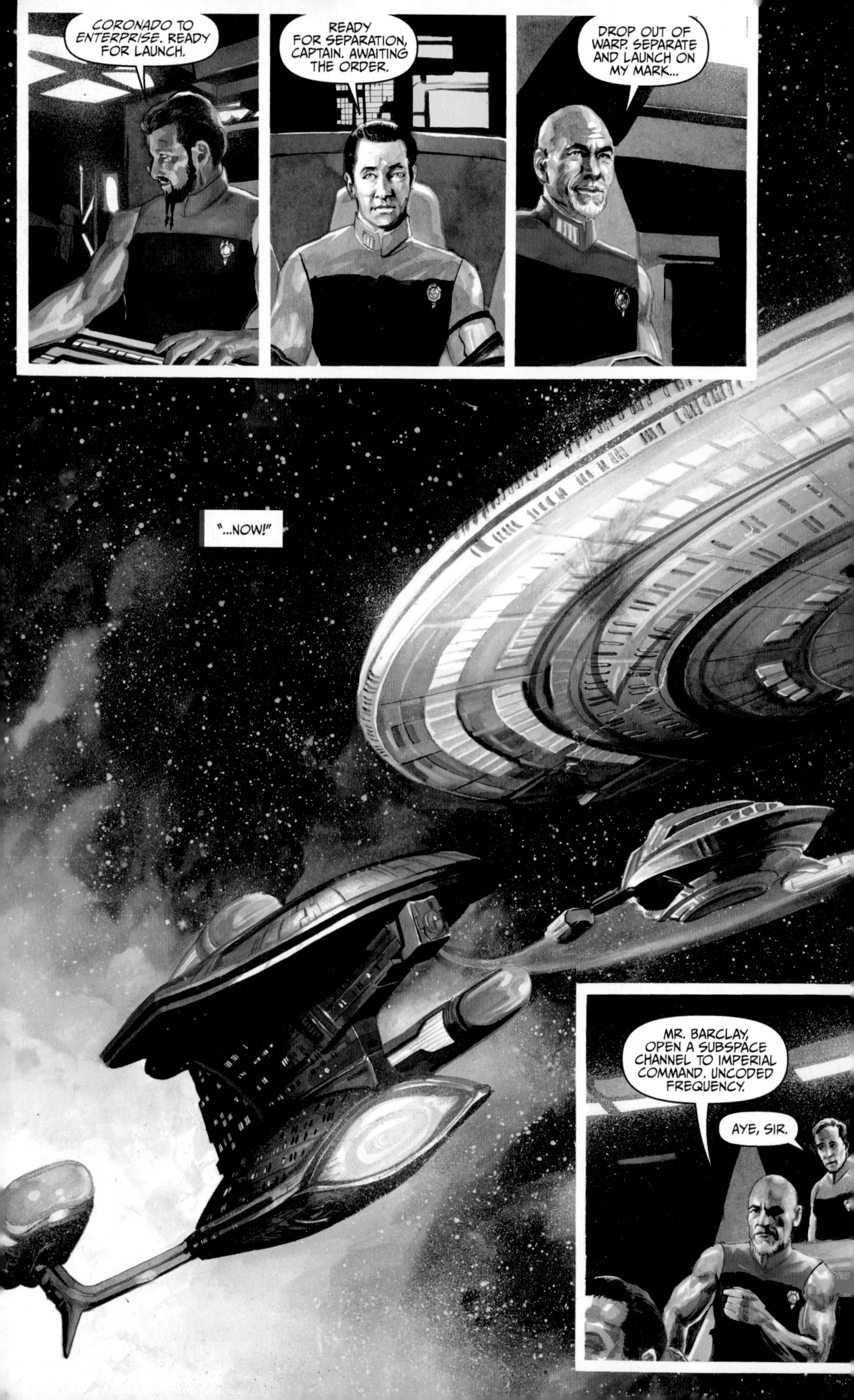
CORONADO TO ENTERPRISE. READY FOR LAUNCH.
READY FOR SEPARATION, CAPTAIN. AWAITING THE ORDER.
DROP OUT OF WARP. SEPARATE AND LAUNCH ON MY MARK...
"...NOW!"
MR. BARCLAY, OPEN A SUBSPACE CHANNEL TO IMPERIAL COMMAND. UNCODED FREQUENCY.
AYE, SIR.

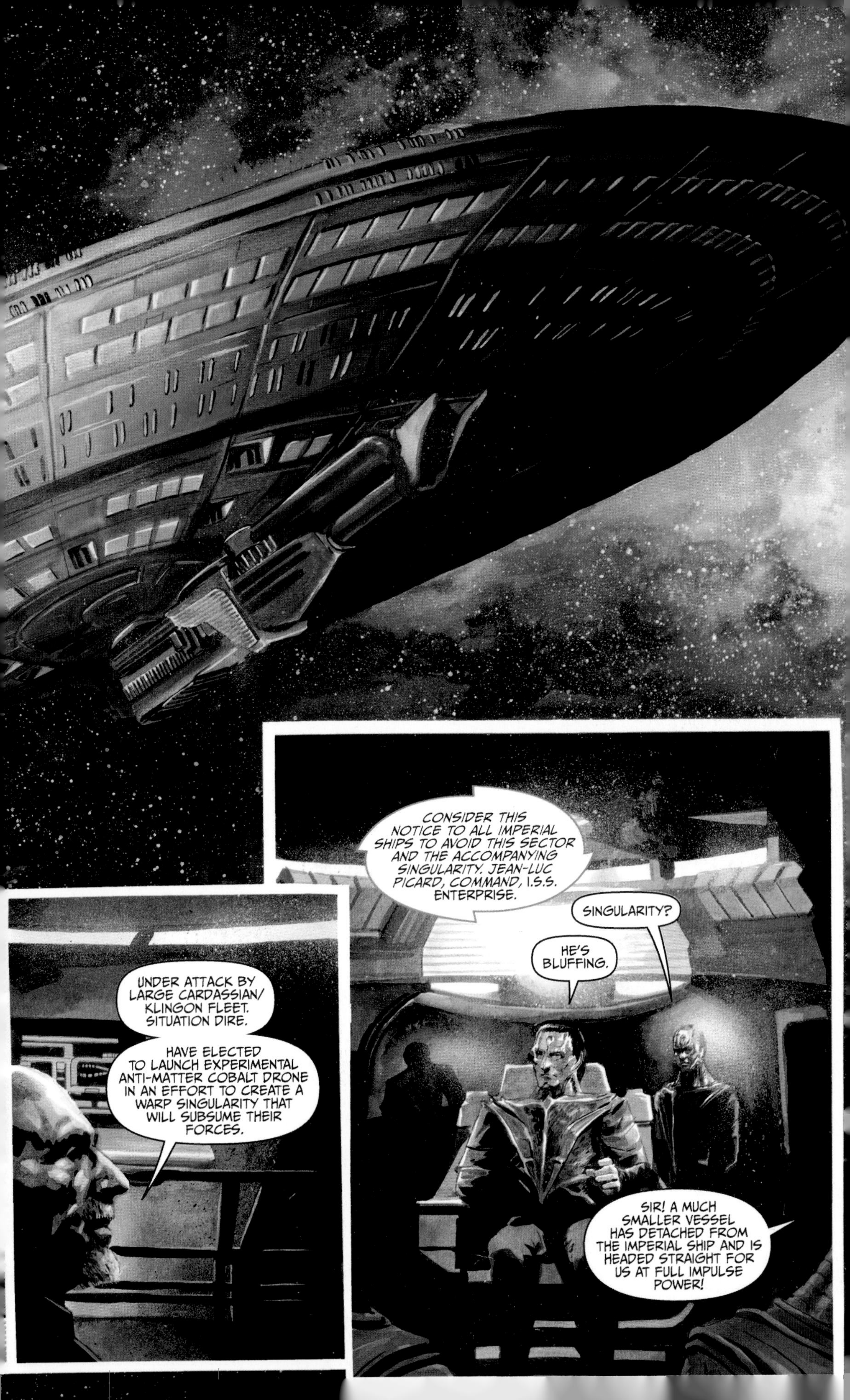
CONSIDER THIS NOTICE TO ALL IMPERIAL SHIPS TO AVOID THIS SECTOR AND THE ACCOMPANYING SINGULARITY. JEAN-LUC PICARD, COMMAND, I.S.S. ENTERPRISE.
UNDER ATTACK BY LARGE CARDASSIAN/ KLINGON FLEET. SITUATION DIRE.
HAVE ELECTED TO LAUNCH EXPERIMENTAL ANTI-MATTER COBALT DRONE IN AN EFFORT TO CREATE A WARP SINGULARITY THAT WILL SUBSUME THEIR FORCES.
SINGULARITY?
HE'S BLUFFING.
SIR! A MUCH SMALLER VESSEL HAS DETACHED FROM THE IMPERIAL SHIP AND IS HEADED STRAIGHT FOR US AT FULL IMPULSE POWER!

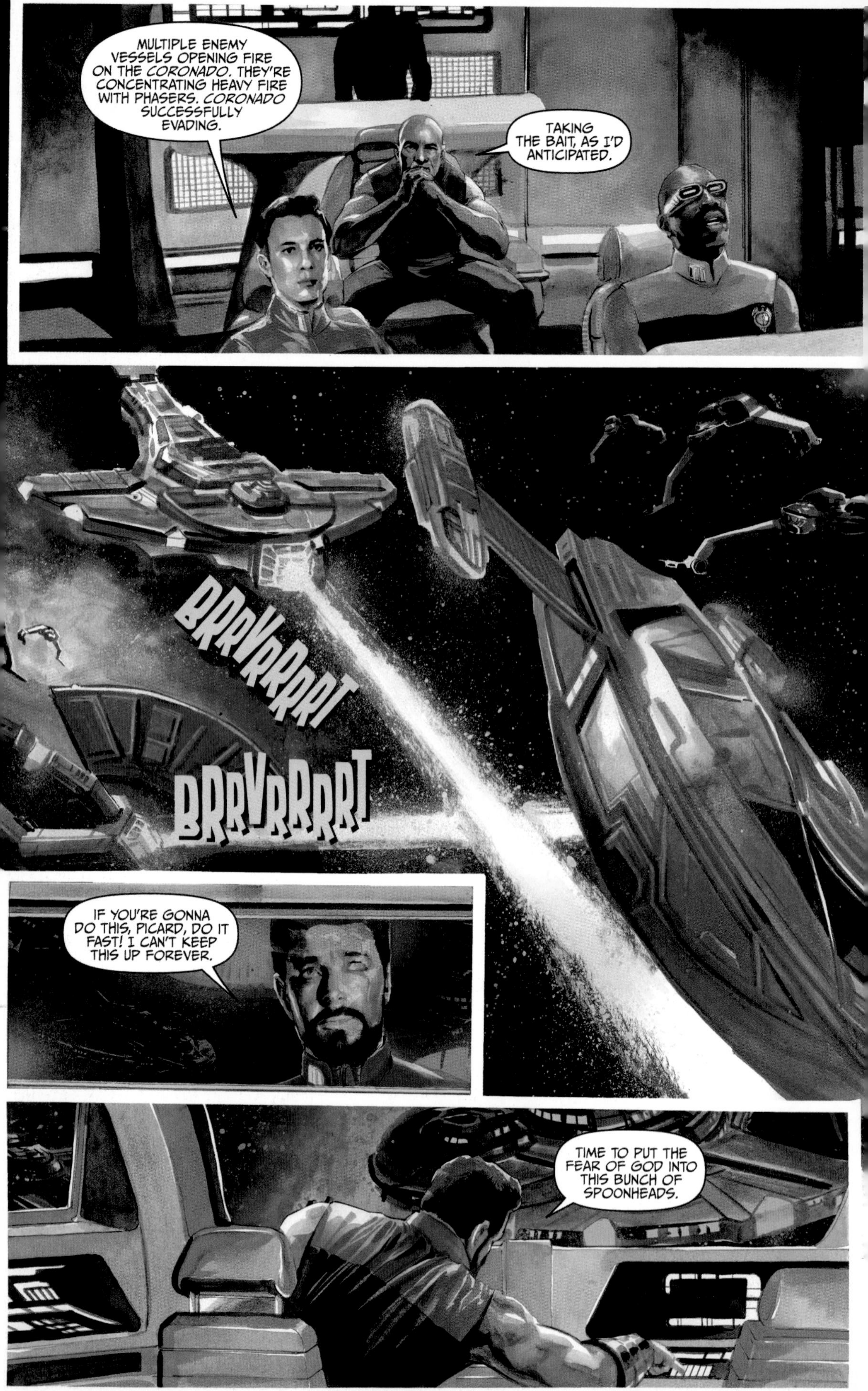
MULTIPLE ENEMY VESSELS OPENING FIRE ON THE CORONADO. THEY'RE CONCENTRATING HEAVY FIRE WITH PHASERS. CORONADO SUCCESSFULLY EVADING.
TAKING THE BAIT, AS I'D ANTICIPATED.
BRRVRRRRT
BRRVRRRRT
IF YOU'RE GONNA DO THIS, PICARD, DO IT FAST! I CAN'T KEEP THIS UP FOREVER.
TIME TO PUT THE FEAR OF GOD INTO THIS BUNCH OF SPOONHEADS.

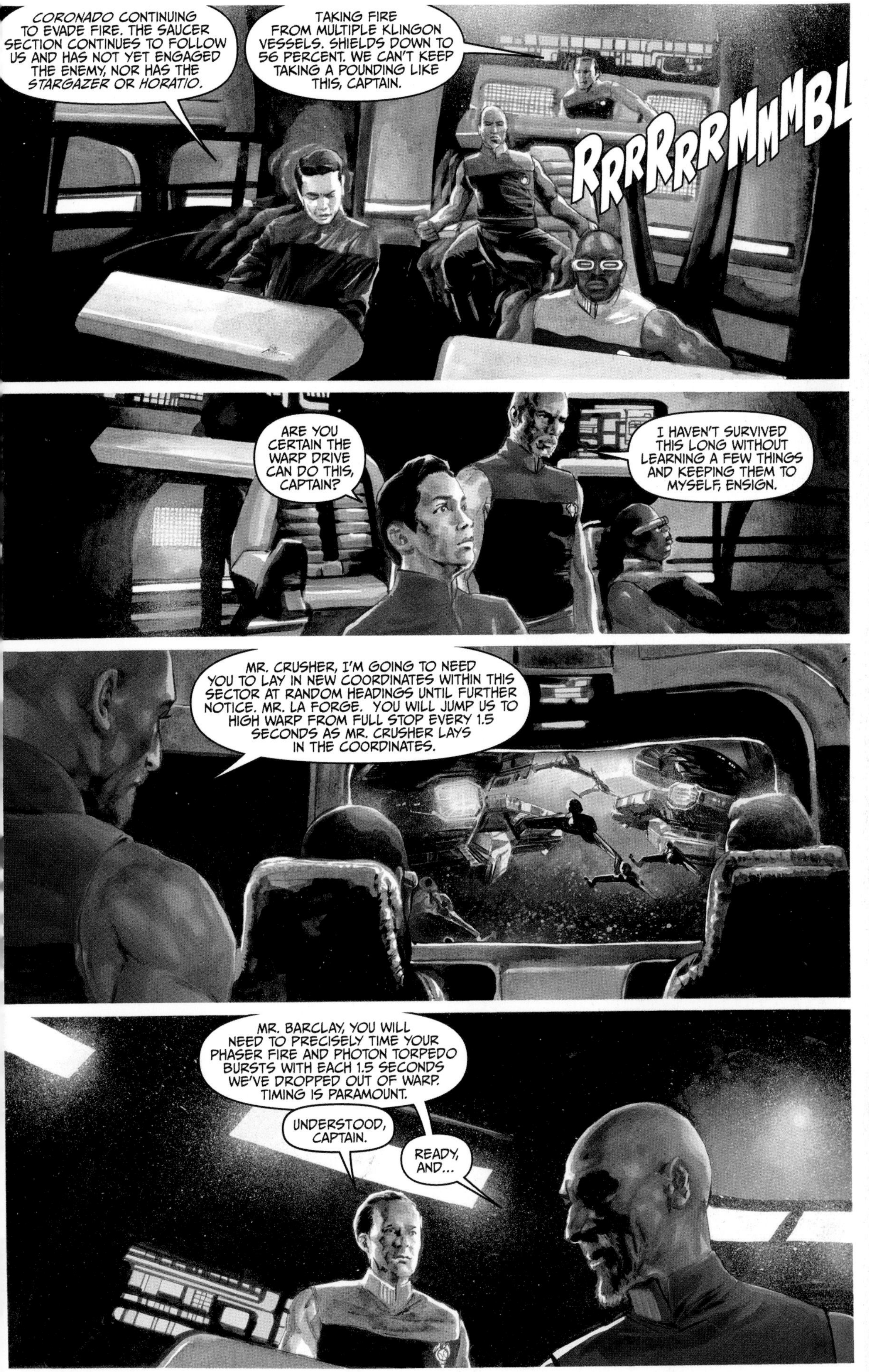
CORONADO CONTINUING TO EVADE FIRE. THE SAUCER SECTION CONTINUES TO FOLLOW US AND HAS NOT YET ENGAGED THE ENEMY, NOR HAS THE STARGAZER OR HORATIO.
TAKING FIRE FROM MULTIPLE KLINGON VESSELS. SHIELDS DOWN TO 56 PERCENT. WE CAN'T KEEP TAKING A POUNDING LIKE THIS, CAPTAIN.
RRRRRRMMMBL
ARE YOU CERTAIN THE WARP DRIVE CAN DO THIS, CAPTAIN?
I HAVEN'T SURVIVED THIS LONG WITHOUT LEARNING A FEW THINGS AND KEEPING THEM TO MYSELF, ENSIGN.
MR. CRUSHER, I'M GOING TO NEED YOU TO LAY IN NEW COORDINATES WITHIN THIS SECTOR AT RANDOM HEADINGS UNTIL FURTHER NOTICE. MR. LA FORGE. YOU WILL JUMP US TO HIGH WARP FROM FULL STOP EVERY 1.5 SECONDS AS MR. CRUSHER LAYS IN THE COORDINATES.
MR. BARCLAY, YOU WILL NEED TO PRECISELY TIME YOUR PHASER FIRE AND PHOTON TORPEDO BURSTS WITH EACH 1.5 SECONDS WE'VE DROPPED OUT OF WARP. TIMING IS PARAMOUNT.
UNDERSTOOD, CAPTAIN.
READY, AND...

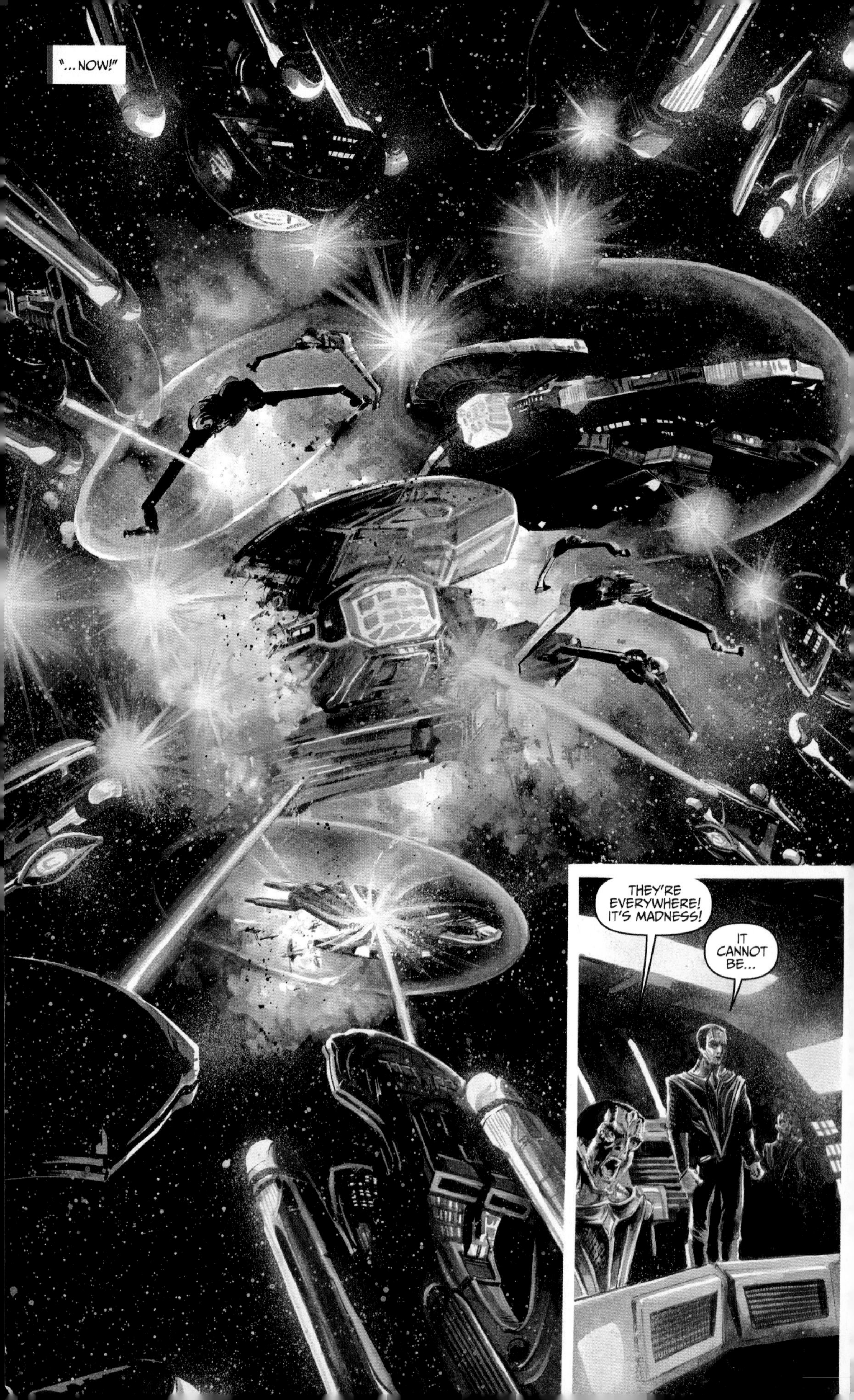
"...NOW!"
THEY'RE EVERYWHERE! IT'S MADNESS!
IT CANNOT BE...

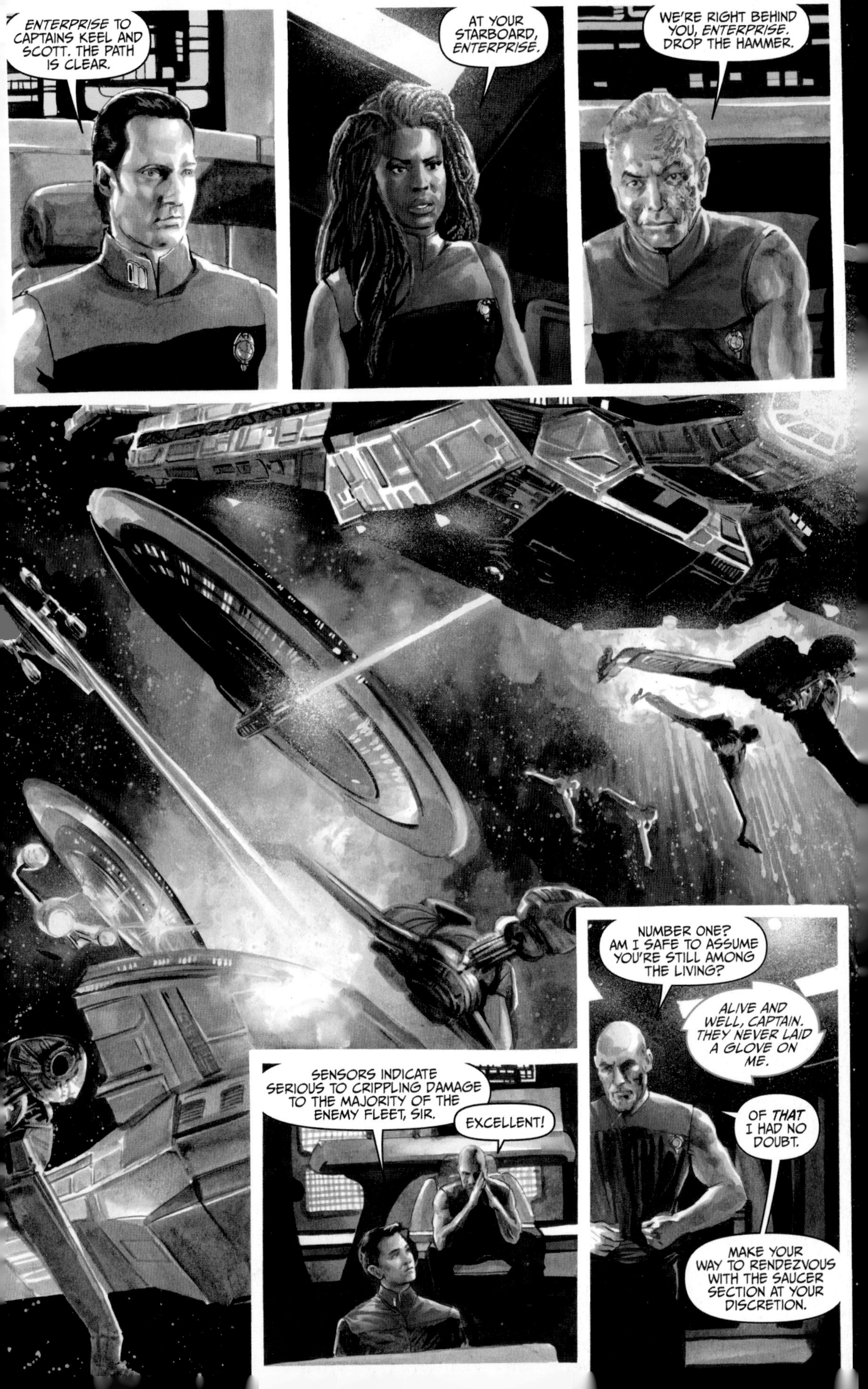
ENTERPRISE TO CAPTAINS KEEL AND SCOTT. THE PATH IS CLEAR.
AT YOUR STARBOARD, ENTERPRISE.
WE'RE RIGHT BEHIND YOU, ENTERPRISE. DROP THE HAMMER.
SENSORS INDICATE SERIOUS TO CRIPPLING DAMAGE TO THE MAJORITY OF THE ENEMY FLEET, SIR.
EXCELLENT!
NUMBER ONE? AM I SAFE TO ASSUME YOU'RE STILL AMONG THE LIVING?
ALIVE AND WELL, CAPTAIN. THEY NEVER LAID A GLOVE ON ME.
OF THAT I HAD NO DOUBT.
MAKE YOUR WAY TO RENDEZVOUS WITH THE SAUCER SECTION AT YOUR DISCRETION.

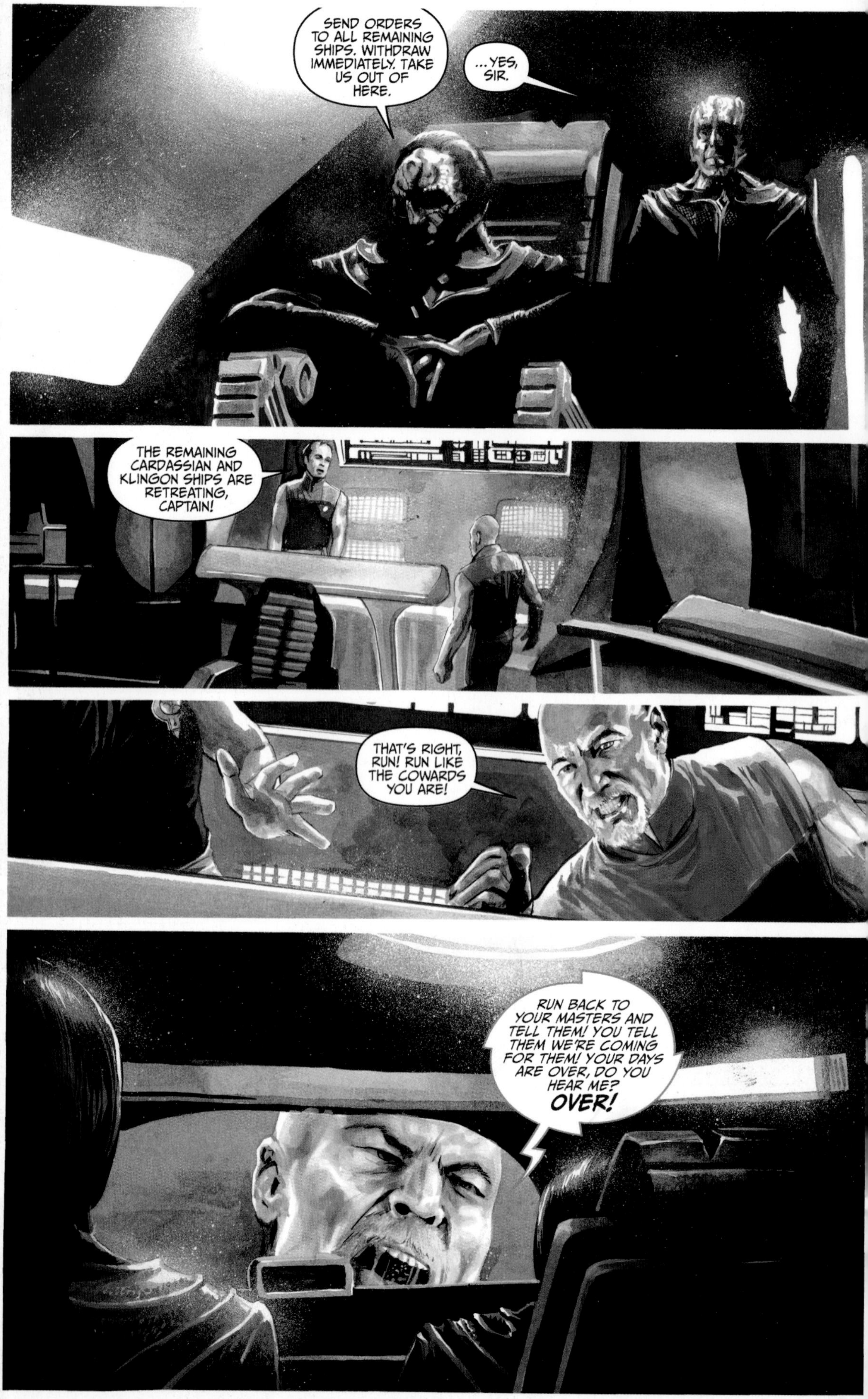
SEND ORDERS TO ALL REMAINING SHIPS. WITHDRAW IMMEDIATELY. TAKE US OUT OF HERE.
...YES, SIR.
THE REMAINING CARDASSIAN AND KLINGON SHIPS ARE RETREATING, CAPTAIN!
THAT'S RIGHT, RUN! RUN LIKE THE COWARDS YOU ARE!
RUN BACK TO YOUR MASTERS AND TELL THEM! YOU TELL THEM WE'RE COMING FOR THEM! YOUR DAYS ARE OVER, DO YOU HEAR ME? OVER!

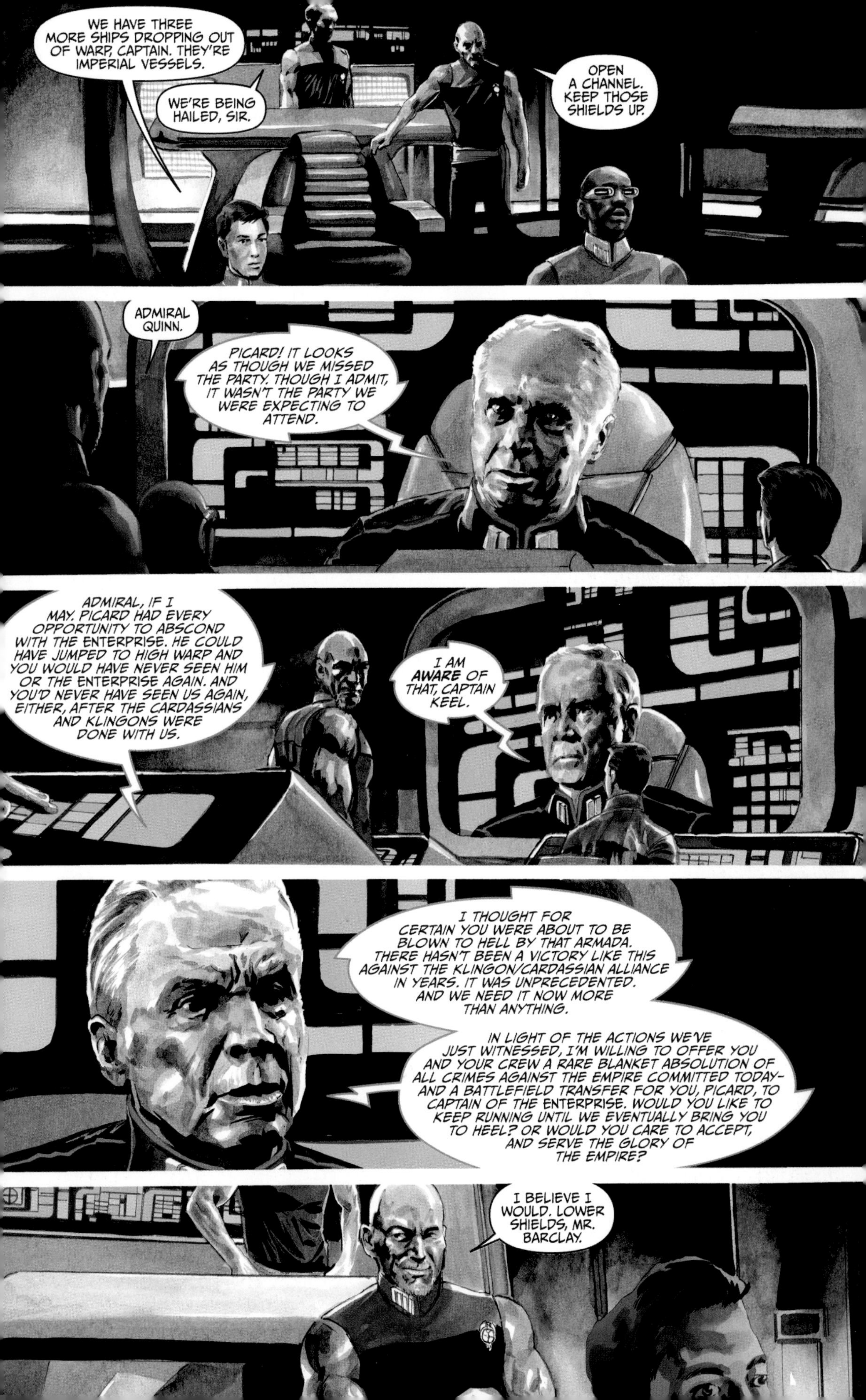
WE HAVE THREE MORE SHIPS DROPPING OUT OF WARP, CAPTAIN. THEY'RE IMPERIAL VESSELS.
WE'RE BEING HAILED, SIR.
OPEN A CHANNEL. KEEP THOSE SHIELDS UP.
ADMIRAL QUINN.
PICARD! IT LOOKS AS THOUGH WE MISSED THE PARTY. THOUGH I ADMIT, IT WASN'T THE PARTY WE WERE EXPECTING TO ATTEND.
ADMIRAL, IF I MAY. PICARD HAD EVERY OPPORTUNITY TO ABSCOND WITH THE ENTERPRISE. HE COULD HAVE JUMPED TO HIGH WARP AND YOU WOULD HAVE NEVER SEEN HIM OR THE ENTERPRISE AGAIN. AND YOU'D NEVER HAVE SEEN US AGAIN, EITHER, AFTER THE CARDASSIANS AND KLINGONS WERE DONE WITH US.
I AM **AWARE** OF THAT, CAPTAIN KEEL.
I THOUGHT FOR CERTAIN YOU WERE ABOUT TO BE BLOWN TO HELL BY THAT ARMADA. THERE HASN'T BEEN A VICTORY LIKE THIS AGAINST THE KLINGON/CARDASSIAN ALLIANCE IN YEARS. IT WAS UNPRECEDENTED. AND WE NEED IT NOW MORE THAN ANYTHING.
IN LIGHT OF THE ACTIONS WE'VE JUST WITNESSED, I'M WILLING TO OFFER YOU AND YOUR CREW A RARE BLANKET ABSOLUTION OF ALL CRIMES AGAINST THE EMPIRE COMMITTED TODAY-AND A BATTLEFIELD TRANSFER FOR YOU, PICARD, TO CAPTAIN OF THE ENTERPRISE. WOULD YOU LIKE TO KEEP RUNNING UNTIL WE EVENTUALLY BRING YOU TO HEEL? OR WOULD YOU CARE TO ACCEPT, AND SERVE THE GLORY OF THE EMPIRE?
I BELIEVE I WOULD. LOWER SHIELDS, MR. BARCLAY.

LATER...

I CHECKED IN ON GUINAN AS ORDERED, CAPTAIN. SHE'S RESTING COMFORTABLY.

AH, MR. BARCLAY! I FELT IT ONLY APPROPRIATE TO MARK OUR VICTORY WITH A CELEBRATION. JOIN US, WON'T YOU?

THANK YOU, CAPTAIN.

NOW, WHERE WAS I? AH YES, DERIMIAN III...

...I WASN'T WORRIED AT ALL. I KNEW THE CORONADO COULD OUTFLY THOSE CARDY CEMENT BLOCKS...

...NOW, WHEN I DISCOVERED THAT MANEUVER, I ONLY EXECUTED IT THE ONCE, BUT I SURMISED THAT OUR THIRD NACELLE WOULD PROVIDE THE STABILITY TO ACCOMPLISH MULTIPLE JUMPS...

...MAYBE YOU SHOULD TAKE IT EASY WITH THAT STUFF...

...I DON' NEEDOO WORRYIN ABOUT ME...MATTAYASSA THASSA TOSSUP...

LIEUTENANT BARCLAY? YOU APPEAR CONCERNED.

NOT CONCERNED, DATA, JUST... UNCERTAIN. I MEAN...

IT WASN'T SO LONG AGO THAT THE ONLY THING I WANTED WAS TO MURDER PICARD. I WANTED IT SO BAD I COULD TASTE IT. AND NOW...

...HOW MANY PEOPLE IN THIS ROOM HAVE FELT THE SAME WAY?

"AND HOW LONG CAN THIS POSSIBLY LAST?"

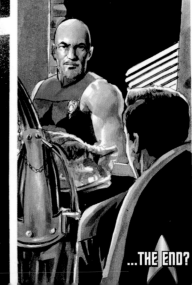

...THE END?

COVER GALLERY

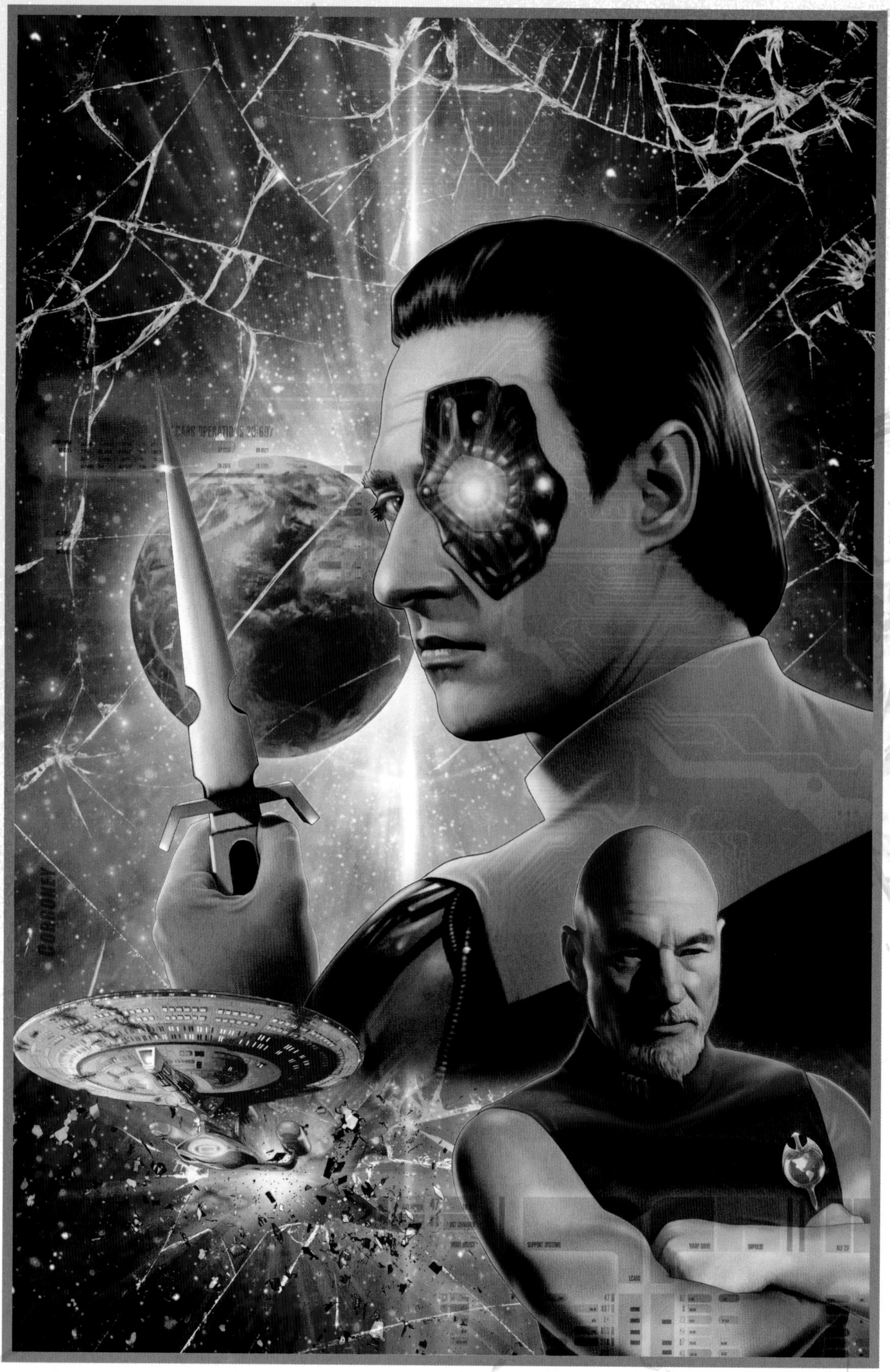
CORRONEY

ART BY
JOE CORRONEY

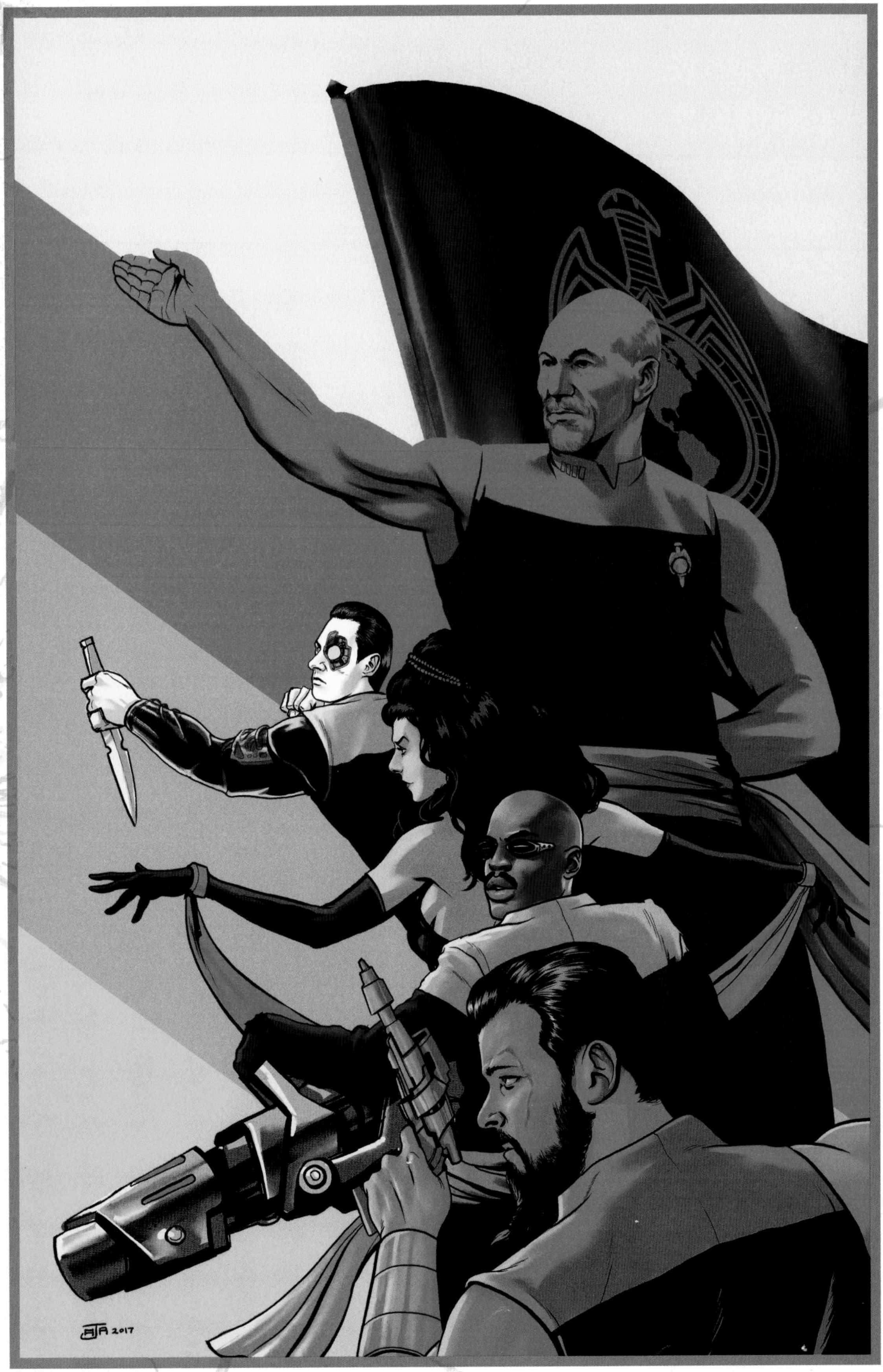

ART BY
ADAM ROSENLUND

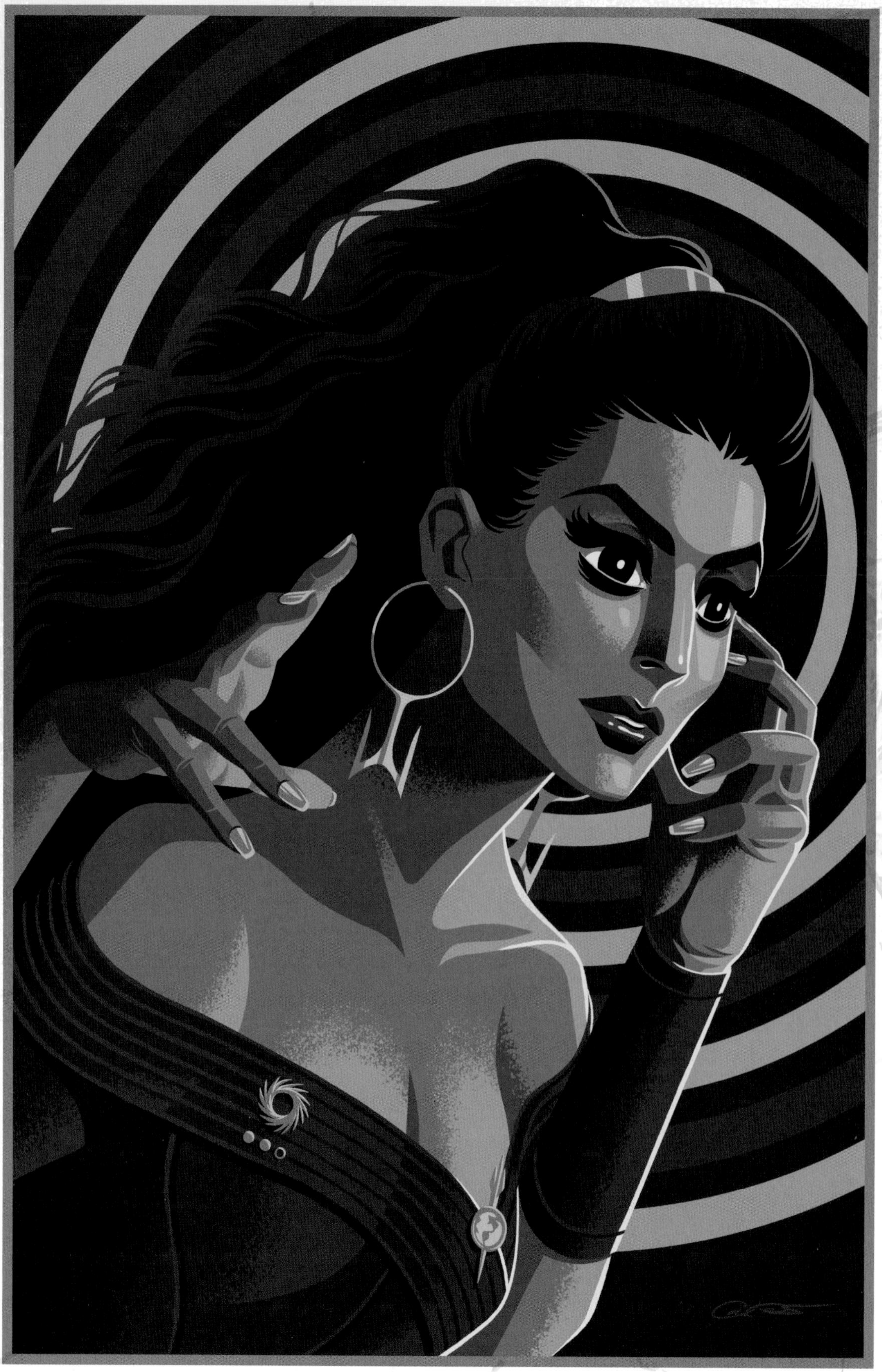

ART BY
GEORGE CALTSOUDAS

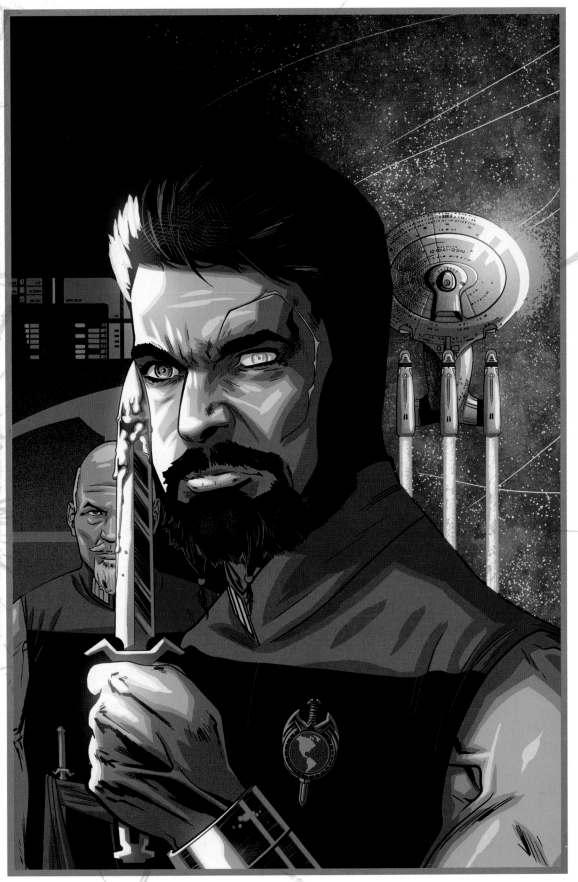

ART BY
JOSH HOOD

COLORS BY
JASON LEWIS

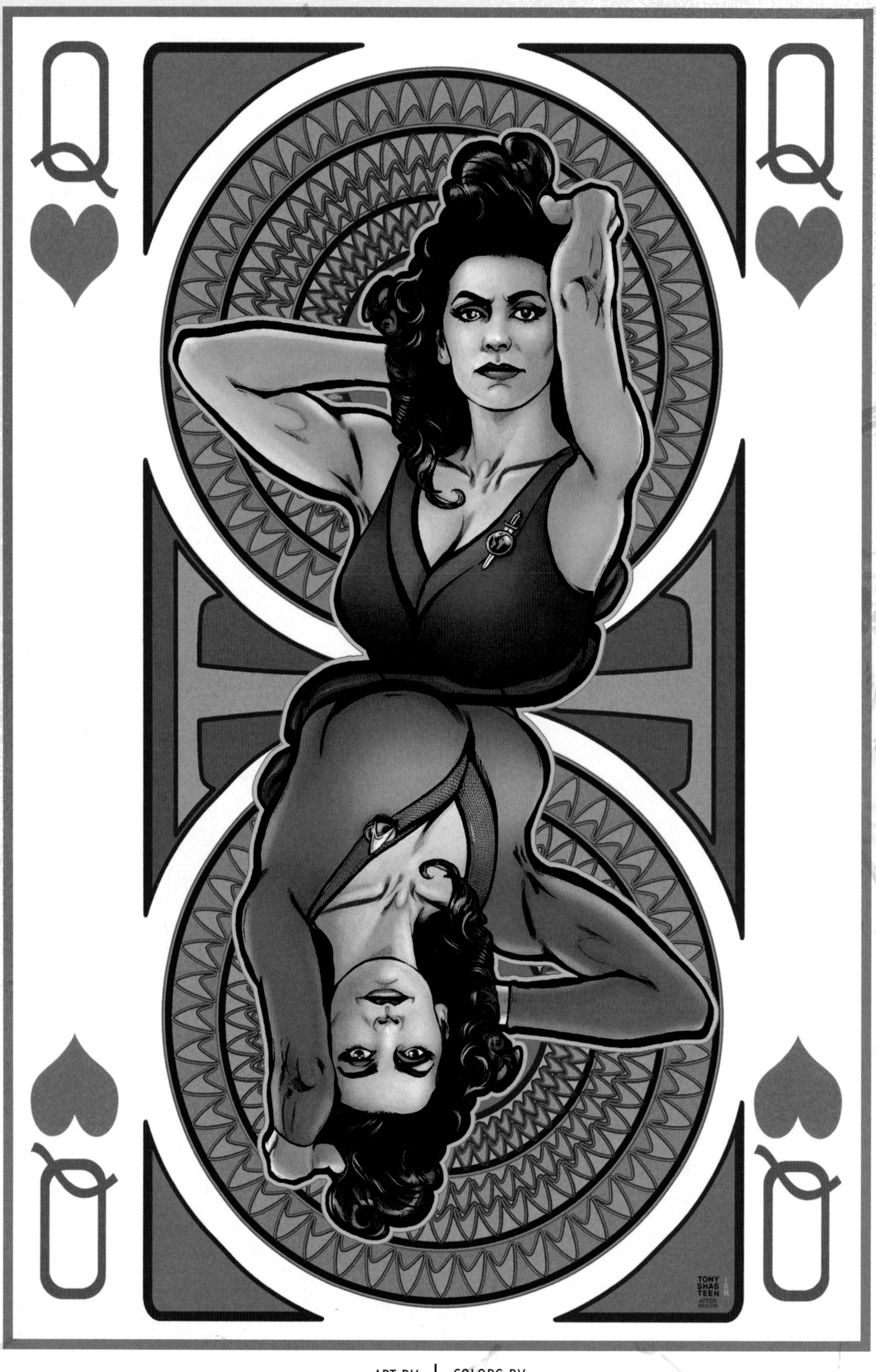

ART BY
TONY SHASTEEN

COLORS BY
J.D. METTLER

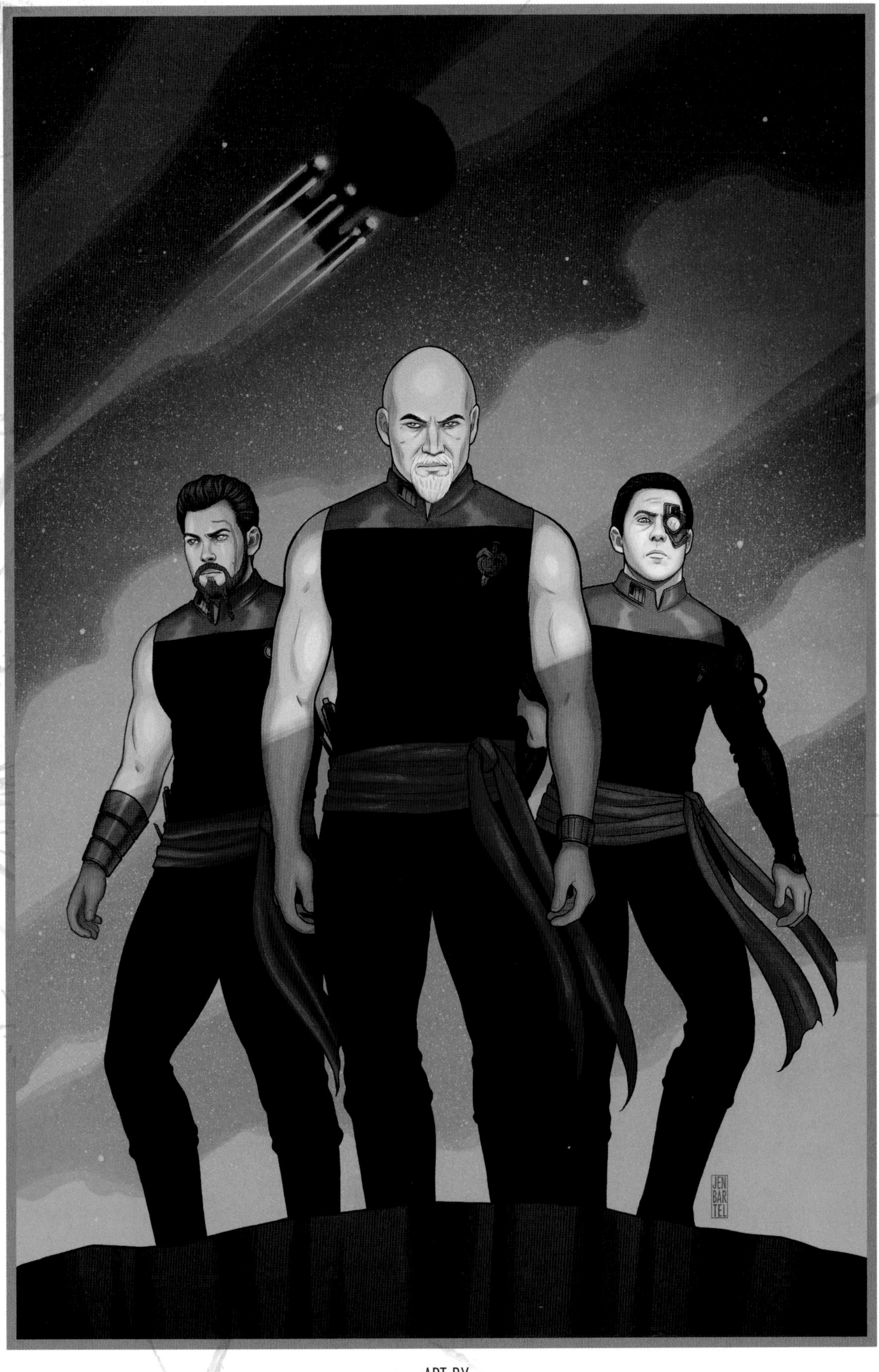
JEN
BAR
TEL

ART BY
JEN BARTEL

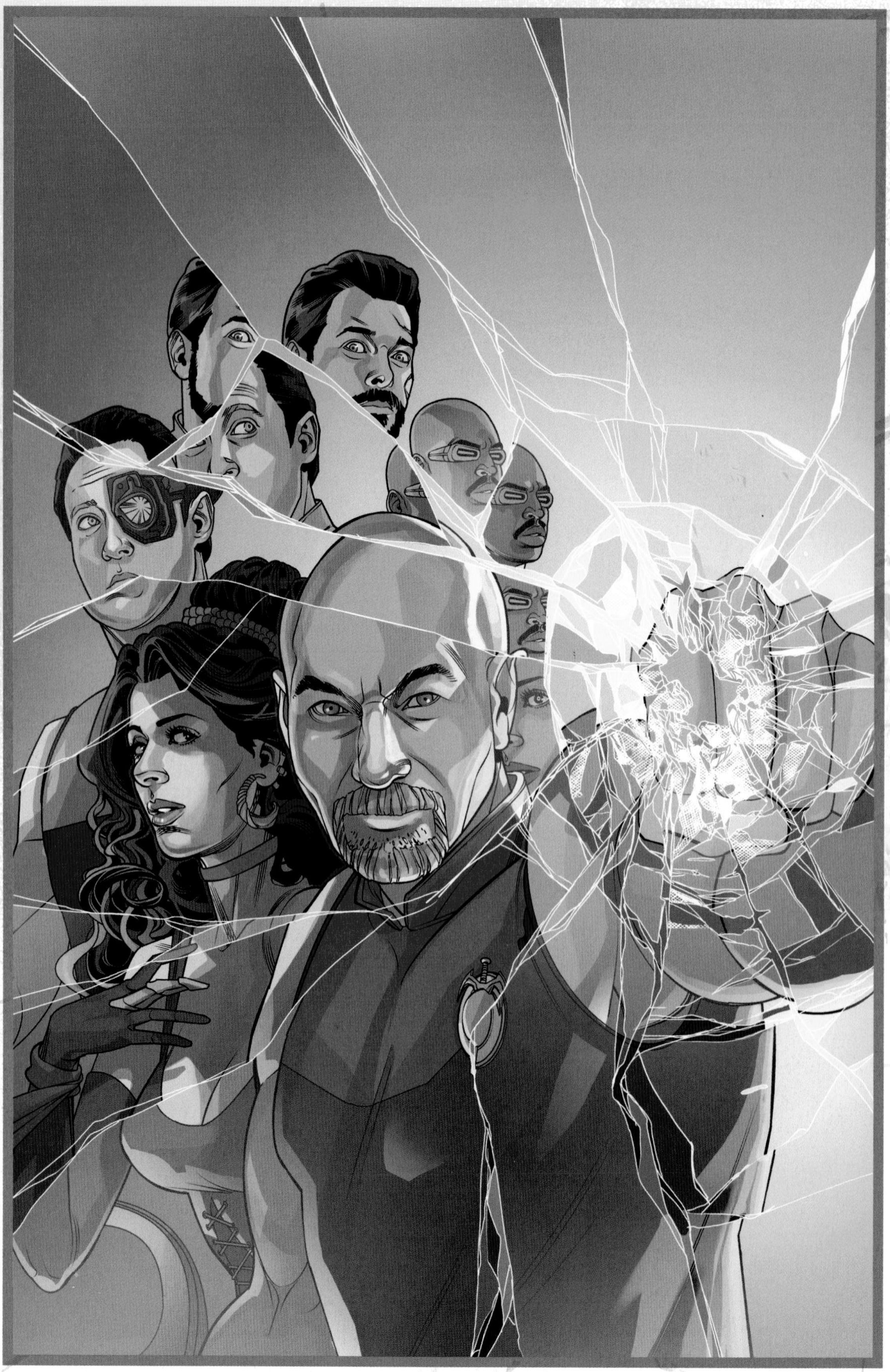

ART BY
RACHAEL STOTT

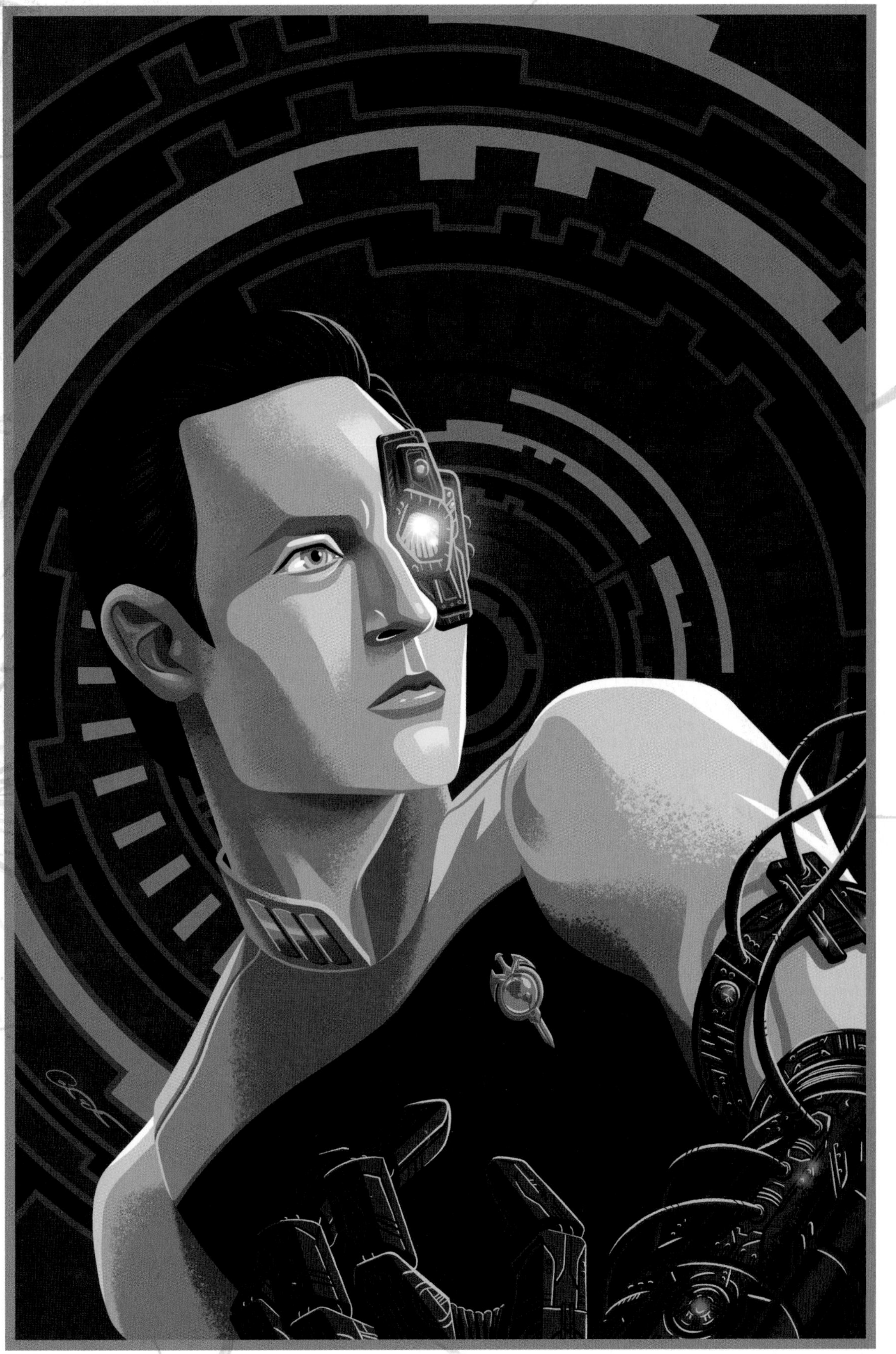

ART BY
GEORGE CALTSOUDAS

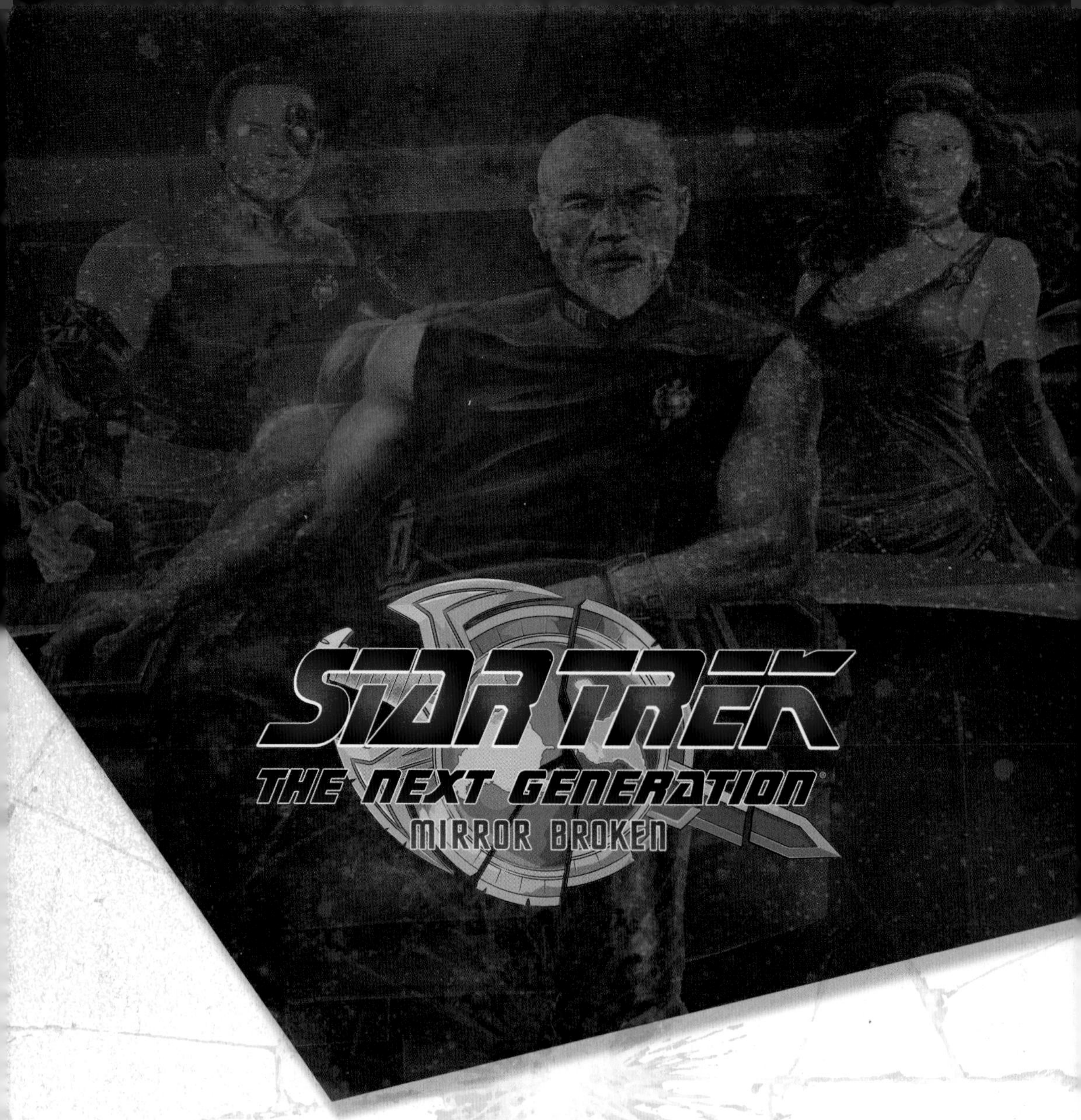
STAR TREK
THE NEXT GENERATION
MIRROR BROKEN